Whispers in the Night

Robert L Hecker

To my darling sister.
Hope you enjoy.

Bob

Whispers in the Night

Published by:

Double Dragon Publishing
PO Box 54016
1-5762 Highway 7 East
Markham, Ontario L3P 7Y4 CANADA

ISBN: 1-894841-46-8

Cover Design by Deron Douglas
First Edition Printing May 18, 2002

Double Dragon Press
a division of Double Dragon Publishing

To my wife, Franceska, whose incredible patience and bright smile have always been there for me.

CHAPTER I

Santa Ana winds, streaming from the Mojave Desert down through the passes in the Santa Monica Mountains, plucked at the old bricks of UCLA's Haines Hall, filling the classroom with a softly chilling moan. Sandi Boeckel hated the sound. It interfered with her concentration as she sat in the last row of the tiered classroom listening to the voice of Dr. Daniel Bradon.

"Self hypnosis. It's a technique you can use when you feel tense or tired. And it's one you can use with clients to help them relax."

His voice was strong and resonant, but because of the moaning wind, Sandi had trouble understanding him.

It was her own fault. The first night in class seven weeks ago she had deliberately chosen to sit near the back. She made believe it was so she could observe the other students, but she knew it was so she herself would not be noticed. Usually, the only drawback to sitting in a back row was difficulty in seeing the professor. Even though she was 5'9" herself, the heads of taller students often cut into her line of view. In most classes, it made no difference. Professors were not known for their good looks. How was she to know that Dr. Bradon would fascinate her from the very first night?

She had expected that the instructor of UCLA's PSYCHOLOGY II University Extension Course would be a wizened professor with the scruffy beard that seemed to be de rigueur for every male psychologist or psychiatrist since Sigmund Freud. But Dr. Daniel Bradon proved to be a surprise.

At the first class session when he strode into the room and placed his briefcase on the table near the podium, she could practically feel his radiated energy. Not her idea at all of someone who had a doctorate in psychology.

For one thing, he was young, probably in his early 30s. True, he had the stereotypical beard, but his was a close-cropped and precisely-cut Van Dyke that suited his broad forehead. His eyes, when they were not sparkling with humor, appeared dark, brooding. His unruly tangle of dark brown hair, trimmed away from his ears, was worn low on his neck. And, although slender, he was far from wizen. When he had taken off his leather bomber jacket and hung if over the back of a chair, it revealed good shoulders. He'd rolled his shirtsleeves up a couple of turns, and Sandi noticed that his forearms and wrists were corded with muscles. He had the flat stomach and slender hips of someone who spent time in a gym or on a track.

He turned to face the thirty students and folded his arms. He said nothing, but before his piercing gaze, chatter quickly died.

Then he smiled, and it was as though sunlight had burst through ice. "Good evening," he said. His voice was soft and warm, but it filled the room. "Welcome to Psychology Two."

Sandi felt a tingle of anticipation. It should be a very interesting class. There was still one vacant chair near the front and she considered moving. It was only her reluctance to draw attention to herself that had kept in the last row.

Now, she again regretted her stupid shyness. During his lectures Dr. Bradon encouraged questions but, although this was the next to last meeting of the nine week course, she had yet to ask a single question. She had formulated several in her mind, but had never actually put them into action. She had convinced herself each time that someone else would ask the same question and she would get her answer. By remaining silent, she could watch and listen without having to expose herself to the danger of ridicule if she asked a stupid question or put forth an opinion that sounded absurd.

At the moment, she was safe from any such faux pas. She had only to listen while Dr. Bradon continued, "Okay. I'll lead you through a session so you can get the hang of it." He began pacing in front of the room, watching as he moved like a hungry tiger. "The first thing is to relax. Start with your forehead. Feel the tension disappear. Now your eyes. Close your eyes. Look into the darkness. Look deep into the darkness." As he spoke the timber of his voice changed from one of authority to a soporific urging. "Just let the tension drain out of your body like water running in a stream. Let your shoulders slump. Let the tension drain from your arms, down through your hands. Look deep into the darkness. Let your mind drift. Let it go."

Obeying Dr. Bradon's gentle commands, Sandi stared into the darkness in front of her closed eyes and concentrated on releasing tension from her body. That's it. Relax. Concentrate on his soft, compelling voice.

"Drain all anxieties, all thoughts from your mind. Let your mind go. Let it drift. Let it seek its own path."

Bradon's soothing voice flowed through her like warm wine. Her mind was a void, dark, except for the balm of his voice. A spurious thought intruded: nature abhorred a vacuum. If she made her mind a vacuum, something would have to pour in. What would it be? Images of her childhood?

No! She quickly shut out the unwanted intrusion. This was supposed to be a pleasant experience not a reason to dig up painful memories.

Relax. Relax. Let the darkness spread and become all enveloping. All enveloping--

*   *   *   *

How strange. I should see a point of light in the darkness. Flickering light. Like the light from a far away candle. No, not one candle. There were two candles. In beautiful holders, holders that appeared to be made of intricately spun strands of silver. They were situated on a small letter-writing table with a delicately inlaid top where I was seated. The candlelight illuminated a spread of Tarot cards arranged on a silken scarf in front of me, and I stared at the cards, fascinated. Using the circular spread designed to forecast events of the year ahead, I had just displayed the twelfth card. The Tower inverted. I touched it with the care due a card of the greater arcana.

The man seated across from me leaned forward to better see the card, and candlelight glinted off his uniform collar. I glanced up and stifled a shiver. The light was reflected from the double rune symbol of an SS officer. Four pips indicated he was a Sturmbannführer, a Major. A colored ribbon around the man's neck suspended a Nazi Grand Cross. On his left arm was an armband with the Nazi Swastika and below it a stripe of oak leaves that indicated the man was a high party member.

In the shadows beyond the candlelight I sensed that other men were standing, watching.

"Well?" the major snapped.

I stared silently at the last card, keeping my fingertips on it, as though I could read its message tactually. I would not be hurried. SS or not, I was the one in control. But that was not the reason I hesitated. Even after years of reading the cards, I still found it difficult to convey bad news. "The twelfth month; the Tower," I murmured. "Its astrological attribute is Mars. It is number sixteen in the major arcana. One and six equals seven making it very powerful. Notice the lightning and the fire. Very powerful forces."

"That is good, no?" the major said.

"Generally, yes. The forces of destiny will destroy something in your life that is working against you. Suffering is ended and your life becomes easier."

"You say 'generally'. What do you mean?"

Again I hesitated. "The card is inverted."

"And this means?" Flickering candlelight made the man's eyes look cruel, dangerous. But his thick fingers, gripped the edge of the table so hard their tips were white, and the timbre of his voice told the truth: he was afraid, afraid of the cards.

When I thought of the forces that had brought this man to power, my sympathy vanished. "Within twelve months the forces of destiny will call down a disaster of great magnitude. You will experience much suffering. And,"--I stared directly into his eyes for the first time--"it will be self-made. Beware the twelfth month."

The man flinched as though he had been struck a blow. Then, with an oath, he swept the cards and the scarf from the table. He jerked to his feet, his callused, powerful hands clinched into fists like mallets. "Stupid!" he snarled. "I don't believe it."

I stared up at him. Standing, he was short and stocky and looked immensely strong. His thinning blonde hair was close cropped and his skin so fair that it was ruddy. Now sweat made it glisten. He was the picture of health, but he would soon be dead. And his death would be violent.

I didn't like him but, even so, the knowledge made my voice husky with compassion as I returned his stare, "I do not control the cards, Herr Sturmbannführer. I only tell you what they say."

The man reached across the table and took me by the shoulders and began shaking and I gasped, "Oh Gott! Gott! Nein! Nein! Nein!" Surprisingly, he replied in English, "It's all right. It's all right. Come back. Come back now. It's all right. Come back. Now."

I blinked as the scene went out of focus. What was wrong? The candles were receding into the darkness until their flames became tiny points like stars.

*   *   *   *

With a wrenching force of will, Sandi opened her eyes. Dr. Bradon! He was holding her by the shoulders and saying, "You're back. That's it. You're back."

Several students were standing near her, staring, their eyes wide in surprise and alarm, and Sandi felt her face grow warm with embarrassment. What on earth had she done? It couldn't have been anything too humiliating because she was still seated in her chair; its writing leaf was still down across her lap so she could not have stood up. "I'm all right," she said, and she saw worry drain out of Dr. Bradon's face.

He straightened and smiled at the students. "Well," he said. "I think we've just witnessed our first spontaneous regression."

"Regression?" someone ask. "What's that?"

After a quick appraising glance at Sandi, Bradon strode down the tiered isle to the front of the room, talking as he moved. "There is a school of thought--arguably, but not without some evidence--that we are all reincarnations and that some people under hypnosis are able to regress back to a previous life."

"I know," someone volunteered. "Like Brydi Murphy."

"That's right. She was probably the most famous regressive, although there have been others. Actually, it's quite common."

Some of the students turned to glance at Sandi, but she hardly noticed. Regression! What had happened to her? And who was the woman with the cards? It couldn't have been she. It just couldn't!

The sharp clang of the bell signaling the end of class jolted her back to reality. The room cleared quickly with a few of the students, as usual, pausing on the way out to speak to Dr. Bradon. Sandi closed her notebook and put it in her carryall bag. She took her time retrieving her sweater from the back of her seat and slipping it on. She did not want to talk to anyone; she was embarrassed enough. And she certainly would have no answers for questions anyone might ask.

But it wasn't one of the students who stopped her when she slowly made her way down the tiered isle toward the door. Dr. Bradon walked over to intercept her. He studied her face, his eyes worried. "You look a little pale. Are you going to be all right?"

Sandi nodded. Pale? It had to be an understatement. She felt weak and shaken as though all the blood had drained from her body. "I'm all right."

She moved to walk around him, but he reached out to touch her arm. "How about a cup of coffee? I think you could use it."

Her instinct was to refuse. An hour ago she--and, she was sure, half the women in the class--would have been flattered by such an invitation from Daniel Bradon. But now she wanted desperately to escape into the night, to get to her home and the security of her room where she could think.

Think?! What good would that do? What kind of answers could she find on her own? Nothing in her experience would explain what had happened. And of more importance, whether it could possibly happen again. But Dr. Bradon was an experienced psychologist. He had to be familiar with such aberrations. What had he said: regression was not uncommon. He must have encountered it before. Maybe he would have some answers.

"All right," she said.

"Good. Where did you park?"

"Lot two."

"Okay. There's a coffee shop near there--the Lu Valle Commons."

She nodded. "I know where it is."

"I'll walk you over there."

She waited in the hall while he slipped on his jacket, closed his briefcase, turned out the lights and locked the classroom door. He seemed to sense that she didn't feel like talking, and he was silent during the walk down the broad hall past the other locked classrooms to the exit and out into the night. As they walked side by side across the broad, night-shadowed Dickson Plaza, the warm desert wind plucked at their clothing and played with Sandi's shoulder-length hair so that she wished she had plaited it into its customary French braid.

Usually she looked forward to walking across the spacious campus. She especially enjoyed walking during the summer nights when the trees, the bushes and the sharp angles of the ancient brick buildings were softened by the shadowed illumination from tall light stands. There were fewer students in the campus quadrangle at night, and instead of the scurrying crowds and the sense of harried intensity that permeated the campus like unseen radiation during the day, at night there was an atmosphere of languid malaise. The students taking night courses were more relaxed and their voices and laughter could be heard as gentle sounds in the darkness. One moonlit evening after leaving class she had detoured to the nearby Franklin Murphy Sculpture Garden where she had wandered from piece to piece in a euphoria of pleasure. During the day, bathed in brilliant California sunlight, the sculptures were harshly beautiful. But shadowed by the dim glow of moonlight and incandescent lighting, they took on an ethereal quality as though the artist's hands alone had formed them instead of hard chisels and molten bronze.

In the classroom, she had noticed a similar contrast between day classes and those at night. Daylight created a no-nonsense businesslike atmosphere that made study and concentration easier.

At night there was a difference, a more informal atmosphere, as though the instructor was a friend instead of a demigod. Perhaps it was because the students were older, usually people with day jobs, families, people without the frantic pressure to graduate top of the class.

Even so, Sandi wished it was daylight. Sitting with Daniel Bradon at one of the small tables outside the coffee shop would not seem nearly so intimate in bright sunlight. She should not be doing this, not at night, not with moonlight filtering through sighing trees. She was engaged to Jordan and, even in daylight, should not be socializing with another man.

But, she rationalized, this was not just another man; he was Dr. Bradon, and this tête-à-tête was simply an opportunity to ask some of the questions about psychology she had been reluctant to ask during class. She was not here because he was ruggedly handsome, or because he had a smile to die for. Business. It was all business.

Watching Bradon return to the table carrying two Styrofoam cups of coffee, Sandi raised her intellect like a shield. Here was a man who could cause her a lot of sleepless night if she let herself be mesmerized by his looks and his charisma. She would not allow him to overwhelm her.

She smiled at the absurdity of the thought. Why should he even try? There were at least a dozen women in the class with stunning good looks and remarkable bodies who she was sure he could have with a snap of his fingers. They certainly weren't sitting in the back of the room so that they wouldn't be noticed.

Yet, she was the one having coffee with him.

One way to keep her objectivity was to avoid looking at him. But she could feel him studying her with his piercing eyes. Under his scrutiny her chest tightened and she had trouble breathing. She had to clutch the coffee cup while pressing it firmly on the table to keep the trembling of her hands from being apparent. Why was this happening? Damn her stupid shyness. It had never before been this bad. Other men did not make her feel like a Victorian spinster.

She took a deep breath. Relax. He was a professor, not a Svengali. She was twenty-two years old, for heaven's sake, and in less than a year would be walking down the aisle with a man every bit as handsome as Dr. Daniel Bradon. She could certainly deal with this nonthreatening situation.

"Susanna Boeckel," Bradon said. "I....

"Sandi," she interrupted. She looked up. "I prefer Sandi." There was enough light so that she could see his eyes were not the deep black she had thought but, rather, were dark blue.

"Okay. Sandi. Two years ago you only needed twelve more units to get your master's in art history. So close. Why did you switch to psychology?"

Her mouth opened in surprise. How did he know that? Her Admissions Resume, of course. But there were more than thirty students in his class. Had he memorized each student's statistics? If not, why her?

"My priorities, uh, changed," she said. How could she explain her real reason: that she was afraid she was going mad. How could she explain the whispering voices that filled her with such nameless fear? Sometimes she would wake up at night bathed in perspiration, shaking uncontrollably. Until she was in her teens she had thought that the whispers were common to everyone. When she realized that she was unique, she had told no one, afraid that they would think her 'odd'. But lately the voices had been growing more insistent. They had to be stopped or she really would go mad. But how? She could place herself in the hands of a psychiatrist, a situation that neither her parents nor Jordan would understand. No. She had to deal with them herself. Knowledge. That was the answer. With knowledge, she could exorcise the voices.

And it was working. Since she had been taking Dr. Bradon's course, she had begun to have more control over the voices. And the fear. Until tonight. Waking from the regression, the fear had come rushing back like water from a broken dam. Was what had occurred in class merely a different manifestation of the same phantoms? Or was it a new threat to her sanity?

"I'm glad your priorities changed," Bradon said with a smile. "Psychology is a fascinating field. We've just begun to scratch the surface. What happened tonight is a case in point."

"Really?" She had to say something. But not the truth. Anything but the truth. Frantically she searched for words that would not make her sound like a fool, and something Bradon once said popped into her mind. "I'd classify it as a rather normal demonstration of a defense mechanism."

The calmness of her voice surprised her. Maybe she could bring this off.

"Possibly." Bradon sipped his coffee. "But defensive mechanisms in the form of regression invariably encompasses the person's own life experiences. The memories might be suppressed to the point of being totally forgotten, consciously. Hypnosis can sometimes dredge up past events and knowledge we don't even know we possess."

"Freud contended that most such memories are based upon repressed fantasies and desires."

"There's a great deal of controversy about that. In any event, such memories never go beyond our own life cycle, our own experiences, fantasies or not."

"Oh? I thought there had been authenticated cases of past life regression."

"Never satisfactorily confirmed."

Sandi was silent. Her own experience was confirmation. There was no denying the stark reality of the scene with the Nazi officer. There was no way it could have been propagated by her imagination.

Bradon sat back and smiled as though he read her mind. "Maybe you'll be the first."

She looked down at her coffee cup. She didn't have to lie when she answered, "I don't know what happened."

"You don't remember any of it?"

She did remember. She remembered too well. "I remember looking at Tarot cards, reading them for a man in uniform." She looked up at Bradon. "He was a Nazi."

"That explains why you were speaking German."

Sandi's brows furrowed. "I don't speak German."

Bradon stared at her. "Not at all?"

"No. Well, I understand a little. My parents speak it, but rarely at home."

"And the Tarot cards? Have you ever used them?"

She shook her head emphatically. "No. Never. I don't even know what they look like."

"I speak German pretty well. Learned it from my grandparents. You were speaking like a native."

"I don't understand it."

"Nothing like this has ever happened to you before?"

Had it? No, the phantoms in her nightmares did not have bodies. They were only vague images, glossolalian voices. Nothing with the vivid reality she had experienced during the regression. Although she had managed to suppress them, she knew they still inhabited some dark recess of her mind. Could they be related to what had happened tonight? Unlikely. There appeared to be no correlation. The regression scene had been sharp, concrete. There had been no real fear, only a dull kind of sorrow for the inevitable death of the young German officer.

The fear had come later, after she had awakened.

"No," she said. "Nothing like it."

Bradon sipped his coffee and studied her. She grimaced in irritation when his direct gaze made her look away.

Robert L. Hecker   13

"How would you like to participate in an experiment?"

All her instincts told Sandi to reject the topic quickly, to run away from this man while she could. Her voice was almost a whisper when she looked up. "What kind of an experiment?"

"A regression." At her flash of panic, he quickly added, "We'll do it in class. Totally controlled conditions. I'll be right there with you."

Something foul stirred in the darkness of Sandi's mind. Were the demons sensing a glimmer of light that meant a door of escape had been opened a crack. She could not allow that. It had taken tremendous effort to lock them away where they could never escape.

Never? There was a vast difference between repressing the demons and destroying them. Perhaps an experiment in regression would bring them into the open. Perhaps, at last, she would have the direct confrontation she had so often prayed for. Then she would destroy the demons, be rid of them forever.

Could she win such a battle? Suppose she could not. What then? Would they then drag her into a madness that would totally engulf her?-- forever!

She could not--she would not take the chance. Like Damocles, it was better to live uneasily beneath the sword than to have it drop.

Yet, wasn't this why she had turned to the study of psychology in the first place?

She should ask Bradon for his opinion. She should tell him that he might be opening a Pandora's Box whose demons he might not be able to control. Did she want to reveal such a dark side of herself?

Her stomach knotted and her fingers clinched around the coffee cup. No. She did not want him, or anyone, to know. If she was insane, it would be her secret as long as she could function rationally. "I'll have to think about it," she said. "It was kind of--disconcerting."

"I can imagine. I'd be scared to death. But,"--he ran the fingers of both hands through his hair--"intrigued too, I guess."

"Why don't you do it yourself?"

"Me?" He chuckled. "I tried once. Nothing happened. I guess I'm one of the new souls."

"New souls?"

"Some religions believe that we go through a never-ending series of births and deaths. Release from the endless cycle can only be done by finding the truth."

"That doesn't make sense," she said. "If the same people keep being reborn, the world population would remain relatively stable."

"True. Another theory is that we're all born seven times. What we are now depends on how we lived in the previous life. Some people are on their seventh cycle; some are on their first. New souls."

Seven times? Sandi wondered if that could be the source of her demons. Could they be left over from a previous existence? If they were, wouldn't bringing them into the open allow them to be extirpated? And yet--she was afraid. She could not afford to take the chance.

"What happens after the seventh time?"

"Depends on your religion, I guess. Transmigrationists think our soul goes into another body, even an animal. Or becomes a God. I like that part. Some think we go to heaven or hell. Nobody really knows, do they?"

He finished his coffee and noticed that she had scarcely touched hers. "You want that heated up?"

Her mind snapped back to the present. "No, no. I . . ." She had to get away. To think. To slow her spinning thoughts. "I really have to be going."

He stood up and came around to pull her chair out for her. "Think about it. This will be your last chance."

Her breath caught. "My last chance? What do you mean?"

"End of the semester. Only one more class." He took a business card from his shirt pocket. "If you change your mind during the week, give me a call."

It irritated her when she saw her fingers tremble as she took the card, wondering as she did so why she bothered. She certainly was not going to change her mind. She'd kept her secret from everyone, even her parents; she would never reveal her demons to a room full of strangers. She tried to think of a reason for her refusal and could find none that sounded plausible, so she said, "It won't work. We'd better forget it."

He raised an eyebrow. "Why not?"

"I'll never sleep in your class again."

He laughed with such ease that she envied him. How long had it been since she had laughed with such delight?

"Touché." He carried their Styrofoam cups to a trash receptacle and returned to the table. "I'll walk you to your car."

She was going to say it wasn't necessary but she noticed that most of the students had gone, and she did not relish the thought of walking alone through the deserted parking structure at this time of the night. There was also a sense of pleasure that Daniel Bradon would be walking with her, a feeling that she quickly pushed aside. Get back there with the other demons, she thought. If I can control them, I can certainly control you.

But when she climbed into her old Porsche and nodded goodbye to him, she felt a momentary loss as though she had cut herself off from something pleasant. Throughout the short drive home the memory of Bradon's voice would not go away. She made a mental note to call Jordan as soon as she got home and set up a dinner date with him as early as possible. The image of Dr. Daniel Bradon was one intruder she meant to deal with quickly and ruthlessly.

CHAPTER 2

Driving through the darkened streets toward his apartment in Manhattan Beach, Dan Bradon fought a gathering headache. There was a smoldering fire in his brain that should be doused with cold rejection. He had no right to experiment with a student's mind. And yet, it was the chance of a lifetime.

He had been astounded when during the self-hypnosis exercise the quiet young woman who always sat at the back of the room had begun muttering in German. He had hurried toward her, afraid that she was having some sort of emotional breakdown that could end in a law suit. At the same time he feared that what he suspected--in fact, hoped-- was occurring might be true. Was it possible? A Regression? His stomach knotted in suspense. This could be his opportunity for professional recognition and, perhaps, some small fortune.

He knelt in front of her, motioning the other student's back. Her eyes were closed, her face taut. She appeared to be in a hypnotic trance, carrying on a conversation with someone in German. He stared at her. Was she faking? She seemed a singularly unlikely prospect for regression. He had paid little attention to her throughout the semester except to note that she always sat at the back of the room, never asked questions and did not participate in class discussions. However, he had noticed that she was very attractive, with startlingly beautiful steel-gray eyes that always seemed to be locked in intense concentration. During his lectures, the other students seemed to accept everything he said as gospel. Not her. Behind her concentrated gaze he had the impression that her mind was analyzing the data like a computer, forming her own conclusions which, judging by the intelligence in her eyes, could well be more conclusive than that of anyone in the class. Von Neumann had been capable of such concentration. The mathematic genius listened quietly to all sides of a mathematical problem, then, after unbelievable mental calculations, came up with the correct solution.

Occasionally, Bradon had been so struck by the intensity of her concentration, that he wondered whether there might be some underlying paranoia. His curiosity had caused him to pull her admissions record. The record had provided her name and age and academic record. But it had given him no insight into her personality, let alone any arcane psychosis.

Even so, of all the students who might be susceptible to hypnotic suggestion, he would have picked her last. Her air of self assurance did not strike him as indicative of a person who would easily release her hold on reality. Yet, she had slipped into a state of trance with astonishing speed. Incredible. Probably due to her inordinate ability to concentrate. More incredible was what had happened then.

He had read about past-life regression but had never encountered it in a patient. Not that he hadn't hoped. If the regressed personality was someone famous or someone connected to history, it could be worth money--a lot of money. Book publishers and TV producers would pay dearly for an account of a good true regression.

But during the regression, as he had listened to the fear in the woman's voice, as he saw the growing anguish in her face, he realized that he should terminate the session. She was exhibiting increasing stress. Then, too, if he allowed it to continue, one of the students might leak the situation to the press and that would be the end of any possible book deal.

Still, he hadn't wanted to bring her out of the trance too quickly. The character she was living should become firmly implanted in her subconscious so that he could easily bring it back another time. But she was obviously experiencing deep emotional anguish. He had to terminate.

Still, he hesitated. He heard one of the students whisper to another, "Could she hurt herself?" Could she? Suppose he didn't bring her out? Would she come out by herself? Or would her mind disintegrate like an overrevved engine?

For a second he experienced a chill bordering on panic. What if he tried and failed? In the past, he had never had trouble bringing a patient out of an hypnotic trance. But this was different. This had gone beyond any kind of trance he had encountered. Deeper. More intense. And thrilling. Here was a person actually taken over by an entity from the past. Did he have a right--let alone an obligation--to break that bond? And if he did, would he be destroying his own chance of exploiting the situation?

Her face suddenly contorted and her voice became shrill, her words halting and slurred. Strangely, her eyes were now open, staring, filled with horror. He had to bring her out!

He took her by the shoulders and shook her gently. "Miss Boeckel. Susanna. It's all right. It's all right. Come back. Come back now. Susanna!

But her eyes failed to focus. Her hands clawed at an unseen presence as her voice rose, bordering upon a shriek "Oh Gott! Gott! Nein! Nein! Nein!"

He shook her harder. Damn. She had to respond! "Come back, Susanna. Come back! Now!"

Relief flooded him when she blinked and stopped talking. He spoke to her, keeping his voice low but urgent, "That's it, Susanna. You're all right. You're all right."

She opened her eyes, and when he saw that she recognized him, he was more than a little surprised at the joy that flooded through him. He might have lost a chance at professional immortality but, strangely, he was glad. That really was incredible. Not like him at all.

Later, after insuring himself that she was going to be all right, he realized he still had a shot at the money. She had regressed once, there was no reason why she couldn't do it again. And next time he would make sure he was in control.

A horn suddenly honked and Bradon jerked his thoughts back to his driving. He had already reached Santa Monica. He noticed with chagrin that, out of habit, he had turned off Wilshire Boulevard and pulled into the parking area next to Marbella's Restaurant. Why had he done that? Having coffee with Sandi Boeckel had made him late getting away from UCLA and he had decided to go straight home. But he had been betrayed by his subconscious which had followed his habit of stopping at Marbella's. Well, what the hell. As long as he was here he could certainly use the surcease of good music. Besides, if he went to bed now with all he had on his mind, he would never get to sleep.

Since it was a week night, the restaurant was not crowded and he was able to take his usual seat at a corner table near the piano bar. Joel, at the piano, acknowledged his presence with a nod and a smile while he continued working his way through a Cole Porter medley. Patsy automatically brought him a Miller Lite and a chilled glass. She glanced at her watch and lifted an eyebrow at him, and he explained, "I stopped for coffee with a student."

The eyebrow remained raised and her chin lifted slightly so he added, "Not bad. If you like gorgeous hair, a great body and compelling eyes. A lot like you."

Patsy grinned and slapped her generous buttocks. "Don't I wish." She moved away, her curiosity satisfied.

Bradon pour a glass of the Miller's but instead of drinking he sat staring at the bursting bubbles. Stopping at Marbella's had been a mistake. It was a place he used as a refuge, an escape from painful memories. Now they flooded in as though they had been seated at the table waiting for him, bringing with them a familiar despair.

He drove the unwanted memories away by turning to his new problem: What was he going to do about that girl? She truly feared another regression. She seemed to sense that she harbored forces that he had no right to unleash. He should let the matter drop. The last time he had played God it had ended in tragedy. There was, also, the promise he had made to himself not to meddle in people's minds ever again; the promise that had made him give up his clinical practice.

He must not break that promise. If for no other reason than that the ghost of Kimberly Hill demanded it.

Ah, but this was different. No psychologist in the world would ever equate Kimberly Hill's psychosis with the regression of Sandi Boeckel. He could handle this one. The trick was control. He had lost control of Kimberly; he would never allow that to happen again.

His chuckle was as bitter as the beer. Right now the comparison between the two women was purely academic. Sandi Boeckel had made it clear that she would never consent to repeating the regression. Her refusal had been oblique but adamant.

Bradon tilted his head back and studied the low ceiling. He was supposed to be good at influencing people. There should be a way to overcome her objections. There had to be a way to change her mind. If that was impossible, to find another way.

Jesus! His head snapped forward and he almost slammed his beer glass on the table. What the hell was he thinking?! Let it go, you idiot! Haven't you learned your lesson?! Remember your damn promise! Stay out of that girl's mind!

But even as he took a determined swallow of beer, he knew that he could not.

CHAPTER 3

When she arrived home, Sandi was surprised to see Jordan's Jaguar parked in the circular drive in front of the house. She pulled her jacket shut against a sharp chill. It was unusual for him to stop by at this time of the night. He was a stockbroker, a partner in Osburne, Delany and Starkey, and it was necessary for him to be in his office by six A. M. so that he could be ready when the New York Stock Exchange opened. He rarely stayed up this late unless it was for some important social function. Something had to be wrong. Oh God. Had something happened to her father or mother?

As she pulled her car into the garage between her mother's Lexis and her father's Mercedes, she quickly used her remote control to close the garage door behind her. Like most residents of Beverly Hills--and anywhere in Los Angeles for that matter--one never lingered in one's car with the garage door open.

She had to use her key to unlock the door leading from the garage to the house and the time it took irritated her. You'd think that with the garage door closed the house would be secure. But her father was almost paranoid about security. He was forever telling how thieves had learned to use variable frequency remote controls to open garage doors, and since most people did not lock the door from the garage to the house, thieves could then walk in and help themselves. So now all doors were kept locked whether or not anyone was home.

Locking the door behind her, Sandi crossed through the laundry and kitchen to the large reception room where she heard voices coming from the library.

The sliding mahogany doors were open and as she entered, she was relieved to see that her mother, looking perfectly healthy, was seated upon one of the sofas in front of the blazing fireplace. Her father was standing next to the fireplace talking to Jordan who was sitting on the facing sofa opposite her mother. Both men were smoking cigars and holding glasses of Beaujolais, and she was immediately struck by how well they fit the setting.

The house was one of the oldest in Beverly Hills north of Santa Monica Boulevard. It had been built in the 1920s and the library reflected the period. The plaster of the high ceiling was patterned in bas-relief. The walls were mahogany paneled. A massive marble fireplace had been converted to burn gas over realistic concrete logs. The floor of polished dark oak was centrally covered by a hundred-year -old Azerbaijani rug. Heavy drapes of floral-patterned, raw linen had been pulled across oriel windows facing the front of the house. Subdued light came from ornate wall sconces. Oil paintings in heavy, gilded frames were appropriately somber portraits of 17th century aristocrats and dark landscapes. All furnishings looked as though they were polished or dusted several times each day but never moved.

Martin Boeckel, posing in front of the fireplace, was wearing dark trousers and a tailor-made, white-on-white shirt. Instead of a necktie, a dark paisley scarf was tucked into his open shirt collar European style. His smoking jacket was of maroon silk with black velvet trim. He was not tall, barely matching Sandi's 5'9" even with 2" heels on his polished loafers, but he kept his weight down so that he looked taller. His dark hair, now shot with silver, had receded and his high forehead and carefully trimmed mustache, already gray, gave him an appearance of great intellect. Pungent smoke wafted from the Cuban cigar he was holding expertly in the same hand as his wineglass. He glanced pointedly toward a grandfather clock softly ticking in the corner.

"Where have you been? You've never been this late. "

"You didn't have an accident, I hope. " Gretchen Boeckel could have been one of Paquin's models. She was taller than Martin with fleshy shoulders and skin as white and fine as alabaster. Her hair, so blonde that at first glance it appeared to be white with age, was worn in a thick roll around her head like an Irish charwoman of the '20s. The high key effect of her skin and hair made her wide blue eyes blaze with color. She wore a Dolman jacket over a long, floral dress whose decorative pattern resembled tiny dark autumn leaves. The Dolman was long, reaching almost to her knees, narrow at the hips and hem and wide and loose across the shoulders. It was made of dark red silk, hand painted with circular designs and patterned with lines of beads. Long tassels hung from the loose sleeves. Its cape-like collar of black velvet hung in wide, serrated folds. Suspended at her throat on a string of tiny seed pearls was a large Brazilian aquamarine that complimented the blue of her eyes. The last three fingers of each hand sparkled with rings bearing diamonds with emeralds, her favorite combination. She sat with her ankles crossed and her glass of red wine poised delicately, her eyes staring accusingly at Sandi.

"No, Mother," Sandi said. "I stayed for a few minutes to talk to the professor. " Calling Daniel Bradon 'professor' sounded strange but it was a term that her parents could appreciate.

Jordan set his glass of wine carefully on a coaster on the green marble top of the Neoclassic Centre table that was precisely positioned between the two sofas. After placing his cigar in an ashtray, he stood up and crossed to Sandi and took her by the shoulders. He had to duck his head to kiss her on the cheek.

"Darling," he said. "We were getting worried about you."

"Why? Is something wrong?"

"Wrong? No, of course not. We were just worried. "

Sandi let her breath out in a surge of relief. There was no emergency. So why was Jordan here? He never came by without calling first. And he knew that she had class on Tuesday night.

"Were you the only one who stayed after class?" Jordan's tone was noncommittal but she sensed an undercurrent of suspicion.

Sandi pulled away from him. "No. " She hated lying, but how could she explain what had happened to her? Her parents would never understand. And Jordan? She had only to look at his intense dark eyes, his absolutely smooth black hair, his tailored black suit, starched white shirt, and dark Paisley tie to know that he, too, would not understand. He had never approved of her decision to go to night classes. He would appreciate even less her having coffee alone with her professor. "There were several of us. We were discussing--child psychology. "

"Child psychology?" Frown lines around Gretchen's mouth looked out of place in the smooth plain of her face. "What on earth for?"

"Right," Martin said. "There's no money in that. If you're determined to pursue this psychology thing you might at least deal with adults."

"There is money in it," Sandi said defensively. "But that isn't why I'm interested. I'd love to work with children. "

"Nonsense," Martin countered. "You've never been around kids with emotional problems. They're bad enough when they're normal. You can imagine what they'd be like when they're psychotic. Drive you crazy. "

"That's why we have universities. We learn to deal with those sorts of things. "

"Well, I think it's a waste of time," Gretchen said. "You've got a fine job in the gallery. "

"Thank you, Mother. But I want something more out of life than selling art to people who don't know a lithograph from an etching. "

Gretchen started to reply but she was interrupted by Jordan's barking laugh. "She can use her psychology on our own children. They'll be the most mixed up kids on the block. "

Martin chuckled, but Gretchen's face remained set in its usual icy planes as she said, "If you must attend a university why don't you go in the day time? I don't like you to be out alone at night. "

"She can't," Martin interjected. "I need her at the gallery. You know that. "

"You only really need her when you're out of town. You can put off any trips for a few weeks. "

"Impossible. I have to--"

"It's all right," Sandi interrupted. They had been through this same argument many times, but again she explained patiently, "I prefer night classes. It will take a little longer but this way I can keep on with the gallery.

"How much time? What about our wedding?"

Sandi dreaded the question. She had told Jordan she wanted to obtain her degree before the wedding, but taking classes only one night a week meant it was going to take more than a year to make up the credits she needed just to qualify for graduate studies. After that, she planned to complete her master's thesis. If she pursued her doctorate, it would take at least three more years of full time graduate studies. There was no reason why she couldn't be married while she was matriculating. But not now. Not until she had exorcised her demons once and for all.

To cut off further discussion, she fell back on her usual excuse, "I'm sorry, darling. It'll only be a few more weeks. I promise. "

"That's what I want to talk to you about. "

As though his words were a well-rehearsed cue, Gretchen stood up, and she and Martin moved toward the door. "You two can work this out," she said.

"Whatever date you pick will be fine with us," her father added.

As she watched her parents leave, Sandi had the feeling that the arrangements had already been made. It was only necessary to fill her in on the predetermined details. "Is that why you came by tonight? Have you three formed a conspiracy?" She kept her voice light, but even she could detect a trace of resentment.

Jordan crossed to a dark walnut sidepiece and took out a wineglass. He filled it from the wine bottle and proffered it to Sandi. She shook her head. "No, thanks. "

He sipped from the glass. "You should try this. 1982 Chateau Ausone. I brought it for you. "

Sandi moved to stand with her back to the fireplace. Although the night had been warmed by the desert winds, the old, thick-walled mansion always seemed to be cold. "Thanks," she said, "but I'm really not in the mood tonight. "

He studied her, his lean face speculative. "Why is it that I have the feeling you're avoiding setting a date?"

His words gave Sandi a shock. Was it that obvious? Perhaps so. They had been engaged for more than a year and had yet to set a date for the wedding. But it was only because of circumstances. Jordan had wanted to have the wedding as early as May, but Martin had made one of his trips to Europe to pick up some Pre-Raphaelites along with Italian and Dutch Baroques that had come on the market, and she had thought it advisable to put off the wedding until he returned. Then in July, Gretchen had come down with the flu and again they had to postpone. During the remainder of the summer Jordan's parents had been away on a world cruise. Now the fall term at UCLA was almost over and there really were no more reasons to wait.

"It's not avoidance," she said. "But we've waited this long, I'd just like to wait at least until I get my bachelor's degree. "

"I see. " He gestured toward her left hand. "Is that why you took off your engagement ring?"

"I only take it off when I go to class. "

"Oh?"

She knew instantly what he was thinking: she took the ring off so that she would appear available to the men in the class. Her voice was icy as she said, "It has eight marquise diamonds. I never wear it at night when I have to be alone. "

"So you admit that place is dangerous. "

One of his arguments against her attending night classes was that universities with their large populations of third world students were dangerous places for a woman alone, especially at night. She had assured him that UCLA was well-guarded; that there were few incidents of women being attacked or mugged. "It's no more dangerous than the parking lot of any market or department store. And I don't wear it there either. "

The sharp edge in her voice made him raise his hand in surrender. "Okay, okay. I'm glad you're being prudent. " He put down the wineglass and came to put his arms around her. She caught the odor of after-shave lotion. He favored the heavy masculine scents that could overwhelm the clinging odor of stale cigar smoke. "I don't mind waiting to be married. But I'm getting tired of waiting for love. "

To emphasize his desire, he put his hand under her chin and held it firmly while he kissed her. She put her arms around him and allowed him to explore her lips while she waited for desire to stir. Instead, she was acutely conscious that his lips tasted of tobacco.

She tried to ignore her faint revulsion, tried to will herself into passion, but there was no response in her body. What was wrong? She was in love with Jordan. Always before when he had kissed her, there had been a tide of desire. But not tonight. Now she just wanted to go to her room where she could think. When Jordan tried to force his tongue into her mouth she kept her teeth together until he gave up. But he continued to kiss her as he released her chin and put both hands around her, low on her back, pulling her hips against him and she twisted away, not wanting to provoke something that would be difficult to stop.

To take the onus from her rejection she smiled at him and laughed. "Don't be so rough. I bruise easily. "

"Sorry. " His attempt at a smile was more of grimace. "I just want you to know how much I want you. "

He reached for her again and she backed away while she continued to smile. "I know. But it won't be long now and then I'm"--her breath caught in her throat--"I'm all yours. "

"Why wait? We're going to be married. We could be spending all this time together. "

It was a question she had often asked herself and for which she had no answer. God knows that these days people rarely waited to be married before leaping into bed, even people who had no intention of getting married. It wasn't because she felt no desire. Jordan was stunningly handsome with chiseled good looks and a fine body. He could have been a male model or one of those Chippendale dancers. She sometimes fantasized about what lovemaking would be like after they were married; she had often yearned for him to take her. So why wait indeed? It would be so easy to let herself go, to lead him up to her bedroom and allow him to arouse her latent passions. It would be weeks before they could be married. Why waste all those nights when they could be enjoying each other's bodies?

Jordan sensed her mood and put his arms around her again, pulling her hard against his hips. He wrapped one arm around the back of her head, holding her so she could not turn away as he kissed her so hard his teeth hurt her lips. If he had not done so, she might have given in, but his abrupt move turned her search for desire into anger and she shoved him away.

"No, Jordan. I want to wait. "

His face contorted in sudden fury, and as quickly smoothed into hard planes as he realized that argument would be unproductive. "All right," he said harshly. "But the sooner you get this psychology nonsense out of your head the sooner we can be married. "

Sandi's chin came up. "Nonsense! What makes you think so?"

"I think I'm perfectly capable of supporting the two of us. You won't be working."

"And what am I supposed to do? Sit home and wait for you?"

"You do what other women do; what your mother does. "

"My mother's idea of a career is planning a trip to Bloomingdale's. If that's what you want, you picked the wrong woman. "

Clinched fists was the only evidence of his anger as he said, "I would think that raising a child would be career enough. "

"She didn't raise me. I've had nannies since the day I was born. And that's another thing that won't happen to any child of mine. "

"What about your career? You can't have both. "

"My career will be children; including my own. "

"Ours," he snapped. "Our children. " Then he smiled and his voice soften the way Sandi was sure it sounded when he was placating an irate client. "I guess you're right. These days a mother needs all the psychology in the world. "

Sandi brought her own anger under control. She touched his arm as thought the light contact would convey her empathy. "I'm sorry, Jordan. But it won't be long. There's so much to do. There's the gallery. And the winter semester will be starting before we know it. "

"Not before I do. " He moved back to her and kissed her on the cheek. "Dinner tomorrow?"

She nodded. "Okay. "

"Eight o'clock. " He picked up the wineglass and drained it. "Too expensive to waste," he explained. At the door he turned back, and she was again struck by his good looks just as she had been the first time she had seen him. He worked out regularly at some gym and looked lean and hard. His suit had to be incredibly expensive because it fit him so perfectly. And the snowy white shirt highlighted his tanned skin and dark hair. His teeth, when he flashed her a grin, were the same snowy whiteness as his shirt. She would have to work on his penchant for cigars. They ruined his clean-cut image. "Four kids," he said. "That would be a nice career. "

She did not move until she heard his car start. Four children? She wondered whether Jordan had worked out the details with her mother and father, deciding that four would be a sufficient number to keep her tied to her home. They might not know it but they were right about one thing: She was going to give her children--whether it was one or a dozen--total commitment, commitment in the form of love. Time without love meant nothing, just as love without time meant nothing. She would have enough of both to go around.

As she slowly climbed the stairs, she tried to picture Jordan as a father. The image was so foreign that she had never given it a thought. When she had met him at a cocktail party sponsored by his brokerage, she had been impressed by his strength of character as well as his sensuous good looks. Martin and Gretchen had been delighted that she was dating someone who had both money and social standing. They had immediately joined forces with him to prepare her for marriage. She was well aware of their scheming, but they didn't know that it was unnecessary. She would never find another man as solid and dependable as Jordan J. Starkey. But Jordan and four children?

The image of Jordan umpiring a Little League baseball game or helping with homework was hard to visualize. Dan Bradon looked as though he would be right at home throwing a football or bringing home a puppy. Daniel Bradon? Why had he popped into her mind? She was going to have a difficult time teaching her children mental discipline when she could not even control her own disruptive thoughts.

That night her sleep was disturbed by familiar voices and vague forms that called her name, urging her into a terrifying darkness. It was the old nightmare again, and she struggled to resist. The darkness was evil. If she gave in, if she entered the darkness, it would close behind her and she would never escape. She must not listen to the voices. She must not.

She awakened with a start, twisted in the bedclothes, perspiring, gasping for breath, her heart pounding. She untangled the bedclothes and got out of bed, shivering when the night air cut through her wet nightgown. She thought she had gained control over the phantoms, but she had been wrong. They were back, as strong as ever. Well, she had conquered them for a long time. She would just have to fight harder. They would never lure her into their alien darkness. Never.

CHAPTER 4

The following Tuesday when Sandi entered the classroom she still had not made up her mind about Bradon's proposed experiment, even though she had been able to think of little else the entire week. She had convinced herself that the scene with the Tarot cards and the Nazis in uniform had no relationship to any of her dream phantoms. The startling regression was an anomaly, conjured up from some unremembered book she had read or an old movie. Either that or it was a chimera created by an overly-active imagination. The experience was now expunged and would not, must not occur again.

But if that was true, if the experience was simply a repressed memory or a traumatic amnesia of some forgotten childhood event, what harm could come of another regression? Perhaps then the slate could be wiped clean and it would put an end to terrifying recrudescence.

Terrifying was the key word. In truth, she was terribly afraid. What if there really were layers beneath layers of ancient memories that could be ripped away like pages from a book? Where would they lead? Into madness? Perhaps the voices, the shadow figures of her nightmares were entities from another life, ghosts who were struggling to push through some membrane of time. If they succeeded, if another regression summoned them forth like Hieronymus demons, could they be forced back into the past after she awakened? It was the fear that they could not that made her decide against participating in the experiment. Her dreams might continue to be filled with the whispering voices of phantoms, but, at least, she now had them under control. Keep the lid on them, she reminded herself. You'll make them die.

She was sitting quietly in her usual place in the uppermost tier in the back of the room when Daniel Bradon entered, and the murmured chatter from the students died. As he took off his leather jacket and draped it over the back of his chair, he looked up at Sandi with an inquiring lift of his eyebrows and she gave a small shake of her head. He continued his preparations, taking papers from his briefcase, but she sensed his disappointment.

"This is our last class of the semester," he said when he had everyone's attention. "Usually I give the test the last thing--that's the test for those of you here for credit--but tonight I'd like to conduct an experiment that shouldn't be interrupted, so we'll take the test first."

Sandi stared at him as a chill shook her. What did he mean? She had indicated that she was not going to participate in any experiment. She set her jaw and continued to stare at Bradon. But he would not look at her. He had better have someone else in mind to be his guinea pig because she certainly was not going to cooperate.

Then it struck her: Of course! He was going to work with someone else. That had to be it. How egotistical of her to think that she was the only person capable of regression. If reincarnation were viable, everyone in the room was a possible candidate.

She was almost smiling by the time the test papers were passed down the row. She would never have been able to concentrate on the test if she knew she was going to be humiliated when it was over.

"It's not my purpose to flunk anybody," Bradon said as he finished handing out the test papers. "I'm sure you won't have any trouble with the true or false or the multiple choice. But I'll be giving a lot of weight to a brief essay at the end." He checked his watch. "I'd like those of you not taking the course for credit to take the test too. It'll help you review what we've been over and it'll keep you quiet for an hour or so."

The test, as promised, proved to be relatively easy. Most of the questions were multiple choice. At the end they were required to write a brief evaluation of the class with suggestions for improvements.

Sandi agonized over the evaluation. She had enjoyed the class, certain that the knowledge gained would in time help her, but to what extent? Had the regression undone the entire semester's work? She ended up leaving the section blank. Bradon might take something off her score, but she was reasonably sure that he would not flunk her. Not after what she had been through.

When everyone had completed the test, Bradon called for a ten-minute break. After the class reassembled, he asked that everyone move down as close as possible to the front of the class. te

A slow anger grew inside Sandi as she gathered textbook and notes and moved with the others from the back rows to seats nearer the front of the room. Damn him! He was going to single her out to be his test subject, knowing that refusing would be difficult in front of the other class members. How dare he again make a fool of her. Well, his ploy was not going to work. If he thought that he could shame her into acquiescing he was badly mistaken. She was stronger than that. She had already taken the test. If he attempted to coerce her, she would gather her books and leave. Still, if she had really misjudged him, he might be vindictive enough to give her a failing grade. Well, so be it.

She found a seat at the side of the room, near the door. She steeled herself for refusal when Bradon began, "You remember that last week we had an interesting example of past-life regression."

To Sandi's discomfort, several of the students turned their heads to glance at her. Her reaction was to stare at Bradon, ignoring the glances and murmurs.

"Tonight I would like to conduct an experiment."

Here it comes, Sandi thought.

"I would like a volunteer. Someone who would like to see if they have a past life or lives."

A volunteer?

Sandi found that she had been holding her breath, and his words caused the tension to drain out of her like water from a broken dam. Many students turned their heads to look at her, but she sat as rigid as stone. To her relief, several students raised their hands. Good. The pressure was off her. Bradon pointed to a young man with dark curly hair. "All right. What's your name?"

"Burnstein. Stan Burnstein."

"Okay, Stan. Come on up in front here."

Bradon placed his chair in a center position, and Burnstein made his way to the front of the room and sat in the chair. Bradon moved to stand behind him. "Now," he said. "I'm going to need all your help with this, so I want each of you to focus your concentration on Stan. Okay, Stan. What I'm going to do is induce a hypnotic state. Just relax and let your mind go. I'm going to try to take you back to sometime in your past. Then I'll bring you back. Or more likely, you'll bring yourself back. Ready?"

Stan Burnstein nodded, "Okay. Oh, one question. Will I be aware of what's going on?"

"Not while it's happening. Your body will be here, but in your mind you will be that other person."

"What if something--something bad is happening? Something I don't want to experience?"

"We'll know about it. If that happens, I'll bring you back."

Burnstein nodded and settled himself in the chair and closed his eyes. He looked as though he was having second thoughts about the experiment, but he could hardly back out now. Sandi could empathize with him. Delving into the unknown was scary. The phantoms of her own dreams were creatures of terror. If they were part of the ancient past, she had no intention of ever finding out.

"Open your eyes," Bradon said and Burnstein did so. "They'll close by themselves when they're ready." Bradon placed his fingertips lightly on Bernstein's temples. "We'll start out with our relaxing exercises. Start here behind your eyes. Let the tension out. Relax your arms, your hands. The tension is flowing from your head down through your neck and shoulders and out through your fingertips. Your arms are growing heavy. Your eyes are growing heavy. You can hardly keep them open."

As he spoke, slowly and gently, Bradon began moving his fingertips from Bernstein's temples, down his cheeks to his neck, his fingers as light as butterfly wings. Watching him, Sandi could almost feel the light caress and the sensation helped her relax. After a moment, Bradon's voice took on a sensuous droning cadence, and Bernstein's eyes slowly closed. Sandi enjoyed the sense of relaxation. It seemed that she had been under constant tension for days, and now she could let it all slough away in the warmth of Bradon's voice. As tension drained, her eyelids grew heavy, and she allowed them to close. Her body was warm, completely relaxed. For some reason Bradon's voice seemed to be coming closer, and she sensed that he had left the man in the chair and was moving up the aisle closer to her. Her eyelids fluttered and his voice urged her to close her eyes and her eyes responded by remaining closed so that all that was left was his voice intoning words that also drifted into darkness.

*   *   *   *

I was seated at a long table in a wide dining room with a high, beamed ceiling. Brilliant light from wall sconces and from two massive chandeliers reflected from a white table cloth and silver and crystal place settings. The plaster walls were bare except for a large portrait of Frederick the Great and a huge red flag featuring a Nazi swastika.

I wore a long, black crepe Jean Patou dinner gown. Its sleeves and the bodice were embroidered in intricate patterns with gold beadwork. My hair was piled atop my head and held in place by combs jeweled with tiny diamonds. My left hand was bare except for a wide gold wedding ring, but on my right index finger I had chosen to wear a large topaz. Next to it on my ring finger I had placed my ruby, the one surrounded by baguette diamonds that Hermann had given me on my twenty-second birthday.

Seated next to me, Hermann, like most of the men, was wearing a tuxedo and black tie. However, Adolph Hitler, seated at the head of the table, was dressed in a dark business suit with a Nazi swastika armband on his left arm. Hermann Goering, as usual, looked like a circus tent in his white uniform. By contrast, Heinrich Himmler should have been resplendent in his newly designed black and silver SS uniform, complete with a black Sam Browne belt. But on him the uniform simply looked ominous.

Reinhard Heydrich was typically arrogant in a similar black SS uniform. By contrast, Ernst Roehm clad in the brown uniform of his Sturmabteilungen brown-shirted storm-troops, looked drab and doughty.

I was surprised that Rudolph Hess wore a tuxedo instead of his Wermach uniform, but he was such a myrmidon that it was probably because Hitler was in mufti.

I was not overly charmed by the seating arrangement that had put Reinhold Ebertin and his mother, Frau Elsbeth Ebertin, Hitler's astrologer, on my right. I would have preferred that she be seated as far away from me as possible. I'm sure she felt the same about me. Although, I don't really understand why she should have any animosity toward me. The woman was a second rate astrologer who used more psychology than facts to produce favorable astrologic charts. She also advocated the work of Martin Pollner and Ernst Tiede and other quack astrologers who stupidly believed that it is possible to cast horoscopes of cities and nations in order to determine their destiny. It had always seemed to me that if astrology was indeed capable of predicting the future, astrologers would be the wealthiest people in the world. Such a waste of intelligence. With few exceptions, astrologers, like chess players, had brilliant minds and if all that effort, all those mental and mathematical capabilities, were channeled into useful pursuits, the world would be infinitely better off.

But I had little time to dwell upon Frau Ebertin's machinations. It was difficult to concentrate on anything because of the way a man seated on the opposite side of the table stared at me. The man really frightened me. He was Colonel Wolfram von Sievers, head of the Ahnenerbe, Hitler's Research and Training Foundation for Ancestral Heritage which many called 'The Occult Bureau.' He had a long, narrow face made to seem even longer by a close-cropped beard and moustache. His deep-set eyes beneath thick eyebrows were dark and piercing. He was one of those individuals who never found it necessary to blink. Seated directly across from me, he persisted in staring as intently as though he were trying to probe my mind. Or to intimidate me. I wondered why. Probably jealousy of my husband. Hermann is a bonafide Count, descendent of a long line of Prussian nobility. The von in Hermann's name came from a three hundred year heraldry while I suspect that von Sievers attribute had been purchased-- and recently at that. Then too, von Sievers was also a latecomer in the Thule Gesellschaft, while Hermann was one of the original, and most influential, founding members.

I also sensed that von Sievers was more than a little disturbed because the Führer had invited Hermann and me without consulting him. In truth, I had been rather surprised when Hermann had received the invitation to attend one of Hitler's rare formal dinner parties even though Hermann is an important Nazi party leader. And lately he had been working closely with the Finance Minister, Count von Krosigk, in raising money for the party and directing party finances.

Trying to ignore Von Sievers' stare, I attempted to concentrate on words being spoken by Professor Carl Haushofer. Seated at the opposite end of the table from Hitler, he was expounding on the concept of Armanenschaft and its relationship to the Thule legend; the necessity for true Aryans to claim Lebensraum eastward as far as the ancient lands of Tibet.

At his mention of Tibet, I inadvertently gasped. That idea had originated in the wild writings of Madame Blavatsky, the Russian medium. I couldn't believe that in 1934 anyone still took her theories seriously.

Hermann inclined his head toward me. "Helga," he whispered. "Are you all right?"

I considered telling him about von Sievers' stare but realized he could do nothing about it, so I nodded. "Yes. I'm fine."

He made a soft grunt of acknowledgement and turned his attention back to the discussion just as Goering said with a laugh, "Tibet? I hope there's room for a little flexibility there. I don't think my Luftwaffe is up to fighting in the Himalayas."

Hitler's eyes suddenly blazed and he slapped his hand on the table so hard that I jumped. "Flexibility!" he shouted. "Flexibility is a sign of weakness. I have achieved success because I would not be flexible. Once I have set a goal I will attain that goal! There will be no turning aside. There will be none of this flexibility!"

I was to remember Hitler's words later in the evening. We were all gathered in the small theater watching Marlene Dietrich in "The Blue Angel", a film that everyone had seen several times but which was one of Hitler's favorites, when someone tapped me on the shoulder. I looked around and was startled to see Heinrich Himmler.

I was sitting in an aisle seat so he was able to put his mouth close to my ear and whisper, "The Führer would like to see you."

I suppressed a faint shiver of alarm. There was an ominous import to the summons. This had to be why Hermann and I had been invited. Although Hitler was known as an occultist, with special interest in the Holy Grail and the Heilige Lance, recently, as though to cover up his penchant, he had been having a number of mystics arrested. Was I to be arrested and sent to one of the infamous Konzentrationslagers?

I did not want to see him alone and as I left my seat, I tapped Hermann on the arm and he got up and followed. When he saw Herr Himmler leading the way, he looked quizzically at me, but I lifted my shoulders in a shrug that said I had no idea what was going on.

Himmler led us to a den room where Hitler was standing with his back to us looking out a large window into the darkness of the night. I was surprised to see that two of the large oil paintings on the walls were sensuous von Stuck nudes.

When he heard us enter, Hitler turned. "Ah, Count and Countess. I hope you will forgive me for interrupting the movie."

"Of course," Hermann said. Like most old-line Prussians he found it difficult to address Hitler as Führer even though he was a member of the National Socialists Party and was deeply impressed by Hitler's dedication to fulfilling Germany's destiny.

Hitler was uncomfortably aware of how the Prussians viewed his proletarian birth and, it was said, his Jew-tainted heritage. He glared at Hermann for a second, his dark brown eyes unfathomable, before he moved to stand in front of me, saying as he did so, "Would you like a glass of wine?"

I knew that Hitler hadn't touched alcoholic beverages since the ill-fated Beer Hall Putsch in 1923, so I declined. Another reason for declining was because I wasn't sure I could hold the glass in my trembling hand without spilling its contents. I tried to keep my apprehension out of my eyes and my voice as I replied, "No, thank you, Mein Führer." I had none of Hermann's compunctions about calling the man 'Führer'. He was not a man to have as an enemy.

"Very well." Hitler moved to stand beside a large desk made of dark oak where he picked up a man's pocket watch from several personal articles on the desktop. I could make out a pocket comb, a wristwatch, a cigar cutter, handkerchiefs, keys, and cuff links. Holding the watch, Hitler said, "I was not aware until recently, Countess, that you have a reputation as a mystic with very accurate psychometric abilities."

My face felt wooden, set in an expression of dismay. My eyes were dry, gritty. If I admitted that I had psychometric talent, would I be incriminating myself? Would I find myself in that whispered place of horror, the basement of the SS-Kommando-Gestapa on Columbia Strasse?

I glanced at Hermann wondering how I should answer, knowing that anything I said would reflect upon him. He saw my distress and answered for me. "I am proud to say that is correct." His eyes flicked toward Herr Himmler. "Perhaps you have heard that she has assisted the police of several cities--including right here in Berlin--to solve some of their most baffling crimes."

"That has been brought to my attention," Hitler said, and I was glad that Hermann had not lied. Hitler undoubtedly had a thick dossier on us. The thought gave me a new rush of apprehension. "As I understand it," Hitler continued, "you can hold an object in your hand and instantly know everything about the owner."

My best, my only defense was the truth. Even so, my smile was far from brave as I said, "It isn't quite that simple. Sometimes I have only the barest glimpse of the person. Sometimes none at all."

"But sometimes the images are very strong. Is that not true?"

"Yes. Sometimes that is true." He had opened my mind to several memories I had chosen to forget, such as the time while working with the police I had been handed a kitchen knife without explanation and had dropped it in horror when I had the vivid impression of the knife being used to brutally murder a young girl, which turned out to be true.

"Very well," Hitler said. "I have a little test for you." There was absolutely no hint in his voice or his eyes that gave a clue to his thinking. Was he a skeptic, searching for truth? Or was he a true believer in the power of the mind? Perhaps he was toying with us, waiting for an incrimination. I knew that I was deathly pale. Lives were at stake here, possibly my own.

Hitler gestured to the objects on the desk. "I have here articles from a number of people. I want you to tell me what you see for each one." He held out the pocket watch he had been holding. "You can start with this."

I stared at the watch, afraid to take it. He must believe that psychic powers could be turned on and off at will. But it didn't work that way. True, I sometimes received vivid impressions the first time I touched an object, especially if events involving it were strong--as with the knife. But usually I received no images at all. Or they came later, sometimes long after I had put aside the instigating object.

"Go ahead, Helga," Hermann said. "Try."

I looked at him helplessly. As many times as I had explained my strange abilities to him, he still did not understand. But then, few did. I glanced at Heinrich Himmler. He was staring at me through the lenses of his wire-rimmed glasses as though daring me to say anything untoward about him. Did one of the objects on the desk belonged to him? Oh, God. Suppose one of them belonged to Hitler himself? I did not have to hold one of his possessions to read his future. He might rise toward the heavens like a holiday rocket, but the world would not allow him to stay there. They would surely bring him crashing down to destruction. One did not have to be clairvoyant to see that.

But I could never tell him.

As though reading my mind, he held out the watch. "Go on. Take it. It's not mine. I will tell you now, none of these are mine."

I was only partially mollified. There was still danger in this exercise. Instead of taking the watch, I bit my lip in nervous consternation and said, "If you don't mind, Mein Führer, I would rather not."

Hitler's face froze in stunned surprise, but it was Himmler who took a step toward me and snapped, "You cannot refuse a command of the Führer! Do you know what happens to people who refuse to submit to the National Socialist doctrine?"

I shot a quick glance at Hermann. His face was as pale as my own. "I have heard," I said.

"Very well. Then you will cooperate. Do you understand?"

I closed my eyes for a second wondering how my country had come to this, that a person such as Himmler could wield the power of life or death. But the reality was that there was no way out. The consequences of defying Hitler would not fall upon me alone but also upon Hermann and, perhaps, other members of our family. I opened my eyes and ran my tongue across my dry lips. "Very well," I said. "I'll try. But I can't promise anything."

"I do not expect promises," Hitler said. "Only truth."

I took the watch from him, careful not to touch his hand, bracing myself. Sometimes images flashed through my mind the instant I touched an object. Often they were so shocking they jolted me like a blow. Not this time. I relaxed and concentrated on the watch. It felt unusually warm. Hitler's hand had to be as hot as fire. Could he be lying? Perhaps it was his own watch and the entire charade was some sort of trap. But trap or not, there was no turning back.

The watch was a fine Breitling. Very expensive, which did not surprise me. None of the Nazis was penurious. I held the watch in both hands and waited for images to form. But there were none. It was as though I was holding a stone. One thing was certain; it was not Hitler's watch. "I'm sorry," I told him. "I'm not getting a thing."

"Take your time," Himmler said. Then he added, "These things take time, Mein Führer."

"I know, I know," Hitler snapped. "Forget that one. Try one of the others."

I placed the watch gently on the desk and stared at the other objects. Which one to take? If I failed totally, Hermann would be *embarrassed. Of more importance, so would Himmler. I was sure he was the one who had brought me to the attention of Hitler.*

One of the objects was a small wristwatch that I suspected belonged to a woman, although it was not a typical woman's watch. If the objects on the desk had been appropriated from the dinner guests, the watch might well belong to Frau Ebertin, the astrologer. Another test? If it did belong to the astrologer, it was a test I would prefer not to take. Hitler might not appreciate my true feelings about astrology. A denunciation of Frau Ebertin might also appear to be professional jealousy.

I was going to pass it by, but when my hand hesitated over the watch I had a fleeting impression of Hitler's body tensing as though he was afraid I would pick it up. And something else. Somehow, I realized that the watch did not belong to Frau Ebertin. It was the property of a young woman. One of the other women at the table? Unlikely. They probably had no secrets that would be of interest to Adolph Hitler. So what was there about the watch's owner that would instill such tension in the man?

I picked it up carefully and clasped it between my two hands, acutely conscious of Hitler's burning gaze. Immediately images began to fill my mind. They were vague and illusionary, but no sense of pain, no apprehension. On the contrary, the watch emitted a friendly warmth, a warmth tinged with sadness. What a strange sensation. Almost like love. But, yet, terribly sad.

"This belongs to a woman," I said slowly. "Rather young. I would guess--" Suddenly I was struck by an image of blood and despair so shockingly intense it was as though the watch was on fire and I almost dropped it, holding it with trembling fingers.

Hitler, his eyes blazing, instantly asked, "What is it? What is it?"

I shook my head, unwilling to answer. Instead, I placed the watch back on desk with the other objects. But Hitler picked it up and handed back to me. "I want to know," he snarled. "I've got to know."

Reluctantly, I took the watch, steeling myself against the expected emotional onslaught. I sought desperately to push my thoughts beyond the awful image, back to a time when I sensed there had been love and affection. "I feel great sadness. She's dead, isn't she?" Hitler did not answer, but his face told me that I was right. Instantly I knew the owner of the watch. Geli Raubal, Hitler's niece. He had been devoted to the girl, more like a lover than an older uncle. It was rumored that she had committed suicide to escape his unwanted attentions. Ironically, she had shot herself in the chest with Hitler's pistol. The shot had not killed her quickly. Instead, she had slowly bled to death. No wonder I had received such a bloody impression.

I held the watch tenderly, desperately trying to regain the warmth I had first perceived. And it was there. But it was not the warmth of love; it was the fire of youth, and of hope. But tempered by an awful despair. I could never tell that to this man. His expression, his tense body told me that the truth would be like a knife in his heart. At the moment he was not the dictatorial leader of one of the most powerful nations on earth. At the moment he was a grieving man who wanted to be told that he was not the cause of his loved one's death. What was the point of hurting him more than he was already hurt? I smiled and lied, "I feel love. This person had great affection for some man, an older man in her life. Possibly a relative."

"Yes, yes," Hitler said. He was so anxious for me to continue that he stood pounding his right fist into his left palm.

"I think she loved him deeply. And her death was,"--what could I say--"because her love was too overwhelming for such a loving heart." Gently I placed the watch back on the desk. "I feel great peace. Great peace."

Hitler let his breath out in a sigh. The sadness in his eyes was tempered by the happiness of knowing that Geli had died loving him. I couldn't help but wonder at the mental stability of a man who could calmly order the deaths of multitudes, but could be so shattered by the death of one. But it wasn't just this man; it seemed to be part of the human psyche that only the death of an individual--or a pet--with whom they have a personal relationship could really touch a person. Which made it all the more remarkable that there were individuals who could feel great empathy for people they did not know personally. Some even jeopardized their own lives to save the lives of strangers. Amazing.

"This one." Himmler pointed to a black fountain pen on the desk as though reluctant to touch it. "Tell us about this one."

I picked up the pen, determined not to provide any information beyond the most innocuous. But even as I took the pen in my two hands I was flooded by such a feeling of evil that I shuddered. Himmler had been watching my face closely, and to my surprise, his lips tightened into a faint smile. "What is it? What do you see?"

It was too late to claim that I felt nothing. How could I possibly conceal the evil that seemed to be radiating from the pen in a foul miasma? Scenes of people being beaten, shot and tortured flashed in my mind with such rapidity that I was overwhelmed with a horrible sickness. I tried to drop the pen and I must have succeeded because I heard myself murmuring, "Evil. Oh God, such evil," even as blackness closed in and I fainted.

*   *   *   *

"Sandi! It's all right. It's all right. Wake up. Sandi It's over. Wake up."

The words seemed to swim toward her and she struggled to grasp them as though they were a lifeline that could lift her from a pit of horror. She had to open her eyes. It would not be over until she opened her eyes. But the horror kept trying to pull her back into the darkness, and she fought to push it away.

"No, Sandi. It's me, Dan. Dan Bradon."

Bradon? Oh, God, what was happening to her? With a will born of fear, she forced her eyelids to lift and by blinking, brought the scene into focus. Bradon? He was on his knees in front of her holding her by the wrists. He peered at her face, his eyes worried under furrowed brows, while he said urgently, "It's all right. Sandi. Come back. Come back now."

Her eyes focused on him and she took a deep breath. Her throat. Terribly raw and sore. Her senses so keyed up she could detect his fear as clearly as she had her own. She attempted a smile to help him end his fearful concern, but she was sure that what she produced was more a grimace. "I'm all right," she croaked.

He smiled and softly said, "Wow. You had me going there."

Then she noticed that the other students were gathered around staring at her, some only with curiosity in their expressions, others with concern. When they saw that she was all right they began chattering with the emotional release of ended alarm. Embarrassed, Sandi began nervously gathering her disordered papers, and she said to Bradon, "I did it again, didn't I?"

"Yes," he said. "You were really gone." His light tone, meant to be reassuring, failed to make her feel better. In his voice she also sensed an edge of guilt. Why? Her mind churned with too many thoughts to focus on one. Lord, she was so tired. Her emotions had been completely drained, leaving her empty of energy. She put both palms to her face and pressed hard against her closed eyes.

"Are you all right?" she heard Bradon ask.

"Yes. But tired--for some reason."

Two or three of the students laughed, and Bradon's face spasmed in quick fury. He stood up and clapped his hands sharply. "All right, everyone. It's already past our time. Go out into the world and sin no more."

The students began gathering their books and papers, moving toward the door. Bradon turned back to Sandi, "You up to coffee again?"

She wanted to say no. She was so tired that she was not sure she could walk the short distance to the parking structure without collapsing. But even if she made it home, tired as she was, she knew she would never be able to sleep, not with all the images swirling within her mind. She had to find out what had happened--had to make some sense out of the images or she might never sleep again. Bradon was her only hope.

"All right," she said. "I've got a lot of questions."

"Me too. But I'm not sure either of us knows the answers."

Sandi gazed at him with a sinking feeling in her stomach. If a professor of psychology couldn't explain what was happening to her, who could? Was she going crazy? Hallucinating? Could anyone help her? Did she even want answers? The truth might be more terrifying that the darkness.

CHAPTER 5

The Santa Ana winds had died leaving warm balmy air that hung softly in the night. As Sandi and Bradon slowly walked across the shadowed Dickson Plaza toward the coffee shop, a sense of tranquility suppressed any desire to talk. Dan Bradon welcomed the silence. He was oblivious to the beauty of the shadowed campus, to other people who passed them. His thoughts were locked in a painful struggle about how much to tell this dangerous woman walking so trustingly beside him. And she was dangerous. She stirred complex feelings inside him that he did not want to surface. The walls he had so painfully built against ever again becoming involved with someone's personal problems were splintering badly. He could not afford to have them fall. The last time he had let down his guard it had cost Kimberly's life and had almost taken his own.

And yet, here he was walking beside this hurting young woman, thinking about how he could use her.

There was something else that was equally disturbing. It had been a critical mistake to watch the play of emotions across Sandi's face as she had fought her battles with the past. Her pain had burned its way into his consciousness like a white-hot iron. She not only possessed the same high intelligence as Kimberly Hill, but she also had a pristine innocence that drew emotions from him like a powerful magnet, emotions that he had sworn would remained buried forever. Stupid. But he knew why. It wasn't just the idea of a book. Admit it. He was more than a little attracted to her.

He stole a glance at her. It wasn't just her subtle beauty. It was the way she moved, the way she walked, with long swinging strides, her back straight and her eyes thoughtful.

And there was her hair. Thick. Dark blonde. Sun streaked. With a natural curl. He liked the way she was wearing it in an unconcerned mane that she unconsciously brushed out of her face with a quick flick of her hand. Dangerous emotions. Emotions he could not afford.

Instead of walking away after the class, like a fool he had invited her to have coffee. He could rationalize all he wanted about wanting to know more about her simply because of her uncanny susceptibility to regression. He also knew it was because he enjoyed being with her. Sex? He couldn't discount the physical attraction. Damn. Such thoughts weren't helping matters.

He should have allowed her to walk away, walk out of his life, then he could resumed battling memories of Kimberly Hill without the distraction of Sandi Boeckel.

But it was a little late to call off his offer. What he could do, however, was keep conversation brief and professional.

When they had obtained their coffee and were sitting at one of the outside tables back in the shadows, he said, "Do you remember any of it?"

His voice was so brusque and cold that Sandi looked sharply at him before saying, "Bits and pieces. It's kind of vague."

"You were speaking German again. Most of it was incoherent but I got the impression that you were at some kind of a party with a lot of Nazi bigwigs. You mentioned Hitler and Himmler, and a woman named Frau Ebertin."

A needle of fear pierced Sandi as his words brought into focus some of the images. But the fear was tempered by a powerful fascination. The fear, she knew, came from memories of the menacing figures she had encountered. But the fascination? That certainly wasn't part of the past. It was of the present. How odd that the two should be so closely linked.

She bit her lip, concentrating, fearful yet determined to probe the images.

"It seemed to be at some sort of a dinner party, in Berlin. Several Nazi leaders were there. I remember Hitler and Heinrich Himmler." She fought back a growing revulsion as more of the image came into focus. "Yes. There was a woman, an astrologer. Frau Ebertin. I didn't like her much."

"Do you know who you were?"

"No." Sandi started to sip her coffee as she attempted to isolate parts of the kaleidoscope, but trembling in her hands made her place the cup back on the table. "I was . . . I was there with someone. My husband, I think."

"You called someone Hermann."

"Hermann. Yes. I remember that name."

"And I had the impression you had some kind of a title."

"That's right. I think I was a countess. Hermann was" --a name was coming into focus--"Count Hermann von Waltz. He was my husband." A name popped into her memory. "Helga. My name was Helga, and I--." She stopped as a kaleidoscope of images numbed her with fear. "There was a desk . . .with objects on it. I was supposed to hold the objects and tell two men--one was Hitler, I believe--about the person the object belonged to. Does that make sense?"

Bradon stared at her as an idea began to form. God. Was it possible? It would explain why she had been so open to his suggestions. "It would," he said slowly, "if you were a medium."

"A medium? A fortune teller?"

"More than that, I suspect. There's a word for it: somebody who can hold an object and tell facts about its owner."

"Oh, Lord. You're right." Sandi's weariness had vanished, driven away by the excitement of discovery. "I picked up a wristwatch. It belonged to a young lady. She had . . ." She was suddenly overwhelmed by sadness and she looked up at Bradon with tears in her eyes. "Her name was Geli. She killed herself."

"Geli Raubal. Hitler's niece. He was supposed to have been in love with her. Before he met Eva Braum."

Sandi scarcely heard him. Something was reaching out of the darkness with fingers of terror. "There was something else. A pen. A black fountain pen. It belonged to a man I met there." The fingers had now reached her, were dragging her into a vivid memory of the scene. She again felt the pen in her hand as surely as though it was real. And with the image came the loathing. "He killed many people, personally. Oh, God. Killed them horribly. And he's responsible for so many more. So many. I can't . . . I can't . . . His name is Roehm. Ernst Roehm."

"Sandi!"

Bradon's sharp voice yanked her back and she jerked in alarm, knocking over her cup of coffee. Her scramble to save her books and notebook from the spreading puddle brought a welcome relief from the dreaded images.

Bradon grabbed paper napkins from a holder on another table and mopped up the coffee. "Did you get any on your clothes?"

"I don't think so."

"I shouldn't have yelled at you. But you . . ." His voice trailed off, and he took the sopping paper napkins to a trash basket.

Sandi was only dimly aware that he had moved away. An icy coldness touched her like the finger of a ghost. It had happened again.

When Bradon returned, bringing Sandi a fresh cup of coffee, she was slumped in her chair, her face pale. "It happened again, didn't it?" she said.

"Well, not really--"

"And this time it was spontaneous. Oh, God. I don't know what's happening to me."

Bradon smiled. "I wouldn't worry about it. I'm sure you'll never be in those particular circumstances again."

"But why did it happen at all?"

Bradon's answer was so soft that Sandi wondered whether he was talking to her or to himself. "Why that particular period?"

Why, indeed? That had been bothering Sandi, too. But then . . . Was it really a mystery? Because another memory was nagging at her. Should she tell Bradon? Should she reveal even a little of her dark secrets? The look of worried compassion in his eyes made her plunge ahead. "Maybe there's an answer," she blurted. "When I was beginning to slide back, there was something--a feeling--of being called. I've . . . I've felt it before."

Bradon slowly put down his coffee cup. This time when he reached across the table and took her hands, she did not pull away, although his touch caused a strange flutter in her stomach. "What kind of a feeling?" His voice was harsh, his eyes boring into hers. "When? What was it like?"

"When?" When had she not had the vague discomfiture as though some ghostly presence were trying to reach into her mind. "Most of my life, I think. But I've learned to shut them out." Oh, God. She'd said it. Something she'd promised herself she would never do. But, in the telling, some of the terror was gone.

"Like walling them up?"

"You could say that." Now! It was not too late to laugh it off as a joke and change the subject. But she had been alone with her fear too long. Maybe it was time to get some help.

She ignored her inner warnings and continued before she could change her mind. "But last week when we were doing self hypnosis, I guess I lost control." The memory frightened her and she gripped Bradon's hands with the strength of fear. "What is it, Doctor Bradon? What's happening to me?"

The fear in her eyes struck Bradon hard. He had seen that same fear in Kimberly's eyes. The best, or at least the most immediate way to defuse it, was to make light of it. So, he grinned at her. "Doctor Bradon?" He looked down at her hands gripping his. "Under the circumstances I think you can call me Dan."

Sandi flushed and tried to release her grip, but he would not let go. She did not insist. His hands were a lifeline, although she was not fooled by his banter. He had deliberately broken the tension. She wished that she had that much control of her own chaotic emotions. But, then, he was a trained psychologist. To him, this whole thing was only an exercise. She was nothing more than a confused client, just as though she was making an office call. Fifty minutes of empathy and a ten minutes break before seeing the next person with a problem. All very impersonal. Any display of concern and compassion was merely a calculated bedside manner.

The realization chilled her and she withdrew her hands. "So? Have you developed any theories, Doctor?" Without his warm touch, her hands felt cold, lost, and she curled them around her cup of coffee.

Bradon's smile was rueful. His touch of humor had dispelled her fear, but it had also returned her cool sang-froid. "It seems obvious that this woman you became--Countess von Waltz--was a medium. That would explain why it was easy to make contact with her."

"It's more than that. As I understand it, regression is supposed to take you back to a past life. That person to whom you return is really a part of you. Her genes are supposed to be somewhere inside you."

"Well, that's the theory."

"So this woman could be--would be, I guess--a distant relative."

"Maybe not so distant. You said the pen belonged to Ernst Roehm. If I remember my history, Roehm and Hitler had a falling out. The Roehm Putch. Hitler--and Himmler--had Roehm murdered in 19--I think it was '34. 1934."

"Murdered. I saw that. That's why there was so much violence, so much--blood."

"It might not have been his. Roehm was head of Hitler's brown-shirts. They were thugs. They murdered a lot of people. Usually they beat them to death. Or tortured them."

"But 1934. That wasn't so long ago. Only two generations."

"That name--von Waltz. It doesn't ring a bell?"

Sandi shook her head. "My parents have never said much about their past. I always thought it was because their parents, my grandparents, died years ago. On both sides. I was too young to remember them."

"Your surname name is, uh, . . ." He twisted his lip in mock consternation.

"Boeckel," she said, smiling. "My name is Susanna Boeckel. Sandi."

"I remember the Sandi. How could I forget it?"

Bradon thought her sudden laugh was the most wonderful sound he had heard in a long time. It signified that for the moment she had dispelled her fear. Of more significance, she was no longer angry. Besides, it brought a new dimension to her face.

"You should laugh more often," he chided. "It lights you up."

Her laughter died as though she hadn't realized that she had laughed until he called her attention to it, and he cursed himself for being such a clod." Laughter hasn't been in much of my life," she said and her eyes grew sad. "You know I don't remember hearing either my mother or father laugh."

Bradon leaned back in his chair and studied her. She could guess what he was thinking. What kind of a home was one without laughter? No wonder she had ghosts trying to get into her head.

"Well," he said, "we're going to have to work on that."

She cocked her head. "Class is over."

"We'll start our own. Beginning tomorrow night, over dinner."

Some primal instinct had warned Sandi that he was going to ask her out; even so, the fact that he actually had came as a shock. Even more of a shock was the realization that she wanted to see him again. Her analytical mind automatically began searching for the reason. Was it because she knew she would enjoy his company? Or was it because he might be able to help her unlock the riddle of her regression? A few minutes ago when she had so easily slipped into the past, her loss of control had been traumatic, filling her with a terrible dread. Suppose it happened again? Would a day come when she could not control such lapses from reality? Didn't that mean she was losing her mind? She had to have answers. It was imperative that she spend time with Bradon. The danger would be in picking his brain without revealing the truth about herself.

Was that the only danger?

She noticed the ring finger of her left hand, the place where Jordan's engagement ring should be--would be as soon as she got home. She had promised that she would have dinner with Jordan and her parents tomorrow. She would find an opportunity to tell Jordan about the regression, and that she was going to discuss it with her professor.

But how could she explain the regression to Jordan let alone her desire to see a psychologist? He would never understand. So many times he had told her how much he admired her control, her mental stability.

Suddenly, it occurred to her that she could never tell him any of this. Nor could she tell her parents. There would be no doubt about their attitude. They would probably hide her in the attic. Anyone who's mind held ghostly images the way hers did would have to be mentally disturbed.

Maybe they were right. She had to know. The need for assurance of her sanity was far more compelling than worries about what would happen if they found out she was conferring with a psychologist.

"I can't make it tomorrow. I'm having dinner with--my parents." Now why hadn't she wanted to mention Jordan?

"Thursday then."

She hesitated. There was still time to escape. "All right," she heard her voice say. Betrayed! Betrayed by something inside her that knew she had no choice. She took back her control. "Just one question?"

"Oh. What's that?"

"Is this dinner for credit?"

He laughed and the tension between them vanished. "Maybe. Wait'll I tell you what the test is."

Sandi knew that he was jesting. Even so, the implication produced a warm feeling that set off alarm bells. How could this be happening to her? New emotions, new feelings were flooding in with such rapidity that she was alarmed. Many were frightening, but one was so pleasant that it dispelled all the doubts. The truth was that she was looking forward to seeing him again. It had nothing to do with psychology. The truth was scary. What she was about to do could destroy her nice, safe, carefully planned existence.

"You still have my card?" he asked and she nodded. "If there's a problem, give me a call."

Sandi swallowed hard. A problem? If Jordan or her parents discovered that she was planning dinner with Dr. Daniel Bradon, there would be problems all right.

CHAPTER 6

It was nearing 1:00 A.M. before Sandi fell into a restless sleep. Her mind had churned with so many disparate thoughts that it seemed as though she would never sleep again. One of the most troubling was an image of Dan Bradon that would not go away. No matter how much she tried to shut him out so that she could concentrate on the mystery of Helga Waltz, he kept popping in. She tried to convince herself that it was only natural that he usurp her thoughts. He was responsible for the regressions and was trying to help her find a logical explanation.

The trouble was that the images of Bradon that crowded her mind had little to do with psychic research. They seemed to focus on his face, his eyes, the way he smiled.

She turned in bed and fluffed her pillow. Stupid thoughts. She was engaged to Jordan. Besides, Bradon had no interest in her personally, only in the research. If it turned out there was nothing to the strange regression, if the entire matter turned out to be nothing but her mind elaborating upon some deeply buried memories, he would put her out of his life in an instant. Or if she said that she was no longer interested in pursuing the subject, that would be the end of it. Wouldn't it? Without the experiment to hold his interest, there was certainly nothing in her personality that was so scintillating that he would be unable to resist seeing her.

He probably had several love interests. There had been ten or twenty women in class who were more attractive than she. Some, with their beautiful hair, their California bodies, California tans and California smiles, were positively breathtaking. She might be as tall as they, and her teeth were just as good. And while her hair, too, was blonde, it was a dark blonde, bordering on reddish-brown. Hardly a golden girl. And he certainly would not be attracted by her body. She was too slender to have the tight, plump buns of the body-builders. Her chest, which she had always thought of as 'adequate', did not measure up to many of those women with really great bodies. Of course, some of their pulchritude was probably the results of plastic surgery. But did men really care? Would Daniel Bradon care?

She turned over and pounded the pillow. Would sleep never come? Would her mind continued to be so damned independent all night? What was Bradon doing in it anyway? She would soon be married. That was the thought she had to hold. Dan Bradon's opinion of her was of no concern. Once this mystery was solved, he would go his way and she would go hers and never their twain would meet.

All right. With that guideline firmly installed, she could think about the regression objectively. Why had it happened to her of all people? Except for the whispers, she was probably as stable, as mentally healthy as anyone in the world. Everyone had nightmares. Everyone had closets in their minds that they would just as soon remained closed. The difference was that most people knew what they were shutting up behind their closed doors. She had no idea what monsters were inside her mental 'closet' banging on the door.

Well, that was one door in her mind that would remain firmly closed and securely locked. Even a new demon, one as strong as Helga Waltz, must not be able to pry it open.

But moments after she slipped into a fitful sleep, Sandi began writhing in anguish as cruel images began to form.

*   *   *   *

Oh, God, what had I done?

I let the newspaper slip from my fingers to the floor. I couldn't bear to read beyond the headline that told in lurid words that Ernst Roehm and several other traitors were dead. Murdered. I had killed them. When I held the pen in my hand and said that its owner was evil, I had signed their death warrants.

It was less than a week since Hermann and I had attended the dinner party, but Hitler had acted so quickly it was almost as though the entire horror had been planned in advance only waiting for my confirmation of the truth to put it into action. Roehm was a monster; a cruel monster. But a traitor to Hitler, to Germany? I had not seen that. It was as though Hitler--or more likely, Himmler--had been looking for an excuse to eliminate him and I had provided it.

With shaking fingers I picked up the newspaper and carried it to Hermann's desk. It was after midnight, but thoughts of the newspaper headlines had kept me from sleeping. Something had compelled me to come downstairs to Hermann's study where he had left the evening paper. I turned on his desk lamp and began reading. They called it the 'Roehm Putsch'. Roehm had been arrested and shot in a prison cell as had Gregor Strasser and other leaders of Roehm's Sturmabteilung brown-shirts. In all more than a hundred so called 'SA traitors' had been arrested and executed.

I heard a sound at the door and looked up, my heart fluttering, certain that some of Goering's Gestapo or Himmler's SS men were coming to get me. Had I, too, been labeled a traitor of the state? I straightened, determined to show that as an innocent person, I was unafraid. Then I saw that the person entering was Hermann. He was knotting the sash of a dressing gown he had donned over his pajamas. His hair was tousled and his eyes heavy with sleep.

"Oh, it's you," he said. "What are you doing up at this hour?"

My legs suddenly refused to support me and I sat down heavily in his big leather desk chair. "I couldn't sleep. I . . . wanted to see the paper."

He glanced at the headlines and nodded. "A bad business. But they deserved it. They were all traitors to the Reich. Why would that keep you from sleeping?"

"One of them was Captain Roehm."

"So? He was the worst of the lot. His brown-shirt swine were getting out of control."

"It was his pen, wasn't it?"

"Pen? Oh, you mean at the dinner. It might have been. What about it?"

"Then . . ." I stood up and moved around the desk on legs of wood. "Then I'm responsible."

"Responsible? For Roehm? Nonsense. The 'long knives' of the SS have been putting together a list of traitors for months. All political, of course. Roehm made the mistake of making enemies of the old Generals, the old families. We've got to have the old guard Wermach and the industrialists on our side if Hitler is going to be appointed Commander-in-Chief. They hated Roehm, so he had to go."

I was glad that my face was in the shadows so that he could not see my expression. "You knew about this? You support it?"

My voice betrayed my revulsion and Hermann, to his credit, couldn't look at me as he said, "Not the details, no. I'm not that high in the Party."

The room seemed to spin. I shoved to my feet and moved to the other side of the desk, needing movement to keep from fainting. When I could speak, my voice was a whisper. "You set up that test."

"It was only a suggestion." His voice echoed his satisfaction as he added, "Himmler thought it was an excellent idea." He came around the desk and took me by the shoulders. "And you, my dear, were magnificent. You saw right through Roehm. You saw exactly what he was. And that part about Geli Raubal was a masterwork. Did you see Hitler's face? He thinks you're incredible."

My heart froze to the point where I thought I was going to faint. It was true; my words had condemned Roehm, and, by association, all those others. Only Hermann's hands on my shoulders keep me from falling.

"Are you all right?" he asked, peering into my face.

I took a deep breath and managed to get some feeling back in my legs. "Yes. I'll be all right."

Hermann's face continued to peer at me. "I know how sensitive you are, Helga. I'm sorry if this has upset you."

I turned to him with the strength of anger. "Why didn't you tell me? I would never have done that."

"Precisely," Hermann said, moving to his chair. "It was better that you were unaware of the importance of the test. But now,"--he chuckled as he sat down at his desk--"Hitler knows your capabilities. And now, there's no doubt of my loyalty. It could not have worked out better."

I walked out of the room feeling ill. He was right about Hitler knowing my capabilities. I couldn't think of anything that filled me with more dread.

*   *   *   *

Sandi's eyes snapped open. She stared into the darkness of her bedroom, perspiring, her heart pounding, her body heavy, leaden. Was she awake or dreaming?

She climbed out of bed and had to stand for a moment, her hand gripping the edge of the bedside table until a wave of dizziness passed. He legs were like wood as she made her way to the bathroom where she turned on every light. In the harsh light she stared at herself in the mirror. Who was she? What was happening to her? It had happened again. And this time it had been spontaneous. There had been no hypnosis, no Dan Bradon making clandestine suggestions. Helga von Waltz had invaded her sleep, had stolen into her dreams, taken possession of her mind while she slept. Was this to be a pattern? Would her mind be taken over each time her defenses were down? She shivered. It was a thought of horror. She slept no more that night.

CHAPTER 7

The Bel Air Hotel is so isolated in one of Beverly Hills' narrow, winding mountain canyons that one could drive past and never know it was there. Instead of the usual towering structure that identified most hotels, the Bel Air is a sprawl of Spanish-type bungalows and low buildings hidden by towering pine, oak and sycamore trees and flowering ferns, shrubs and bushes. Scattered flowerbeds blaze with impatiens, peonies and Bird of Paradise. In the cool canyon the air is rich with the scent of mock-orange, gardenia and jasmine. The only sounds are the chirping of birds, trickling water from innumerable fountains, and the occasional murmur of a passing Rolls Royce or Bentley.

The hotel's dining area features indoor and outdoor dining. Indoors the dining areas are separated into small nooks and rooms of various sizes so that intimacies do not have to be shared with strangers. It is much the same outside. In addition to a large central area, several tables are set into individual coves overlooking a garden with a gazebo that is in demand for weddings. On a nearby pond, white swans glide as though to suggest that no aberrant thoughts should be allowed to violate the serenity.

Sandi was thinking about the swans as she sat with her parents and Jordan at a table nestled in one of the secluded coves of the outdoor dining area. How wonderful it must be to drift through life with no thoughts whatsoever to interrupt your halcyon existence. She realized that if she wanted it that way her own life could be equally placid. Her parents had plenty of money; she didn't have to work; she didn't have to think beyond the moment if she didn't want to. Marrying Jordan would perpetuate such a problem-free existence.

And that is what it would be, 'existence' instead of living. Like the swans, she would drift through each day depending upon someone else to give her food, shelter and a safe environment. There were negative aspects, of course. If a swan ever gave a thought to what life was like beyond the pond, it could not leave without losing everything. For a swan, freedom meant not only the loss of serenity, it might also mean death. Loss of freedom, however, might be a small price to pay for total serenity. If you happened to be a swan.

A sommelier poured a small amount of wine into Martin's glass and Martin said to Jordan, "I think you'll like this. It's a fine young Riesling I discovered last year."

"I'm not that much of an expert on wines," Jordan admitted.

"You should be," Gretchen sniffed. "It creates a good impression with business associates."

"I'll look into it."

The sommelier waited impassively as Martin sniffed the aroma from the light amber liquid, then took a tentative sip and rolled it around his tongue. After he swallowed, he pursed his lips and looked up at the sommelier. "Let me see the bottle."

The sommelier turned the wine bottle so that Martin could read its label. "Schloss Johannesburg Rosalack Auslese, as you requested, Monsieur Boeckel."

"This is '86. I ordered '76." Martin smiled at Jordan. "'76 was one of the best years in their history."

"I beg your pardon, sir," the sommelier said. "Are you certain you said '76?"

Sandi would have been embarrassed, except that this little scenario had happened so many times during her life that now there was only a weary resignation. Martin had indeed said '86. But he knew all along that he would deny it so that he could impress his guests with the fine discrimination of his palate.

"Of course, I'm certain. I distinctly said '76. You do have it?"

"Yes, sir.

"Oh, and bring the proper glasses, s'il vous plaît. These are for young Beaujolais, not young Riesling."

The sommelier turned with a fixed smile, "Sorry, Monsieur Boeckel. I'll have it taken care of."

As the sommelier moved away, Martin said to Jordan, loud enough so that the man could hear, "You have to watch them. It's not like the old days."

Sandi had seen her father play his little game many times. What was in his psyche that made him want to display his knowledge of oenology in such a demeaning way. He knew perfectly well that the glasses were correct for the Riesling; Beaujolais glasses were slightly smaller. But his guests were not likely to know the difference and, after all, the entire performance was for their benefit. Its purpose was to illustrate that Martin Boeckel was not only a Knight of the Vine but a man used to giving orders. In this instance it was designed to show Jordan that Sandi came from a family steeped in breeding and savoir-vivre. A psychologist would probably label it a classic example of low self-esteem.

"That's true about most help these days," Jordan agreed. As though to illustrate his point he turned to a Latino bus boy wearing an immaculate white jacket who was pouring water for them. "Excuse me," he said with a smile, "but liquids are always served from the right."

A waiter had arrived to take their order and the bus boy shot him an apprehensive glance as he quickly amended his procedure to pour from the right. The waiter's face was impassive as he stood waiting.

"We're not ready," Gretchen told him. "We just arrived, for heaven's sake."

"Of course," the waiter said. "I'll be back in a few minutes."

"Do that," Gretchen commanded.

Sandi signaled her disapproval of Gretchen's hubris by deliberately closing her menu and placing it on her plate.

Gretchen's chin came up. "You've got to learn patience, my dear. Older people don't read as fast as you."

Sandi said, "I know, Mother. Take your time. They have your favorite, John Dory."

"Oh," Gretchen folded her menu. "I believe that's what I'll have. Thank you, my dear. Now, where is that waiter? They're never around when you want them."

Later, after an acceptable wine was poured and they had ordered, Jordan said to Sandi, "Now that the semester is finished, how many more units do you need for your degree?"

Sandi turned from staring into the shadows of the fragrant gardens. "Eight to qualify for my bachelor's. I've already signed for winter and spring classes."

"Then you'll be eligible for the state certification tests."

"Well, no." Sandi decided that she had avoided the subject long enough. Better that Jordan know the truth before they were married. "Actually, I'll have to matriculate for my master's degree. Then I'll have to complete a year of graduate studies and at least five thousand hours of practical experience before I can practice."

"Five thousand hours!" Jordan grunted. "That's more than two years."

"Most professions take longer than that to become established," Sandi pointed out.

"Practice?" Gretchen exclaimed. "You intend to work?"

"People do, Mother."

"In some clinic?" Martin snapped. "With deranged children?"

"They're not 'deranged' the way you mean it."

"Then why do they need psychiatric help?"

Jordan tapped the fingers of his right hand on the table. "Let me get this straight: After we're married, you intend to continue attending classes at the university, then work in some clinic--for two and a half years?"

"Well, yes. It's similar to a medical doctor interning in a hospital."

Martin said, "Your husband might have something to say about that."

Sandi's jaw tightened and Jordan quickly lifted his hand. "I'm not one of those Old World patriarchs. If Sandi wants to spend a couple of years helping people, I guess we can work that out. But no night classes. The nights will be ours."

Sandi nodded. "All right."

Martin carefully put down his glass of wine. "Well, maybe I am old-fashioned, but I think a woman's place should be in the home."

"Taking care of her own children," Gretchen added pointedly.

Sandi did not answer. She knew how this conversation would turn out. Each time she had attempted to discuss her views of the future with her parents the conversation always ended with her feeling like a traitor for even considering a career. There was no point in pursuing the subject now. If would be best to discuss her plans with Jordan when they were alone. Besides, she was having trouble concentrating on the future. Her mind was still trying to cope with her experience of last night. In the past her nightmares had been filled with vague voices that she had been able to keep buried in the darkness. But last night one of the phantoms had slipped through unbidden.

A familiar chill traveled down her spine. Had the regression she experienced in class opened a door she might never get closed?

She sipped her wine, willing her hands to be steady. If she could not control the monsters in her sleep, she might be able to attack them while she was awake. The best defense was an attack. And there was no better time than now.

When there was a break in the conversation she turned toward Martin. "Father, you've spent a lot of time in Germany. Have you ever come across anyone named von Waltz?"

The effect of her words was startling. Martin paused in the act of lifting his glass to his mouth as though frozen, and her mother's hand jerked, almost knocking over her glass of wine.

Jordan's eyes widen at their startling reaction and he said, "Good God!"

His voice broke the spell and Martin slowly put down his glass. He looked at Sandi, his eyes dark with a quality she had never before seen. At first she thought it might be anger, and she wondered why he should be angry because of such an innocuous question. Then she noticed that his hands were trembling, and she realized that the look in his eyes was not anger; it was fear.

"Where did you hear that name?" His voice was so low that Sandi had to lean forward to hear him.

She was not certain how to answer. She had been prepared to tell them the truth even though she was sure they would not believe her. But in light of their surprising performance, the truth was out of the question. She needed evidence more concrete than a name plucked from a dream. "I, uh, read it somewhere," she said.

"Read it?" Martin's voice said that he did not believe her.

"Where?" Her mother's voice was equally incredulous.

"Well, I'm not sure. I suppose I could find it again. Why? What difference does it make?"

Instead of answering, Martin said, "You must read hundreds of names. Why remember that one?"

"I don't know. It seemed sort of familiar, I suppose."

"You suppose?" Gretchen said. "What do you mean?"

"Nothing. I have no idea why it even stayed in my mind."

Gretchen started to say something else but stopped when Martin lifted a finger. His smile was strained as he said to Sandi, "Darling, it's not important. Let's just drop the whole thing."

But Sandi had no intention of letting it go. It was perfectly obvious that the name had some meaning for them and their avoidance of her questions only piqued her curiosity. "I think it might have some importance," she said. "I can't seem to get it out of my mind."

"I've had that experience," Jordan said. "Only with me it's generally a song or a name I can't remember, never one I can't forget." He patted her hand. "Don't worry, they always go away sooner or later."

"That's right," Martin agreed. "Just forget it and it'll fade away."

Were they right? Would Helga Waltz simply fade away? Sandi knew better. She also knew that her parents would never again allow her to bring up the subject. So now she could not afford to let the matter drop, even though she hated the role she was forced to play.

Sandi looked at her father so insistently that he could not meet her gaze. "You know that name. What is there about it that makes you so frightened?"

"Frightened? I'm not frightened. It's just that it reminded me of someone very unpleasant. An art dealer I had some business dealing with in East Germany a few years ago. His name was von Wolfe. A most unpleasant person. He actually threatened to kill me. Obviously, nothing came of it. But your mention of the name did cause a slight, ah, discomfort."

"That's right," Gretchen hastily agreed. "Von Wolfe. You were too young to remember, my dear. But you must have heard us mention the name. Finding this other name that sounded so much like it must have triggered your memory."

"Association," Jordan said. "That's one of the memory techniques. Associate a name with another or with some object that you can remember."

If the images in her mind had not been so vivid Sandi might have believed them. But she could no longer doubt what she had seen. "No," she said. "Her name was Helga. Countess Helga von Waltz."

This time the only effect was a glance between Martin and Gretchen before Martin said quickly, "That's correct. Helga was the name of Herr Wolfe's wife. You have a remarkable memory, my dear. You couldn't have been more than four or five years old."

"Precocity runs in our family." Gretchen smiled at Jordan. "She was talking before she was a year old."

Jordan chuckled. "Albert Einstein didn't speak well until he was nine. I didn't talk until I was two. I always said it was because I didn't have a whole lot to say."

"Girls mature faster than boys," Gretchen said. "You'll see that when you have your own."

"I'm going to Germany," Sandi interrupted.

It was as though she had frozen time.

Then Jordan slowly lowered his glass of wine, his eyes wary. "Germany? When?"

"As soon as possible."

"You mean before the wedding?"

"Yes."

She heard her words as though they was coming from another person. Only seconds ago she had no thought of making such a trip. Then it had simply popped out. Now she realized that it was her subconscious telling her that if she was ever going to get to the bottom of the dreams, if she was ever going to exorcise the ghosts, she had to find their genesis. And that was in Germany. "I'm sorry, Jordan. But I've got to do this."

"But what about your classes? You said you've already signed up."

"They don't start for almost three weeks. If I leave right away I should be back by then."

"But why? What's gotten into you lately?"

"Nothing really. I just want to . . ." She hesitated, wondering how much she could tell them. Should she say that the voices in her head, voices that she had heard most of her life, compelled her to go. Such an explanation would sound more like psychosis than curiosity. "I need a vacation."

"A vacation?!" Gretchen said. "If you want a vacation, there are other places that would be better."

"Hawaii," Martin interjected. "You loved it there when you were twelve. Or was it thirteen?"

"Germany," Sandi insisted. "Our roots are there. I'd like to see the country before I," --she took hold of Jordan's hand--"settle down."

"Well," Jordan said. "Right now would be an awkward time for me. If I'd had a little advance notice . . ."

"You don't have to come, darling." Sandi prayed that he would not change his mind. It was going to be difficult enough to conceal her real mission. If she had to make excuses for her every move, it would be impossible. "I'm perfectly capable of looking after myself."

Martin looked at his wife and a current seemed to pass between them. "I suppose I could go with you," Gretchen said. "I haven't had a vacation for some time."

"That would be nice," Sandi said. But she had no intention of taking her mother. She would have to concoct come reason for going alone or, more believably, create some irresistible reason for her mother to remain in town, such as discovering some major event attended by social elite and movie celebrities where she could display her jewelry and a new evening gown. With such an opportunity, dynamite could not propel Gretchen Boeckel out of town.

CHAPTER 8

It was difficult for Sandi to keep her dinner date with Dan Bradon. Her mother and father had both looked at her with suspicion when she said she was going out. It was not unusual for her to go to a movie or some event with a girl friend, and she often went to dinner with Jordan, but this was the first time she had lied to her parents about where she was going and they seemed to sense it. It had also been necessary to lie to Jordan. If she told her parents she was going somewhere with Jordan, then he called asking for her, it would be disastrous. She managed to carry off the deception by promising herself that it would never happen again.

Driving along the Pacific Coast Highway toward the setting sun, she found herself humming. She would have whistled if she knew how. At first she thought her mood was because she was going to meet Bradon, an anticipation that she found to be disturbingly exciting. She had been avoiding an analysis of the effect he had on her as a child avoids thinking about a fearsome movie, because she knew that the association was dangerous and should be avoided.

No, her euphoria was due to something else. This was an exhilaration she had not experienced since she was a little girl, and it took her some time to identify what it was: freedom. Never in her memory had she totally escaped the supervision of her parents. Always when she was away from them, they knew exactly where she was, with whom and for how long. But this time no one knew, not even Jordan. She could drive forever, fly to the moon, and no one could stop her. The feeling was heady but, also, a little frightening. Suppose something happened to her, an accident? Could she take care of herself? And could she ever explain being this far from home?

Well, she would just have to be super careful. This meeting with Daniel Bradon was too important to miss because of a few trepidations. It was also worth a few white lies.

The restaurant proved to be near Malibu on the ocean side of the highway. She was delighted when she walked inside to discover that the dining area was cantilevered out over the water. Breaking waves rumbled against a rocky barrier directly under the restaurant.

Bradon saw her and came to escort her to a table next to windows that overlooked the ocean. Far on the horizon she could make out the shadowy outline of Catalina Island. The huge disc of the sun, distorted by the atmosphere, was just slipping below the horizon, leaving a shimmering path along the flat expanse of water. A magnificent panorama of colors, ranging from violent crimson to the most delicate pink, painted the broad canvas of the sky.

Sandi stared in awe, mesmerized by the enormity of the scene. Bradon stood beside her studying her face instead of the sunset. "I'm glad you appreciate it."

Sandi was unable to take her eyes from the remarkable display, enchanted by the subtle change of colors. "It's incredible," she breathed. "I don't think I've ever seen a sunset so brilliant."

Bradon chuckled. "I arranged the whole thing for you."

Sandi glanced toward him without turning her head. "Thank you, God."

"Ah," Bradon said with a smile. "Now you know."

During dinner Sandi realized that her conversation was far from scintillating. Her attention was centered upon the beauty of the descending dusk. She watched, fascinated, as the colors of the sunset transmuted and paved the surface of the ocean with an increasingly dense patina of darkness until, at last, the dark sea merged with the night sky, leaving only darkness and the constant sound of the surf. It was not until, one by one, faint stars began to pierce the darkness that she was able to turn her attention to her dinner--and to Bradon.

He looked at her with a quizzical smile. "Hello. You're back."

She brushed her hair back with both hands and looked down at her empty plate. "What did I have for dinner?"

Bradon shook his head in mock dismay, "The most expensive item on the menu and you don't even remember it."

"I'm sorry."

"Don't be. The only thing I've ever seen more beautiful than the sunset is you watching the sunset."

She looked at him, intending to join in his smile. Their eyes locked for an instant and to Sandi it was as though someone had touched her with an electric shock. Her smile froze and she quickly looked down at her plate so that he would not see her confusion.

It was an unnecessary gesture because Dan Bradon had just as abruptly turned his head to stare out the window. He had been keenly aware as he watched her revel in the beauty of the sunset that powerful emotions were taking control of him. But he was sure that he could handle them. He'd had two days to prepare his defenses. Then her cool gray eyes looked directly into his and it had been as though a sledgehammer had struck a mighty blow against his impregnable walls.

He blinked and looked away. He could not allow himself to fall into the depths of those luminous eyes. It would ruin everything.

When he turned back, she was looking down at her plate which made it much easier for him to regain his control. In order to keep her hypnotic attraction at bay, he concentrated on his real purpose for being with her.

"I feel kind of guilty," he said, and his voice sounded to him as though it had all the warmth of a pitch by a used car salesman.

She looked up then, but the power was gone from her eyes as though she too had closed a forbidden door. "Guilty? You mean about . . .what happened?"

"Yes. I, uh, should have stopped it sooner."

"It wasn't your fault. You didn't know I was so . . .susceptible."

He almost didn't tell her. He had her trust now. Why take a chance on losing it? It would be easy to allow her to continue thinking that he was trustworthy. On the other hand, by confessing to her, by showing her how terribly contrite he was, he could entrench himself farther into her confidence. Unless, of course, she rejected him outright in righteous anger. Which could happen.

But, studying her, he didn't think she could do that. He decided to take the chance. "I mean about the second time. In class."

Sandi stared at him wondering what he meant. Why should he feel guilty for something over which he had no control? "But you weren't trying to---" She stopped as a thought slammed her and she straightened in her chair. "You set that up! You knew what would happen!"

He looked away unable to meet her accusing gaze "I didn't really know." He braced himself against the temptation to slide back into a lie and added, "But I had a pretty good idea it would."

She tilted her head back in disgust, rubbing her hand hard across the back of her neck. "God. I was so damn naive. You knew I was susceptible. All you had to do was get me to concentrate on the right words. Burnstein wasn't your target. I was."

His silence was her answer.

"And it worked. You pushed me back. And I didn't want to go! I didn't want that! Why?" When he did not immediately answer, she slapped her hand down on the table. "Answer me, damn it." Bradon reached for her hand, but she yanked it back. "Why?"

He grimaced and sat back in his chair. "I was quite sure what would happen."

"So why did you do it?"

"I wanted to find out if what had happened before was an anomaly or whether there really was something there."

"But you knew I didn't want to do it."

"I know. But I had to find out. Most regressive people don't always go back to the same place in time, become the same character. That's what was so unique about Brydi Murphy. But you did too."

The anger had drained out of Sandi leaving a depression of weariness. "I know. That woman . . . She came back again."

"Again? You mean in the class?"

"No. That same night. I was sleeping. Or I think I was sleeping. It happened again."

"Without hypnosis?"

He had leaned across the table and was staring at her intently, his eyes bright with the fervor of discovery and she nodded. "Yes."

"You went back to the same time, the same character?"

"Yes. Her name is Countess Helga von Waltz."

Bradon leaned back in his chair without taking his eyes from her face and he was silent for a long moment before he said, "Spontaneous regression. Jesus."

"Yes, and I'm scared silly."

"Why? I'm sure it won't hurt you."

"Because I don't have any control over when it will happen. It could be right now, or while I'm driving, any time."

"Oh, I don't think so. I don't think an entity could take over a fully conscious mind."

"I hope you're right." Sandi stared out the window into the darkness.

Bradon ran his fingers through his hair. This girl could be a gold mine. Unless for some reason she was faking the whole thing. Except that if she was, she had to be the best actress in the world. He would swear that her fear, her anxiety, was real. In a way, it didn't really matter. Faking or not, if he could induce regression any time he wanted, the situation could be priceless.

For an instant, doubt stabbed him. Suppose she wasn't faking. She was terrified of this regressive character; he had no right to put her through that kind of pain.

He quickly dismissed the thought. It would be in her best interests if he could get to its roots. Of course, her fear might be so great that she would refuse to cooperate. He would have to find some way to reduce her fear.

"This person, Helga, does she seem malevolent? Someone who would want to harm you?"

"Oh, no. I don't think she could knowingly harm anyone."

"Then,"--he had to word this carefully--"why not pursue this? Find out why she's trying to communicate?"

"With more regressions?"

"Yes."

"Because . . ." Sandi hesitated. It was a question she had been avoiding asking herself. Although the question frightened her, she was almost glad that he had asked. Why not another regression? If she could uncover the truth about Helga von Waltz through regression, she would not have to make the trip to Germany.

Still, the thought of another wrenching journey into the past made her stomach churn with dread. "Because I have a bad feeling about it."

"Bad? In what way?"

"I don't know. It just terrifies me that I might let something loose I can't control."

Bradon was silent for a moment, and she sensed that he had withdrawn from her as though she had told him she had some terrible disease. She drew a sharp breath of relief when he said, "It seems to me that sooner or later you're going to have to confront this entity, whatever it is. You won't get any peace until you do."

Her voice was a whisper, "That's what I think too."

At her reply he looked at her sharply and Sandi thought she saw pleasure in his expression. It had to be because he was concerned for her and happy that she had made the correct decision. "Good," he said. "Will you let me help you?"

"I don't think that will be necessary."

The warmth drained from Bradon's face leaving it set in icy lines of hurt. "Why not? I feel responsible. The least I can do--"

"It isn't that," she interrupted. "I . . . I don't want to find out that way. I mean by regression. I'm afraid of it. Of her."

"Then what? How else are you going to find out?"

"By going to Germany."

He blinked as though she had slapped him. "Germany? You're going there? Why?"

"I've got to find out if Helga von Waltz really existed. Or if she's just a figment of my imagination."

He nodded slowly, his eyes speculative. A smile tugged at his lips. "Maybe that would be better. If we can prove she really existed, that the things you've experienced really happened, it would be fantastic."

"But . . . There wouldn't be any need for another regression. I'm sure I can find out all I need to know from records."

Bradon nodded. "Great. When do you plan on going?"

"As soon as possible."

"Fine. That gives us a little more than three weeks before the winter semester starts."

A flush of pleasure warmed her. "Us?"

"Sure. I was in on the beginning of this. I'd like to be in on the denouement."

"You want to come with me?"

"Of course."

Sandi was so frozen with surprise that it was difficult to speak. "But . . . that's impossible."

"Why? I speak German. Read and write it too. You'll need some help."

"But . . ." Sandi didn't know how to proceed. The thought of traveling with Bradon was incredibly exciting. But how could she possible carry it off? He seemed so blasé, as though knocking about Europe with someone he hardly knew was the most natural thing in the world. Maybe it was natural for him, but it certainly offered insurmountable complications for her. "I don't think so," she said. "I couldn't do that."

"Why not?" He saw the worry in her eyes and hastily added, "Separate but equal. I pay my way; you pay yours."

"It isn't the money."

"Separate rooms. Me in the basement; you on the top floor. We converse only by telephone. Cross my heart."

Sandi laughed. "We wouldn't have to go that far."

"Then it's settled. When do we leave?"

"Wow," Sandi exclaimed. "Things are happening a little fast for me. I just decided to go yesterday. I haven't made any plans."

"Then now is the time. I guess Berlin would be the place to start." Bradon took a pen from his jacket pocket and waved to a waiter. "Excuse me. Do you think you could find a piece of paper for me? And bring some coffee, please. Lots of coffee. And," he said to Sandi, "start calling me Dan."

He was so elated that Sandi wondered how she could tell him that what he was suggesting was impossible. If Jordan ever found out that she had gone to Europe with a man, it would be the end of everything. And what about her parents? She had never traveled alone. Her mother might insist upon accompanying her. But she could not allow that. She would have to convince her mother that she didn't need a chaperone. She was no longer a teenager. The thought made her smile. Traveling with Daniel Bradon would certainly put an exclamation point on the end of her innocent teens. Not that anything untoward would happen. They would, of course, have separate rooms.

But just the idea of being alone with Daniel Bradon for days--and nights--would mark the beginning of a new era in her life, a new independence. She thrilled at the thought.

Then, the old fears crowded in as she remembered why she was going. Maybe it was a good thing that Bradon would be going with her. The demons she could be unleashing might be too much for her to control alone.

CHAPTER 9

Once they were in the air and she was comfortably ensconced in the airplane's window seat, some of Sandi's tension drained away. After days of uncertainty, days of white lies and hasty preparations, her journey was actually happening. A brief thrill shook her. Now there was no turning back. Now she was committed. The muted power of the plane's engines gave her quest a solid reality that had been lacking throughout the preparations.

She leaned her forehead against the cool plastic of the window and concentrated on the diorama of earth and sky. She had absolutely no fear of flying. Rather, she never failed to be delighted and awed by the way such a huge machine could bore through the thin air with such ease. She also enjoyed staring down at the earth unreeling far below and fantasizing about people in ox-drawn covered wagons plodding step by step across the mountains and the prairies that she was streaking across in such comfort.

She smiled and rested her head against the headrest. In a way, those pioneers had it easy. They had not been subjected to abstract fears. Their fears were based upon solid reality, such as finding food and water, dealing with the weather and the prospect of being killed by wild animals or marauding Indians. Her stress was based upon elements that could not so easily be grasped. Voices in her head. Ghosts from the past. Hers was an ingrained fear that had existed through history: fear of the unknown, fear that could not be faced behind the solid protection of a rifle, fear that ate at her brain like acid.

Still, she was facing it. This trip was solid proof. Further proof was the fact that there had been no new regressions since she had made her decision. It was as though the phantoms knew she was now the pursuer instead of the victim. She would seek out the phantoms; she would meet them face to face; and she would conquer them just as pioneers had faced and conquered their real fears. Of course, she thought ruefully, a lot of them failed.

She had another worry that the pioneers did not have to face. And he was seated beside her calmly reading the airline's magazine. Traipsing around Europe with a virtual stranger was not exactly conducive to one's peace of mind. If her parents ever found out she had not made the journey alone, they would be furious. She'd only been able to dissuade her mother from accompanying her by promising to telephone her every day. And Jordan! Suppose he somehow found out. Did he love her enough to trust her traveling with another man? Would anyone?

Actually, if it hadn't been for Bradon she might have abandoned the trip. His enthusiasm had given her the strength to stand up to pressure from her parents and from Jordan. They had pointed out that she knew nothing about the pitfalls and dangers of foreign travel. Besides, this was the off-season in Europe and many of the most interesting attractions would be closed. There was also the danger of a young and inexperienced woman traveling alone.

And that was another way Bradon contributed to her peace of mind. He was an experienced traveler. There was comfort in knowing that if she ran into any real problems she would have the protection of a strong man. She smiled to herself at the sheer sexism behind the thought. Today any woman who admitted, even to herself, that she felt more secure because a man was with her was considered a traitor.

Those things, however, while worrisome, were not what gave Sandi the most apprehension. Was this whole program a wild goose chase? She had no real proof that such a person as Helga von Waltz ever existed. Her only evidence was some strange aberration inside her mind. A hurried investigation before she left Los Angeles had failed to produce any reference to either Hermann or Helga von Waltz.

Even a search of the internet had turned up nothing.

Of course, the reference books she had examined were in American libraries, although the UCLA library had a large collection of foreign books, including books in German. However, to her amazement, she did find many books about Hitler--and others in the Nazi hierarchy--being involved with the occult and with mysticism.

Suppose that in Germany she did find evidence that Helga von Waltz had actually lived. What then? It had been more than half a century since the end of the war. The Countess had to be deceased. How else could she be a ghostly spirit? Perhaps she would discover that there were living relatives. Then what? Did she expect to knock on their door and announce that she had been in communication with their dead mother or grandmother?

It all sounded so foolish and so nebulous that if it hadn't been for the fear of appearing a coward to Bradon, she would have cancelled the journey.

Turbulence jarred the plane and Bradon's magazine slipped to the floor. They both reached for it. Their hands touched and for an instant, Sandi thought that the plane had been struck by lightning. She jerked her hand back and Bradon, after shooting her a quick glance of surprise at her reaction, picked up the magazine.

Sandi slumped back in her seat. There had been no lightning. The shock had come from Bradon's touch. Static electricity? Not likely. His hands were steady as he calmly turned the pages of his magazine. How could they create so much tension in her by a simple touch? They gave no evidence of extrasensory power. The hair on their backs was dark, fine as silk, the skin bronzed by California sun. The fingers were slender, but looked strong. No rings. Nor was there evidence of a discoloration that indicated that he had worn one. His nails looked healthy which, she remembered from some magazine article, meant that he had a healthy body.

But what about his mind? Was it equally healthy? Maybe she was putting her trust in someone with mental aberrations. She was keenly aware that psychologists sometimes had more problems than their patients. Proof was the unusual number of suicides in the profession.

She really knew very little about Daniel Bradon. Until a few days ago she hadn't even known if he was married. For all she knew, he could have had a wife and eight children.

But she was not stupidly naive. As soon as she had agreed to his accompaniment, she began an investigation. She had no intention of going anywhere with Bradon until she knew more about him.

The problem was that she had no idea about how to proceed. How did one go about determining the background of a person? She could probably find out Bradon's credit rating and perhaps his bank account without too much trouble. But it was his character that was in question. Would she be safe with him? Did he have a criminal record? Was he a rapist? The idea of secretly prying into a person's life was distasteful, but her safety was more important than any threat to her moral sensibilities. She considered hiring a private detective, but that was even more distasteful, like asking a stranger to peek over Bradon's transom. No. It would be better if she did her own investigating. Two places where she could get background information were the university and the American Psychological Association.

But obtaining access to UCLA records proved to be embroiled in red tape that would take days to untangle. And there was no branch of the American Psychological Association in Los Angeles, and her phone calls to their headquarters in Washington, DC ended in frustration. They would release no information without proper court documentation or permission from the psychologist in question.

In desperation, with time running out, she had gone to a private investigation company. A day later they had given her a report that had put her in awe of their efficiency and, at the same time, had calmed her fears about Daniel Bradon.

According to their report, he was Dr. Daniel Sean Bradon. 6'1" tall. Weight: 175 lbs. No brothers or sisters. Never married. No children. He had been born 29 years ago and grew up in El Centro, California where his father owned an automobile agency. His grandparents on his father's side were from Ireland. His mother's parents had emigrated from Germany.

His mother died when he was 10 years old; his father was retired, still living in El Centro.

He received his master's degree and doctorate from UC San Diego. His internship and graduate work were accomplished at UCLA.

He had then gone into private practice as a clinical psychologist with an office in Manhattan Beach. After two years he had abruptly terminated his clinical psychology practice, fired his receptionist/secretary, and switched to industrial psychology. Currently, he was developing psychological tests for corporate hiring and job placement.

In addition to his practice, he taught classes for the UCLA Extension Program. His credit rating was excellent, and he was making mortgage payments on a $350,000 home in West Los Angeles. $350,000? It couldn't be a very large home for that little money; not in West LA. His current balance on the mortgage was $l78,000 dollars. He drove a two-year-old Pontiac TransAm for which he was making payments of $438.57 per month with a balance due of $8,472.27.

His health was good with no known major illness or problems with drugs or alcohol. No arrests, no outstanding warrants. His hobbies were ocean surfing, swimming, cycling and jogging. At UCSD he had been on the track team that had won several NCAA championships.

After reading the brief report, Sandi felt somewhat more confident of her safety. She wished that the report had provided more insight of his personality. For instance, why did he dislike being called Doctor Bradon? Why had he made the switch from clinical to industrial psychology? And why had he never married? Was he currently involved with someone?

She assumed that the long flight to Berlin would give her time to learn more about the real Dan Bradon. Spending several hours seated side by side would allow her to couch her questions about his personal life in friendly conversation.

She cleared her throat. There was no time like the present. Then she saw that Bradon had put his magazine down and appeared to be napping.

With a sigh, she pushed the button that tilted her seat and leaned back a little. She wished that she could fall asleep so easily. This had to be how soldiers felt going into battle from which they probably would not emerge whole. Bradon, on the other hand, had nothing to lose. He did not have the fear that he might become a casualty in their quest. Or was it just that he was one of those people who possessed such self discipline that he could relax even when heading toward an unknown peril?

Would there be peril? What about her courage? While she could tell herself that she would not play the coward, how was one to really know?

What about Bradon? If her mettle had never been tested in combat, neither had his. It had been several hours since he'd had an opportunity to shave and the usual sharp outline of his Van Dyke beard and moustache was blurred by sprouting whiskers that gave him the tough look of a fighter. But how strong was his courage? If he ever had to fight, how would he handle himself? Would his calm assurance shatter under pressure? Would his brilliance disintegrate in the face of physical danger?

He did not have the look of someone who would wilt under pressure.

He appeared to be physically strong enough to take care of himself. In fact, he practically radiated power. At the same time he looked so vulnerable with his eyes closed and the hard plains of his face relaxed. She had an almost overwhelming urge to run her fingers through his hair, to brush back errant locks from his forehead.

A pulse under his jaw throbbed in a slow, steady beat that fascinated her. She wondered if her own heartbeat would match his. Feeling slightly foolish, she checked the pulse at her wrist. To her surprise her pulse was racing. How could that be? She was relaxed, in control. She took a deep breath and willed her pulse to slow, to become one with Bradon's. To her consternation, her pulse rate increased. This time, the reason was not a mystery: She had been wondering what it would be like to touch the pulse beneath his jaw with her fingertips, to brush it with her lips. His own lips looked soft and warm. How would they feel on hers? Would they be tender or savage? Would his tongue be demanding? Would he--

As though he sensed her thoughts, Bradon opened his eyes, catching her staring at him, and she quickly looked away, feeling her face grow warm.

"Having second thoughts?"

She turned toward him determined to appear coolly competent. "Not at all. I'm looking forward to laying this mystery to rest."

"I mean about me."

Chagrined that he had so easily read her thoughts, Sandi lied, "Not really. If I didn't think that I could trust you I wouldn't be here."

"But you really don't know a damn thing about me."

A pang of guilt shook her. She knew a great deal about Dr. Daniel Bradon. She covered her embarrassment by saying, "As much as you know about me."

"Not really. I had access to your records."

"And they told you all about me?"

"Well, there were a couple of points that were a little vague."

"Such as?"

"Such as your favorite color; your favorite music. What you do in your spare time. If you like sports. Where you got that little scar on your chin. And why you haven't been carried off to an ivory tower by some lothario by now."

His persiflage had changed with the last question, and she wondered why. Maybe he thought there was some psychological reason why she was not married. Since he was a psychologist, he probably attached a deep and sinister psychosis to her matrimonial status. Well, let him. That was his problem.

Except that she did wonder why he was so interested in her personal life. Was it possible that his interest went beyond their project? The thought gave her a strange sensation in the pit of her stomach. Perhaps she had misread his motives. Perhaps his only reason for being with her was sexual.

Even if it wasn't, could he keep his testosterone-driven instincts under control for several days? They would be spending a lot of time together and for some men opportunity triggered a call to action.

Still, she was certain that Bradon was not that type. He was not a Neanderthal who would allow his desires to gain control of his intellect. But suppose she was wrong. What if his only interest in her was her body? Well, there was no turning back now. She simply would be on her guard.

A new thought made her smile. If his only interest in her was sexual, there was no reason for the sense of intellectual inferiority she had been harboring. Dan Bradon might have a Ph.D., but he was also a man who seemed to be hitting on her like any ordinary male.

"My favorite color," she said with a disarming smile, "is blue. Music? Just about everything. Especially rhythm and blues--and Latin--because I like that kind of dancing. Sports? I don't follow any teams really. I like to run--not jog--run. And I play tennis. Swim sometimes, but it's kind of boring. Like aerobics. Oh, and the scar. I fell off my bicycle when I was seven."

He lifted an eyebrow, waiting for an answer to his question about her marital status and, for reasons she could not articulate, she chose to avoid it by saying, "Now your turn."

His wry smile said that he was very much aware that she had evaded the question, but he did not press for an answer. "Tan," he said. "Music? Eclectic, like you. But a penchant for jazz. Not the modern stuff that passes for jazz. I mean Brubeck and Miles Davis. And flamenco guitar. De Lucia. Sports. I'm a Raiders fan, wherever they are. Baseball--Dodgers when they had players whose names I could remember. Basketball and hockey? Only the playoffs. They play too many games during the season. One game doesn't mean anything."

The report from the detective had indicated Bradon's athletic abilities, but she didn't want him to know how much she already knew about him so she said, "You look as though you're in good shape. Don't tell me you're one of those body builders."

"No. Too boring. I go more for the triathlon."

"Triathlon?" The report had not mentioned a triathlon and his answer surprised her. Triathletes were a breed in themselves, unquestionably the best conditioned athletics in the world--except, arguably, boxers. A triathlon consisted of an ocean swim of two miles, followed immediately by a bicycle ride of one hundred miles, followed immediately by a full twenty-eight mile marathon run. Certainly, not the type of sport one would expect from a psychologist.

As though he saw the doubt in her expression, he said, "Not the big one. That would kill me. I go for mini-triathlons."

"What are they?"

"Half mile or a mile swim, twenty-five mile bicycle and ten kilometer run."

She was still impressed. In fact, more impressed. A major triathlete had to be so dedicated to his physical development that he had little time, or thought, for anything else. Such narrow dedication had to be terribly stultifying, ruling out a diversity of interests or relationships. Of course, there were some professional men whose dedication to their careers was equally focused, to the exclusion of any but the most superficial of outside interests. Apparently Bradon was capable of enjoying life outside his profession.

"And the scar?" she said.

"What scar?"

"Everybody's got a scar."

For some reason Bradon hesitated. It made Sandi wonder whether, if he did have a scar, it might not be physical. Then he smiled and said, "Mine's from an appendectomy." He cocked his head to look at her impishly. "Want to see it?"

"Only if your appendix was on your arm."

He grinned, looking at her out of the corners of his eyes. "You didn't answer my last question."

She returned his grin. "I guess I forgot it. It couldn't have been important."

He studied her face for a moment before he leaned back in his chair and closed his eyes. "You're right," he said. "Not important."

Sandi turned to gaze out the window hoping that he was right and that the question of her engagement to Jordan had no bearing on their project. What really disturbed her was why she had found it difficult to tell him she was engaged to be married. Also, by refusing to discuss the subject, she had closed the door on questions about his own commitments. Was he involved with someone? Perhaps he, too, was thinking about marriage.

But then, what difference did it make? This was strictly a business trip. It would proceed precisely the same whether either of them was involved with someone or not.

She leaned back in her seat and closed her eyes. Very well, Dr. Daniel Bradon, she thought. I'm as good as married, and I'll assume that you are too. That would make the journey less difficult for both of them. One thing was certain: He would not be having an affair with her.

But as she drifted off into a light sleep the thought that lingered was that Bradon's lack of interest in her had also taken an edge of excitement from their project, leaving only the dull ache of fear.

CHAPTER 10

When their plane landed at Berlin's Tegel Airport, the weather was warm and clear, although puddles of water gave evidence of a recent rain. During the taxi ride from the airport on a wide and modern freeway, Sandi stared in fascination at the unfamiliar city. She had expected some lingering evidence of the immense destruction that had been wrought upon the city during World War II, but except for an occasional odd juxtaposition of new structures with old, there was no evidence that the city had been virtually reduced to rubble.

Bradon leaned forward and gave directions in German to the driver and Sandi caught the words 'Kaiserdamm.'

Soon the driver turned off the freeway onto a busy boulevard and headed toward a distant group of skyscrapers.

"This route takes us through Tiergarten Park," Bradon said, "toward the Brandenburg Gate."

Recalling her map, Sandi said, "Good. I'd like to see that, and Unter den Linden."

"We'll have to make that another time. We're going to turn off through the Ku-damm."

"The what?"

"Ku-damm. It's an abbreviation of a boulevard called Kurfurstendamm. Only now it stands for a district, kind of like Times Square in New York."

From Ernst Reutes Platz the taxi swung onto a boulevard named HardenbergStrasse which was jammed with slow moving automobiles and buses and led into canyons of tall, modern buildings housing restaurants, hotels, theaters and cafes. Bradon was right about the area being like Times Square, except that the cleanliness of the streets and the colorful umbrellas over tables at sidewalk cafes were nothing like New York.

Leaving the Ku-damm district, the taxi proceeded southeast and the structures soon changed to older buildings, apartments, shops and stores. They seemed to be heading away from the business district and Sandi said to Bradon, "Aren't we going in the wrong direction?" She indicated another cluster of tall buildings in the distance. "That looks like the city center."

"That's the old center. Used to be East Berlin. We're headed for a district called Kreuzberg. It's close in and nicer."

And probably less expensive, Sandi thought. Martin had given her a list of the best Berlin hotels, but she had no idea how much money Bradon made as an industrial psychologist. She had not wanted to embarrass him by making reservations at one of the expensive three or four star hotels such as the Hilton or the newly liberated Grand Hotel in East Berlin. The large mortgage payment on his house and the fact that he was augmenting his income by teaching at night, indicated that he was probably struggling to make ends meet. So, to preclude any embarrassment, she had left it to him to make the reservations. It also seemed logical since he had been to Berlin several times. However, Berlin was a tourist mecca and, although this was the off season, she was worried about the suitability of a mid-price hotel, especially one for which reservations could be made on short notice.

She grew more apprehensive as the buildings they passed appeared to be older and more drab and the streets narrower. She again considered telling Bradon that she had enough money for the best hotel, but decided against it. It was probably best if he didn't know her financial situation. She would pay any exceptional expenses by claiming that it was, after all, her mission. If necessary, she would make it clear that she would not accept some bug infested flophouse.

Her apprehension continued to increase as they passed through a section that still showed the effects of World War II bombing.

After passing a park where there was a hill topped by a huge iron cross, she was on the verge of protesting when they entered a charming district of tree-lined, cobblestoned streets. The buildings were old four and five storied structures with stuccoed facades, many with wrought iron balconies and bay windows. On their ground floors most of the structures housed small restaurants, markets or shops.

"Kreuzberg," Bradon said. "This is what Berlin looked like before the war."

It was not hard to believe. The area had been relatively untouched either by the war or by modernization, and Sandi had lost most of her apprehension by the time Bradon directed the taxi to a halt on BergmannStrasse in front of an ancient brick and stone building that looked as though it had been an apartment building at one time. Now a discrete bronze plaque next to the door indicated that it was the Hotel Viktoria.

They got out of the taxi, and Bradon reached for his wallet to pay the fare, but Sandi stopped him. "No. Remember. It's my mission."

Bradon nodded. "Okay, boss."

He translated the driver's stated amount for her, and Sandi paid the fare using Euros she had obtained in Los Angeles. If Bradon felt embarrassed, he gave no indication. He even helped her count the money, adding a suitable but not ostentatious tip.

An ancient bellman hurried out of the hotel pushing a dolly, and Bradon helped him load their heaviest bags. Bradon picked up their two carry-ons, and they followed the bellman into the lobby.

The floor of the small lobby was of polished parquet and, as they approached a small reception desk, their steps echoed from a high ceiling and dark, oak-paneled walls. The concierge, a plump, balding man wearing a baggy black suit with a white tuxedo shirt and a red bow tie, came forward to meet them with his hand extended. "Ah, Herr Bradon. Willkommen. Ich frene mich, Sie nach zo langer feit wieder zu sehen."

"Danke, Herr Olbrich," Bradon answered. "Es ist gut zurük zu sein." He turned to Sandi, "Herr Olbrich, may I present my associate Fräulein Boeckel? Sandi, this is our concierge, Herr Olbrich."

Sandi took the offered hand, saying, "Sehr angenehm."

"And I also," Herr Olbrich gushed in English. "You are most welcome. I have everything ready for you."

As they presented their passports and prepared to register, Sandi experienced a moment of unease. Had Bradon reserved separate rooms, or would he try to pull a fast one by booking them both into one room? She was preparing her defenses as she signed the register, but the concierge placed two keys on the counter.

"Number 23 for Fräulein"--he consulted the register--"Boeckel. And number 25 for you, Herr Bradon. They are adjoining as you requested and have a magnificent view of the street."

Adjoining? As you requested? Sandi said nothing, but she wondered why Bradon had requested adjoining rooms. Suddenly she felt very vulnerable. She was a stranger in a strange city where she knew little of the language and where she had placed her welfare in the hands of a man she hardly knew. She drew courage from the knowledge that the Germans were essentially respectable people, and if she screamed bloody murder someone would likely come to her aid. Maybe it would be prudent to ask immediately for a different room. But if she were mistaken about Bradon's intentions, she would look like a fool. It would also send a signal to Bradon that she didn't trust him. She decided to deal with the room after she saw it. If it was unacceptable, she could use it as an excuse to change.

After taking a creaking, open-lattice elevator to the second floor, she was still reviewing her options when the bellman ushered her into a spacious room with large windows facing the street. The oaken floor, overlaid with several throw rugs, was polished until it shown, as did the darker wainscot. The walls appeared to be freshly painted and were decorated with a number of old oil paintings that looked as though they should be in museums. Heavy linen drapes flanking the large windows were drawn back, and afternoon sunlight filtering through trees festooned with tremulous autumn leaves made the room bright and cheery.

Sandi loved the room until she noticed a door that connected to the adjoining room. Bradon's room. She almost turned back until she saw that the door could be secured from her side by means of a deadbolt. She assumed that the other side of the door had an equally imposing deadbolt. Good. Bradon could sleep secure in the knowledge that she would not attack him.

Bradon had followed them into the room, saying, "The place is old and the rooms are kind of small, but I think you'll like it."

Except for the suspicious door Sandi already liked it. Except . . . Where was the bed? In most inexpensive hotels the bed occupied the center of the room. Again her eyes turned toward the ominous door.

"This is the sitting room," Bradon said before she could comment. "The bedroom and bath are here."

He opened an opposite door to reveal a large bedroom with a huge four-poster bed and Sandi said in surprise, "It's a suite."

"Of course. Not like the Hilton maybe but better than a Motel 6."

"I love it," she said. "Better than the Hilton."

"And it's within walking distance of most areas we're going to want to visit."

"Good. When do we start?"

He glanced at his watch. "I'm still on L.A. time." He turned to the waiting bellman. "Wie spät ist es hier?"

The bellman took a large watch from his vest pocket. "Es ist genan dreiund zwangzig minuten und füfzehn sekunden nach drei uhr nachmittags."

"Danke." Bradon turned to Sandi. "Three thirty. That gives us plenty of time before dinner. They don't eat until about ten here. Think you can hold out, or do you want to get something at one of the sidewalk cafes?"

"I'm not hungry really."

"Maybe you'd like to take a nap. Get rid of some of that jet lag."

"No, I napped on the plane. Besides, I'm too keyed up to sleep. What I'd really like to do is find a library and get started."

"It's a little late in the day for that, don't you think? Why don't we take a walk? I'll show you some of the city."

"Walk? Is it safe?"

"Safer than New York or LA."

"That's not much of a recommendation."

"Don't worry. In this area, it's safe."

Sandi glanced out the window and suddenly the idea of a walk sounded delightful. She always enjoyed seeing new places, new surroundings, and walking through Berlin in the sunshine of a late autumn day sounded exotic and exciting. "Fine," she said. "I can be ready in, say, a half hour."

"Good. I'll rap on your door."

Alone, Sandi carried her large bag into the bedroom and placed it on the big bed where it almost sank out of sight into the puffy, down-filled mattress and bedding. "Ho boy," she chuckled. "I hope it's cold tonight." She dragged the bag from the depths and placed it on a straight-backed chair where she opened it and began hanging her clothing in a large armoire that smelled of camphor.

In the spotless bathroom, it took her a few minutes to unravel the mystery of the shower above a four legged bathtub, and while the pipes rattled when she first turned on the water, they quickly settled down. As she scrubbed herself under the delicious hot water, she had the disquieting feeling that she was also scrubbing away her familiar world. From now on she would be treading an unknown trail that would be full of pitfalls and leading she knew not where. Instead of being frightened she found that she was looking forward to the challenge. Strange. It wasn't like her to be so adventurous. What had come over her? A month ago--no, not even that--two weeks ago, the idea that she would be in a strange country accompanied by a man she hardly knew would have been acutely absurd. But here she was on a quest for long forgotten Nazis that now seemed slightly foolish, perhaps even dangerous. Nazis. Despite the heat of the water, she shivered.

She had just finished dressing when she heard Bradon's tap on her door. She made a quick appraisal in a full-length oval mirror that was held in a beautifully carved wooden frame. She had decided to wear something comfortable for walking. It was early fall and the evening would probably be cool so she had selected a long, dark, loose-fitting wool skirt and a high-necked knitted blouse. For footwear she chose dark brown, calf-length boots with western heels. Looking at herself in the mirror the ensemble seemed somewhat drab so she added a colorful hand-painted Lester jacket of heavy silk cut in the pattern of a man's bomber jacket. She wondered about a hat. Did women in Berlin wear hats? She hadn't noticed any during the ride from the airport so she decided to compromise by pulling her hair back and securing it with a knotted scarf. If she felt out of place she could convert the scarf into headgear.

When she opened the door she was glad she hadn't dressed too formally because Bradon was wearing pleated slacks, a turtle neck shirt and a suede-leather jacket. He made no comment about her own clothes but his lingering gaze when he asked, "Ready?" gave her a glow of satisfaction. As they took the small elevator to the lobby and went out onto the street, she was wondering why she had been so pleased by Bradon's look of approval. His opinion of her should be of no consequence. She put the thought down to ego, the pleasure that anyone would have if they detected admiration in someone else's look or words. But a warm glow stayed with her as they headed west on Bergmann Strasse.

She enjoyed walking, and she had the impression that Bradon glanced at her with surprise when she matched his stride. He had probably thought that her idea of a good walk was the leisurely stroll they had taken across the UCLA campus and she would wilt after a block or two. He would discover that she could easily keep up with him unless he broke into his triathlon run.

The sidewalks were often made narrow by outdoor tables so that passing people occasionally caused Sandi to crowd against Bradon. Each time their shoulders touched she resisted an urge to take hold of his arm by placing her hand in her skirt pocket. Odd that she should feel such a desire. It had to be because of the delightfully crisp air, the exhilaration of being free from her parents, even the tiny thrill of apprehension about being in a strange and exotic city. When their shoulders did touch, Bradon did not pull away, and she wondered whether he also was under the spell of the time and place. She glanced at his face, but he was taking in the sights and sounds of the city as though he had no other thought on his mind. Obviously, the romance of the situation had no effect on him.

Her smile of relief was tempered by a twinge of disappointment. Any woman would like to think that she was attractive to a man as worldly as Daniel Bradon.

They left the close-packed apartment buildings along Bergmann Strasse and turned north on a street called Mehringdamm. The old tree-lined street was fronted with small shops, restaurants and art galleries. From time to time a passing subway train vibrated the pavement.

"They call this area the 'Kiez'," Bradon said. "Kind of like Glendale except that Glendale managed to get its independence from Los Angeles, but the 'Kiez' never made it. It's still part of Berlin."

"It doesn't look as though the war did much damage around here."

"Yes and no. What you've got here is a mixture of old and new. It's strange the way fire--or bombs, for that matter--can devastate some buildings and leave others relatively unscathed. But don't forget that the 'new' is around fifty years old. It's getting harder to tell the difference."

"In California they tear everything down every few years and start over. We don't have many really old buildings."

"They're starting to do that in Europe. You don't see many really ancient buildings any more, except in places like Prague or Budapest." He gestured toward the northeast. "Over in Süd-Ost thirty-six there are hundreds of industrial buildings and apartments that look like they might be a hundred years old."

"Süd-Ost thirty-six?"

"That's a zip code. We're in the Kiez's 'artists-and-intellectual' district, zip sixty-one."

"I see a lot of shop signs in English."

"This is the heart of what was the American sector. Checkpoint Charlie--the old Checkpoint Charlie--is straight ahead."

"It sounds like you've spent a lot of time here?"

"Not really. But when I'm in an interesting city like this, I do a lot of walking. Besides, my mother's roots are here. You look at a place a little more closely when you realize that your ancestors might have walked the same streets."

Sandi was silent as she thought about his reply. Had the woman she was seeking walked this same street? Had she seen the same sights, experienced the same odors, heard the same sounds? If so, why didn't she now feel an increased empathy? She was suddenly aware that she had been harboring a hazy impression that if she ever did walk in the footsteps of Helga von Waltz, that she would have a strong cognition like a bloodhound picking up a familiar scent. But here she felt nothing out of the ordinary. Which meant that either her supposition was wrong or the woman had never walked this particular sidewalk. She did not have enough information to form a logical conclusion.

"I suppose ancestors of mine could have walked here too," she said. "My grandparents on both sides are from Germany."

"Really? Where were you born?"

"San Francisco."

"My mother was German, but not a Berliner," Bradon said. "My dad was Irish."

"Oh." Sandi tried to sound as though the information was new to her. "So Bradon is Irish."

"Right. County Mayo, or one of those God forsaken western counties."

The sidewalk had become increasingly crowded and they were forced to make their way through a group of people who had appeared from a subway entrance. Many of them were speaking English. "Mehringdamm Station," Bradon explained. "A lot of Americans around here. The American library is right around the corner."

Excitement tugged at Sandi. "It might be a good place for us to start looking in the morning."

"That's what I was thinking. I've never been there, but I'll bet they've got a lot of information about Hitler and the war."

"At least it might give us some leads."

"Yeah, but don't be disappointed if it doesn't. The Germans always kept meticulous accounts, but the war destroyed a lot of the old records. We might not find anything."

Sandi refused to believe that. Somewhere in the labyrinth of this vast city were threads that would lead her to the truth.

A sharp edge of doubt stabbed at her resolve. Did she really want to know the truth? Perhaps it would be better to abandon the entire idea and return home where she could settle back into cozy predictability. She could marry Jordan and allow her life to drift smoothly like a river flowing within secure banks; a river whose course was charted and its depth known. She had lived all her life suppressing the voices inside her head; she could continue to do so. Before the fateful episode in Bradon's class they had been growing fainter. In time she was sure they would die altogether and she would really be free.

But, then, if the voices died, she would never learn the truth. Somehow they had led her this far, she could not give up now. Tomorrow. Her chin came up and her stride increased. Tomorrow she would find the thread that would lead her to real--and lasting--peace.

CHAPTER II

Sandi awakened slowly, her thoughts as warm and pleasant as the down-filled mattress of the bed. She lay with her eyes closed, almost afraid to analyze the source of her euphoria for fear that it would go away. Could it be because she was actually in Germany, actively perusing her goal? Maybe. Perhaps her euphoria was because she was with Dan Bradon.

She blinked. Jolted fully awake. Impossible! Still, she had suddenly become so warm that she had to throw aside the heavy comforter. No. Not Bradon. He was simply a means to an end. Nothing more. There had to be some other reason for her sense of bliss.

A new thought yanked her to a sitting position. The voices. In her head. They were gone. Silent. For the first time in her recent memory, she was free.

She sat in the cocoon of the bed, her eyes closed, a blanket pulled to her chin, enjoying the silence. This surcease might be temporary and she had to make the most of it while she could.

Minutes crawled by. Not a sign of the voices. Slowly she began to relax. Oh God. They were gone, really gone. Did this mean that she could abandon the quest?

Suddenly, as though her thought had shattered a barrier, the voices were back, subtle, subliminal, like ephemeral ghosts, more felt than heard. Her warm euphoria fled, driven away by the whisperers

Her gloom was further darkened when, glancing out the window, she saw that during the night a storm had moved in and a lowering mass of ragged clouds spewed a cold drizzle. She had been aware of the vagaries of Berlin fall weather and had brought a long raincoat and waterproof leather boots so the thought of walking in the rain did not dismay her. But this was to be the first real day of the quest, and with the return of the voices, she could not shake a growing apprehension about where the search would lead.

Were the voices trying to warn her not to meddle in the past? Or were they calling her? The past could well be filled with quicksands waiting to drag her under.

She set her jaw and climbed out of the cozy bed. The hell with them! She was committed. There was no turning back.

As she showered, she rationalized that her malaise was in part caused by jet lag, and as soon as her metabolism caught up with the clock, she would be her usual self. Although, of late, her usual disposition hadn't been the best in the world. Still, the quieting of the voices, if only for a while, had given her a much needed rest. If she could get the information she needed at the American Library, it could be a good day after all.

Dan Bradon must have also felt the import of the day because his greeting to Sandi when they met in the hotel lobby was a taut smile accompanied by a curt "Good morning." During breakfast at a small cafe around the corner from the hotel, he was unusually quiet.

His pensive mood suited Sandi just fine. She did not like engaging in pointless repartee. Bradon's silence also revealed that he had a quiet thoughtful side, which rather surprised her. Outgoing, optimistic people, who appeared to enjoy life to its fullest often became bitter and mean when their mood changed. Bradon's quiet mood seemed to be more introspective, but leavened by an innate awareness that he was still a part of humanity and should not burden others with his problems.

After breakfast, he suggested they take a taxi to the library, but Sandi told him that since the rain was only a drizzle she would prefer to walk. She didn't tell him that she really wanted the time to marshal her resolve, to use the unfamiliar sights and sounds of Berlin as reminders that she had set sail on this course and would follow wherever the wind took her.

The American Library was not large, reminding Sandi of a modest community library. Light was provided by several windows and indirect fluorescent lights. Bookcases lined the walls. Others were precisely spaced in back-to-back rows in the center of the room. A checkout desk was near the front entrance. Three long dark oak tables surrounded by oak chairs occupied the other end of the room. Quietness was assured by a dark green carpet of such a hard weave that it looked at though it would survive a cattle stampede.

In the silence, their steps thudded faintly on the carpet as Bradon led the way to the information desk. Behind the desk a plump middle-aged woman with light brown hair pulled back and tied in a severe bun, looked up with a smile. "I can be of help, no?"

"Perhaps," Bradon said. "I would like to locate a German family."

"Oh, yes." She turned to a bookcase behind her. "A directory we have."

"No, no. This is a family who lived here during the war. Before the war, actually. I believe they were nobility."

"Oh. What name? Perhaps I know."

"Von Waltz. Count Hermann von Waltz."

She shook her head. "No. That name I do not know."

"Perhaps a book on heraldry," Sandi said. "Probably of the old Prussian families."

"Oh. We have such books, yes. Come. I show you."

She led the way to a back section of bookcases and removed a large volume on Germanic heraldry. "This one is in German. You read German, ja?"

"Enough to get along," Bradon said.

She handed the book to Bradon. "Others we have in English but not so good as this."

"Thanks. If we need help, I'll come and ask you."

"Ja, Ja. I am here to help."

She moved away and Bradon carried the heavy book to a study table where he held a chair for Sandi. Sitting down next to her he angled the book so they could both look at it. "How do you think it's spelled: W.A.L.T.Z.?"

"That sounds right. It's a place to start."

"Right."

The layout of the book was similar to an encyclopedia with names followed by a brief history of the individual. As Bradon leafed through the pages, Sandi's heart began beating faster and her lips became dry. Was she about to find her ghosts? Perhaps something as simple as a name and a few printed words would exorcise forever the dread that had been a constant part of her life.

Bradon ran his finger down a page. He paused at a name. Sandi stopped breathing, waiting. "Waltz. Kurt Wilhelm Waltz. Noted orthographer. Orthographer?"

Sandi let her breath out in a soft sigh of relief. This could not be the right man. "The art of writing. Study of words and spelling."

"Couldn't be our guy. No 'von' either. Let's see. We've got four more Waltzes. No 'vons'."

"Let me see."

He angled the book so that Sandi could get a better view and they studied each of the names. Of the four other Waltzes listed, three were deceased professors. There was a Count von Walzer, but he had died in 1837. None of the others had a background remotely connected with Prussian nobility and none had wives named Helga.

"Could there be another way to spell it?" Bradon said. "Maybe W.A.L.Z.?"

"I doubt it. That doesn't sound German."

Bradon closed the book. "Then there's nothing here."

Sandi had ambivalent feelings of relief and disappointment. Maybe it was all a wild goose chase and she could now go home knowing that at least she had tried.

Bradon saw the look on her face and interpreted it as disappointment. "Don't worry. We'll find it." He pushed to his feet and picked up the book. "This is only one book. There are plenty more."

But an hour later his confidence had waned. They had searched both German and English language books on German genealogy without success. There were numerous people with a family name of Waltz but no link they could find to Count Hermann von Waltz.

"Maybe we're going about this backward," Bradon mused. "You said that Helga was a psychic, psychometric."

"That's right."

"Well, let's see what we can find out about her."

It was after 11:00 o'clock and several more people had entered the library. They were forced to wait at the information desk before they could speak to a short, balding man who had replaced the woman, probably for her lunch break.

"We're looking for anything you have," Bradon said, "linking some of the high ranking Nazi officers--Hitler, Himmler, Heydrich, Goering---to the occult."

The man's bored expression vanished and he stared at Bradon as though he had asked for his wife's phone number. "Occult? You're interested in the occult?"

He spoke English without an accent and Sandi was quite sure he was an American, probably retired military.

"That's right."

The librarian's fingers began drumming on the top of his desk. "Well, we don't have much on the occult. Hardly military, you know."

"I understand Hitler had an occult bureau," Sandi said. "I believe it was called the Ahnenerbe. Maybe you have something on that."

The librarian worried his lower lip with his teeth and his fingers continued their restless affair with the desktop. "The Ahnenerbe. I've heard of that. Never believed it though. Hitler was a lunatic but not that crazy, if you know what I mean. Horoscopes and mediums and that sort of thing. Occult. No, no. It's a little out of our scope. Most of the records for that sort of thing were destroyed before we could get our hands on them; if they ever existed. Hitler's orders, I've heard."

Sandi stared at the man wondering why he had become so defensive. His arrogant dismissal set her temples throbbing and, impulsively, she placed her hands on top of his, forcing them to stillness. She stared into his eyes, trying to make her own as sexy as possible. "It's important." She tinged her voice with urgency, keeping it warm and intimate. "Please help me."

Under her palms she could feel the man's hands tremble and he had trouble meeting her gaze. "We, uh, we really don't have that sort of information here. But, uh, there are some old books on the subject. I could,"---Sandi felt his hands stiffen--"give you a name."

She released his hands and gave him her most devastating smile. "Oh, thank you," she breathed. "I would really appreciate it."

The librarian hastily grabbed a pencil and on the back of a form used to request books, he scribbled an address, then thrust the paper into Sandi's hands. "If there is anything," he said, "Herr Burger will have it."

"Thank you. Thank you very much." Clutching the paper, Sandi headed for the exit with Bradon walking beside her.

"Wow!" he whispered, "You'd make a hell of a used car salesman."

Sandi smiled. "Sincerity. It works every time."

Bradon chuckled softly. "The most sincere people I know are con men."

"You see. It works."

"For you. He wouldn't have given me the time of day."

Outside the entrance they paused beneath an overhang to study the address on the paper.

"Terrible handwriting," Bradon sniffed.

"I think he was a little nervous."

"It looks like an address on WinterfeldStrasse. That makes sense. The Schöneberg district is famous for its bookshops. Feel like walking or should I get a taxi?"

"How far is it?"

"A couple of miles, back the way we came. We could take the S-Ban, but I'm not that familiar with the routes."

"I like to walk. See the city. We can stop for lunch on the way."

"If you can hold out until we get there, I know just the place."

"I can make it if you can."

"Probably better," he said with a smile.

Sandi pulled up the collar of her raincoat and they moved into the drizzle. They were walking back along FriedrichStrasse toward Mehringdamm, their hands in their pockets and rain dripping from their hats, before Sandi voiced a thought that had been bothering her.

"I wonder why he was so nervous?"

"The librarian? I got the impression that he didn't want anything to do with Hitler. A lot of Germans are like that."

"He isn't German. He's American."

"Because he didn't have an accent? Some of them speak better English than we do."

"Oh."

Sandi walked in silence for a few steps. She knew that it wasn't the mention of Hitler that had made the man nervous. When she had instinctively touched his hands it was because she had sensed his fear and had wanted to reassure him that there was no reason to be afraid. "It was the occult," she said. "He didn't want to talk about it. And he is American. But of German heritage. From Chicago."

Now why had she said that? She was almost as startled by the statement as was Bradon who stopped and stared at her.

"Chicago? What gave you that idea?"

The drizzle was chilling against her face but she scarcely felt it in the wonder of the moment. "I have no idea. It was just a--a hunch."

Bradon's eyes were speculative as though he did not really believe her. "A hunch. Uh huh."

To break the tension, Sandi began walking. "Where is this restaurant?" she said. "I'm starving."

Bradon had to trot to catch up. "It's raining harder," he said. "Let's grab a bus. At least down to Victoria Park."

"Okay," Sandi agreed. The sooner they found the bookstore the sooner she could find out whether she was searching for a real person or slipping toward insanity. She experienced a faint irritation at the delay when a short time later they alighted from a bus and Bradon began leading the way toward a beautiful white building with an incongruous clock tower.

"Rathaus Schöneberg, the town hall. Can you believe it was built in the early nineteen hundreds?"

The pristine building appeared new. Its green lawns, dark roof and white facade seemed untouched by time. "I guess it wasn't touched during the war."

"Restored. This whole area was hit pretty hard. They were after Tempelhof Airport and the railroad marshalling yards."

Sandi thought of the tons of bombs and artillery shells that had rained down on Berlin and shivered. "Not a good place to be living."

"Yeah. Incredible the way times change. This place we're standing is called John F. Kennedy Platz."

"Really? Why?"

"It's the place where he said, 'Ich bin ein Berliner!'." He glanced from his watch toward the clocks on the tower. "In a minute you'll get a real treat."

"Don't tell me a cuckoo pops out."

"Better."

Sandi's gaze was drawn to a flag that was struggling to fly in the light rain. In the center of the flag on a white field between top and bottom stripes of red was the silhouetted figure of a bear. "Why does it fly a California state flag?"

"The bear? It's been Berlin's heraldic symbol for God-only-knows how long. Notice that it's wearing a five-pointed crown. That's a reminder that Berlin is still an imperial city."

Sandi's reply was interrupted by the clear peal of a bell in the tower as it struck the hour of noon. As the strokes rang forth in warm timbre, Bradon said, "Another indication of how times change. That's a replica of our Liberty Bell. A gift from the same Americans who killed a lot of people here."

"And vice versa," Sandi replied dryly.

Bradon nodded. "True. We can be glad we were born when we were." The last mellow tone of the bell began its journey to infinity and Bradon took hold of Sandi's elbow. "So much for history. Let's take advantage of the present."

He began to lead the way into the building, but Sandi paused. "I'm really not in the mood for history."

"There's a restaurant in the basement. Great food."

"Great. I don't know why, but I'm hungry."

"Thinking is hard work."

"You've got that right."

Before they went down stairs to a Ratskeller-style restaurant, Bradon showed her a room at the base of the tower that contained 17 million American signatures expressing Berlin-American solidarity when Berlin was still a divided city.

In the small restaurant, at Bradon's suggestion, Sandi sampled beer that had been sweetened with a dash of raspberry syrup. "Poor man's champagne," he explained.

After Sandi finished a lunch of delicious catfish taken from the nearby Havel River, she sipped a second glass of the red-colored beer. It seemed a good time to ask Bradon a question that she had wanted to ask sooner but had put the question aside until she felt she knew him well enough to delve into his personal life.

Keeping her voice offhanded, she said without looking at him, "I was wondering--and you don't have to tell me if it's something personal-- but . . ."

She hesitated, waiting for an invitation to proceed and he said, "What? My age? I'm twenty-eight. Way over the hill. So you have nothing to worry about."

She looked up then with her most innocent expression. "It isn't that. I was just wondering why you switched from clinical to industrial psychology."

His smile stayed, but a curtain seemed to block the sparkle from his eyes. "That's easy," he said. "Money. It's a lot easier to collect from a corporation than from a disturbed patient. And I don't have to deal with malpractice insurance."

Sandi hoped that her own face was as noncommittal as she said, "I guess you're right."

He was lying and she wondered why.

As though to make sure the subject was closed, he got up and came around to pull her chair back. "We'd better get started. What was that address?"

Walking up stairs, Sandi dug the piece of paper from her pocket. "100 WinterfeldStrasse."

"Right. That's not far."

It had stopped drizzling, but the sky was still dark beneath low hanging, windtorn clouds. Sandi yanked tight the belt on her raincoat and pulled her hat low. The brisk wind prevented conversation, but it also gave a sense of intimacy as she and Bradon braced against its clawing fingers, their shoulders almost touching.

As they walked, Sandi tried to focus her thoughts on what might be waiting for her in some antique book in a musty Berlin bookstore, but her thoughts kept slipping back to Bradon. She wondered why he was so reluctant to talk about his clinical work. Could he be harboring some dark secret? Something dangerous? Nonsense. It would have shown up in the detective's report. Maybe he just didn't like people prying into his personal affairs. He probably discussed his work freely with other friends. Friends? Could she really say they were friends? More likely he thought of her simply as a colleague.

Actually, it was best that he did. Many psychologists believed that the male animal was incapable of a pure plutonic friendship with any woman who was younger than his mother; sometimes even if they were older. During the twenty or more times a minute that thoughts of sex crossed the mind of the average male over the age of ten, some of it was bound to take the form of fantasies about any woman he happened to be with.

A gust of wind caused Bradon to miss a step, and he brushed against her side. She interpreted the brief contact to be a sign that she was right. Bradon's mind might view her as his colleague, but his glands undoubtedly viewed her as a potential bed partner. She would have to keep her guard up.

She put a little more distance between them and increased her stride, ducking her head into the wind while she concentrated on the street scene. They had moved into a district of narrow, elm-lined streets. Small shops occupied the ground floors of old two-and-three-floor apartment buildings. The footing on the narrow sidewalk was made treacherous by a layer of wet golden leaves shed from trees that lined the street. Once she slipped despite her caution and Bradon steadied her by taking hold of her upper arm. Instead of letting go after she had regained her balance, he slid his hand down until he could entwine their fingers as they walked. Sandi's mind shouted at her to pull away from his unexpected intimacy. Such an abrupt move would probably damage his ego. Besides, she was probably reading meaning into the gesture that was not there. As Shakespeare had said, "You jest at scars that never felt a wound."

Bradon's touch had occupied her thoughts and she was surprised when he stopped and said, "Here we are." They were in front of a small shop with a sign over the sidewalk that proclaimed it to be 'Burger's Buchs.'

He released her hand and she felt a sharp sense of loss as though she had suddenly been deprived of a part of her body. She hid her consternation by thrusting her hand deep into her pocket as she said, "Good," and led the way into the shop.

Reflected in the shop window she saw Bradon make a rueful smile and shake his head as he followed her inside. She was right. His gesture had been more than concern for her safety. Somehow the thought did not make her angry.

Inside the shop the only light came from the large front window. In the dim light, Sandi could see that the shop was filled from floor to ceiling with bookcases. Each case held a polyglot collection of old and, by comparison, new books. Some of the books were in orderly rows, but most looked as though they had been pawed through for years and discarded with contemptuous disregard for order. Layers of dust on the shelves and on many of the books was a major contributor to the shop's gloomy ambience.

A thin man sat at a small desk near the door reading a book that he angled toward light from the window. Sharp features and a stubble of gray beard made it difficult to determine his age, although Sandi guessed he was in his fifties. He was wearing a thick, knitted sweater over a shirt and a loosely knotted tie that looked as though they had been worn every day for decades. Thin strands of once blonde hair sprouted through the open top of an eye shade like weeds in a planter's box.

The man's dark, cavernous eyes flicked up when they entered. His thin finger marked his place in the book. He sighed, as though miffed that they had interrupted his reading. "Ja?" His voice was as dry and dusty as his books. Sandi noticed that the book he was reading was written in English.

"Herr Burger?" Bradon said. The man stared without answering as though to say who else would he be. Bradon eyes grew bleak as he reacted to the man's arrogance, but he continued to smile. "We were told that you could help us locate some books on the occult."

The man replied in German. "Ich spreche kein englisch," and turned back to his book.

Switching to German, Bradon said, "You have, I suppose, heard of World War Two? Adolph Hitler?"

Herr Burger's thin shoulders stiffened and he looked up at Bradon but did not speak.

"We are looking for someone who was one of Hitler's psychic advisors. We would appreciate any help."

Herr Burger reached for a light switch on the wall and clicked it on and dusty lights in the ceiling reluctantly put forth a dim glow. Herr Burger nodded toward the jungle of books. "You are free to look."

Sandi could see that Bradon was struggling to hold his temper, and she stepped forward. "Herr Burger," she said in English, her voice icy. "I am a psychic, working with the police. If you do not cooperate, I can promise you that misfortune will fall upon your head. The choice is yours."

Burger's mouth had come open and he stared at Sandi with eyes that now held interest. "You are psychic?" he asked in English.

Sandi stared at him, her eyes as cold as his had been. "You do not know?"

Burger blinked and licked his lips. Slowly he lowered his book to the desk and, as he stood up, the pages ruffled, losing his place. "What do you want to know?"

Bradon took a step toward him. "Hitler's occult bureau, the Ahnenerbe. We are looking for a man who could have been associated with the bureau. His wife was one of Hitler's psychics."

"His name?"

Sandi was relieved that Burger had not denied that there was an occult bureau nor that Hitler had employed psychics. "Hermann von Waltz," she answered. "Count von Waltz. His wife's name was Helga."

Burger looked away as he ruminated and Sandi wished that she actually was psychic so that she could tell what he was thinking. Did he know of von Waltz and was debating whether or not to lie? Or was he honestly searching his memory?

Burger shook his head. "I never heard of that name." He saw the disappointment in Sandi's face and added, "But that means nothing. There were many occultists involved with the National Socialists. Especially in the early days. Dietrich Eckart, Karl Haushofer, Stein, Rudolf Steiner, von Sebottendorf, whose real name, you know, was Rudolf Glauer."

"What about astrologers? Psychics?"

"Hitler, Himmler, Goering. Even Goebles. They all had connections with the occult. Astrologers, Tarot readers, readers of auras, palmists, clairvoyants, so many. None remained in power very long."

Sandi's voice was a dry whisper as she said, "What about psychometrics?"

Burger's thin face lifted and he almost seemed to smile. "Ah," he said. "Psychometrics. A special talent. But no. I have no knowledge of such a person being involved with the Ahnenerbe. You must remember, many such people were arrested and their records destroyed in the 1938 purge."

Suddenly, Sandi felt drained of energy. She closed her eyes and pressed her fingers against the sides of her nose as she tried to absorb this latest rebuff.

Bradon nodded toward the bookracks. "Perhaps the answers are somewhere in there. Can you make any suggestions?"

Without a word Herr Burger walked back into the dark aisles, followed by the two Americans. He began selecting books from the cluttered shelves in seemingly random fashion. Once he paused, asking, "Do you read German?"

Bradon said, "Yes," and the desultory selection continued until Herr Burger had seven books. He then carried the collection to the front desk. Without a word he studied the price penciled on the inside cover of each book and wrote them on the back of an envelope. He totaled the figures and handed the envelope to Bradon who reached into his pocket.

"I'll get it," Sandi said hastily, opening her purse.

Bradon's hand came out of his pocket clutching Euros. "I've got it. You can reimburse me later."

Sandi nodded. "Be sure you keep track."

"You'd better believe it," Bradon said with a tight smile as he counted out the proper amount. "Every farthing."

"Pfennig."

"Whatever."

Herr Burger wrapped their purchases in old newspapers to protect them from the rain, and Sandi led the way outside. She took a deep breath of the fresh air. Even being in the drizzling rain was better than the decay and depressing gloom of the shop.

"Did you get the feeling," she said as she and Bradon walked away, "that he didn't want to talk about it, just like the man at the American Library."

"It? You mean the war? A lot of Germans are like that, especially the older ones."

"Not the war. The occult. The Nazi connection."

"Oh. Well, even that's understandable. Maybe not so much to an American. But you've got to remember that the people of Europe are not far removed from a time when superstition was a big part of their lives. Even today out of the big cities, in the rural areas, they still retain a lot of the old myths and superstitions."

"Maybe that's why Hitler was so much into the occult. He grew up in a kind of backwater region."

"In Hungary. Yes, I would think so. That whole Transylvania area has been a hotbed of superstition."

"No wonder. More Gypsies live there than any place in the world, with all their ancient superstitions and curses. Hungarians still revere Vlad Tepes."

"Yes. The Impaler. They say he was the prototype for Bram Stoker's Count Dracula."

Sandi smiled as she felt a familiar childhood dread. "Those old movies with Bela Lugosi and Boris Karloff used to give me nightmares."

"And you're an American. Think how those legends must have given nightmares to the people who grew up in those grim mountains and black forests with their old castles and stories of vampires and werewolves. No wonder they were big in the occult."

Bradon's words swirled amid Sandi's thoughts as she walked through the rain. Maybe she, too, was a victim of superstitions, a victim of repressed stories from her childhood, memories buried deep in her subconscious? "Superstitions," she said quietly, "are a lot like stereotypes: they often have their roots in facts."

"True. But facts as they were known at the time. Today we know better. That's why we can laugh at those old wives' stories."

"You mean like stories about psychic regression."

Bradon laughed, his voice warm in the chill air. "Could be. Maybe you're right about truth being at their roots."

"Truth as we know it now," she said, echoing his words. "In a hundred years we'll look back on this and laugh."

"A hundred years." His voice had softened, became musing. "Wouldn't it be nice to be together then?"

Sandi's breath caught in her throat. She had to take several steps before she could begin breathing. What he had meant? A joke? In response to her own? Or were there deliberate implications in his remark? Did he envision them going through life together, and beyond? He was probably thinking of a reunion in heaven with all his colleagues. What else could it mean?

To break free of the disturbing thoughts, she gestured toward the package of books that Bradon was lugging balanced on one shoulder. "Those must be heavy. Let me carry some."

"I'm okay. But I am curious about what it is we've got here. It was too dark in that place to get a good look at the titles."

"Me too. Let's stop at a coffee shop and take a look."

He glanced at her. "Are you buying?"

"Sure," she said. "It's only fair. You bought the books."

He laughed again, and the sound filled her with such pleasure that Sandi vowed never to be gloomy when she was with him. Which would be easy since he seemed to chase away all her morose feeling anyway. One more thing to worry about. Why the devil couldn't he be old and grouchy? It would certainly make this entire trip a lot easier on her mind.

Sitting at a small table in a cafe, their hands warmed by holding hot cups of cappuccino coffee, they tore the wrapping from the books and examined the titles. They included "Sword and Swastika" by Telford Taylor, Francis King's "Satan and Swastika", Shalar's "The Nazis and the Occult", "The Dawn of Magic" by Pauwels and Bergier, "Science of the Invisible" by Shepard, and two books in German which Sandi interpreted as "Urania's Children" and "Uralinda Chronicle".

Bradon thumbed through one of the books. "No pictures. And I hate small print."

Sandi studied their small library. "A lot of reading. I wonder if we can find a restaurant where they don't mind if we read at the table."

"As long as the waiters don't get a look at the titles. We might get poison in our soup."

This time it was Sandi's turn to laugh, and when she saw the look of pleasure on Bradon's face, her smile felt as though it would never go away.

CHAPTER 12

Bradon was having difficulty concentrating on the book he was reading and making notes on hotel stationary. He and Sandi were sitting in her room on opposite sides of a small table where they perused the books they had purchased. Outside the afternoon sunlight had dissolved into dusk and then into night. The only light in the room came from a reading lamp on the table. Classical music--Bradon thought it was Beethoven--came faintly from a small radio sitting atop the unused TV.

The time, the place, the setting, as well as the urgency of the research, were conducive to study. So why was he having so much trouble concentrating? Stupid thought. He knew the reason. He was acutely conscious of Sandi's presence on the other side of the table, so close that their knees almost touched. He could practically feel the warmth of her soft breath. He couldn't control the way his eyes kept flicking from the pages of the book to her slender hands only inches from his own. And her face, as she frowned at the book she was reading, drew his glances like a magnet. Damn! That soft skin beneath her ear was the perfect place for a nuzzling kiss. And double damn! Why had she shaken her glorious hair loose so that the incandescent light gave it the color and texture of spun honey, honey that cascaded from her shoulders each time she bent forward to study the pages? From time to time she used her left hand to brush aside recalcitrant strands that hindered her vision. The movement was unconscious to her but it always caused him to lose his place as his gaze leaped to her breasts where the cloth of her sweater was tightened by her gesture.

In desperation he propped his elbows on the table and cupped his hands across his forehead like a visor so he could not see her. It failed to help. As though they had a mind of their own, his senses remained tuned to the sound of her breathing, the faint smell of her perfume, the nearness of her knees beneath the table.

But there wasn't much he could do about it short of getting up and moving to the couch or another chair, preferably one about a mile away.

Stupid thought. He was totally incapable of moving. The building could fall down and he would have been locked in his chair as long as she remained so near.

She obviously was having no trouble concentrating. She had almost completed all of the books written in English, making copious notes, while he had yet to get through one in German. Apparently his nearness had absolutely no effect on her. Perhaps she was one of those women who never thought about sex until given some reason to think about it. He smiled to himself. Hell, most women required some external stimulus to bring sexual images into their thoughts. And then they were usually negative. So why was it that women, with all that brain power perking along and no thoughts of sex to impede concentration, weren't the rulers of the world? Sandi and he were archetypal: his concentration was disrupted by erotic thoughts while she was totally absorbed in her work.

It was a good thing that she was the one in control of their relationship. One intimate look from her, one intimate gesture, and he would be unable to resist. And that would not be good for either of them. She was already hurting. A romantic fling was the last thing she needed. Sex was too damn powerful an emotion to fool around with. He already knew the tragic consequences that could occur.

He terminated the temptations by glancing at his watch and turned his book face down on the table. "Almost eight. You getting hungry?"

Sandi looked up, blinking to refocus her eyes. "Eight? Already?"

"Five to. I vote we call it a day."

"Okay. I should call my mother." Sandi put her pencil in the book to mark her place and closed the pages. "Besides, you must be bored stiff reading this stuff."

Bradon stifled a chuckle. Bored? If she only knew. He would like this time to go on forever, sitting with her, watching her face, her hands, her hair, her nearness filling him with a warmth that brought every sense alive.

He stood and moved toward the door. "How about a half hour?"

Sandi also stood. "Fine. Uh, what should I wear?"

Bradon paused, his hand on the doorknob. Her words conjured images that brought a warm flush to his face and he was grateful for the dim light. "Cocktail dress, I think. After dinner we'll hit a couple of clubs."

Sandi glanced down at the books on the table. "I'd really like to get back to these, if you don't mind."

She had no way of knowing that was precisely what he would also like to do. Sitting close to her, alone, in the quiet room, with the soft music from the radio was a fantasy come true. But a dangerous fantasy. There would be far less hazard in being in a club surrounded by people and blaring music.

"We can do that in the morning. You've got to see a little of Berlin's nightlife. No telling when you'll get back here."

Sandi hesitated. "All right. I guess it would be best to get a fresh start in the morning." She moved toward the bedroom. "A half hour. Okay?"

"Bueno. And don't wear walking shoes. We'll take a taxi."

Her hair swirled as she turned her head to say over her shoulder, "Damn. I've got some mountain boots that'd go great with basic black and pearls."

"Good. In Berlin you can wear anything."

"Just like in L.A."

"Right. Just like L.A."

In his room, Bradon hurriedly stripped off his clothes and stepped into the shower, leaving the water on cold.

By the time he began dressing he had his glands under firm control, a control he was determined would not slip again.

Later when he gently rapped on Sandi's door, he steeled himself for the impact he knew she would produce when he saw her. She had been bewitching when bundled against the chilling rain. She had been devastating in a sweater and long skirt. What would be the effect of a cocktail dress?

She opened the door and he froze, stunned.

God, she was tall.

Sandi saw the way his jaw slackened and she stepped back. Had she made a mistake? Was the way she had dressed so inappropriate?

She had chosen an Ungaro long-sleeved, wide-shouldered, high-necked, minidress of dark purple silk decorated with bands of purple paillettes down the front and around the waist like a belt. Her panty hose were taupe. For shoes she had chosen black Bally sling pumps with four inch heels. She had fastened her hair up in order to better display pendant earrings of pearls and brilliant cubic zirconium. Usually she wore little or no makeup except for lip-gloss, but she had taken the time to touch up her eyelids and lashes. The mirror had told her she looked fine so she could not understand Bradon's astonishment.

"Is it all right?" she said. "I can change."

Bradon gave a little shake like a dog coming out of water and hastily said, "No, no. It's fine. Great, in fact." He indicated her earrings. "Are those real?"

"The pearls are Mabes. But the diamonds are cubic zirconium."

"Good. Berlin isn't as safe as it was a few years ago. I'd hate for you to lose real diamonds, just in case."

"Maybe I'd better leave them here."

"No, don't change a thing. I like being the envy of every guy in the joint. Have you got a jacket?"

His words of approval gave Sandi a thrill of pleasure, immediately followed by a flash of guilt. She was engaged; practically married. Why should she care what he thought of her appearance? Stranger still, why had she gone to so much trouble to look her best?

She picked up a beaded jacket from the back of a chair and he held it while she slipped it on. Was she mistaken or, for an instant, did his hands linger on her shoulders before he stepped away?

"Maybe you'd better bring something warmer," he said. "It'll be cold later."

"I just have my raincoat. It's got a lining."

"Fine. I'll carry it."

As she took the heavy raincoat from the closet near the door, she said, "What about you? Shouldn't you have a topcoat?"

He was wearing black boots with Cuban heels, dark gray pleated slacks, a black turtleneck sweater and a dark blue Blazer. On his whipcord body the combination gave him a casual elegance that he wore easily. "I'll be warm enough," he said. When she brushed past him on the way out the door she heard him mutter, "Maybe too warm."

Riding in the taxi he chose to sit with the full width of the seat between them and Sandi wondered why. It wasn't that they had to sit thigh to thigh like lovers but there was something chilling in the distance he deliberately put between them. Maybe it had something to do with his mutter about being "too warm". The words had made her heart skip a beat, but she must have misinterpreted the meaning because there was a sheen of perspiration on his wide forehead. The turtleneck sweater with the wool jacket did look warm.

The restaurant was on the top floor of the Grand Hotel, one of the tallest buildings in East Berlin. Sandi could well believe that the hotel had been in the hands of the Communists. The decor of oaks, plushes and leathers was sumptuous but terribly overdone, as though a decorator had used photographs to imitate such renowned California restaurants as the Beverly Hills Hotel's "Polo Lounge" or the old "Chasen's." There was even a small dance floor and an orchestra that played American songs from the 1940's and Teutonic versions of rumbas, sambas and tangos.

The restaurant afforded a view of the city's dark skyline. Looking out at the neon signs and the traffic in the street below, Sandi could almost believe she was back in Los Angeles.

But this wasn't Los Angeles and while her dinner of Venison Scaloppini with Spaetzle and Preiselbercu, ending with Black Forest Cake, had been excellent, the German cuisine reminded her that she was in Berlin and that she was here for a purpose.

After dinner they sat having coffee with glasses of Amaretto. Bradon's silent gaze, along with his usual expression of sardonic amusement, made her uncomfortable. Was he laughing at her?

"I take it," she said, "that you didn't find anything pertinent in the German books."

Bradon's eyes lost their humor. "Not so far. Except that those Nazi panjandrums were pretty deep in the occult."

"I got the same impression. If what we read is really true."

"Oh, I'm pretty sure it is. There are too many cross-references. It's just that so many of the specifics are missing, like reading about the theory of relativity: you know it's true but you can't quite get a handle on it."

"Like some people always have a curtain over their mind. You can never really know them."

"I know. Someone once said that every person is a moon with a dark side that is never shown to anyone."

Sandi looked away, unable to endure Bradon's pensive gaze. She had already revealed more of her dark side than she intended. And yet, that was the reason they were here, to dredge up her dark side and hold it to the sun. But it was a side she dreaded revealing, even to herself.

Bradon sensed her discomfort and said, "Listen. They're playing our song. Would you like to dance?"

'Our song' was appropriately enough 'Smoke Gets In Your Eyes.' When Bradon took her in his arms the song's words of warning echoed in Sandi's mind. This wasn't the way it was supposed to be. Only Jordan, the man she was going to marry, should be able to elicit such a sense of pleasure.

She rationalized that it had to be because she loved to dance. She would enjoy the moment just as much with anyone who danced as well as Bradon. For he was a smooth dancer, moving with the ease of someone who feels the rhythm and mood of the music. After her first tentative steps she lost herself in the music, moving in easy grace, feeling his chest against her breasts, his thighs against hers. The sensation was so erotic that she broke the contact.

Bradon stiffened and for an instant he lost the rhythm. Then his lips twisted in an amused smile. When he resumed the dance, he was careful to keep their bodies well separated.

The next dance was a tango, and she started to return to their table but Bradon caught her hand. "Want to try it?"

Sandi hesitated. She knew how to tango. Months of cotillion when she was in her early teens had brought out a talent for dancing that had delighted her. She enjoyed all the dances, but the tango was her favorite. Unfortunately, Jordan never danced the tango so it had been a long time since she had given herself to the exotic beat. What made her hesitate was the dance itself; if done properly, the tango demanded intimate body contact. There would be no escape from Bradon's touch, from the nearness of his lips. Would her own body betray her? Should she take the chance?

The decision was taken out of her hands when Bradon pulled her into his arms, using his strength to hold her tight against him as his feet began the gliding steps. Instinctively, Sandi followed, her body rigid with apprehension, but her feet responding with the automatic sense of a dancer.

The floor was almost deserted, giving them room to perform the intimate, lingering steps. As Sandi became absorbed in the carnal rhythm, her instincts took over and she began to relax, moving easily, letting long ago memories combine with Bradon's expert lead to sweep her into mesmerizing joy. She had forgotten how very much she loved the complicated dance. She pressed close against her partner, her legs, her arms, matching his in the erotic ritual. The sensuous throb of the music robbed her of inhibition. She danced without thought, her body responding to the sensation of the moment, abandoning herself to her partner's arms and his compelling eyes.

When the music ended with a crescendo, Bradon bent her back in a low sweeping turn before he pulled her back into his arms and held her close, their legs intertwined, their bodies straining against each other. For a blinding instant, Sandi's eyes were locked on Bradon's in a gaze as intimate as a kiss.

Gradually, she became aware of the sound of applause. The sound grew louder, calling her back to reality, and Sandi broke the mesmerizing bond with a strangled gasp.

She stumbled across the floor to their table, not knowing how she made the short journey without bumping blindly into intervening tables and chairs.

At the table, without waiting for Bradon, she grabbed her purse and walked quickly to the rest room. Sitting in front of a mirror, she opened her purse with trembling fingers. But she took nothing out. Instead, she sat staring at her flushed face, peering into her wide eyes, glazed with tears, feeling as though she was looking at the face of a stranger. What had caused her to lose control? It must have been the music. The exotic rhythm, the romantic ambience had made her forget all ties of home and family.

She stared into her eyes in the mirror and admitted the lie. It wasn't the music; it wasn't the time or the place. It was Bradon. How was it possible for him to have such a powerful effect on her? It was beyond analysis. She was behaving like a schoolgirl away from home for the first time, which, however, was close to the truth.

She closed her purse with a snap. Bradon was trying to seduce her. That was the answer. But he was not going to succeed. It had to end. Right here and now. She must not jeopardize her purpose with some stupid adolescent infatuation.

She stared at herself in the mirror. The eyes that returned her stared were no longer filmed with tears. They were hard, steely with resolve. Good. That's the way they would stay.

When she returned to the table Bradon was gazing out across the lights of the city. He saw her and stood up, and she noticed that he avoided looking into her eyes when he moved to hold her chair. She hoped that he had made the same decision as she. But whether he had nor not, it made no difference. She was now firmly in control of her emotions.

Bradon had taken his seat and she noticed that the usual sardonic twist of his lips was missing as he said, "I guess we should go back to the hotel."

"I thought you wanted to go to a disco club?"

"Well, I did but, uh, . . ." His eyes came up to hers. "Maybe we'd better call it a night."

Her gaze was steady as she looked directly into his eyes. "Why? Don't you like to dance?"

He studied her level gaze, then his own eyes regained their amused

glint. "Okay," he said. "But let's go some place where they don't play the tango."

Walking toward the door, Sandi wondered if she might be making a mistake. Any dance with someone as charismatic as Bradon, even separated disco dancing, could put a strain on her resolve.

Her back straightened and her chin came up. Being close to Bradon would allow her to exercise her willpower. And everybody knew that exercise made a person stronger. Besides, her feet were beginning to hurt and sore feet could make the most romantic dance in the world a complete failure.

CHAPTER 13

The next day Sandi and Dan Bradon paid a visit to the magnificent Staatsbibliothek library in the Tiergarten district's Kulturforum. When they left late in the afternoon, their eyes gritty from hours of reading, they were both discouraged. An entire day wasted with no results.

By unspoken consent, instead of taking a taxi, they began a slow walk along ReichpietschuferStrasse on the side of the street bordering the Landwehrkanal. As they walked in silence, Sandi idly watched the U-Bahn trains follow the snaking curves of the canal. But her eyes failed to register the images. She was thinking about their failure to find even a single clue to the mysterious Baron Hermann von Waltz or his wife, Helga.

That morning, they had finished examining their small library of books on the occult. After a quick lunch, they had taken a taxi to the huge State Library. Sandi felt as though she would go mad if she had to read one more German biography.

"While we're here," Bradon said, "we really should take a look at the Gedenkstatte Deutscher Widerstand."

It took a moment for Sandi to focus on his words. "Widerstand? What's that?"

"A memorial to German resistance."

"Resistance to whom?"

"Hitler."

"I didn't know there was any."

"It's pretty hard to resist when it could get you shot. That's what the memorial is for."

"The ones who were shot?"

"Yes. Following the attempt to assassinate Hitler in 1944."

"Maybe we should see it. It would suit my mood."

She was walking with her head lowered, her steps dragging. Bradon glanced at her. "Cheer up," he said with a broad smile. "We're just getting started."

Bradon's good cheer was not infectious. Sandi remained wrapped in a gloom of failure. How could she have been so wrong? All the signs, all her instincts, had lead to this city. She felt empty, as though she had been betrayed by her convictions.

After a few minutes of silent walking, Bradon broke into her introspection. "Are you sure about the name?"

"Von Waltz? Yes. That's the name I heard. The name I saw."

"But don't forget, the images were coming out of your head. There was no actual hard evidence. They could have been--twisted, changed."

"But not the time, or the place. I saw her with Hitler."

"Saw whom? Some woman named Helga von Waltz. Where did you get that name?"

Sandi stopped. Where had she first heard the name? It had just been there, a part of the images. "Himmler called her by that name. I remember that."

"Himmler was part of the illusion. He called you by a name that came out of your head. It could have been wrong."

Sandi stared at him as a glimmer of hope began to form. It was quickly thrust aside by returning doubts. "If it was wrong, we're finished. We have nothing else to go on."

"Not necessarily."

"What do you mean?"

Bradon did not want to be looking at her when he told her what he had in mind, so he took her arm and turned to begin walking again. "There is a way we can get more information, more clues to go on."

"How?"

"You can go back again."

He expected her to turn upon him in quick anger. She had made it clear that she had no intention of ever again going through the nerve-shattering experience of regression. Instead, she continued walking, her head down in thoughtful contemplation.

"I hate that," she said. "I really hate that."

"I know. But I can't think of anything else."

"It might not work. I have no control over it."

"I know that too."

She went on as though she was not listening to him. "I might not go back to the same time. I could be a different person entirely. If it worked at all."

"Maybe I can control that."

His words penetrated her musing and she looked at him. "You can? How?"

"When I put you under--when you regress--I'll ask for Helga."

Sandi nodded without replying. Actually, she knew instinctively that it was not necessary to ask for Helga. The German woman was apparently one of the strongest voices in her mind, practically demanding to escape. The problem was not in letting her out; the danger lay in putting her back. Each time she became Helga, the woman became stronger. If she continued these regressions, would a time come when Helga would take over her mind completely so that Bradon could not bring her back to reality? Would it happen this time?

The thought was still in the forefront of her mind as she sat in her room at the hotel and listened to Bradon begin the familiar ritual. "Close you eyes. Relax. Just listen to my voice."

The room had been darkened by drawing the curtains and the only sound besides Bradon's voice was the muted rumble of traffic on the street.

It was difficult for Sandi to let go of her fear so that she could concentrate on Bradon's warm voice. She was tense with apprehension, struggling to cooperate, but, at the same time, resisting giving up her hard won control of the voices in her head.

Bradon realized her mental struggle and he moved behind her chair. Keeping his voice low and patient, he slowly led her through the relaxation exercises. When her fluttering eyelids and slack muscles indicated that she had been able to release her fears and was completely relaxed, he began the next level. "You are completely relaxed, safe and warm, feeling wonderful. You are going back. Looking for her, looking for Helga. She is there waiting for you . . . .

*   *   *   *

It was cold in the subterranean chamber. I shivered. But my chill was caused as much by apprehension as by the cold. If this entire macabre ceremony was not so deadly, it would be comical. Watching, I felt foolish, like being part of a bad melodrama.

Hermann, I knew, felt none of my perturbation as he dutifully performed the ostentatious SS initiation rites. Nor was there any hint of hypocrisy from any of the other participating men. They were caught up in the ritual and spirit of the ceremony as profoundly as were Cardinal initiates of the Vatican.

When it was Hermann's turn to drink the purified wine, he stepped forward smartly and took the silver chalice from the hands of Reichsführer-SS Himmler. The chalice was supposed to represent the Holy Grail and the wine the blood of Christ, and Hermann was properly solemn as he presented the cup to the four quadrants of the cross before taking a sip of the wine. He glanced toward me. His face was impassive but his eyes gleamed with triumph. He handed the chalice back to Himmler, then returned to his place with the four other men, standing as stiff and imperious as a Prussian soldier.

Although I detested the ceremony and all its implications, I had to fight against a wave of pride. Hermann was half a head taller than the other men who, in truth, did not match my expectations as the elite of Aryan Germans. Two of them, no matter how much they strained to stand like soldiers on parade, had the heavy stomachs and rounded shoulders of men who spend their time behind desks. The other two had thick bodies and short-fingered hands. Their features had a brutish look that reminded me of prison guards. Even their new--and I had to admit, ominously impressive--black and silver SS uniforms, including black riding breeches and gleaming black boots, could not make up for their lack of military bearing.

But by virtue of this SS ceremony they would take their place in the order of the new Reich as the elite of the elite, the fairest of the fair. And, I thought with a shudder, the most brutal of the brutes.

The ceremony had been designed--by Himmler himself it was said--to resemble pagan initiation ceremonies of the old Thulean 'Black Order' with augmentation from Masonic and Templar Knight initiation rites. Himmler particularly liked the swearing of allegiance to himself as Reichsführer-SS, a procedure that had its roots in the Jesuit Order and their sworn to-the-death loyalty to Ignatius Loyola and the Catholic Church.

As the ritual proceeded with much flourishing of daggers and kneeling while taking oaths, I had the chance to study the odd room. SS headquarters had been established in an old Westphalian castle. It was being refurbished to Himmler's specifications by several hundred slave laborers, at the expense of many lives I had heard. The large, dungeon-like room we were in at the base of the castle's north donjon had been aptly named 'the well of the dead.' The walls of the circular room were made of rough-hewn stone blocks and decorated with heraldic arms and shields of German heroes. Light was provided by flaming torches mounted in wall sconces. A circular pit in the center of the floor had been sunken more than a meter into the solid rock foundation. Plinths had been implanted around the edges of the sunken pit. Each plinth supported an urn that was slated to contained the ashes of some high-ranking SS hero, provided his death was heroic.

The ceiling was very high and shaped like an inverted funnel, to act as a chimney for the smoke of the burning torches, I supposed.

The rites seemed to go on forever. At one point a ring bearing the Death's Head image of the SS Totenkopf Division was slipped on each man's finger. I could not fathom how Hermann could tolerate such a horrible symbol on his hand. I would have nightmares every second of the day or night thinking of all the dead people it represented.

My legs were tiring to the point where I was having difficulty standing in the required attitude of attentive contemplation when, at last, the ritual was concluded by a brief address from Himmler that ended with the admonition: "Never forget we are a knightly Order, from which one cannot withdraw, to which one is recruited by blood and within which one remains with body and soul so long as one lives on this earth. "

It was a relief to move forward and congratulate Hermann and the other men. When I embraced Hermann and kissed his cheek, he whispered in my ear, "You see. It is more than you thought. Much more."

He was referring to my skepticism regarding Himmler and his so called "Schutzstaffel" staff guard. I had made it clear to him that I considered the SS to be a group of thugs who hid behind Hitler's protection while committing barbaric crimes. I had to admit, however, that they were a powerful organization and, under Himmler's dictates, were growing ever more powerful.

And now Hermann was one of them. I knew that in his heart, like most old order Prussians, he had as much disdain for Himmler and his SS thugs as he had for Hitler. But he was a realist and being an officer in the

SS gave him entry to the upper echelons of the Third Reich's elite. It also imbued him with the power--and, indeed, the responsibility--of inflicting terror.

I was reminded of the SS's ability to evoke fear when Hermann put on his hat and I saw the Totenkopf Division's Death's Head symbol above the hat's shinny bill. The sight was like an icy wind and I crossed my arms over my chest, rubbing my shoulders.

"Are you cold?" Hermann said.

I was wearing a knitted gown with long sleeves, but I'd been forced to leave my jacket in the castle hallway because it was not the obligatory white color that Himmler demanded all women wear while attending the ceremony. "I am a little," I admitted. "It's chilly in here."

"Good," Hermann said. "It'll be a good excuse to get out of this mausoleum."

We were walking toward the door when Himmler moved to intercept us. "Ah, Countess von Waltz. I'm delighted you could witness our ceremony."

He took my hand and I flinched when he clicked the heels of his boots. He made a perfunctory bow and pressed his thin lips to the back of my hand.

"The honor is mine," I lied.

Hermann smiled, relieved that I hadn't expressed my true feelings. "She had a sudden chill. We were going for her wrap."

Himmler nodded. "Of course. Wearing these heavy uniforms I sometimes forget it can become chilly at this time of the year."

"We will see you at the reception," Hermann said.

We started to move away but Himmler stepped in front of us. "We have a little time," he said. "Would it be convenient for you and your wife to come with me?"

I experienced the same spasm of terror I'd felt the time I had been summoned to an audience with Hitler. The difference was that this time I knew what this man wanted. This was not a dreaded SS or Gestapo summons that could end with a disappearance in Nacht und Nebel 'Night and Fog.' He wanted a psychic reading. I wondered who the victims would be this time. Maybe I would be lucky and the images would be positive. But if they were not, if I saw deceit--or worse--what would I do? Could I possibly devise some means of evading a pronouncement that would most likely cost someone his life?

I retrieved my jacket before Himmler led us through the austere castle halls to a suite of rooms in one of the south towers that I assumed were his quarters. The suite was furnished with heavy oaken tables and chairs. On the walls were tapestries and Teutonic shields bearing coats of arms. It looked as cold and barren as I'm sure it had been when the castle was originally constructed four hundred years ago.

Himmler led the way to a room that I took to be the castle's library since there were shelves of books that appeared never to have been touched. A large fireplace with a smoldering fire occupied one wall. Above the mantel was an ancient portrait of a medieval knight seated on a rearing white horse and brandishing a long sword.

Himmler saw me staring at the painting and said, "The Saxon king, Heinrich the First. They called him 'the Fowler', presumably because of his penchant for hawking. I have reason to believe I was named for him." Through the lenses of his thick glasses, his eyes fixed me with a stare that raised Goosebumps on my arms. "Tell me," he said. "Do you believe in reincarnation?"

Unsure of his desired response, I hedged by saying, "I have heard that it is possible."

He brought the palms of his hands together with a slap that caused me to jump. "I knew it," he almost shouted. "You see I would not be surprised if I were not the reincarnation of King Heinrich. At the least, I'm certain I bear his blood in my veins."

"I can well believe it, Reichsführer," Hermann agreed. To me he said, "It was King Heinrich who was responsible for uniting the Germanic duchies. And it was his brilliant defeat of the Magyars that saved the nation, just as our Reichsführer Heinrich is saving the nation today. Did you know that the Reichsführer has founded a Heinrich Memorial Institution dedicated to reviving the spirit and deeds of the King?" Hermann turned to Himmler with a broad smile. "In truth, Reichsführer, I believe it would be appropriate if historians designated you King Heinrich."

I stared at Hermann in no little awe. Not only because he had become an abject sycophant, but because I had no idea that he was the lest bit knowledgeable about ancient history. It seemed that he had made it a point to acquaint himself with Himmler's penchants.

Hermann's obsequiousness was lost upon Himmler who nodded in agreement. "Perhaps someday they shall.

"With your knowledge," Hermann said, "you should write the history of the Third Reich yourself."

"An excellent idea. I believe I shall do so--after my retirement, of course."

"Who better to do so," Hermann said. "Don't you think so, my dear?"

"I would never have thought of it," I murmured. Why had Himmler brought us here? It could not be for a lesson in history. My apprehension was so strong that I felt as though the room was icy cold, and I moved to stand in front of the fire, staring into its smoldering flames so that I would not have to look at either of the men. The black and silver SS uniforms, which every one thought were so splendid, always made me nervous, and now Hermann wore one of them. I was so sick at heart that I could hardly stand and I clutched the fireplace mantel for support.

Neither of the men were aware of my revulsion. I heard Himmler's boots thudding on the carpet as he came toward me and I stiffened. "Countess," he said when he was standing beside me. "I have been most impressed by your psychometric abilities. You could be of great benefit to the Reich, and to me personally, if you would help me with a slight, ah, mystery."

He was staring at me intently and the light of the fire reflecting from the lenses of his glasses made it appear as though his eyes were blazing with some inner fever. "A mystery?" I asked. "What sort of mystery?"

I felt stupid asking the question. He clearly wanted me to help him identify a potential enemy. Why had Hermann allowed this to happen? I had told him that I could never repeat the incident of the dinner party that had caused the death of Ernst Roehm and Lord only knows how many others. He should have made it clear to Himmler.

I looked at Hermann but he was engrossed in examining a book he had taken from a shelf. My fear and anger increased when he turned his back and seated himself comfortably in one of the chairs. I saw that the book was about bird watching, a subject of no earthly interest to him. He had thrown me to the wolf and was turning his back on the slaughter. I could only stare into the fire and hope that my psychic muse was as dead as my heart.

Himmler took a small, flat jewelry case from his inside jacket pocket and opened it. Inside the case, resting on a bed of crushed velvet, was a man's diamond ring. He took the ring out and placed the case on the mantel.

"Here." He extended the ring toward me. "Tell me what you can about the owner of this ring. I am especially interested in his future."

Every fiber of my being screamed at me not to take it. Himmler would not be so anxious to discover the ring's secrets if they were not of great importance. And if I could discern its secrets, would it lead to another death? Did I have a choice?

Actually, I had three choices. I could do exactly as he asked and tell him everything I could learn from the ring and damn the consequences. I could lie. Unless he already knew so much about the ring's owner that a lie would be detected. In which event, the resultant death might be my own.

And the third choice: I could refuse to cooperate. Probably with the same dire results.

Like a coward, I took the ring. It was expensive. Gold, with a large diamond surrounded by smaller stones. Although a man's ring, it had a distinctive feminine look. I held it gingerly in the tips of my fingers. Perhaps if I did not clasp it, perhaps if I did not make it the center of my thoughts, I would receive no images at all and I could safely evade a direct answer.

Himmler saw the way I was holding the ring and the fire in his glasses seemed to leap. "Is there a problem, Countess?"

"No, no," I answered hastily. "I'm, uh, I'm getting nothing. But as I

told you, sometimes--"

Hermann had put down the book when he heard Himmler's rebuke and he quickly crossed to me. "You've not holding it correctly," he growled. He snatched the ring and placed it in my palms, forcing them together where he held them tightly. I could feel the ring burning into my palms like an ember and the image of a young man exploded in my mind. It was him. Himmler himself.

I stifled a gasp, but Himmler heard it and said, "Ahh. You see it."

Images kaleidoscope through my mind, but I could sense no ominous import. There were impressions of a young Himmler, ambitious, unhappy, scheming and ruthless. The images gradually changed into scenes of such horror that if Hermann had not held my hands in a terrible grip I would have flung the ring from me. "Oh, God," I cried. "Don't! Let me go, Hermann. Please!"

But he refused to release his grip. "What is it? What do you see?"

I shook my head, unwilling, actually, unable to speak. The images had changed from masses of dying men, women and children to an image of Hitler's body, burning. And Himmler . . .

"Betrayal," I gasped before I could stop myself. I had seen Himmler betraying the Führer, surrendering to enemy forces. I could not tell him that.

"Betrayal?" Himmler shouted. "Someone betrays me?! Who?! Who do you see?"

"No," I gasped. "There is nothing. Nothing."

"Tell me!" Himmler demanded. "You! Make her tell me."

Hermann increased the pressure and twisted until my wrists felt as though they would break. "Tell him," he gritted. "Damn it! Tell him!"

I shook my head, moaning with pain. "Hermann. Please."

In reply, Hermann let go with one hand and slapped me across the face. The blow was so hard and stunning that it snapped my head back and my temple hit the edge of the mantel. Sparks exploded in my head and a geyser of red blossomed and became an overpowering blackness"

*   *   *   *

Sandi became aware of a sound. A voice. Its words came into focus slowly. Someone was talking to her in a voice that struggled to remain calm but was tinged with worry, "Sandi. Come out of it. It's all right. Come back. Come back. Sandi. Sandi!"

She desperately wanted to open her eyes, but an apprehension about what she might see made her keep them tightly shut. Where was she? Why did her head hurt so much? Oh, God, yes. Hermann had hit her! But the voice. It was not Hermann's. And it called her Sandi!

Her eyes snapped open. She blinked. Focused.

Her eyes fastened on the anxious face of Dan Bradon. He was

bending over her, pressing a damp, cool cloth to her forehead. Bending over her? She should be sitting in a chair!

She lifted her head and found that she was lying on a couch in her hotel suite. It had grown dark outside and the only light came from the desk lamp. "Bradon?"

Her voice was a croaking whisper but Bradon's face lost its taught lines of worry; his lips attempted a smile that she was sure was only for her benefit, like someone trying to reassure a hurt child. "Well," he said. "Glad to see you back."

Sandi put her hand up to touch her temple. She expected to encounter blood but there was none. Still, her temple was sore and, she was sure, bruised. "He hit me," she said. "Hermann hit me."

"Then you remember?"

She tried to push herself into a sitting position and Bradon helped with an arm around her shoulders. His hand felt warm on her bare skin and her eyes swiveled to find out why. Her blouse! It was open to her waist and pulled away from her shoulders. Her breasts were half out of her bra, almost totally exposed. Her anxiety was swept aside by a surge of anger. "What the hell is this?" she cried, wrenching away from him. "What were you doing?"

Bradon yanked his arm away from her shoulders as though he had been caught in an illicit act. "You were unconscious, hardly breathing. I started to give you CPR."

Sandi pulled her blouse together and, with trembling fingers, began refastening the pearl buttons. "You don't have to take off somebody's clothes for CPR."

"You do if you think their heart has stopped. I was ready to start heart stimulation."

Some of the suspicion had gone out of her voice when she said, "It was a hypnotic trance. You knew that. Or is this all part of your routine?"

Bradon jerked to his feet. "My God, Sandi! I thought you were dead. What the hell happened?"

Sandi stared up at him, suddenly feeling weak and vulnerable. His anguish could not have been faked unless he was the greatest actor in the world. She wanted to close her eyes but was afraid to, afraid that if she did she might slip back into that awful nether world. She licked her lips, discovering that they were dry and rough. Her throat, too, felt dry as though she had been breathing through her mouth. Had Bradon begun mouth to mouth resuscitation? Had his lips been on hers? Were they warm and tender? Or had he been rough? Savage? Forcing her mouth open mercilessly, perhaps even putting his tongue--

She surged to her feet. "Water," she said. "I've got to have a drink of water."

She swayed and Bradon quickly slipped a steadying arm around her waist. "Sit down," he said. "I'll get it."

As he eased her to a sitting position on the couch, Sandi was surprised at his strength. When they had danced in the club, his muscles had felt hard, powerful. But she had no idea of his real strength until now. She wondered if he worked out at one of those body-building gyms.

After he headed for the suite's bathroom, Sandi put both hands on her cheeks. Her palms were sweaty and while her cheeks were equally hot, they were dry as though all moisture had been burned away. It wasn't like her to be so upset. It had to be the after-effect of the regression.

But that was over. Never again would she allow herself to be so open, so vulnerable. If they could not find Helga, if they could not find the source of her voices with purely scientific evidence, then they would never be found. She would continue to live with them just as she always had, whatever the cost to her sanity.

Bradon returned with a glass of water. While she drained the glass, he studied her, his face impassive. Then he took the empty glass and sat holding it as though it provided a personal contact with her. "Feel up to telling me about it?"

She wanted to scream 'no!' She never wanted to talk about the horrible experience. She wanted to lock the entire situation in a far corner of her mind where it could never bother her again. The awful images, however, once so sharp and terrifying, were already beginning to fade, diminishing their power of fear. Perhaps, it was best to tell Bradon what had happened before she forgot many of the details.

He listened to her explanation quietly, only interrupting to ask pertinent questions. When she finished, he got up and paced the floor. "It would seem," he said, "that the Count and Countess were not the happily married couple we had assumed."

"I think they were," Sandi corrected. "In that age and, especially, here in Germany, the husband was expected to be dominant."

"I guess you're right. The Count might have been a son-of-a-bitch, using his wife to further his career, but he was no different than a lot of others. Men and women."

"It seems to be a unique characteristic of the human species, riding on the coattails of others."

Bradon stopped in his tracks and turned to face her. His face wore a peculiar expression as though she had detected some shameful secret. But the expression vanished so quickly she was not sure it had ever existed.

"You weren't able to find out anything that would give us a clue about their identity?"

"No. Nothing new."

"Hmmm. What was it that Helga got from that ring that made her refuse to tell? Can you remember?"

"Some of it. The ring was Himmler's, of course. She got the impression of thousands of people dying by his hand."

"I can understand that. It was Himmler and his SS Schutzstaffel who rounded up the Jews and Gypsies and ran the death camps. Their blood had to be on his hands."

"There was more. Betrayal. He was a traitor."

Bradon stopped pacing. He tilted his head to gaze at the ceiling in concentration. "Let me see. I think it was Himmler, right at the end of the war, who offered to surrender Germany to the Allies. Except for Russia. He was scared to death of the Russians."

"I know. When Hitler found out about it, he was furious."

"But it never happened. Himmler was too late. A few days later Hitler killed himself in that bunker. Not far from here, by the way."

"Himmler committed suicide. I got that from the ring too."

"No wonder you couldn't say anything. He wouldn't have believed you."

"If he had, he would have been forced to kill both Hermann and me. I mean, Helga."

"I wonder if he did--have them both killed."

Sandi slowly shook her head. "I don't think so. I didn't have any sense of that."

"Well, I guess--" Bradon stopped talking so abruptly that Sandi looked up in surprise. He was standing in the middle of the room staring at her. "I thought that psychometrics could only see the past, things that had already happened."

"Oh, no. They sometimes see the future. Remember when Helga told Hitler about,"--she had trouble saying it--"about those people he had killed. Ernst Roehm and the others."

"Yes. But that was all past history to you, to Sandi Boeckel."

"To me, yes. But not to Helga. She had to be seeing the future."

"Well, maybe. But I don't see how that's going to help us." Bradon sank into a chair. "Too bad you didn't ever try to work with an object that belonged to Hermann."

Bradon had made the remark with bitter casualness, but the impact of the words brought Sandi's head around and she looked at him with wide eyes. "Of course," she whispered. "Psychics can never get a reading about themselves. But Hermann . . . . If Helga wanted to, she might be able to see his future."

Bradon looked up with sudden hope. "That chalice. With the wine. Hermann used it. If it exists . . ." Then he made a gesture of despair. "I don't think it would work. What you've seen has always been a reenactment of history, of something that actually happened. Helga never tried to get a reading from the chalice. You couldn't make her do something that never happened. Could you?"

Sandi got up and went to the window. The room had become small, airless. The walls seemed to be closing in on her. She pulled the heavy drapes aside and stared out at the traffic moving along the darkened street. Out there was reality, people going about their daily lives, far removed from the horrors of the past. Why couldn't she be like them? Why did she have to be cursed with the awful voices? Her life would be so sweet, so uncomplicated if she were only--the word that leaped to her mind was 'normal.'

But she wasn't normal, and the only way she ever would be was to track down this whispering ghost and destroy it. Then maybe--just maybe--she would be like everyone else.

Sandi put her hands to her throbbing temples. "I don't know. It seems that I'm like a--a channel to the past. I don't think I could change it."

Bradon's voice was heavy with concern when he said, "It doesn't matter. You can't go through that again."

Sandi took a deep breath of relief. Thank goodness Bradon agreed with her decision. "I don't think I could."

Bradon rubbed at his chin. "Maybe there's another way. That place where you were. It was some kind of a castle. Right?"

"Yes. They were going through initiation rites."

"For the Schutzstaffel." The excitement in his voice made Sandi turn to look at him. Exhilaration had driven him from the chair and he was standing behind her, his eyes glowing. "I'll bet they've got records there."

Sandi felt her tension fade. Maybe she would not have to endure the pain of another regression. "Yes. I'm sure they have." Then her relief was shaken by a sudden doubt. "If the castle still exists. It might have been destroyed in the war."

"We'll have to find out. Where was it? Those books about the Nazis and the occult. They mentioned such a castle. God, where was it? It was a strange name. Started with a W."

"Westphalia?"

"No. But it was in Westphalia." Bradon's voice had climbed with anticipation and he began moving around the room in agitated pacing. "Anyway, it doesn't matter. I've got it in my notes. In Westphalia. Somewhere near Paterborn. I've never been there, but I know where it is. West of here. Close to Hanover. Too close to fly. We can go by train." He glanced at his watch. "We can start first thing in the morning. Get to bed. Get some sleep. We'll get an early start."

He was rushing toward the door when Sandi said, "Before I go to bed I usually like to have dinner."

"Dinner?"

He turned to face her with a smile. "Sorry. Forgot all about it. Okay. Let's slow down a little. First, a good dinner. Then we can make plans." He looked at her for a moment and his voice deepened as he added, "You're a wonder; you know that?" Then the excitement took over again and he said, "See you in fifteen minutes."

"Fifteen minutes? You call that slowing down?"

"Okay. Twenty. I'll look up the name of the castle." He crossed to her, and before she could move, he grasped her shoulders and quickly kissed her. "We're going to find it," he chortled. He rushed out, leaving the door open behind him.

Sandi slowly crossed the room and shut the door. The kiss had lasted less than a second but it had jolted her like an electric shock. Her lips still burned from the heat of his lips; her shoulders still tingled from his touch.

She shook off the euphoria. The kiss was nothing more than a sudden burst of joy. Nothing more.

Her thoughts turned to where they would be going tomorrow, and the warmth of pleasure turned to the chill of dread. That horrible castle. Suppose they did find it and there were no records? What then? Would she have to regress once more? And if she refused, would the voices grow more demanding, driving her into submission? Also, if she refused, would Bradon abandon the quest? And if she did try to regress once more and failed, what then? She drew a shuddering sigh. Each alternative led to disaster.

As she began unbuttoning her blouse to change for dinner, she was reminded of when she had opened her eyes after the regression and found Bradon's face so close to her own. He'd said he was preparing to give her CPR. Had he already begun? Suppose she had awakened when his lips had been on hers? Would she have stopped him? Or would she have twined her fingers into his hair to hold him captive while her tongue explored his mouth? Would she have . . .

Her suddenly clumsy fingers tore the last button free and the ripping sound snapped her back to reality. She stared at herself in the mirror, her gaze centered on her lips. Had Bradon kissed her? Really kissed her? Her lips seemed to be fuller than usual. Had they been bruised into sensual sensitivity?

She shook off the thought. She had enough battles to fight. She didn't want to add one more.

Later that night as she drifted into sleep, the images that flooded her mind were not of the Countess Helga von Waltz. They were visions of strong arms around her and warm lips on hers.

CHAPTER 14

When she saw Wewelsburg Castle, Sandi had a horrible sinking feeling in the pit of her stomach. For a moment the sunshine of the beautiful fall day changed to a heavy, dark overcast. The castle seemed to be waiting, like a crouching beast, waiting to devour her.

Bradon put a hand on her shoulder. "Are you all right?"

With an effort, Sandi blinked away the image. She was standing with Bradon beside their rented car, staring at the castle on the distant ridge. "I'm fine," she lied.

Bradon studied her face and the pallor of her cheeks. "What is it? You saw something."

She shook her head. "Not really. It was kind of deja vu."

Bradon's concern could not overcome his elation. "Good. That has to mean that Helga really was here."

He held the car door for her and she climbed back into the passenger's seat with all the enthusiasm of a Marie Antoinette being led to the guillotine. They followed the paved road across a wide meadow, giving her time to study the castle.

As they approached the castle, it began to lose some of its foreboding. Up close it looked more like a government office building than a castle. It was a huge, sand-colored box sitting on the crest of a low ridge. Most of the surrounding trees had lost their leaves, giving the castle a drab, wintery look. The main structure, four stories high, was covered by a dark, peaked roof pierced with dormers. The north end of the building was rounded like a large castle donjon. Looking as though they had been stuck on as an afterthought, two huge towers at the corners of the other end of the building were topped by dark, strangely pointed, Welsh domes. Several colorful pennants and flags, fluttering gaily from atop the roof and turrets, could not ameliorate the ungainly ugliness of the structure.

The road curved down into a shallow canyon where they passed over a stone bridge that spanned the Alme River. Winding up the far side, the road ended in a parking area near a guardhouse. This was the off season for tourists and there were no other cars in the spacious lot.

When they left the car, Sandi considered taking her jacket, but the day was warm and the sky clear. She wore jeans and a long-sleeved cotton shirt and even though fall weather could change quickly, she should be warm enough.

Inside the guardhouse they were greeted by a pretty girl wearing the Paterborn area's native garb of a dark skirt and a snowy white, long sleeved blouse. A long, white scarf encompassed her neck. One end of the scarf was looped over her head and fastened with an ornamental pin near her right cheek. Her hair, her eyebrows and lashes were dark and her eyes a rich brown. She reminded Sandi of a Gypsy girl, a comparison she was sure the girl would not appreciate.

"Hello," the girl greeted in English. "Welcome to Wewelsburg Castle."

How had she known they were not German? Sandi was beginning to feel as though she was wearing a sign that said: Ugly American.

"Good afternoon, Fräulein," Bradon said. "I understand the castle is open for visitors."

"Yes. I will be your guide."

Bradon paid the visitor's fee and the guide began her presentation by pointing to an artist's drawing of the castle. "The castle was first constructed in 1603 by Dietrich von--"

Bradon held up a hand to stop her. "That's very informative. I hope you're not offended but we're only interested in the World War Two period."

The guide's plump face crinkled into a smile as though nothing any visitor could say would offend her. "Of course," she said without a trace of irritation. "This way, please."

She moved to an adjoining room where the walls bore several photographs and a flow chart of work that had been done on the castle. "Here we have an exhibit of the period from 1933 to 1936. It was during this period that the castle was leased from the village for one Mark a year by the Schutzstaffel. Renovation was begun to turn the castle into a Reich school for SS leaders. Labor was--"

Again Bradon interrupted, "Please excuse me, Fräulein, but do you have records of the SS officers who went through the initiation ceremony here?"

She shook her head sadly. "No. They do not exist."

Bradon looked at Sandi and gritted his teeth. "I might have known."

The guide shot him a puzzled look. "I said something incorrectly?"

"No, no," Bradon said hastily. "May we go inside the castle?"

"Of course, but we should first review the other periods. The exhibits go right through 1945."

"Thank you. We've read about the castle. We would just like to see it."

The guide's face brightened. "Oh, gut. Then we can go right in."

They followed her out of the guardhouse and across a small flagstone-paved court, heading toward a short ramp that led into the main hall of the castle. As they approached the forbidding structure, Sandi fought a desire to turn and flee. "Do we have to go in?" she whispered to Bradon.

"As long as we're here," he whispered back. "We might find something."

They continued to follow the guide who strode ahead with her arms swinging. Sandi wished she had such carefree energy. Her feet were leaden with dread, her body cold. What would she encounter inside the castle? She was only sure of one thing: it would not be pleasant.

The guide looked back over her shoulder. "We are lucky the walls were not destroyed by the demolition. The interior has all been restored since 1979. But it is authentic in every detail."

Sandi felt a glimmer of hope. "Demolition?" Maybe there was little remaining of the evil.

The guide glanced at her with a look that asked why Sandi didn't know about the demolition if she had read so much. "The castle, as I'm sure you know, was virtually destroyed by an SS task force just at the end of the war. The restoration took thirty years almost."

Bradon said, "Were all the articles--the furnishings--were they all destroyed?"

"Unfortunately, yes. The destruction was very complete. Except for the crypt in the north tower and the Hall of the Supreme Leaders."

Bradon quickly said, "Could we see those?"

"Of course." Then she added reprovingly, "Information about them was in area three of the guard house museum."

The guide led the way through an inner courtyard to a door in the large north tower. Above the door was an ancient inscription in German that read: "My House Shall Be Called A House Of Prayer". It had to have been part of the original castle. Sandi wondered why Himmler had allowed the contradictory statement to remain. Perhaps he thought, as did so many Generals, that God was really on the side with the most firepower and that the inscription was a monstrous joke.

Inside, it was evident that the huge room had once been a chapel. The ceiling was high, supported by marble-faced columns. The marble floor was inlaid with a large sun wheel, a swastika and a stylized SS victory rune. In a number of places the numbers 3 and 12 were also inlaid in the marble.

In the center of the room was a large round table. Facing the table were thirteen throne-like seats.

"Thirteen," Bradon said. "I suppose that's significant."

"Yes," the guide said. "For Reichsführer Himmler and his twelve apostles."

"I wonder why the SS demolition team didn't destroy this?" Sandi mused.

"Superstition, I'll bet," Bradon said. "Isn't the 'Hall of the Dead' just below?"

The guide's brown eyes were unusually round as she said in German, "Superstition. I never thought of that."

Bradon turned to Sandi. "Do you remember any of this?"

"No." She turned to the guide. "Do you know when this part of the work was completed?"

"In 1943, I believe."

She said to Bradon, "1943. Helga was here before that. She couldn't have seen this room."

"I was afraid of that." Bradon said to the guide who was staring at them, trying to make sense of their conversation. "Can we go down to the crypt?"

She nodded quickly. "Oh, yes."

She led them back through the courtyard and outside the walls of the main building. Crossing a causeway over a gully that might have been an ancient moat, they entered another door in the tower. Electric lighting revealed a narrow flight of concrete stairs.

Cautiously following their guide down the stairs, Sandi experienced a growing uneasiness. The farther they descended, the greater was her sense of familiarity--and fear.

They exited the stairs into a circular room and Sandi gasped. She clung to the balustrade as her knees threatened to buckle. It was all there: the pit in the center, the walls decorated with heraldic shields and standards, the circling plinths with their horrible urns.

Bradon put his arm around her waist, but she scarcely noticed it. Her brain was churning with horror and the sound of imprisoned voices. She put her hands over her ears in an attempt to shut out their cries.

The guide was staring at Sandi as though looking at a ghost and Bradon grasped the young woman's arm. "The chalice? Where is the silver chalice?"

"Chalice?"

"The one used in the SS initiation ceremony. Where is it?"

"Oh." Her eyes swiveled to look at him. "It was never found."

With an effort Sandi said, "Bradon." He turned to her and she formed the words. "There's nothing here. Let's go."

Her face was drained of color, her hands clinched on the stair railing. Her body felt so heavy that she was afraid her legs could not support it. At the same time her head wanted to float away, her mind spinning.

Bradon took hold of her arm, "Sandi?" He said to the guide, "We'd better leave."

The guide rushed ahead of them as Bradon gently turned Sandi and led her unresisting form up the stairs.

Only when they were outside in the waning sunlight was Sandi able to shake off an awful claustrophobic fear. With the setting sun, a chill breeze had begun to stir and she felt cold and hot simultaneously.

The guide looked at her white face and trembling hands and ran to fetch a glass of water while Bradon led Sandi to a stone bench. Her pain-filled eyes and rapid breathing gave him a pang of guilt. He had brought her to this. If he hadn't pressed the issue, she would be home now with her family enjoying the California sun.

Dropping to one knee in front of her, he took her by the shoulders and using the same urgent tone he had used during her hypnotic trance, he commanded, "Sandi. Come out of it. Come back. Sandi! Sandi!"

He tightened his grip on her shoulders, aware that he was hurting her, and shook her gently. "Sandi. It's me: Bradon! Sandi! I'm here. I'm here."

To his relief she sighed and blinked before she said, "You're hurting me."

"I know. I'm sorry." He relaxed his grip on her shoulders, but did not let go. He wanted to sooth her with soft words. He wanted to take her in his arms and hold her, to quiet her fears with his strength and his concern.

Instead, as though commanded by some perverse entity, he said, "What did you see there? What did you see?"

She looked toward the setting sun as though to reassure herself that she was alive and in this time and place. She brushed back her hair in a familiar gesture that brought Bradon a sense of relief. She was going to be fine. But he had to know what she had seen before the scene faded from her memory.

"You're all right now. I'm here with you. You can tell me what you saw."

"I saw . . ." Her voice was a harsh whisper. "I saw death. So much death. It surrounded me. I thought it was going to pull me down into that--that awful place."

Bradon rose from his knees and sat beside her, pulling her close against his chest. "Is that all? You didn't see any articles, any objects that might have been used by Hermann?"

"No. Nothing. Nothing but death."

The guide hurried up with a glass half-filled with water and Bradon took it from her with a quick, "Danke." He pressed the glass into Sandi's hands. "Here. Drink some of this."

She raised the glass to her pale lips and sipped. As the cold liquid soothed her throat, color returned to her cheeks and she attempted a smile. "I'm sorry. Did I ruin it?"

"No, no," he said hastily. "There was nothing to ruin."

The guide's voice was pinched.. "Are you all right, Miss? We have a doctor in the village."

"I'm fine," Sandi said. "It was just a touch of claustrophobia."

For a moment the girl's face was blank, then she smiled. "Oh, yes. Phobia about closed-in places. Many people have that feeling in the crypt."

Mention of the dungeon-like room caused Sandi to shiver and Bradon said, "It's getting chilly." He turned to the guide. "Is there somewhere we can go where it's warm?"

"The gatehouse," the guide said. "The castle is always cold."

Bradon helped Sandi to her feet. She turned a little and one of his forearms rested against the softness of her breast. She was unconscious of the touch, but Bradon felt as though his arm was on fire.

He released her so abruptly that she stumbled. He reached to catch her but she straightened. "Sorry," she said. "I guess I'm still a little unsteady."

Bradon put his arm around her waist. "Here," he said. "Lean on me."

As they moved toward the gatehouse, he asked the guide, "Is there a hotel in the village?"

"Oh, yes," she said, "There are several. You will enjoy."

"Thanks. Danke."

Walking with his arm around Sandi's waist, Bradon could feel the movement of her muscles and her shirt sliding across her silky skin. She smelled faintly of perfume and sunshine. Her hair, brushing his cheek, made him want to turn his head and bury his face in its softness. The temptation was so strong he was almost glad when they arrived at the gatehouse and they had to separate to enter through the narrow door.

"Here it is warm," the guide said. "But there is no place for the sitting."

In the warmth Sandi immediately felt her strength returning. "It's all right," she said. "I'm feeling much better."

"Are you sure? Maybe we'd better check with a doctor."

"No, no." Away from the castle and its compelling terror, she was able to regain her equilibrium. "I just had to get away from that room."

A group of tourists entered and their chattering voices resounded through the small room.

The guide said, "Excuse me, please. If you are now well, I must go."

Sandi formed a reassuring smile. "I'm fine. And thank you very much."

Bradon said, "Oh, one moment, Fräulein."

He handed her five Euros as a tip but she waved it aside with a "No, no. Thank you."

Bradon said, "Well, thank you. Thank you very much."

She said, "It is my pleasure."

The voices of the visitors grew louder as they began discovering exhibits on the museum's walls, and Bradon said, "Let's see if there's some place quieter."

Sandi did not mind the noise. The sound of happy voices helped drive away memories of the dark crypt. But she allowed Bradon to lead her around a partition into a quieter area.

Exhibited on the walls of the small room were diagrams of the castle as well as pamphlets and official papers. Books were displayed in cases with glass-windowed doors. In the center of the room glass-topped cases held various utensils and other memorabilia from the castle.

"Look," Bradon said, "if you don't want to talk about it, I understand. But . . . I think you saw something in there."

Sandi closed her eyes. She wanted to tell Bradon what she had experienced. At the same time, she wanted to wipe the images from her memory. Perhaps telling him would help. "I'm not really clear about it myself.

They were not images exactly. They looked like men in black SS uniforms with terrible faces. Skeletons. There was a--a feeling--of death."

She was trembling and Bradon put his arms around her and pulled her close. "Okay," he said. Then he surprised himself by saying, "It's over. If you'd like to, we can call this whole thing off."

He held his breath waiting for her answer. If she decided to back out now, he would be left with nothing to write about, nothing but vague suspicions. No publisher would buy a book based upon suspicions unsupported by facts.

"I don't know," Sandi murmured. "I thought we were getting--" Her voice broke off with a sharp intake of breath and Bradon felt her stiffen with shock.

"What is it? What's the matter?"

She did not answer. Her breathing was short, gasping. Her gaze was locked on the display case, her eyes wide, her body rigid. He turned his head to see what had caused so much terror. Inside the case were several rings, each bearing the SS death's head.

Before he could catch her, Sandi pushed away from him, backing away from the display case, her mouth making faint sounds of anguish. She was brought to a halt by bumping into a bookcase.

Bradon quickly went to her and put his arm across her shoulders. "It's okay," he said. "Its only an exhibit. Let's get out of here."

"No."

Her voice was so faint that he could scarcely hear the word. He couldn't stand the pain in her eyes. "I think we should. Put this whole damned place behind us."

He started to turn her toward the door, but she resisted. She was staring at one of the bookcases. Behind its glass doors were several old books that looked as though they had been rescued from a fire. A sign over the case was in German and English, reading: "Mementos From The Suite Of Heinrich Himmler".

"Look." Sandi pointed to one of the books. The book was badly battered, its title virtually obliterated.

"A book? What about it?"

"I saw him reading it."

"Who? Himmler? When?"

"No, no. Hermann. When we were in his suite. Hermann was reading that book. I saw him."

Bradon peered more closely at the book. He could just make out part of its German title. "Bird watching? He was reading a book on bird watching?"

"He didn't care what it was. He wanted to withdraw while Helga was reading for Himmler. The book was his way of doing it."

Bradon stared at the book as excitement built. Hermann hadn't owned the book. But he had used it. It still might carry his imprint. If it did

. . . if he could talk Sandi into another regression while holding the book, as Helga she might be able to generate some real insight into Hermann von Waltz. He had to get that book.

Bradon rubbed his hand across his face, thinking. Would the museum sell the book? Unlikely. Museums didn't sell things. Could he borrow it? Again, unlikely. They would want to know why he wanted it. And he did want it. There was only one way.

He would have to work fast. The new visitors were still in the entrance room. He could hear the guide telling them about the various display areas, which meant that they might be coming this way at any second.

He quickly took a key ring from his pocket. On the ring was a small penknife and one of its blades was a screwdriver. Prying open the blade he slipped it into the crack next to the door's lock and pried.

Sandi's eyes widened. "What are you doing?"

"Borrowing a book," he said. "I forgot my library card."

There was a sharp snapping sound and for a moment Bradon was afraid he had broken the glass. Then the door swung open. Bradon reached in and pulled out the book. He thrust it under his arm while he attempted to wedge the door shut. But the damaged lock would not retract. He handed the book to Sandi. "Hold it a second."

Her eyes were wide, staring at the book as he thrust it into her hands. Using his knife blade, he was able to press the tongue of the broken latch back far enough to secure the door. Only a close inspection would show that it had been jimmied open. If things went well he could replace the book tomorrow before anyone noticed it was gone.

He turned back to Sandi, saying, "Maybe we can--" He stopped. She was clutching the book in both hands, her grip so tight that her knuckles were white. Her eyes were shut, her face frozen in a look of intense concentration. Her mouth moved as though she was attempting to speak but could not force out the words.

Bradon stared at her, mesmerized. My God. She was into it. And without hypnosis. But they only had seconds. That crowd would come pouring through the doorway any second. He put his hands on top of hers, locking them around the book. "Von Waltz, Sandi," he urged, his voice quiet and intense. "Find out about von Waltz."

"Not . . ." Her lips struggled to form the words. "Not . . .his name."

Oh, damn, damn. She must be getting impressions of someone else who had held the book, maybe Himmler himself. It was a hell of a long shot to think she could have zeroed in on von Waltz when he'd only held the book that one time. "What name? Who is it," he said.

"Luckenwalde. Not . . .Waltz. Luckenwalde."

Suddenly her eyes rolled back and her knees sagged. Bradon released her hands and grabbed her around the waist and the book slipped from her hands. Gently he eased her to the floor and checked her pulse.

It was strong and steady. Thank God. It was only a faint.

He could hear the group approaching from the other room and he scooped the book from the floor, wrenched open the bookcase door, and shoved the book back into its place. He had just secured the door and was bending over Sandi's unconscious form when the guide, her voice preceding her, led her group through the doorway. She stopped abruptly when she saw Bradon bending over Sandi.

"Wie das?!"

Bradon lifted Sandi and cradled her in his arms. "It is all right," he said in German. "She is not feeling well. I will take her to the hotel."

Without waiting for a reply he made his way through the silent group of tourists and out the door.

Carrying Sandi to the parking area, he cursed himself for not anticipating her reaction. God. No wonder she had slipped so easily into the regressions. Her psychic abilities had to be incredible. Touching the book must have hit her like a jolt from a stun gun.

He looked at her face so still and white. Her cheek was pressed against his shoulder like the trusting touch of a child, and he hated himself even more. He had no right to force her so close to madness. The chill wind stirred her hair so that it brushed across his face in a tender caress. Her lips were parted, looking incredibly soft and so close he could feel her warm breath. In his arms her body felt strong but incongruously vulnerable. And she was vulnerable. For some reason, she was desperate to find the roots of her obsession. It would be so easy to exploit those vulnerabilities, and not just to write a book. If he worked it right, he could have her in bed before she realized what she was doing.

Oh God. Stop thinking like that. He was already seducing her mind. He had to respect her body.

Just before they reached the car, Sandi stirred and her eyes fluttered. She felt lightheaded and had trouble focusing her thoughts. She became aware that she was being carried by strong arms, her cheek nestled against a muscular shoulder. Bradon. He was carrying her, his strides sure, his even breath brushing her cheek. It felt wonderful. She smiled and gave herself to a feeling of warmth, of security.

She reached up and locked her arms around his neck. She closed her eyes and snuggled against his broad chest, pressing her cheek closer against his shoulder.

Maybe, she thought, he would walk forever and she would never have to let go.

CHAPTER 15

The two-storied von Luckenwalde house was large enough to have been a hotel. The lower floors were fronted with brick. The upper floors were of white plaster interlaced with dark beams. The sharply sloping roof, broken by numerous dormer windows, was covered with gray tiles of slate.

The surrounding grounds were park-like, clean and precisely groomed. Manicured lawns and flowerbeds were shaded by strategically placed copses of trees. A long macadam drive wound from an ornamental iron gate in a surrounding wall to a flagstone-paved circle in front of the house. The effect was one of programmed solitude, as though serenity was the objective of wealth.

The woman who opened the door for Sandi and Bradon looked as though she belonged in this house. She appeared to be in her seventies, heavy with excess weight, but she moved with studied dignity. Her light brown hair, streaked with gray, was pulled back and tied in a bun. Wide hips supported a heavy, wool skirt. The skirt, her shoes and her loose fitting sweater looked as though they had been selected with care from shops catering to the haut monde. Around her ample neck she wore a gold chain that supported a heavy pendant shaped like a lion with diamond eyes. Her fingers glittered with rings. Sandi was certain that the rubies, tourmaline and emeralds were authentic.

Bradon smiled. "Frau Hofstaetter?"

Her broad smile flashed glimpses of gold. "Ah, Fräulein Boeckel, Herr Bradon. You made good time."

They had called from Berlin before making the fifty-kilometer drive south to the village called Lucke-walde. The village name was eponymous, having been taken from the von Luckenwalde family somewhere around 1427. The family estate on the outskirts of the city was still known as the Luckenwaldebesitz.

"The drive," Bradon said, "was beautiful. German autobahns are the best in the world."

"True, true. We still have good roads. The rest of the country may be falling apart, but we do keep up our roads. Come in, come in."

The interior of the house was as meticulously organized as the exterior. The hardwood floors of the foyer and the oaken balustrade of a curving stairway shone as though untouched by shoes or hands. The white plaster walls gleamed brightly, their smooth expanses broken by oils of landscapes and dark, brooding portraits. Crystal chandeliers, dangling on long chains from the vaulted ceiling, gleamed as though newly minted. It was difficult for Sandi to believe that someone actually lived in the house. It had to take an army of service people to maintain such sterility.

Frau Hofstaetter escorted them through double doors to a large room furnished in French Baroque. Between beautifully inlaid sideboards was a massive fireplace with an intricately carved limestone mantel. The floor, gleaming with wax, was parqueted with blonde spruce and dark oak. A huge oriental rug in subdued russets and tans covered the center of the floor, which seemed a shame to Sandi. She would have displayed the exquisite parquet in its full glory.

When they were seated Frau Hofstaetter tinkled a small bell and an elderly manservant entered wheeling a teacart. He wore a dark, vested suit with a white shirt and a black bow tie. The shirt's collar had been starched to a stiffness that made it cut into his neck but he did not seem to mind.

Without a word he began pouring three cups of tea from a silver service, adding a generous dollop of milk to each before handing a cup to each person. He picked up sugar tongs and a silver cup filled with miniature lumps of sugar. He paused in front of Sandi expectantly. She did not want sugar but felt that he should be rewarded for his attention so she lifted an eyebrow, realizing that it would be gauche to actually ask. Reading her gesture perfectly he placed one lump into her cup. Advancing upon Frau Hofstaetter he dropped two lumps in her cup automatically. He turned to Bradon without going toward him and Bradon responded correctly with an infinitesimal shake of his head.

The man returned the sugar and tongs to the service and placed three coasters made of thick embroidery on the coffee table. That done, he turned to Frau Hofstaetter. Some secret signal passed between then and he made a slight bow. His shoes made tiny squeaking sounds when he crossed the waxed parquet and took up a station beside the door.

Frau Hofstaetter sipped her tea and smiled at Sandi. "You're American, aren't you?"

"Yes," Sandi admitted. She felt as though something more was required and added, "From California."

"I've never been to California. I lived for several years in Chicago. That was when my husband was with the Deutsche Bank." She spoke with only the trace of an accent on her Ws and Vs.

"That explains your excellent English," Bradon said.

"Thank you," she answered with a smile. "I was afraid I'd picked up a Midwest accent."

Bradon carefully put his nearly full teacup on a coaster. "Frau Hofstaetter, I apologize in advance for being so abrupt, but the reason we contacted you is because of this house."

Frau Hofstaetter continued to sip her tea while her eyes watched Bradon with the placid benevolence of someone who had no fear of the past.

"Not the house, actually," Bradon corrected. "The family who lived here."

Her eyes remained calm. "You are referring to Colonel Rostov?"

"Rostov. No. I was referring to Count von Luckenwalde."

Her eyes remained serene but her teacup paused briefly on its way to her lips. "Ah. That was a long time ago."

Sandi had been smothering her impatience, but now it bubbled forth. "Did you know them: the von Luckenwaldes?"

Frau Hofstaetter lifted one precisely arched eyebrow. "You mean the Count. He was never married."

Sandi's hand holding her teacup jerked as though she had been struck. She stared at the woman. "But he was. To Helga. Helga von Luckenwalde."

Frau Hofstaetter slowly shook her head. "No, my dear. I'm quite sure he never married."

Sandi's throat had closed so tightly she was unable to speak and it was Bradon who said, "How can you be sure? You didn't know them."

"The Count is well remembered in this area. There was even talk of changing the name of the village--to erase the stigma, you understand."

"Stigma?" Sandi's voice was harsh but she could not keep silent.

"Because of how he died."

Sandi felt her mouth go dry. "I don't understand," she said.

Frau Hofstaetter's small eyes moved rapidly from Sandi to Bradon and back. "You don't know?"

Bradon said, "Know what?"

"He was hanged by the Allies. At Nuremberg Prison. In 1946."

A dark mist swirled through Sandi's head, clouding her vision and she swayed in the chair. Bradon was at her side instantly, and he took the teacup from her nerveless fingers.

"Easy," he said.

The butler hurried toward them and Frau Hofstaetter told him in German, "Water. A glass of water."

The man rushed away, and Sandi pushed her hair back from her forehead with both hands. "I'm all right," she said. She was so anxious to hear more about von Luckenwalde that she would have come back from the grave. "Why?" she aaid. "Are you sure?"

"Of course. He was tried as a Nazi war criminal. Very high up in the party. I'm sure it's all in the American records."

"We'll check," Bradon answered.

The butler returned with a glass of water and Sandi drank it greedily. The cold liquid hardly helped her parched throat at all, but it cleared the darkness from her mind.

After the butler took the empty glass and retired to the kitchen, Sandi turned back to Frau Hofstaetter. "Are you certain he wasn't married?"

"Quite. We didn't know him, of course. But in researching the estate we've learned a great deal about him."

"Can you tell us?" Bradon asked.

"As much as I know." As though to prepare for a long story Frau Hofstaetter placed her cup on a coaster and straightened in her chair. "This house has a rather strange history. From what I've been able to gather, it was constructed by Count Hardenberg of Prussia for members of his family in 1815 following the Napoleonic wars. Perhaps he did not actually have the building constructed but, rather, had it restored. You know he was devoted to architectural reconstruction. In any event, at that time it was a huge estate and included the village.

When the Prince died in, I believe 1820, the estate was acquired by Baron Ernst Brunn."

Sandi listened with growing impatience as Frau Hofstaetter recounted the house's heredity. The woman's memory of details was extraordinary. It gradually dawned upon Sandi that the woman was bored sitting home alone day after day and, to relieve her boredom, had made an exhaustive study of the house. They were probably the only people who had ever asked her about the place and she was pouring out her wealth of knowledge with an evangelical zeal. Sandi glanced at Bradon. He had picked up his cup of tea and was sipping it resignedly while he stared at Frau Hofstaetter as though wondering how she could regurgitate such a steady flow of names and dates.

Suddenly Sandi heard the name Count Axel von Luckenwalde and she snapped to attention.

"--acquired the estate in 1906. That was the halcyon Bismarck era just before the first World War. I believe he was some sort of officer in the Prussian army. His son, Count Hermann von Luckenwalde, was born here in 1898. He inherited the estate when his father died in 1933. He resided here until 1945 when he was arrested by the Americans."

"And he never married?" Sandi interrupted. "Don't you find that odd?

"Not really. The war interrupted many lives."

"So there were no children."

"No. I told you he never married."

"Brothers? Sister? Any living relatives?"

"Not that I know of." It was the first time Frau Hofstaetter had to admit a failure of information, and it appeared to unsettle her. Then her eyes sharpened and her voice took on an edge as she said, "There is no problem with title to the estate. The East German Socialist Republic took it over in 1945. When their government collapsed, it was appropriated by the German Republic. We purchased it in an entirely legitimate transaction. The papers are all on file in Berlin."

"Oh, no," Sandi said hastily. "I'm sure it's perfectly legal. We're only interested in the von Luckenwaldes for a--a book we're writing. About famous German homes."

Warmth returned to Frau Hofstaetter's voice. "How very interesting."

"We were wondering," Bradon said, "if there are any articles or mementos left in the house by the Count."

"Oh, I don't think so." Frau Hofstaetter's smooth forehead wrinkled in thought. "The house was occupied by Russian army officers for more than forty years. It was in terrible shape when we acquired it. Everything required restoration."

"You did a fantastic job," Bradon told her. "It's beautiful. But do you suppose the Russians brought in their own furnishings? Or did they keep those that were here after the war?"

"I suppose they kept those that were here. They certainly looked finer than anything I ever saw in Russia, even though they were badly used."

"What did you do with them?" Sandi's voice was faint with anxiety.

Frau Hofstaetter looked at her as though she had asked a very stupid question. "Why we disposed of them, of course. They were hardly fit for use after forty years of occupation."

Tension drained out of Sandi like the last breath of hope to be replaced by a familiar despair. "Everything? Did you dispose of everything?"

"Everything of any consequence. You can see that my furnishings are all new and very exclusive."

"Yes, yes. They're beautiful. But you said 'of any consequences.' Were there things, articles of any kind, that you might have saved?"

"Saved? No. Why on earth would we want to save anything?"

"Oh." Sandi felt so weary she could scarcely hold her teacup. Another dead=end. She had ridden such a roller coaster of hope and despair that now she had no desire to press for more information. Besides, what more could the woman tell them?

She hardly heard Bradon's voice as he said, "I realize you had to redecorate all the rooms, but what about the basement?"

"The basement?" Frau Hofstaetter stared at Bradon without comprehension.

"You didn't redecorate the basement too?"

"Of course not. What would be the point?"

"Did you clean it out?"

"I suppose so. I would never set foot in a basement."

"What about the Russians? Do you think they might have cleaned it out?"

"Not unless there was something to take."

Sandi's hopes were again riding an upward spiral and she stood up, her eyes again bright with interest. "Would it be all right if we looked?"

"Whatever for? There's nothing there except the furnace."

"But would you mind?"

Frau Hofstaetter studied Sandi, her eyes speculative as though wondering if these people were entirely honest. Her curiosity overcame her suspicions and she said, "Very well. But nothing is to be removed."

Sandi did not blame the woman for being cautious. She probably thought they were spies searching for something sinister. Or thieves after anything of value. "Naturally," she said. "You can come with us if you'd like."

Frau Hofstaetter gasped, as though Sandi had asked her to accompany them into hell. "I? Certainly not!" She picked up the small silver bell and shook it daintily. Its tiny tinkle was still sounding when the doors opened and the butler entered. He stopped in front of Frau Hofstaetter expectantly and she nodded toward Sandi and Bradon. "Would you please take the lady and the gentleman to the basement."

If the request seemed bizarre, the butler gave no indication. His face retained its marble-like cast and he said, "As you wish, Madam."

Again there was an invisible communication between the two before he backed two steps and turned with the precision of military training. He walked to the doors where he waited for Bradon and Sandi without so much as glancing in their direction.

Sandi led the way toward the door. Passing Frau Hofstaetter she said, "We should only be a few minutes."

"Oh, take your time. Have Wolfgang bring you back here when you're finished."

Wolfgang? The name had a forbidding ring, and Sandi lost a little of her enthusiasm as she and Bradon walked into the hall. They waited while Wolfgang closed the doors before he led the way toward the rear of the house with strides as purposeful as a Prussian soldier on parade.

"Do you think it's true?" Sandi said to Bradon. "About the Count not being married?

"If it is, maybe we've got the wrong man."

Sandi's fists clinched as tension shot through her. If von Luckenwalde was the wrong man, if this was the wrong house, their search had once again come to a dead end.

They entered a kitchen that was large enough to cook for an army. Although the floor was paved with white brick and the appliances were all modern, the room felt as though it belonged in the days of curling linoleum, coal stoves and ice boxes. Wolfgang clicked a light switch beside a newly painted door. He opened the door and led them down a flight of wooden steps that had the solid feel of being constructed to last several hundred years.

The basement consisted of a single large room with floor and walls of concrete. Light came from bare overhead bulbs in porcelain reflectors and from a series of narrow windows set high in the walls. A number of substantial pillars supported the floor beams of the house. A huge oil furnace occupied the center of the room like a giant octopus, its tentacles of ducting snaking off in all directions. A large workbench was set against one wall. Tools were hung on a pegboard above the bench with the care and precision of artwork.

The room was as immaculate as the rest of the house. There was not a speck of dust on the floor or the workbench. The windows were spotless, even though mud had to splash on them with every rain. Sandi was sure that if she ran her fingers along the top of the heating ducts, they would come away clean. If there had ever been any articles left over from the von Luckenwalde estate they had been removed with the dust.

Bradon surveyed the room with a grimace. "Talk about German efficiency. I wish they had a little Yankee slovenliness."

Sandi shivered. She crossed her arms and hugged her shoulders. "I don't like this house," she said. "It's more like a museum than a home."

"I know. If there was ever anything here, it's gone now."

They climbed the stairs with Wolfgang following. Sandi felt a sense of relief when they stepped into the kitchen. "What on earth do these people do with old things?" she said as much to herself as to Bradon. "They can't throw everything away."

"Yeah. It isn't natural. You should see my place. Half the time I think I'm living in somebody's attic."

Sandi jerked her head around to stare at him and, at the same time, his eyebrows rose. "The attic," they said together.

Bradon turned to Wolfgang who had just turned off the basement lights. "The attic," he said in German. "We would like to see the attic."

He was rewarded by Wolfgang's chiseled features sagging in surprise. "The attic? It is not presentable. No one goes to the attic."

"Good," Sandi said. "Take us there."

Wolfgang was frozen like a soldier who had just been ordered to his death. The thought that stabbed through Sandi's mind and raised a banner of hope was that he was hiding something. If it was something he did not want them to know, it had to be about von Luckenwalde. That was assuming he understood English and had overheard their discussion with Frau Hofstaetter.

Wolfgang led them to stairs at the rear of the kitchen. On the second floor he unlocked a door near the end of a carpeted corridor and pulled it open with some difficulty. He carefully reached inside and clicked on an overhead light. A narrow flight of stairs led to a closed door at the top. When Bradon and Sandi climbed the stairs, Wolfgang followed with all the enthusiasm of a condemned man climbing the gallows steps.

Bradon had to put his shoulder against the upper door to force it open, releasing the odor of dead air laden with dust. The instant that Sandi peered into the attic, she knew what Wolfgang was hiding: shame. The attic was the antithesis of the basement. The light was dim, filtered through layers of dust on dormer windows and on bare light bulbs, those that worked at all. The wood floor showed their footprints when they moved to the center of the low ceilinged room, sending dust motes swirling. Sandi breathed in shallow gasps to filter as much of the dust as possible.

But when her eyes adjusted to the light, she involuntarily sucked in her breath. The room was a treasure trove of old pieces of furniture, abandoned personal articles, such as broken bicycles, and old clothing. All were covered with layers of dust that must have taken years to accumulate. It was exceedingly unlikely that the Russians or Communists officials who had occupied the house for the past forty years had set foot inside the attic for many years, if at all.

Bradon had the same impression because he said, "This stuff was probably stored up here in 1945 when they cleared the house so the Russians could take over."

"Then it must have belonged to the von Luckenwalde family."

"Let's hope so. Somebody might have lived here between the Luckenwaldes and the Russians."

Sandi gazed at the welter of dust-laden articles. "It's going to take a while to sort this out."

Wolfgang, who had been standing just inside the door, cleared his throat before saying in German. "If you will excuse me, I will so inform Madam."

"Okay," Bradon answered in English. "Tell her we might be an hour or more."

Wolfgang bobbed his head stiffly in acknowledgement and turned to go. He was reaching for the doorknob when Sandi said, "Leave the door open, please."

Wolfgang's step faltered as though he could not stand the though of leaving such a mess open to view, but he left the door open.

"I would hate to be stuck up here," Sandi explained to Bradon.

"I don't trust him either," Bradon said in a low voice. "He looks too much like Bela Lugosi."

Sandi smiled. Wolfgang did look like the actor. But that wasn't why she had wanted the door left open. It was because the musty room gave her the same uneasy feeling she had when visiting a graveyard. She didn't think she could stand it if the door accidentally slammed shut and they couldn't get it open. As Bradon watched with an amused twinkle in his eyes, she carried an old dining chair to the door and braced it so the door could not be blown shut.

"It always slams shut in the movies," she explained.

"That's right. You can learn a lot by watching movies. Like not getting trapped in an attic with a snake or a monster."

"I choose the monster. He could break the door down."

Bradon grinned and turned to survey the attic. He slipped off his jacket and rolled his shirtsleeves up over his forearms. "Just what exactly is it we're looking for?"

"Anything that would give us a lead on what happened to Helga."

"That rules out the furniture and old clothes."

Bradon didn't say it but Sandi had the impression he was going to add, "If there ever was a Helga."

"What I'd really like to find," she said, "is a diary. Or letters."

"Pretty slim odds. Let's see if we can find something they might be stored in."

Moving gingerly to keep from stirring up more of the dust than necessary, they began working their way around the scattered articles. Sandi blinked away dust-induced tears as she searched for a trunk or suitcase or briefcase that might contain papers. The articles in the center of the room were easy to identify. They were mostly broken pieces of furniture. But those in the darker corners of the room had to be inspected closely. This sometimes involved crawling under the low beams of the ceiling.

After almost an hour of searching, Bradon stood in the center of the room and shook his head. "Nothing," he said. "Not a note or scrap. Nothing but junk."

Sandi was desolately exploring the drawers of a dirt-smudged writing desk that had a broken leg and chipped top. She had given up hope of finding anything significant a half hour ago when their initial enthusiastic search had turned up nothing. Since then her optimism had waned farther with every empty drawer and barren cabinet. "I guess you--"

Her voice broke as she peered closer into a small side drawer she had jiggered open.

Bradon was by her side in two quick strides. "What is it?"

"I'm not sure." Her eyes had caught a dull glint from a thin gold chain that was hanging from the back of the drawer. She pulled the drawer all the way out of the desk and turned it around so she could see the opposite end. Against the back of the drawer, suspended by the thin chain, was a round silver locket. The chain had caught in a sliver of wood so that the locket had not fallen from its precarious resting place.

Sandi gently manipulated the chain to free it from the wood. "It looks like the kind that opens," she said. "Maybe it has a picture in it."

"If it has," Bradon growled, "it's probably of the family dog."

Sandi had the locket free and she took it in her hands intending to search for a latch. But the instant her hand closed around the cold metal, she felt a tingle like an electric current and she almost dropped it. Her involuntary "oh" caused Bradon's shoulders to straighten.

"What?" he said. "What is it?"

"It's hers. It belonged to Helga."

Bradon did not question her source of knowledge. "Open it," he said softly. "See what's inside."

Sandi found a tiny latch and depressed it while she used her thumbnail to pry apart the two halves of the locket. Each half contained a faded black-and-white photograph. They looked as though they had been scissored from snapshots.

One was of a young woman with dark hair that was pulled back away from her face and held in place by two silver-edged combs. Her widely spaced eyes under thick, beautifully arched eyebrows, stared gravely at the camera even though her lips were smiling. She was not a beautiful woman. The planes of her face, and her probing eyes, made her appear more handsome than beautiful. But she was striking. No one could ever look into that face and forget it.

"Helga," Sandi said. "It's her."

"He must be the Count."

Bradon was referring to the opposite portrait. It was of a man who appeared to be in his forties. His hair was slicked back close to his head making his features appear sharp and angular. He, too, was staring at the camera but he was not smiling. His eyes were hawkish, menacing. No, Sandi amended her thought. Not menacing. Calculating. And his lips, though finely chiseled, were a little too sensual to have strength. But she knew him. She had seen him in her regressions.

"It's Hermann," she said. "Count von Luckenwalde."

Bradon straightened. "I don't know how much good it will do us. We have no proof that she's Helga. And even if she is, it still doesn't answer the question of what happened to her. It doesn't give us a clue."

"Maybe. But I'd like to keep this."

"Right. But I don't think we'd better tell Frau Hofstaetter."

Sandi disliked the idea of taking the locket without permission. That would be stealing. But suppose Frau Hofstaetter refused to let them have it? Actually, it wouldn't really be stealing. The woman did not know the locket existed. And how could one steal something that did not exist?

She knew she was rationalizing. Stealing was stealing. Except that if Helga did exist, she might be a relative. So the locket was probably more hers than it was Frau Hofstaetter's.

"You're right," she said. "And, besides, it can't be worth much. It isn't old enough or unusual enough to be an antique."

"I'll put it in my pocket," Bradon said holding out his hand.

Reluctantly, Sandi parted with the locket. It was difficult to relinquish the one concrete link to the past that she'd been able to find. All their other evidence had been in the realm of suppositions, implications and simulacrums. The locket at least proved that the woman in her visions had actually lived; assuming that the people in the pictures really were the von Luckenwaldes. Who could they ask? Not Frau Hofstaetter. She wouldn't recognize the von Luckenwaldes if they sat in her living room.

"Don't lose it," she said.

"Don't worry. It'll be safe, unless Wolfgang is a pickpocket."

"Maybe he'll want to search us. We have been here a long time."

Bradon looked from Sandi's grimy face and clothes to his own dusty clothing. "Are you kidding," he laughed. "He wouldn't touch us with a ten foot pole."

The image of Wolfgang's horror brought a burst of laughter to Sandi's lips. It was the first time she had laughed in weeks, and she allowed the laughter to build. She knew she was approaching hysteria and Bradon was watching her with increasing concern, but she couldn't stop herself. The laughter cut through the suffocating worry and apprehension in a flood of joy that felt so wonderful she had no desire to check it.

She didn't know when it happened, but she became aware that Bradon had put his arms around her. He held her against his chest while he whispered, "It's okay. It's okay."

His words sounded odd until she realized that her laughter had turned to tears and she felt a burning humiliation. What must he think of her to lose control that way? She wanted to push away, to show him that she didn't need his support. But something deep inside kept her cheek pressed against his shirt that was damp from her tears. His chest felt strong, reassuring, like the circle of his arms. She could hear his heart beating in a rhythm that seemed faster than it should be. After the hard work in the attic she could smell the heavy odor of masculine sweat.

It would be so pleasant to stay locked in his arms and forget the outside world. She was even isolated from the voices in her head. Nothing could reach her. Here she was safe.

Bradon could not believe he was holding her in his arms. He had been fighting this fantasy since they had started the journey. He stared at her face. Smudges of dust had softened her imperious beauty leaving a tear-streaked urchin. When her laughter had turned to tears, the urge to cradle her in his arms had been overwhelming, and he had pulled her close. Now the desire to keep her there was equally overwhelming. Feeling her trembling body and her warm tears soaking through his shirt, had brought forth a savage protective impulse that he had not known he possessed. It was an impulse he had to resist. When you were planning to destroy someone the last thing you wanted to do was feel protective toward them.

Tears still oozed from beneath her closed eyelids and he took his handkerchief from his pocket and, putting one hand under her chin, he tilted her face and gently wiped away the damp smudges. If her eyes had remained closed he would have been all right. But they slowly opened. They were so luminous with tears, so incredibly beautiful that he was drawn into their depths. Then his lips were brushing her cheeks, moving to caress the softness beneath her ear. She moaned softly. A tremor rippled her flesh and brought an answering moan from his throat. His lips caressed her delicate eyelids, her fluttering lashes. His hands left her face and slid down her back, thrilling to the feel of her warm skin through the thin fabric of her shirt, his mind was numbed by the wonder that instead of pulling away she pressed her soft breasts against his chest.

The contact unleashed a volcano in his mind. His arms locked around her slim waist, molding her to his body. He groaned in anguish and his lips left her eyelids, searching for the warmth of her mouth.

At the sound, Sandi's eyes flew open as though she had been struck. Her head snapped back; her hands wedged between them, pressing against his chest. "No," she whispered. "Please no."

For an instant she thought that he was not going to release her. If he did not, if he pulled her even tighter against his lean body, if his lips found hers, she didn't think she could resist. Her body was trembling with spasms of such intense pleasure, her lips ached so much for his touch, that her tiny spark of control would be consumed by a raging fire.

But he did let her go. With a low growl of frustration, he dropped his arms to his sides and stepped back. Without his arms around her, Sandi thought her knees were going to buckle. She felt chilled. Lost.

She recovered quickly, turning so that he would not see her flushed face. She found her purse where she had left it by the door and extracted a tissue that she used to scrub at her face. It did not matter that Bradon had already wiped away the smudges with his handkerchief; she had to do something to take her mind off her betraying desire.

Bradon picked up his jacket from the back of a chair and slipped it on. "Let's go," he growled with more grit in his voice than necessary. "I don't think there's anything more to find here."

Sandi nodded. She was not sure she could speak. Her throat felt tight and her legs were incredibly weak. When she took the chair away that was propping the door open, she wondered what would happen if she allowed the door to slam shut, locking them inside. How many hours would it be before someone came searching for them? Could she keep her sanity while locked in a warm, dark attic with Dan Bradon? What did she want to happen?

As though the thought itself was the monster of the attic, she turned the legs of the chair like a lion tamer and with a determined thrust, tossed it inside the attic. When Bradon walked out past her, she closed the door with a hard pull. There. The monster was contained and she would never let it out.

CHAPTER 16

It had been unbelievably easy to leave the von Luckenwalde house. When Frau Hofstaetter had recovered from the shock of seeing their dusty clothes and dirty faces, she had been happy to escort them from the premises. Walking past Wolfgang, who was resolutely holding the door, Sandi had deliberately lurched, brushing against him. Wolfgang's granite face blenched and he cringed away as though they were lepers. Sandi and Bradon laughed throughout most of the drive to their hotel in the village.

Neither of them mentioned the incident in the attic. It was as though each knew that it should never have happened; that it was a sudden giving away to carnal impulse, and it would never be allowed to happen again. At times their laughter sounded strained as they strove to ignore the powerful currents that passed between them.

By the time they reached their hotel, each had managed to bury the incident under a thick layer of denial. It had never happened, therefore there was nothing to discuss.

After showering and changing clothes, Sandi descended to the hotel's combination pub and restaurant. A hefty waitress with amazingly red cheeks and braided flaxen hair showed her to a table in front of a bay window where Bradon was waiting.

It was difficult for Sandi to sit across from Bradon and not look in his face. Judging by the way he was avoiding her eyes, he was having the same difficulty.

As soon as they had placed orders for meatball sandwiches, Sandi asked, "Did you bring the locket?"

Bradon took it from his pocket and handed it to her. She held it to the light coming from the window, trying to keep her fingers from trembling. The thin chain was ordinary, links of gold with an unsubstantial clasp. The chain looked as though it had not come with the locket, which appeared to be made of stainless steel. One side of the locket was totally smooth. The other side was almost as smooth, but in the strong light Sandi could make out the faint outline of a heraldic symbol.

She pointed the symbol out to Bradon. He took the locket and tilted it so that the surface was a bas-relief. "Looks Prussian. If that means anything."

Taking back the locket, Sandi opened it and held the pictures to the light. But they revealed nothing new. She held out her hand to Bradon. "Lend me your penknife."

He dug the knife from his pocket. "What have you got in mind?"

Using the thin knife blade, she began carefully prying Hermann's picture from the locket. She reasoned that if she damaged it, it was the least important of the two.

"What are you doing?"

"Sometimes people put names on the back of pictures."

"That's right. I'll bet they're Hermann and Helga."

The picture had not been glued in place and, with a minimum of effort, Sandi was able to prize it free. While she was working on the second picture, Bradon examined the first. "No name. But there is a date: April, 1932."

Sandi checked the back of the second picture. "Same here: April, 1934."

"Which means they could be anybody."

"I don't think so. They're the man and woman I saw. Only younger."

"Are you positive?"

Sandi studied the pictures. Were they Hermann and Helga? There was a strong resemblance. But she could not be absolutely sure. "No. But even if it is them, I don't see how it's going to help."

"One more chink in the armor. Maybe somebody will recognize them. Or we might find some old pictures and we can compare them to these."

"Kind of a long shot at best."

"Right. But still a shot."

"I wonder why Frau Hofstaetter said that the Count never married?"

Bradon shrugged. "She probably didn't know. Don't forget, she never met them."

"I'll bet people who did know them refuse to admit it."

"I wouldn't be surprised. The Zeitgeist in 1946 wasn't conducive to admitting you hobnobbed with Nazis." He handed the locket to her. "They might have pictures of the Count in the local library. We'll check after lunch."

Sandi fitted the pictures back in the locket, then dropped it in her purse. "Maybe. That whole period from the 1930s to 1946 has been removed from a lot of libraries."

"And out of a lot of minds," Bradon said.

That night while transcribing notes for his book, Sandi's words came back to Bradon. She had been right. The village library held surprisingly little information about the von Luckenwalde family and most of that was prior to the l930s. It was as though historians had been interrupted by the formation of Hitler's National Socialist Party and had never resumed their records after the war.

The heraldic symbol on the locket might be traced to some long ago family ties--if it could be made out at all--but it would most likely be the crest of the Count's family and, thus, would provide no insight into Helga and her origins. And when the Nazis had systematically destroyed records of their occult connections in 1934 and again in the last days of the war, they had effectively destroyed any evidence of a psychic named Helga von Luckenwalde. Apparently Hitler and Himmler--and Count Hermann von Luckenwalde himself--had wanted to erase any connections with Helga.

Provided, of course, there ever had been a Helga. Perhaps she only existed in Sandi's mind. Still, there had been a Count von Luckenwalde. And there were the pictures. But was the woman in the picture truly Helga? He had only Sandi's word for that and she had not been absolutely positive.

What it boiled down to was that his chances for a best selling book were nil. Without proof that the images in Sandi's mind were based on reality, he had nothing. Books about regressions were a dime a dozen, on the same order as books about people abducted by flying saucers.

Strangely, he was not terribly disappointed. Exploiting Sandi's fear was putting a real strain on his conscience. If he had been successful in remaining totally objective, he might have been able to carry it off. But the longer he remained with Sandi, the more his objectivity became as strained as his conscience.

On the other hand, if he abandoned the book, he could give free rein to his growing affection.

Later, as he drifted into sleep, his last thought was wondering whether he was falling in love or falling in lust. It was one emotion he did not feel compelled to sort out.

For her part, Sandi was having no such ambivalent feelings. Her thoughts as she readied herself for bed were not about Bradon; they were about Helga. How could the woman have created such strong images during her regressions if she had never existed?

Before she climbed into the hotel's huge double bed with its oaken head and foot boards, she took the locket from her purse. She sat on the edge of the bed and reexamined it in the light of a bedside lamp. She tilted the locket so that the light shown on the metal surface at different angles, hoping to bring out more detail in the worn family crest. But it was useless. The surface was hopelessly worn, leaving only faint outlines of a shield topped by what appeared to be an eagle and a bear. There had to be hundreds of heraldic crests with those attributes.

She opened the locket and stared at the pictures inside. The people in the pictures stared back at her, their eyes as blank as their minds. Could she really have their blood in her veins?

Sandi swallowed her disappointment and snapped the locket shut. She was about to put it back into her purse but, impulsively, slipped the chain around her neck. She turned off the light and climbed into bed, lying on her back so that the locket rested in the hollow of her throat. It felt so heavy that she took it in both hands and held it while she tried to go to sleep.

However, a disturbing image kept flashing through her mind. It had a face, a form. Bradon! She could not keep her mind from remembering how good it had felt to walk with him, his thigh touching hers, his hand holding hers. How wonderful it had felt to feel his lean, hard body against hers when they had danced. His dancing had been so smooth, his control of her so commanding and, yet, so tender, his eyes so intense, his breath so hot. And in the attic . . . She could still feel his lips caressing her eyelids, the play of hard muscles beneath her hands, his hips pressed hard against hers. Her face grew warm as she realized that she had not given ground; she had thrust her hips equally hard against his. And all the time his lips had been ravishing her face. Thank God she had come to her senses before he had actually kissed her.

She was smiling when she drifted into a sleep that was warmed by memory and a strange heat in her loins.

Then Bradon's face became stiff and rigid and dissolved into the blank, faded face of the man in the locket picture. He held her in his arms while he stared at her with eyes that did not blink, eyes that filled her with fear.

She had to get away from those burning eyes. But the man's grip was too strong. She moaned in fear when he lifted her, carrying her locked in his arms while he slowly mounted a scaffold that terminated in a platform where a hangman's noose awaited.

She tried to scream. But no sound came from her throat.

She tried to break free. But his grip only tightened.

It was Helga who saved her. She was standing at the top of the platform and as the man took his place beneath the hanging noose, Helga pulled Sandi from his arms. She lifted Sandi as she would a small child and carried her down from the platform.

And Sandi was a child with Helga looking into her face as she held her. Helga's eyes were no longer blank but filled with sadness. Her lips moved, and Sandi though that she was going to tell her that she had nothing to fear, that she would be protected. Instead, Helga whispered something that Sandi could not make out. She strained to hear, but it was as though Helga's voice was as ephemeral as a summer breeze with no form, no beginning and no end.

Her message delivered, Helga glided away. Sandi held out her arms to her, silently calling for her to remain. But the woman's form dwindled into an ethereal distance and was gone, leaving Sandi reaching toward an empty sky.

She awakened with such a sense of hollowness in her chest that it was difficult to breathe. She was still clutching the locket but it no longer gave her a feeling of comfort. She obeyed an overwhelming urge to strip its chain from her neck.

After turning on the bedside lamp, she opened the locket. She could hardly bring herself to look at the pictures, afraid of what she might see. But they had not changed. The faces continued to stare at her with their blank eyes.

Taking a nail file from her purse, Sandi pried the picture of the man from the locket. Then she snapped the locket shut. Leaving the man's picture face down on the bedside table, she replaced the locket around her neck.

She instantly felt a subtle change in the locket. It seemed lighter, as though a malevolent weight had been removed.

This time when she clasped the locket in her two hands and waited for sleep, she knew that she would no longer be terrorized by a hangman's noose.

But she could not sleep. For some reason, the locket felt peculiarly warm in her hands and, abruptly, she sat up in bed. She knew what the woman had said!

Desperately afraid that she would forget the words, she turned on the bedside light and found a pen in her purse. There was a note pad on a small desk and she wrote the words that burned in her mind.

She tore the paper from the note pad and clutched it in her hand while she struggled into a robe. She held the paper tightly, afraid that it would vanish like the image of the woman. She opened the door and went down the dimly lighted hall to Bradon's room.

She knocked softly, afraid that she would awaken other guests, although it did not seem likely. The hotel was small; there were only two other rooms and she had seen no evidence that they were occupied. Still, she did not relish the thought of someone seeing her knocking on Bradon's door in the middle of the night wearing only her nightgown and a thin robe.

She was about to rap again when she felt the floor tremble with approaching footsteps and the door was partially opened. Bradon, in his pajamas, his hair tousled, blinked at her. "Sandi?"

She slipped inside his room. "Close the door," she whispered.

He closed the door softly, then turned to her. Keeping his voice low, he said, "What is it? What's wrong?"

"Not wrong," she said. "Right. We've got to go to Switzerland."

"Switzerland?"

"Yes. All the money from the estate is in a bank there."

Bradon combed his unruly hair with his fingers. "What are you talking about? What money?"

"Money from the von Luckenwalde estate. It's in the Zuger Bank in Interlaken." She held the paper out to him. "See."

Bradon, now wide-awake, took the crumpled paper and smoothed it so he could read the words Sandi had scrawled. "Zuger Bank of Interlaken." He looked up at her. "Where did you get this?"

"I,"--this was going to sound strange--"I had a dream. The woman in the locket, Helga, she told me."

To her relief, Bradon did not laugh. Rather, his face cleared as though relieved of a depressing worry. "My God," he said. "You've really got it."

"Got what?"

"Psychometric. Just like Helga. She had to be a relative, probably your grandmother."

Sandi's hand went to the locket she still wore around her neck. "I thought of that," she whispered. "But . . . it's not possible."

"Did you know your grandparents? Did you ever meet them?"

"Well, yes. On my father's side. But my mother's . . . She said they died when I was a baby."

"So it is possible."

"No, it isn't. Her name wasn't Helga Waltz. Or von Luckenwalde."

"So how did you get the message?"

"I was holding the locket. But it could be coincidence."

"That's what I thought when you held that book--back at the museum. But twice? That's more than coincidence." He took her shoulders in his strong hands. "Honey, you've got it."

Sandi felt a thrill of pleasure. Honey? Then the pleasure quickly ebbed. In his excitement he had simply used the first expression that came to mind. He probably called every woman 'honey' just as some women called everyone 'darling'. And his grasping her shoulders was also reflex action. In the heat of discovery, he would have grasped anyone the same way.

Except that he didn't immediately let her go. He stood with his hands holding her shoulders, looking into her eyes, and his broad smile slowly vanished. It was replaced with a look of such longing that Sandi swayed toward him, her body, her lips, feeling incredibly receptive.

The tip of his tongue touched his lips and his hands tightened on her shoulders. He began to pull her close while his head poised to kiss her. Sandi wanted to resist; she had to resist. But she could not, and she felt her own lips grow warm as they slowly parted, waiting for his kiss.

Then his arms stiffened and his face hardened. The sardonic smile returned to his face as he gently thrust her back to arms length. "I knew you were special," he said. "It doesn't matter now whether we find Helga or not."

Sandi blinked at him, trying to bring her thoughts back into focus. "What do you mean?"

Bradon released her, and again she experienced a penetrating sense of loss, as though she had been set adrift. His smile became rigid and he quickly explained, "I mean, I, uh, hope we find her, of course. But this psychometric ability opens up new possibilities."

"Maybe not. Maybe it only works when I'm thinking of Helga."

Bradon's face twisted in quick disappointment. "Oh God. I hadn't thought of that." His smile reappeared as though on command. "Well, that's all right. It should be enough."

"Enough? Enough for what?"

Again he answered quickly, "To find out about Helga, of course." He moved away as though to avoid contact with her. "Switzerland, huh?

Okay. We'll leave in the morning." He was reaching for the knob of the door when he stopped. "Oh, damn."

"What?"

"Most of those Swiss accounts are secret. They use numbers instead of names. Even the bank people don't know the name of the account holder."

"Oh, no," Sandi corrected. "Not any more. They passed a law in, I think it was 1992. At least two bank officers have to know the name of the account holder."

"Okay. But without the account number, they won't tell us anything."

Sandi grimaced. "The account has to be fifty years old. Maybe they'd welcome an inquiry."

"Well, we can hope that they're looking for heirs or something. But if it's a big account, they're probably happy to just sit on it and collect the bank charges."

"We'll have to try."

Bradon smiled at her and with his smile her spirits lifted. "Yes," he said, "we've got to try."

CHAPTER 17

It took less than an hour for Bradon to drive a rental car from the Bern airport to Interlaken. Coming out of the clouds from the top of Jaun Pass, Sandi gasped in awe as the panorama of the Bernese Oberland burst upon her senses. Clouds obscured the peaks of the highest mountains, but Sandi had a magnificent view of Brienzersee and Thunersee, the twin lakes at the base of the mountains. The city of Interlaken, their destination, was located on a flat isthmus between the lakes.

She had rarely seen such picturesque beauty. The water of the nearest lake, the Thunersee, was cobalt blue. It was cradled in the arms of mountains that were carpeted with dark green forests and emerald green meadows, backed by gigantic, snow capped peaks. It seemed that a separate village nestled in each small cove of the lake. The stark white of the two and three storied homes with their red tile or dark, slate roofs were in startling contrast to the blue waters of the lake and the green of the shore. The villages seemed incredibly tiny and vulnerable beneath the formidable peaks.

Driving along the edge of the lake, Bradon pointed to a group of craggy, mist shrouded peaks. "That's the JungFrau Region. Those three are probably the most famous trio of peaks in the world. That's JungFrau, the Virgin. The middle one is Mönch, the Monk. And that's the famous Eiger, the Ogre. Over there,"--he pointed to a distant misty peak--"is the Schilthorn. There's a restaurant near the top. You might have seen it in one of the James Bond pictures. As long as we're here, we should go up."

Sandi studied the sheer face of the mountain. "There's a road up there? I don't think I'd like that."

Bradon chuckled. "Not a road. A cable car. This is ski country. These mountains are laced with ski lifts and funiculars and cable cars."

"Sounds like fun," Sandi said, but there was little enthusiasm in her voice. The wall of ragged peaks looked like the fangs of vicious dogs. They appeared to be crouching over the villages and towns as though waiting to pounce when least expected. She recalled reading that people who live among forbidding mountains such as these always were a little afraid of them. She could understand why. They made one seem fragile, insignificant. They would endure forever. Man was a puny creature whose footsteps would scarcely leave a mark.

As they entered the outskirts of Interlaken, Sandi was thinking that compared to the mountains, her life might be short, but hers was filled with excitement and tensions that the mountains would never know. Although she wouldn't mind trading a little of that tension right now for some of the mountain's serenity.

The city of Interlaken gave Sandi the feeling that at last she was seeing the real Switzerland. Situated at the very base of towering ranges of sawtooth peaks, the small city was postcard perfect. Outside the city one and two storied homes were scattered haphazardly across the plain. Although it was October the big winter storms had not yet arrived and the main street, lined with shops, restaurants and hotels, still retained vestiges of its famous bordering flowers.

A stop at the tourist office in the Hotel Metropol provided a list of available hotels and guest houses. Bradon suggested they stay at the Metropol since they were already in the lobby, but Sandi was intrigued by pictures of hotels that looked like Swiss chalets. "As long as we're here," she said, imitating Bradon when he suggested the trip to the Schilthorn restaurant, "we should go Swiss."

Bradon agreed without protest. He would have been willing to stay in a tree if it brought a sparkle of joy to Sandi's usually somber eyes.

They selected a small chalet in the Unterseen district that offered spectacular views of the Thunersee and the JungFrau. Before they entered the hotel, Sandi gazed in awe at the blue jewel of the lake and its circling snow capped mountains with their skirts of varying shades of green. The scene looked so incredibly pristine that she could not help but think that this would be a fantastic place to live.

The same thought had occurred to Bradon but with a reservation. "Great place to visit," he said. "Boring to live."

"Boring? How could anyone be bored with this beauty."

"Like a beautiful woman with no personality. She can change her clothes four times a year, but eventually you want something with a little more excitement."

"Like Los Angeles?"

"Well, it may not be a beauty queen, but it sure ain't boring."

"I think after we find this Zuger Bank, this won't be boring either."

Before she changed for the trip to the bank, Sandi telephoned her mother, explaining what had happened. When she told her about visiting the von Luckenwalde estate and that they were now in Switzerland, Sandi was pleased that her mother wanted to know all the details. Finally she was beginning to believe her.

After dressing, she debated about wearing the locket. Even without the Count's picture inside, the feel of its weight hanging from her neck was upsetting. It didn't matter whether or not it was some kind of a link between her and the voices; it was a bomb that could blow up at any moment, sending her spinning into eternity.

At the last moment, obeying a strong impulse, she slipped the thin chain around her neck and allowed the locket to hang outside her blouse, unwilling to feel it touching her flesh like some cold, dead hand reaching out from the grave.

They found the Zuger Bank near the west end of Höheweg Street sandwiched between a restaurant and a shop displaying a fantastic array of watches and Swiss Army knives. While Sandi had not expected the Zuger Bank building to be an ultramodern steel and glass structure such as the bank buildings in most large cities, she did not expect it to be a three storied, whitewashed structure that, except for double, glass entrance doors, could have passed for a Swiss 16th Century home.

The interior, however, looked more like a bank should look, with men in dark suits sitting at desks handling customer services. She and Bradon approached a desk with a sign on it in German that indicated the man behind it was in charge of Foreign Services. The man appeared to be in his mid-forties, with the girth, the dark suit, the steel-rimmed glasses and thinning dark hair that spelled career banker. A computer monitor and keyboard sat on a small table next to his desk.

He was filling out a money transfer form with a fat, gold pen and he looked up with irritation when Bradon said, "Guten Morgen."

"Ja?" His voice had an impersonal hardness that sounded as though it was more used to saying "No" than "Yes". "Kann ich ihnen helfen?"

"Ich hoffe es," Bradon said. "Wir brauchen auskunft über eins ihrer koten."

The man stood and smiled, but his eyes behind his glasses remained watchful. "I see," he said in excellent English as he extended his hand. "I am Herr Gluck, Senior Executive for Foreign Services."

"I'm Dr. Daniel Bradon of the University of California," Bradon said as he shook the man's hand. "This is my associate Dr. Sandi Boeckel."

Sandi almost smiled. Doctor?

"Delighted." Herr Gluck shook Sandi's hand with a firm, cool grip. He motioned to chairs at the side of his desk. "Won't you sit down, please."

When they were seated, Herr Gluck picked up his pen and held it expectantly. "You mentioned an account? Is there a problem?"

"No," Bradon assured him. "No problem. It's, ah, rather a complicated story." Herr Gluck sat back in his chair and his eyes that had softened when Bradon said there was no problem, became watchful again. "My associate and I are doing research work in genealogy. We've come across an interesting family with origins in Germany, the Prussian district, that is especially fascinating. The family name is von Luckenwalde."

Bradon paused, watching to see the effect of the name on the man but there was none. He had either never heard the name or he was a good poker player--or Swiss banker--because his eyes revealed nothing.

"Count Hermann von Luckenwalde," Sandi said. "His wife's name was Helga."

"Yes?" Herr Gluck said. "And how does this involve the Zuger Bank?"

"Von Luckenwalde was executed by the Allies as a war criminal. At some point during 1945, Helga von Luckenwalde liquidated their estate and left Germany. We believe she deposited the money in a Swiss bank.

This one."

Herr Gluck's eyes did not change expression but he rubbed his palms together in front of his chest. "You believe?"

Sandi said, "We have no proof. Most of the family records were destroyed during the war or immediately afterward."

"So how did you come to the conclusion that the funds might be in The Zuger Bank?"

Bradon looked to Sandi for a plausible answer and she said, "That too is complicated. But unless there's another Zuger Bank, I'm sure it's this one."

"I see. And you have the codes to this account?"

"Codes? Well, no."

Before Herr Gluck could reply, Bradon said, "We're really not interested in the account itself. We only want to trace the movements of Frau von Luckenwalde."

"Well," Herr Gluck said, "Not all of our holdings are confidential, although all are discreet. If you will wait here, I will see if there is such an account. And, if so, whether or not it is protected."

"Of course," Bradon murmured and Herr Gluck got up and walked to stairs leading to upstairs offices.

"Do you think he'll tell us?".

"Depends. First, does such an account even exist? If it does, is it confidential? And even if it isn't, I doubt he'd tell us anything. The Swiss are so damn protective of their banking he could end up in prison."

"So you think he's just going through the motions?"

"I'm afraid so."

"But we have the name and the date. That should be enough to tell if the account exists."

"Some people don't want anyone to know their account exists."

They saw Herr Gluck descending the stairs. Sandi tried to read some hope in his expression but the man's face might have been sculpted in plastic.

At the desk he sat down and carefully pulled up his chair. He folded his hands on top of the desk. "As you no doubt know," he began in a voice as impersonal as a recording. "Swiss banking is very strictly controlled by banking regulations and by Swiss laws. If I were to breach any one of these regulations, I could be sent to prison for several years."

He paused and Sandi took the opportunity to say, "Then the account is confidential."

Herr Gluck's smile was wintery. "I did not say there was such an account." Sandi opened her mouth to reply, and Herr Gluck held up a hand. "I can tell you this without breaching any regulations. We have no record of anyone named von Luckenwalde."

The look Bradon turned upon Sandi was skeptical. The ball was in her court. Sandi groped for words, some method of explaining the unexplainable. How could she prove that the words she had heard were real?

She reached up and clutched the locket in her left hand. Could she be wrong? Had her vision been nothing but a chimera, a sham, the figment of a disintegrating mind? As though in answer to her unspoken thought, she felt a searing pain in her head as though a burning iron had branded an image on her brain.

She gasp and Bradon half rose from his chair and Herr Gluck said, "Are you all right?"

"Yes, yes," she said. "Let me have your pen."

Without waiting for his answer, Sandi picked up the pen and scribbled a name and series of seven numbers on the edge of the money transfer paper lying on the desk. "That is the name and the account number. We want all the information you have on that account."

Herr Gluck's composure had been shattered. He sat with his mouth slack, his glasses askew before his bulging eyes.

Bradon reached over and turned the paper so that Herr Gluck could see the number. "You wanted a name and the confidential account number. There they are."

Herr Gluck recovered his composure and stood up. "Why you did not give me this before?"

"A test," Bradon said. "We wanted to be certain that the account was truly confidential."

The bewilderment in Herr Gluck's eyes turned to anger. He breathed in sharply through his nose and his face hardened into its usual set planes. He picked up the paper and turned to leave. "I will be right back."

"One moment, Herr Gluck," Bradon said. He picked up the pen and copied the name and numbers on the top page of a desk calendar and ripped off the page. He smiled at Herr Gluck. "Thank you. We'll wait here."

Gluck, clutching the paper, turned and walked away. Bradon looked at Sandi with a quizzical expression. "Helga Waltz?"

"That was the name that came to me."

"Maybe that was her maiden name. She must have gone back to it when Hermann was executed."

"That sounds logical."

Bradon's gaze shifted to the locket. "It was the locket, wasn't it?"

"I don't know. But I was touching it." She ran her fingertips across its smooth metal surface and shivered. Unable to bear its touch a moment longer, she unfastened the clasp with trembling fingers.

She was going to drop it in her purse but Bradon held out his hand. "Let me see it."

She handed the locket to him, glad to have it out of her hands. It might be a door to another life but it was a frightening door, one that she did not enjoy opening. Bradon examined the locket with more care than he had the first time he had looked at it. When he snapped it open and saw only one picture he looked up at Sandi. "What happened to the other picture?"

"I . . ." Should she lie? And what lie could she possibly tell that he would believe. "I tore it up."

"Tore it up?!" The look of disappointment and anger that shot across his face made her flinch back in her chair. "For Christ sake, why?"

Why was Bradon so angry? It seemed all out of proportion to loss of the picture. "It . . . He frightened me."

"How the hell could he do that?"

"I . . .I saw him in a . . .a dream. He was . . .evil."

"But that was no damn reason to destroy it. Why didn't you just save it? Or give it to me?"

"I had to destroy it."

Bradon studied her stricken face and took a deep breath, "Okay. No harm done, I guess. There should be other pictures of him in military archives."

"Other pictures? Why would we want them?"

Bradon snapped the locket closed. He smiled and warmth returned to his voice. "No reason. It's just that after all the problems we had getting the blame thing, I just hate to lose any part of it." He handed the locket back to her. "Don't lose it. It might be the only picture we'll have of Helga."

"You're right," Sand answered as she fastened the chain around her neck. "But to tell the truth, I'll be glad when I can forget her."

Herr Gluck was approaching the desk and they turned to him. He sat down and placed a file folder on his desk. "May I see some identification?" he said.

"We told you," Bradon said. "We're not the account holders."

"I understand. This is simply for the record."

Sandi and Bradon showed him their passports and he carefully copied their names on a form. He opened the file folder and placed the form inside and took out another paper. He cleared his throat and began speaking in a voice that betrayed his reluctance to impart information. "The account was opened in 1945, as you indicated, in the name you gave me: Helga Waltz."

"What was the opening sum?" Bradon asked.

Herr Gluck consulted his paper. "Fifty-five million, three hundred twenty-seven thousand, eight hundred Swiss francs."

"Fifty-five million?" Sandi could scarcely believe what she had heard.

"That is correct."

"And the current balance?"

Again he checked the paper. "The account has been depleted over the years. It is now forty-three million, seven hundred thousand, two hundred eighty-four Swiss francs."

"What would that be in dollars?" Bradon said.

Herr Gluck made a rapid calculation on a pocket calculator. "Fifty two million, four hundred forty thousand, three hundred forty-seven dollars."

Sandi put her hand across her mouth. Such a sum was almost inconceivable. "You said the account has been depleted. How?"

"It bears interest, of course, but as instructed by the current account holder, sums have been systematically transferred that cut into the principle."

Sandi's heart began pounding and her palms grew sweaty. It had to be the answer to what had happened to Helga. "The current account holder? You mean Helga Waltz? Where is she?"

"Helga Waltz's will was executed in 1956."

Sandi's heart seemed to stop as thought she had been struck in the chest by a hard blow. "Her will? So she is dead?"

"That's usually the situation when a will is executed."

Sandi sank back in her chair. She felt spent as thought she had reached the top of a mountain after a long, arduous climb. It was over. They had all the answers. There was no reason to continue the quest.

The telephone on the desk beeped and Herr Gluck picked it up. "Ja," he said, "Herr Gluck sprechen."

He listened for a moment, then put the phone back in its cradle. He closed the file with a slap of finality. "If that will be all."

"Just one more thing," Bradon said. "To whom was the money transferred. And where?"

Herr Gluck stood up. "I'm sorry. I can tell you nothing more." He held out his hand to Sandi. "I am honored to have met you."

Sandi stood and shook his hand, murmuring, "Thank you." But Bradon did not move.

"We would like the name of the current account holder," he said.

Herr Gluck's heavy jaw quivered. "That is confidential," he snapped.

"We have the account number. It is no longer confidential."

"But you are not the account holder. Good day."

Bradon was prepared to argue but Sandi touched his shoulder. "It doesn't matter," she said. "We got what we came for. There really was someone named Helga."

Bradon looked up at her, then nodded. "Okay." He stood and without extending his hand to Herr Gluck, said, "Thank you."

Sandi took hold of Bradon's arm and they walked to the door. As Bradon opened the glass door, Sandi glanced back and saw Herr Gluck staring at them. Just as the glass door of the bank closed behind them, Herr Gluck quickly picked up his telephone and began rapidly punching a number. For an instant, Sandi felt a tingle of alarm, wondering why the man should make such a hasty call. She dismissed the thought by rationalizing that Herr Gluck was no doubt reporting their departure to his superiors with relief. He probably had never experienced such a traumatic confrontation in his entire career.

During the ride back to the hotel, Sandi's mind was filled with thoughts about Helga von Luckenwalde.

Prior to her husband's death in 1946--perhaps with his help--she had liquidated the von Luckenwalde estate and placed the funds in the Swiss bank, using her maiden name.

After Hermann's execution, she had probably left Germany, although Sandi could not be sure of that. In any event, Helga was dead. Why hadn't she realized that.? Helga had to be dead for her spirit to take over during a regression. Assuming that such a thing was possible.

Sandi had a strange feeling of revulsion. To have had another person invade her body, to take it over, made her feel unclean. It had to be the same feeling experienced by a rape victim.

From the driver's seat, Bradon muttered, "I wonder where she went?"

Sandi looked up. So Bradon was wrestling with the same thoughts. "It doesn't really matter," she said. "What does matter is that she actually existed. I'm not going crazy."

"I never thought you were."

"Not even a little?"

Bradon smiled, his eyes twinkling. "Eccentric, maybe. Crazy, no."

To Sandi's surprise she found that she had been tense, waiting for Bradon's answer. Now the tension vanished, leaving her with a glow of relief and pleasure. Bradon had no reason to lie. He didn't believe that she was losing her mind. And she could certainly live with being thought eccentric. She relaxed in her seat, her lips forming a tiny smile. Her mission was finished and she had survived, body and soul. She felt wonderful.

Bradon had been studying the distant peaks of the JungFrau. "When do you have to get back?"

"To the hotel?"

"No. L.A."

"Oh. No particular time. Why?"

Bradon gestured toward the towering Alps raising spectacularly to the south. "Let's to up on the Schilthorn for lunch. We can be there in an hour."

The sun had burned away the mists from the mountains and the thirteen thousand foot peaks of the JungFrau thrust toward the sky in sharp relief. Sandi stared at the snowy slopes of the mighty Schilthorn with a tingle of fear and anticipation. The view from its famous restaurant had to be one of the sights of the world. "Okay," she said. "But I'm going to put on my winter clothes."

"Good idea. I'll dig out the long johns."

"You'll look cute," Sandi said with a grin. "Don't forget your hat."

An hour later Sandi had to work hard to keep her light hearted mood as Bradon headed their rental car out of Interlaken. Almost immediately they plunged into a wide canyon between overpowering mountain walls. The two-lane highway followed the banks of a small river, winding through incredibly green forests and meadows.

"Over there," Bradon said pointing to the escarpment on their left, "is Trummelbach Falls."

"I don't see it."

"That's because it's inside the mountain. You've got to see it. It's incredible. Maybe when we come back."

"This whole place is incredible."

"You should see it in winter."

"I'd love to."

"Okay. It's a date."

Sandi's lips were suddenly dry. She should tell Bradon about her engagement to Jordan if only to halt any thoughts he might have about her availability. But she sat silently, all the while damning herself for not telling him, rationalizing that there was plenty of time.

To change the subject she said, "Reminds me of Yosemite."

Bradon smiled. He knew she hadn't answered his invitation. "Yes. Carved out by glaciers the same way."

Sandi looked at the fields of snow that still clung to the upper lips of the canyon walls. "One big difference. The people in Yosemite don't have to worry about avalanches. I'd be on pins and needles living here."

Bradon pointed to the fifteen-hundred-foot wall on their right. "Think of the people up there. They've got to worry about being swept over the edge."

Sandi ducked her head to peer through the windshield at the steep cliff. "There's a village up there?"

"Two of them. Right on the edge. You'll see them when we get there."

"Oh." Sandi leaned back in the car seat. This jaunt was beginning to seem less and less like fun. "All I can say is: the food in that restaurant had better be terrific."

Leaving the car at Stechelberg, they walked the short distance to the cable car station. Sandi stared in dismay at the cables stretching up the almost sheer slope of the escarpment. "We're going up there?"

"Only the first leg. To Gimmelwald. Then over to Mürren where we change cars for the Schilthorn."

Sandi had no real fear of heights. She had ridden the Palm Springs cable cars without fear. But this was different. They were going to be suspended by thin cables over deep canyons. If anything went wrong, it could take hours, maybe days, to get help. But Bradon was doing his best to please her, so she was determined to enjoy herself.

When they entered the car, Bradon said, "You're going to love this. This is the heart of the Alps. You'll get a view of the whole region."

She hoped that he wouldn't notice that her smile was a little stiff. "I can hardly wait."

Her apprehension only subsided a little when she saw that there was an operator inside the cable car. She reasoned that if the operator had enough confidence to ride the car back and forth all day long, it must be safe.

The car was large but there were no other passenger. "In the winter," Bradon said, "it's probably full. This is big ski country."

The car's doors slide shut and with a lurch, the car started upward. Sandi's grip on the handrail tightened and as the valley floor dropped away rapidly, she sucked in her breath. Despite her apprehension, the expanding view was so spectacular that she watched in awe, her lips parted in wonder.

To Bradon, looking at her was a greater pleasure than any view. She reminded him of a child who had never been allowed to play, then had been turned loose in a carnival.

As the cable car inched upward, sometimes swaying thrillingly over ridges and canyons, Sandi held her breath. Gradually she became used to the car's movement and, as Bradon pointed out the incredible unfolding vistas, she forgot her fear.

They had passed the Gimmelwald station and Bradon was pointing out the distant peaks of the JungFrau Region when movement reflected in the glass window caused Sandi to turn her head. It was the car's operator. He was standing in the center of the car with his feet braced against the swaying, a revolver in his hand.

She gasped and Bradon's head jerked around to see what was causing her alarm. The man motioned with the gun. "You vill not try anything," he snarled. "I vill shoot."

Bradon tensed but did not move. "What do you want?"

The man pointed to the locket around Sandi's neck. "Gif me that."

Bradon shifted his feet and Sandi sucked in her breath. Bradon was going to attack. But the man was too far away. He would be killed! She put her hand on his arm. "No. Don't."

Bradon glanced at her, his eyes narrowed with suppressed anger. "All right." He turned back to the man. "Easy. Just take it easy."

The man motioned with the gun. "Gif me the locket."

Sandi's hand went to the locket. "It has no value," she said. "It's nothing."

In answer the man stepped forward and with a swift move, yanked the locket hard, breaking the thin chain. He glanced at it before dropping it into his pocket. Bradon crouched, and the gun centered on him. "No." Sandi said quickly. "It isn't worth the chance."

Bradon straightened, his eyes wary and Sandi knew that if he saw even the smallest opening, he would attack. The thought filled her with fear. The locket, their money, nothing was worth Bradon's life.

The man stepped back and the apprehension that had been paralyzing Sandi's mind was overlaid with a growing terror: What was the man going to do when they reached the Mürren station? How could he possibly escape? A phone call to the police would have them waiting for him at the bottom. What was he going to do?

Her puzzle was answered when the man pulled the emergency handle on the car door and slid it open so that wind swirled dust from the floor. My God! He was going to make them jump! Even if they lived, they would be too badly injured to reach help for hours.

Bradon also realized what the man intended, and he sucked in his breath. He was not going to die without a fight. The man looked husky, in good shape. And he had the gun. But with luck, he might be able to take him. Better to be wounded or even killed by the gun, than to go without a fight.

The man evidently sensed his resolve because he leveled the gun at Bradon. "Sorry about this," he said calmly.

Sandi's eyes were locked on the gun and the man's finger on the trigger. Horror froze her as she saw his knuckle tighten. Her arm seemed to move of its own accord and she saw her purse arching toward the man.

The movement caused the man to shift his eyes for a fraction of a second, and Bradon sprang in a low dive. The blast of the gun exploded in his ears as his shoulder came up under the man's extended arm. Bradon rolled, coming to his feet in one movement. The man's gun was coming up for another shot and Bradon smashed the man's wrist with the edge of his rigid palm. The man grunted with pain. But he didn't drop the gun. He was swinging it up to fire when Bradon's fist crashed against his jaw.

The man's head snapped back, his eyes glazed. He stumbled back on rubbery legs and struck the side of the open door. His eyes started with horror as his feet slipped through the opening. He dropped the gun and frantically clutched at the bottom edge of the door, his feet dangling in space. Bradon reached for him, but wind whipped the man's body sideways, tearing his fingers from their grip. He screamed in horror as he began a long plummet to a tree choked canyon far below.

Bradon's move had carried him to the edge of the open door. He teetered, half out the door, clawing for support. Sandi sprang forward and grabbed his jacket and, with strength she didn't know she possessed, pulled him back inside the car where they fell to the floor.

They lay locked in a tight embrace, clinging together, their breathing unsteady, unwilling to trust letting go. Gradually, holding Sandi in his arms, Bradon's fear began to subside, and with it came the realization that he hadn't been afraid for himself; he had been deathly afraid for Sandi. He would have given the man anything he possessed if it would have kept Sandi from being harmed. It was a prayer that the man would take their money and leave them alone that had kept him frozen.

But the man had no intention of allowing them to live. The realization had propelled him into action. But if Sandi hadn't thrown her purse, they might both be lying at the bottom of a gorge.

He began aware that she was quivering in his arms, and that tears were streaking her face. "It's okay," he whispered. "He's gone."

"Oh God," she sobbed. "I was so afraid he was going to shoot you."

Bradon lifted his head. "Me? You were afraid for me?"

"Yes." Her sobs stopped with a gasp and her eyes opened wide. "Are you all right?"

"Yes. He missed me."

Her breath went out in a rush and her arms tightened around him. "Oh, God, God," she breathed. "That was awful."

Bradon's fingers gently brushed the tears from her cheeks. "I know. I know."

Somehow his fingers were replaced by his lips and he brushed them across her cheeks, tasting the salt of her tears. Then his lips were brushing hers.

At first, they did not even realize that their lips were touching. Then, in a subtle shifting, his lips were on hers and he was lost in a mindless joy. Her lips were incredibly soft and warm. With his senses rapidly spinning out of control, his kiss grew deeper, harder. He could feel her breasts soft against his chest, her thighs hard against his own. His tongue caressed her lips and sought her mouth. To his delight, her own tongue touched his as warily as a startled doe. And, like a frightened doe, when his tongue plunged deeper, in sudden panic, it fled.

She pushed herself away from him, sitting up. She pressed her hands to her face, breathing deeply as she tried to restore her perspective.

Bradon, too, sat up. "Sorry," he said. "I guess it was the adrenaline. I, uh, got carried away."

"I know," she murmured. "I did too."

He stood and helped her to her feet. Looking out the front of the car he could see that they were rapidly approaching the Mürren station. He picked up the man's gun and tossed into the void before he slid the door shut and latched it.

"Why did you do that?" Sandi said. "The police--"

"It would be better if we keep our mouths shut," Bradon interrupted. He began searching for the place the man's bullet had struck the car.

"But . . . we've got to tell the police."

"If we do, we'll be stuck here for days, maybe weeks."

"But they'll find out and we'll be worse off."

"If they ever find his body, there's nothing to connect us to him." He pointed to a small hole in the metal under the seat at the rear of the car. "See. Even the bullet hole is almost invisible."

"But he's the operator. They'll wonder what happened to him."

"I'll bet there won't be anybody at the station. He wouldn't want anybody to know we were even on the car." He picked up her purse and handed it to her. "Believe me, Sandi. If we report this, the red tape will be murder. Or we can just walk away. All we've lost is the locket."

"I'm not really sorry about that," Sandi murmured. "It was . . .depressing."

"Well, I'm sorry we lost the picture. But the best thing is to forget the whole thing."

Slowly she nodded, her head scarcely moving. "I guess you're right. It's just that--"

"It goes against your moral principles," Bradon finished for her. "I understand. But this time expediency is more important that principle."

The car reached the station and settled into its berth with a solid clank. Bradon push the 'open' button at the operator's console and the door slid open. After they exited, Bradon leaned in and pressed the 'close' button and they quickly walked out of the station. He had been right; the station was deserted.

Outside, Bradon led the way down a side street. "There's a cog train we can take down to Lauterbrunnen. We'll be long gone before the operator is missed. If he was the operator, which I doubt."

If she had been alone Sandi would have notified the police. But Bradon's grip on her arm reminded her that she would not suffer any consequences alone. Bradon would also suffer. She said nothing and they walked rapidly along the picturesque streets of the village. The sunlight was warm and bright; the towering snowcapped mountains spectacular. It was a day that made one glad to be alive.

CHAPTER 18

The 747 cruised effortlessly at 40,000 feet. Sandi, in a window seat, was awakened by morning sun glinting off an endless field of clouds far below. She glanced at her watch. Only two more hours to Los Angeles. She had slept as though she was drugged.

In a way it seemed as though she had been drugged, because the voices, the images that usually plagued her sleep were gone, left in the wake of the plane boring through the blue. Forever, she hoped.

Her eyelids were heavy, poised on the edge of sleep, her body pleasantly logy. She luxuriated in the release of the tension that had been her constant companion for days. The difficult part was behind her: during the drive from Interlaken to Bern to turn in the rental car, she had keep looking over her shoulder for the flashing lights of a police car. The most anxious part had been waiting in the Bern and the Munich airports for departure, expecting any second for a policeman to tap her on the shoulder.

Only after hours of flight and no orders to turn the plane around and return to Munich, did she begin to feel safe.

She sensed that Bradon, too, felt a sense of relief. He had displayed his usual insouciance during the journey to the airport and the nerve shattering boarding of the plane where they were most likely to be apprehended, but she suspected that, inside, he was as tense as she.

"You're awake. You had a nice sleep."

Sandi's eyes popped open. Her eyes felt heavy, gritty. She couldn't have slept long. She pressed the button bringing her seat back up a little. Bradon, sitting beside her, had the desktop down in front of his seat. He had been writing in a large, spring bound notebook.

She stretched and rubbed her eyes. "Yes. Did you sleep?"

"For a while. I don't sleep well on planes."

"I haven't been on them enough to know. This is really my first long flight. Except for the trip over. But that doesn't count. I was really hyper."

"You weren't what I'd call relaxed last night."

"I know. I expected to be arrested any second."

"No reason to worry. It's over."

"I hope so." She started to relax back in her seat, then straightened. "There's something I don't understand."

"About what?"

"About what happened on the cable car. Why did he want the locket?"

"I guess he thought it was valuable."

"It was just a picture locket. It didn't look valuable."

"I guess it did to him."

"You'd think that if he wanted money, he would have taken my purse."

"Good thing he didn't. We'd probably both be dead."

"I know, but . . . Could he have been after the locket?"

"I don't think so. Nobody knew anything about it except us."

"The banker. He saw it."

"But he couldn't know anything about it. To him, it was just a locket."

"I guess you're right." Her sigh was of relief, not regret. "It is over, isn't it?"

Bradon's smile drove away any lingering doubts. "Well, the bad part is. The good part is still ahead."

Sandi leaned her head back against the headrest and allowed her eyes to close. Bradon's words echoed in her mind. The good part was ahead. Soon they would be landing in LA and she could return to her comfortable, predictable life. Maybe not so comfortable. She would have to begin preparations for her wedding. Jordan would not be put off any longer. And now, with the voices gone, knowing that she was not a mental case, there was no reason not to be married as soon as possible. So why did the thought fill her with sadness?

Bradon had resumed writing and Sandi found herself studying him. He was intent on his work, his slender fingers gripping the pen firmly. He had taken off his jacket and turned the cuffs of his shirt up so that she was able to watch the play of muscles in his corded forearms. With his head bent low, a lock of hair fell across his wide forehead, its darkness in sharp contrast to the white of his skin.

His lips reflected his thoughts as he wrote, reacting with tiny smiles, frowns and tight pressure. Those were the same lips that had been on hers in the cable car. The same lips that had caressed her cheeks, soothing her tears. The same lips that had captured hers so tenderly, then had turned savage with her response.

She couldn't believe she had responded so fiercely. It was as though the escape from danger had heightened her senses until she had been unable to control a frantic desire for Bradon's arms, his lips, his body. Strange that her relief had taken such a direction. Would it have been the same if she had been with Jordan? Would Jordan have reacted with such swift violence when the gunman was going to shoot? When the danger was passed, would he have held her and kissed her as though he never wanted to let her go?

She blinked, breaking the tension. But she couldn't keep the memories at bay. Since that fearful, wonderful moment, Bradon and she had been stiffly formal as though each wanted to pretend it had never happened. But her lips remembered every tender caress, every savage thrust. And her body remembered the feel of his hips against hers, his chest crushing her breasts, his strong legs entwined with hers. Remembering, her breathing deepened and heat grew in her thighs. Her stomach contracted, fluttering. She could feel every pulse of her heart that surged through her body. Perspiration beaded her upper lip. The seat suddenly seemed too small, cramped, and she shifted uncomfortably.

Beside her Bradon swore gently.

Startled, she gasped. "What's the matter?"

"This damn pen gave out on me. Do you have one?"

"I'm afraid not. I lost mine somewhere, as usual."

"Maybe the stewardess has one I can borrow. Be right back."

He folded up the desk shelf and carefully secured his notebook in the pocket in front of his seat before he walked down the aisle.

Sandi searched for the airline's magazine in the pocket in front of her seat but there was none. There was one visible, however, in Bradon's seat pocket and she reached over and pulled it free. In the process his notebook also came free and fell to the floor. Sandi picked it up to put it back in the pocket, and a sheet of paper slipped from between the pages. She caught it quickly and was about to return it to its place when she noticed the letterhead at the top of the paper. Random House. They were book publishers. Could Bradon be writing a book?

She realized it was none of her business but, even as she slipped the letter back inside the notebook, her eyes involuntarily scanned the first lines. Two words leaped out at her: psychic regression.

Her hand froze. She had no power to stop reading the letter, and its words burned into her brain. They said that Random House would be very much interested in a case study of psychic regression. They would be especially interested in an account of his attempt to locate the woman who was the source of the regression! Oh, God! It was about her. She sat stunned. Hurt. Bradon was writing a book about her! He was not interested in helping her; he only wanted material for his book!

With trembling fingers, she opened his notebook.

"What are you doing?"

He was standing in the aisle, holding the borrowed pen, his eyebrows hooding his eyes in fury. He leaned over and snatched the notebook out of her hands, revealing the letter resting on her lap.

She picked it up. "What is this?"

Bradon's face went from dark red to a pale white as though an arctic wind had blown through his mind. Slowly he lowered himself into his seat. He made a small dismissive gesture with his hand as he said, "I'm sure you've figured it out for yourself. Random House is interested in a book I'm working on."

"A book about psychic regression."

"Well, yes. Part of it. Actually, it deals with several forms of the paranormal and its psychologic ramifications."

"That's a lie, Bradon. You know that's a lie. It's about me."

"Only part of it--"

"I knew it. I knew you set up that second episode."

"I told you I did."

"But you lied to me about why. It was just another chapter for your damn book."

"No. That's not true. I made notes, of course. I'm a practicing psychologist--"

"You're a psychopathic liar. That's why you came with me, so you could get material for your book. You didn't give a damn about my feelings.

"Only at first, I swear." Bradon reached for her hand but she yanked it away. "That was before--"

"Before you realized that you might have a chance at getting my body as well as my mind?" Her blazing anger abruptly gave way to a sense of despair so profound that her lips quivered and tears welled in her eyes. "Oh, Dan, I trusted you."

Sharp words of protest died on his lips. "All right," he said. "I have been thinking about a book. But that has nothing to do with the way I feel about you."

Her impulse was to turn away, to shut out Bradon and the world. But that would leave her forever drowning in pain. "I think," she said, "it has everything to do with it."

"You're wrong. I want to help you."

"I'm sure you do. If you succeed, it'll make a nice final chapter."

"That isn't the reason and you know it."

"I don't know it. You've never made any attempt to find out how I feel. You don't know what it means to me to find out about myself, to end this. To you it's nothing but a game. You don't give a damn about what happens to me. You don't care about anybody but yourself."

Bradon's face had drained of color. "That's not true," he whispered. "Not any more. Look, Sandi--"

Sandi interrupted by tossing the letter onto his lap. "Here," she said. Her tears had vanished, scorched dry by a bitter pain as sear as winter leaves. "Write your book. But from now on you'll get no help from me."

Bradon picked up the letter and for an instant, Sandi thought he was going to tear it up. Her glint of happiness vanished when, instead, he placed the letter back in the pages of his notebook. "I don't know how to convince you you're wrong."

"Don't try. I've had enough of your convincing."

"I'm trying to tell you--"

Sandi's hurt and anger burst forth in a grim warning. "Stay out of my life!" Her voice was quiet but she might as well have been screaming. "That's it! Just stay out!"

Bradon stared at her, his jaw working, before it clinched in tight control. The depth of her anger surprised him. He had not thought that anyone with such soft, warm eyes and such an evident, almost helpless, vulnerability could harbor such strength. Had her strength been there all the time and he had missed it? She was right about one thing: he had failed to see her as she really was.

It didn't seem possible that he could have been so wrong. Perhaps she had acquired the strength during their odyssey. Not likely. One did not acquire such hard-edged resolution overnight.

So, she must be right. He had been stupidly oblivious to her deeper feelings. Not that it made any difference now. She had made it very clear: She would never work with him again. She would probably never speak to him.

He gripped his chin with the palm of his hand, struggling to focus his thoughts. There had to be a way to regain her confidence. His mind seemed dead, refusing to respond. Maybe it would be best if he did get out of her life. A clean lobotomy. He could finish his book without her on his conscious. Once finished, there would be no reason to even think about her again. Any ghost of some long dead woman she might have inside her head was her problem.

Virtually the same thoughts were churning in Sandi's mind, but not for the same reason. It was best that she and Bradon were parting company. He had been occupying more and more of her thoughts, creating disturbing fires that had nothing to do with their quest. He was a specter insinuating himself between her and Jordan. Their relationship had to end. Relationship? It was all one-sided. Bradon's only interest in her was financial. The moment the plane landed he would be out of her life--forever. Never again would she see his smile, hear his voice, never feel his arms around her. So be it. If she could exorcise the other ghosts from her head, she could also exorcise him. Couldn't she?

Their parting outside the Bradley Terminal at LAX was stiff and formal. Her instinctive good manners made her say, "Thank you for your help."

Bradon's reply was equally cool. "Yes, well . . . If there's anything I can do to help, let me know."

She turned away, saying, "I don't think so."

And it was over.

She took a taxi to her home. She had deliberately refrained from informing her parents and Jordan of her arrival day. She knew they would disregard her instructions not to meet her at the airport, and she certainly didn't want them to see her with Dan Bradon. How could she possibly explain to Jordan why she was leaving the plane with her university professor? He would surely recognize Bradon from her descriptions. In addition to his Van Dyke beard not many men would have a sardonic twist to his lips that could shift from a cynical twist to a laugh-provoking grin with the bewildering elusiveness of liquid mercury.

She sat up straighter and focused on the passing scenery. She had to stop thinking about Bradon? Her respect for him had been shattered on the rock of perfidy. And when respect is gone, everything is gone, including love. No. Not love. She couldn't allow herself to believe what she had felt was love. Infatuation. Nothing more.

The taxi turned off the 405 Freeway at Sunset Boulevard and she caught a glimpse of the new Getty Museum high on a hill. How different her city was from those of Germany and Switzerland. She should be elated that she had concluded her mission. Instead, she felt bone weary, devoid of energy, with absolutely no sense of accomplishment. Homecoming should be a time of pleasure. Instead, she was filled with bitter tension. It was all Dan Bradon's fault.

Darn! He was doing it again, invading her mind. She had to forget him!

She sighed. What a fool; the truth was that she would never be able to forget Dan Bradon. But what to do about it? Instead of fighting the memories, she had to place them in a corner of her mind where they could gather cobwebs. Eventually, they would be absorbed into the warp and woof of her life's pattern where Bradon would simply become a single thread in a vast carpet of time. The day would someday come when she would not be able to sort him out from the thousands of other threads.

There was another thread that she intended to lose in the intricate paradigm of her life. This thread was labeled 'Helga Waltz'. If the voices ever returned, she now had a concrete personage she could deal with. No longer would she have to fight the stultifying fear that she was going crazy. Somehow this woman had invaded her mind from beyond the grave. If she ever tried it again . . . well . . . Armed with the weapon of truth, she could counter any new onslaught. "Back to your grave," she would say. "I want nothing to do with you."

Back to your grave?

Sandi jerked to attention. What if Helga Waltz was not in her grave? Many survivors of Hitler's Germany were still alive. She might be a woman in her eighties, or even nineties, but it was possible that she was still alive.

Sandi shook her head. Impossible. The banker had said she was dead. Besides, didn't regression mean that the spirit of the dead person took over the spirit of the living? How could Helga do that if she was still alive?

Sandi settled back in the seat. The argument was academic. Alive or dead, the woman called Helga was out of her life. Forever.

CHAPTER 19

Sandi should have been paying attention to the dance music. When she missed a beat, Jordan tightened his arm around her waist until she caught her balance.

"Sorry," he said.

"My fault," she answered. "Sorry." The music. Concentrate on the slow beat. Forget the last time she had danced. Forget that night in Berlin when the arms around her had belonged to Dan Bradon. Those days and nights, were part of the past. Now she must look to the future.

But the iron control she imposed on her mind was lost upon her body. Jordan's hand upon her back did not burn through the thin material of her dinner gown as had Bradon's. Jordan's hand holding hers did not have the same strength and tenderness as had Bradon's. And Jordan's body pressed against hers did not send waves of heat coursing through her stomach and thighs. Why? Why was her heart not thudding completely out of rhythm with the music as it had when she danced with Bradon?

"Damn," she muttered as she missed another beat.

"What?" Jordan said. "Is something wrong?"

"No, no. I guess I'm just out of practice."

"I suppose so. Want to sit down for a minute?"

Sandi said, "Yes," not because she didn't want to dance but because she wanted to make her body stop its betrayal. Especially since the betrayal was so false. Dan Bradon was not the man she loved, the man she was going to marry. It was Jordan. And her body had just better get that through its head.

Jordan held her hand, almost pulling her off the small dance floor. This was their first time together since Sandi had returned from her trip, and Jordan had suggested dinner at the Prescott in Santa Monica because the cuisine was superb and they had a small dinner orchestra. Ordinarily, Sandi loved dancing, but tonight she wished they had gone somewhere else.

In fact, it would have been better if she had postponed their date since she had absolutely no appetite, no energy.

At their table Jordan refilled her glass from the bottle of 1987 Cabernet Sauvignon he had carefully selected. Their dinner had arrived as they were dancing, and the waiter whisked away the metal covers that had been keeping the food warm. The aroma of perfectly prepared Colorado Lamb Loin with Guava and Mustard Tarragon Cabernet Sauce was tantalizing, making Sandi believe she really was hungry. After the first few bites, however, she resorted to picking at the food so that Jordan would not notice she was not enjoying the meal.

One more thing to make her feel guilty. Jordan had gone to a great deal of trouble to make sure their first date since her return was perfect. She had never seen him so warm and so solicitous of her every wish. If he noticed that she was not devouring the roast lamb with gusto, he chose to ignore it.

"I think December would be good. Just before Christmas."

Sandi looked up from her plate. "December?"

"For our wedding. I can arrange my schedule to be free by then." He mistook her solemn stare for skepticism and he added, "I know you want to wait until after your winter semester. But you can miss a class or two. I promise I won't interfere with your studies after that."

"December will be fine," Sandi said. She hated the listless quality in her voice. For Jordan's sake, she should exhibit some enthusiasm. "I've . . . I've cancelled my winter semester."

"Cancelled?"

The joy that appeared in his dark eyes turned the sharp knife of guilt in her stomach. He would be devastated if he knew that she had only cancelled so she would not have to be in the same room with Dan Bradon. "Yes," she said. "I think I'll transfer to USC or Pepperdine."

Disappointment replaced his joy in his eyes. "Oh."

Sandi reached across the table and put her hand over his. "But not until spring. We'll have the whole winter to ourselves."

He smiled, and breathed a low sigh. "Whew. You had me worried for a minute." He took her hand in both of his. It should have been a romantic gesture, but the thought that crossed Sandi's mind was wondering how he kept his hands and nails so immaculate. His hands always looked as though he had just scrubbed them with Boraxo. There was never a speck of darkness under his nails. Never a chip. Never a hangnail. Each nail was precisely trimmed the same length as though measured by micrometers. Her own nails seemed to attract dirt and destruction like magnets. It seemed that all she had to do was pick up a piece of paper, and she had then to scrape away grime and repair damaged polish. Some people had all the luck.

She became aware that Jordan was talking to her. "I know something's bothering you. I wish you could tell me what it is so I could help."

The concern in his voice made Sandi catch her lower lip in her teeth and tears misted her eyes. "It's not important. I'll work it out."

"You're the most stubborn person I ever met," he said with a rueful smile. "But I won't push. I just want you to know that I love you."

"I know. I love you too."

But her hand being held in his felt dead as though it belonged to someone else. She consoled herself with the thought that all she needed was a little time. Time would cleanse her memory, wipe away the past few weeks like images in a fading picture. December. Only a little more than a month. Would that really be enough time? It would have to be.

She began her healing process by going back to work in the art gallery. This filled her days with activities far removed from anything related to psychology and Dan Bradon. At night she kept his memories at bay by dates with Jordan and by helping her mother and father prepare for the wedding.

Her parents were jubilant. It wasn't only because of the wedding, although that was reason enough. It was also because Sandi had given up her ill-conceived search for some woman of the past. She had not told them all the details of her journey. But she had told them that the woman's name had turned out to be Helga von Luckenwalde. They had stared at her in silence as though expecting some cataclysmic pronouncement, and had shared her disappointment when Sandi had explained that nothing had come of her investigation.

Gretchen threw herself into planning for the wedding as though she wanted to get Sandi married before she could change her mind. "It'll be a big wedding, of course. Traditional. I've made reservations for the church. It seats five hundred."

"Five hundred," Sandi gasped. "We won't have that many."

"Almost," Gretchen exclaimed happily. "We'll be sending out at least two hundred invitations. And then there's Jordan's family. You'll have to help me with that."

"All right," Sandi agreed. Working with Jordan to develop the guest list and sending out invitations would fully occupy her mind, leaving no room for unwanted memories.

Her resolve was shaken, however, when her mother said, "Something old, something new, something borrowed, something blue. I'll see what I can find. There might be something in the attic. I think my old wedding gown is up there. I was about your size then."

The word 'attic' shot through Sandi's head like a driven spike; vivid images of the last time she was in an attic flashed through her mind. Her voice quivered with anticipated anguish when she asked, "Do you want me to look?"

"No, no. You've got enough to do. I know where things are."

Sandi unclenched her fists. Thank God. She wasn't sure she could cope with poking around a dusty attic. Maybe in fifteen or twenty years, but not now. "All right," she said. "Just be careful of those stairs."

Throughout the remainder of the day Sandi fought to suppress the memory of Dan Bradon and her in the darkness of the von Luckenwalde attic. If her mother insisted on rummaging through the attic for some old family memento, let her. If she fell down the stairs, if she got cobwebs in her hair, well, it was her idea.

But the attic seemed to exert an attraction that she found increasingly difficult to resist. Was the attic one more ghost that was going to haunt the rest of her life--like Dan Bradon? Well, she couldn't confront him, but she certainly could confront the ghosts in the attic. Then, when nothing happened, when there were no shattering memories, she would know that she was completely over Dan Bradon. Beside, she rationalized, there was a certain amount of danger involved. Her mother really could be hurt trying to climb the narrow stairs.

On the other hand, if it was dangerous, perhaps she shouldn't go up there alone. If she got hurt, who would know? But who could she ask to go with her. Her mother? Her father? Except that they were having lunch at the country club, probably inviting more people to the wedding. Gretchen had become so obsessed with making plans that she had signed up with a health spa and was exercising every day so she would look good at the wedding.

Who else could she ask? Of course. Jordan.

She picked up the telephone, hesitated, then slowly put it down. Jordan would never go any place that was filled with dust and cobwebs.

She snorted with disgust. Rationalizing again. The real reason she didn't call was because she could never go into an attic with Jordan. Not even with her mother or father. It was best that she challenge the memories alone whatever the peril.

Moving quickly so she wouldn't have time to change her mind, she changed into a T-shirt and jeans and knotted an old scarf over her hair.

At the end of the second floor hallway she paused in front of the door to the attic stairs. She reached for the knob, then stopped. Her heart thudded in an irregular beat, and her palms were slick with perspiration. What a fool she was! Only an idiot would force herself to do something she knew was going to be exquisitely painful. Turn around. Run.

Even as she struggled with doubt, her hand was turning the knob of the door. She took a deep breath, pulled. The door failed to budge. Was it locked? Or simply stuck from long disuse? Either way. it was the excuse she needed to give up.

She turned away, her heart already beginning to slow. But she couldn't give up. If she could not stop the memories, she had to find out if they had any power over her.

She wiped her damp palms on her pants legs, then grasping the knob in both hands. She braced herself and pulled hard. With a groan of protest, the door broke free. She swung it open and stood staring at the narrow flight of stairs that led upward into darkness.

She found a light switch inside the doorway and clicked it on. She was faintly surprised when a bare bulb at the top of the stairs illuminated. She'd expected that the lights wouldn't work after such long disuse.

There was no door at the top of the stairs and she saw with relief that lights had also come on inside the attic.

She started up the stairs, moving fast. But with every step, her pace slowed. The closer she came to it, the more the top of the stairs seemed like the entrance of a tomb.

She stopped, half way up the stairs. She needed time to prepare for the ghosts. Strange that in all the years she had lived in the house she had never been in the attic. It was one of those places that she knew existed, like the North Pole, but had no desire to visit.

She swayed and clutched the handrail to keep from falling. Why was she forcing herself into a test she could not win?

But she had to do it. She had to know.

She made it to the top by using her arms to pull on the handrail. Step by tortuous step she climbed, her eyes locked on the top of the stairs, staring, unblinking, her heart thudding wildly as though she expected a dark form to come hurtling toward her.

At the top of the stairs she paused to get her bearings. Since the house was constructed in the French style, the attic ceiling was low but flat all the way to the walls, creating a fairly large room. The floor was bare wood--pine it looked like--and, as she anticipated, covered with dust. Light from low-wattage bulbs scarcely disturbed the darkness.

Unlike the attic in Germany, this room was almost empty. Her parents were not savers; used objects and clothing held no sentimental value for them. The only items were a small suitcase, a wicker hamper, and a steamer trunk with rusted hinges and corner plates.

If the gown was here, it had to be in the trunk. She walked toward it, moving cautiously. Her footsteps stirred the dust, and a painful memory stabbed her. Why did dust smell the same the world over? A different odor would not have triggered such overwhelming desires. She could almost feel Bradon's arms around her, his lips on hers. Warm. Tender.

She had to get out! The attic was destroying her hold on reality as surely as Bradon's dark image.

She bolted to the stairway where she stopped, clutching the handrail for support. She would never make it down the steep stairs. Her legs were too weak. She was forced to wait, trying to thrust the memories aside so that her heart could slow and her strength return.

Damn the memories! Why did she have to be so stupidly weak?! Was she going to allow a brief encounter to destroy her life? No way! She was stronger than a memory.

She released her grip on the rail and wiped at her eyes. Tears? She had been crying! How dare he do that to her! "Damn you," she muttered. "I'm going to marry Jordan and no ghost is going to stop me!"

She turned and strode to the trunk. After a brief struggle with its rusty latch, she was able to raise the lid. Inside, on top of other old dresses, was her mother's wedding gown. The trunk had protected it from dust and she lifted it out tenderly. It was a beautiful soigne gown, obviously expensive, with a beaded, white satin bodice and a full skirt of peau de soie. A yoke of intricately woven Irish lace flared over the shoulders to form wrist-length sleeves that ended in scalloped lace cuffs. A long train of tulle was suspended from the bodice, and Sandi carefully held it clear of the dusty floor.

She held it against her. Her mother had been right about the size. With a few modifications, it did look as though it would fit.

She turned to carry the dress from the attic and almost fell when her foot caught on the edge of the nearby suitcase, stirring fresh motes of dust. She stared at the suitcase. It looked out of place, as though it was trapped in the attic. What could be in it that her parents thought worth saving? She poked it with her foot. It was light, dusty. Probably empty. Most likely it was just an old suitcase they had stored for future use and forgotten. But it was intriguing.

She carefully replaced the gown in the trunk and knelt to open the suitcase. At her touch its catches sprang open with loud clicks. She raised the top, half-expecting evil spirits to come swarming out. Old clothes. Nothing but old clothes, three old blouses and a black skirt. Under the skirt was a letter envelope of yellowing paper. Sandi reached for it. "Oh!" The sound exploded from her and she jerked her hand back. Something was terribly wrong! Her fingers trembled, and she was engulfed by a foreboding that made her stomach feel hollow.

Oh, God. Sandi hated the sensation. She knew what it meant and she hated it. Always it portended a shocking revelation of fear and violence, an assault on her mind that burned in new images like acid.

She reached to slam the cover! Damn! She could not! She could not!

She was frozen, staring at the letter. She dreaded touching it. But something would not allow her to walk away. If she did--if she could somehow simply refuse its impelling--the letter would burn in her mind with a haunting guilt.

In the vain hope that she could ameliorate the pain, she sucked in a breath and snatched up the letter and crumpled it in her fist!

Nothing!

There was no image! It was simply a wad of paper whose sharp edges pressed painfully into her palm. She had been fearful for nothing.

With a deep sense of relief, she closed the cover of the suitcase and used it as a table to smooth the envelope. There was a faded address: Mrs. Dennise Winters, 356 Michigan St., San Francisco, CA.

Winters? That was her mother's maiden name: Gretchen Winters. But who was Dennise? Sandi did not recall her mother ever mentioning a relative named Dennise.

Inside the envelope was a single sheet of stationary, folded in the center. She extracted the sheet and opened it. Wham! Shock slashed through her mind with an image so sharp and vivid that she gave a gasping scream and dropped the letter. Too late! Violence! Fire! Death! The woman who wrote the letter had died in shattering violence. The agony of her death was imbued into the fabric of the letter as surely as the ink of her writing.

Sandi's stomach churned. She swallowed hard. Who was the woman? How could her letter induce such a powerful image? How did such a shattering letter come to be in a suitcase belonging to her mother?

Sandi stared at her hands, willing them to stop trembling. But they were as much out of her control as was her pounding heart. She had to read the letter. She made her trembling fingers pick up the letter, steeling herself for the horrific shock. It did not come. It didn't need to. The image of death was seared into her brain. Why? She had to find out why.

Held in her trembling fingers, she could not read the letter. She had to hold it flat on top of the suitcase. In the dim light the faded writing was difficult to see. She blinked, trying to bring her eyes into focus. The writing was cramped, tremulous, as though written under great stress, the words marching across the unlined paper with an increasing slant. It was dated 4/12/75.

Dearest Dennise,

I've been trying to call you but something seems to be wrong with your telephone. I just found out the strangest thing. I was talking to mother and she let it slip that she had been married before she married dad. I think it was in Germany before she came here. I tried to find out more. She wouldn't say anything. She did warn me to be careful. She said something bad was going to happen. That kind of scared me. You know how psychic she is sometimes. Do you know anything about this? Call me, call me, call me.

Your loving sister,
Gretchen.

Gretchen? Her mother? Impossible. Her mother didn't have a sister. Besides, it was not her mother's handwriting. And the woman who had written the letter was dead. She had seen her die. In a horrible, fiery accident?

Who was she? How could she cause such terrible images? Could the answer be in the letter?

As much as she dreaded it, she had to pick it up. Perhaps nothing would happen. She could not remember a time when the initial shock had been repeated.

Gingerly, holding her breath, Sandi picked up the letter. When nothing happened, she breathed deeply and pressed the letter between her palms.

Nothing. No image; no sensation of any kind. "All right," she gritted. "Come on; come on."

After a frustrating moment, she folded the letter and replaced it in the envelope. Why had she been cursed with such a 'gift' without controls? It was not fair that an object could jar her with unwanted images. Then, when she desperately needed information, it refused to obey her summons.

She tried to recall what she had seen. As usual, the image had appeared as a jolting flash, like a scene revealed in a nanosecond burst of lightning.

She closed her eyes and concentrated on the brief chimera. An automobile. The woman who wrote the letter had been riding in an automobile. An auto accident! Of course! But where? San Francisco?

Sandi pressed her fingers to her temples where a nascent headache was beginning to throb. She had to get out of the attic. There was too much pain closing in from the dark shadows.

Her mind reeling, she stumbled down the stairs. She reached to turn out the light. The awful letter. It was still in her hand! She dropped it, recoiling as though from a serpent.

She stared at the envelope. It looked so innocuous lying face down on the bottom step. She licked her dry lips. It should not be left there. And she desperately wanted to ask her mother about it.

Squinting with anxiety, she picked up the envelope. Again, there was nothing. No shock. No image. It was as though the letter had conveyed its message and was now dead.

Holding the letter by one corner, she turned out the attic light and closed the door. Only then did she remember the wedding gown. She should go back and get it. But she could not. Not yet. At the moment the attic was the home of more ghosts than she could handle.

In her father's den, she got out the family photograph album and leafed back through the pictures, trying to find a clue to the identity of Dennise. There were not many pictures. Her parents had never been obsessed with keeping photographic memories. Most of those in the album were of herself during her early years. There were few pictures of her mother or father before they had married. And no reference at all to anyone named Dennise.

It had been years since she had looked through the album, and now, slowly examining the pages, it began to dawn on Sandi that there were no pictures of her mother's parents. There were a few of Martin's mother and father, looking stiff and uncomfortable in their Sunday clothes. But there was not a single picture of Gretchen's mother or father.

She was still puzzling over the pictures when she heard her parent's car entering the circular driveway. Carrying the album and the letter she went to meet them. As they entered the door, she asked them to come into the living room. Her mother noticed the photograph album and a deep furrow appeared between her eyes, "Is that our album?"

"Yes," Sandi answered. "I get a kick out of some of these old pictures."

"I hate them," Martin said as he led the way into the living room.

"They make me feel old."

While her father made Martinis for himself and her mother at the corner bar, Sandi picked up the letter. "I was in the attic today," she began, "looking for your wedding gown."

"That wasn't necessary," Gretchen said. "I told you I'd get it."

"I know. But I was impatient."

"Understandable," Martin said. "I'd like to see it myself. Bring back a lot of memories."

"Next time," her mother said, "don't go up there alone. If you got hurt there'd be no one to help you."

"There was an old suitcase up there too." Sandi held up the letter. "I found this letter."

Martin scarcely glanced up, but Gretchen took a quick step toward Sandi. "Let me see that." Her voice had an icy ring that brought back memories to Sandi of when as a child she had done something terrible and could expect punishment.

But she was no longer a child and, as she handed the letter to her mother, her own voice was firm. "I don't understand. It looks like a letter from you to someone named Dennise Winters. Who was she?"

Martin's hand jerked, sloshing liquid from his drink. Gretchen's fingers, caught in the act of opening the letter, froze for an instant and color drained from her face. Then her lips tightened and she opened the letter. She scarcely glanced at it as though she already knew its contents and only wanted to confirm its authenticity. "I suppose you're mature enough to know," she said. "Dennise Winters was my sister."

Sandi stared at her mother. "Sister? You never mentioned having a sister."

Gretchen touched her tongue to her lips as though they had become dry. She sat down on the couch and stared at the letter accusingly as though it was at fault for interrupting the smooth flow of her life. "She did not lead an . . . exemplary life. We chose to pretend she did not exist."

"But in the letter you asked her to call you."

"It was only because of that dreadful rumor. I wanted to know if she knew anything about it."

"About your mother being married once before?"

"That's right."

"What did she say?"

"Nothing. She was killed in an automobile accident."

So the image was true. There had been an accident. Sandi thought her mother was strangely dispassionate about the loss of her sister. But, then, she'd said that they were not close.

"Fortunately," Gretchen continued, "the whole thing proved to be nothing more than gossip." She put the letter back in the envelope and tossed it toward Sandi in a gesture of total indifference. "Please put this back where you found it."

Sandi picked the letter up from the floor. She knew that her mother did not want to discuss the matter further, but she could not allow the door to be closed until she had more answers. "It didn't look like your handwriting."

Her mother's eyes narrowed. "I was younger then. And I would prefer not to discuss it."

As a child Sandi would have cringed at her mother's cold stare and fled the room. Even now it was difficult for her to hold her ground. She extended the photograph album. "Is her picture here? I'd like to see what she looked like."

Her mother made no move to take the album. "No. I have no pictures of her."

"Not even when you were children?"

Martin said, "Sandi. Your mother has said she doesn't want to discuss this. Let it drop."

Sandi stared at their set faces. When they had that look, further discussion was useless. She put down the album, but kept the letter as she went to the door. Before she left he room, she turned back. "Where was the accident?"

Martin lifted his hand. "Enough," he snapped. "The subject is closed."

Her mother's chill stare said that she agreed. The subject was closed.

Sandi started toward the attic, then stopped. She wanted to examine the letter more closely. In her room she held the letter under a strong light, but could find nothing she hadn't seen before. The only difference was the knowledge that the accident was real. Dennise Winters was dead. But there was no indication of when the accident could have occurred nor where. But since Dennise had not answered the letter, the accident must have occurred reasonably close to the date of the letter. She checked the date again: April, 1975.

Putting the letter aside, she examined the envelope. The post office cancellation stamp read San Francisco. That was not surprising. Her mother had grown up in San Francisco. If it wasn't for the unfamiliar handwriting, she could dismiss the letter from her mind. Her mother simply had a sister of whom she had been ashamed for some reason. She had died in an automobile accident. Her mother harbored no grief at the loss. She wanted the incident closed.

Folding the letter Sandi placed it back in its envelope, then put it inside the drawer of her bedside table. Tomorrow she would return it to its place in the attic. There was no reason, except for her curiosity, why she should not respect her mother's wishes to drop the matter. She had managed to lock away her own ghosts, why shouldn't she allow her mother to do the same with hers?

But that night as she prepared for bed after returning from an uneventful dinner with Jordan and her parents, she couldn't stop thinking about the letter. How could her mother's handwriting have changed so much? And was Dennise Winters an older or younger sister?

She sighed and shook her head. That's all she needed: another quest. The search for Helga Waltz had been traumatic enough; there was no point in disrupting her life again by chasing another will-of-the wisp.

She opened the drawer in the bedside table, intending to move the letter as far away from her as possible, short of returning it to the attic. Going up those stairs at night was something she could never do. Reaching for the letter, she paused. The letter was gone! Sandi pulled the drawer all the way open. Except for a note pad she always kept in the drawer, it was empty.

Had she put the letter there? Yes. She remembered clearly that she had. Could she have moved it and forgotten? She searched her memory, retracing her preparations for dinner with Jordan and her parents. No, she had not moved the letter; she was sure of it. So who had?

It could have been her mother or father. After dressing for dinner, she had waited for them downstairs, talking to Jordan. So they had the opportunity. But why? Were they afraid that she would lose it? It was only a letter, for heaven's sake. Not even important according to her mother.

Sandi gritted her teeth in irritation. She had intended to put the letter back in the suitcase. Didn't they trust her to do so? Obviously not. Well, it was gone, out of her life. So that was the end of it, except for a lingering doubt about her mother's motives. Plus a recalcitrant curiosity about Dennise Winters. What had she been like? It would be nice to have an aunt, even a black sheep aunt.

The incongruous thought made her chuckle. The events of the last few weeks must be making her mother think that Sandi was another black sheep. No wonder she had taken the letter. Her daughter was acting crazy enough without having some peculiar letter throwing gasoline on the fire.

Sandi was still smiling when she snuggled in her bed and waited for sleep. But it wasn't an image of the letter that invaded her sleepy mind. It was the face of Dan Bradon. She missed seeing him; she missed the warm look in his eyes when they talked, his smile that came so often and easily. Damn. Why had he ruined their friendship by lying? Why couldn't he have told her about his plans for a book? If he had been honest, she might have given her permission, perhaps even helped him. Then they could have remained friends.

Even as the thought gave her a warm sense of pleasure, she knew that it was impossible. She and Bradon could never be just friends. There was some dark attraction between them that eventually would have spilled over into . . . into what? Not love. What she felt for Jordan was love. Bradon was like the devil trying to steal her soul. What she had felt for him was fascination, like a moth drawn to a flame. It was best that she had snuffed out the flame before it could consume her.

Sometime in the night during a dream of Bradon's lips on hers, a dream of his strong, sensitive fingers caressing her back as they held each other close in a sensual tango, the dream dissolved into a blur of trees swept by a car's headlights as it sped along a two lane road.

*   *   *   *

Richard was driving fast but carefully, not outrunning the headlights. He would take no chances with her sitting beside him and holding their baby in her arms.

Then, suddenly, she gasped as out of nowhere the dark form of another car appeared beside them dangerously close. Richard shot an angry look across at the other car and shouted, "Turn on your lights, you--"

His voice broke off as the other car swerved, smashed into them. The thudding impact yanked the steering wheel out of Richard's hands, sending the car hurtling off the road into darkness that she knew was a canyon. The car seemed to hang in the air forever and she cradled her baby. She was not frightened. The thought that went through her mind was a wonder of what it was going to be like to be dead. Then there was a thundering crash, and a bright burst of light.

*   *   *   *

Sandi jerked to a sitting position in her bed. Her heart was pounding, her breath laboring. Her nightgown was wet with perspiration. Richard? Who was Richard? And who was the woman? It was not Helga. Of that, she was certain. Dennise? Her mother's sister. And the baby? Had the baby survived?

What had triggered such a horrible nightmare? Could it have been the letter? No. It was something her mother had said, something about her sister having been killed in a car accident. The suggestion must have triggered her imagination.

She sat on the edge of the bed and clutched at her hair with both hands. Why on earth did she have to be so susceptible to suggestion? Why couldn't she just go through life like other people, living her own life, only hers. It was something she was definitely going to work on right after she got back from San Francisco.

She snapped on her beside lamp. Back from San Francisco! Where had that stupid thought come from? Her parents had been dead set against her going to Europe; they would have apoplexy if she told them she was going to San Francisco. This time she would not be able to hide the reason.

Her father and mother were not fools. They would suspect it was because of the letter even if she told them a lie.

The best course was to just go. She remembered a quotation: 'It is easier to obtain forgiveness than to obtain permission.'

She would leave a note so they wouldn't worry, then explain when she returned. Explain? She couldn't even explain to herself. She only knew that she had to go; she had to know more about the death of Dennise Winters.

CHAPTER 20

The following morning, Sandi checked into the tower of the Fairmont Hotel where she and her parents had stayed on her only previous visit to San Francisco. As before, Sandi was both fascinated and terrified in riding the hotel's glass-walled, outside elevator. Since the Fairmont was situated atop Nob Hill, the ride began at a fearful height above the city. Even though a glorious panorama of San Francisco Bay widened as the elevator crawled up the outside of the tower, Sandi would have turned her back if she could have done so without feeling like a fool in front of the accompanying bellman.

Only from the safety of her suite, did she begin to enjoy the spectacular view. In the bedroom, it took but a few minutes to unpack her single suitcase. Since she had no intention of going out on the town in the evening, she had only brought day clothing warm enough for November, plus one dinner ensemble. With any luck she would complete her research in one day and by tomorrow night be on a plane back to LA.

She checked her watch. 10:00 A.M. After freshening her makeup, and making sure she had a note pad and pen in her purse, she rode the elevator to the lobby. This time with no bellman to impress, she did face away from the view, turning for a quick peek only when the elevator neared the ground floor.

On the street she considered asking for a taxi. But the day was cool and the sun glorious so she decided to walk the few blocks to the San Francisco main library. Even though she loved Los Angeles, it was so spread out that there were few places one could reach by walking. But San Francisco, hemmed in by water on three sides, was compact so that a person could walk from place to place, if you didn't mind trudging up and down a few hills.

The hills reminded her of San Francisco's cable cars and, although it was a little out of the way, she walked to Powell Street and swung aboard the first car that came by. She gawked like an awe struck tourist as the car rumbled down Nob Hill to Market Street.

In the central library she asked for all back issues of the San Francisco Examiner of April and May, 1975. Her mother had said that Dennise had been killed in an auto accident before she could answer the letter, so it must have happened some time in April or, possibly, May.

The back issues were on microfiche and the librarian showed her how to use the viewing machine. At first Sandi was all thumbs but after a little practice she was able to skim rapidly through the pages of the paper, searching for automobile accidents.

It took her more than an hour to examine all the pertinent pages of April issues. There was an abundance of auto accidents reported, but none mentioned anyone named Dennise Winters.

She moved to the May issues and in the issue of May 2nd a small item caught her eye. The headline read "FAMILY KILLED BY HIT AND RUN". Scanning the article, a name leaped out at her: Dennise Winters!

Holding her breath as though afraid the least tremor would destroy the delicate image on the screen, she began reading the article. It told a story of a young man, Richard Banks, who was killed while driving at night on a back road in the Montara Mountains near Half Moon Bay. Apparently, his car had been struck by a hit and run driver and forced off the road. Also killed in the accident was his passenger, Dennise Winters, sister of Bank's wife, Gretchen.

Sandi stared at the print. Bank's wife Gretchen? It had to be a reporter's error. She scanned the remainder of the article. The only survivor of the accident was Dennise Winters' infant child. Banks and his sister-in-law had been on their way to Half Moon Bay to visit Helen Winters, mother of Dennise and Gretchen.

Sandi's throat tightened and she swallowed painfully. A confusion of names, places and voices swirled through her mind as though the walls she had so painfully built had burst. She put her hands over her ears in an attempt to shut out the cacophony but there was no shutting out the discordant voices. "What is it you want?" she murmured. "What do you want of me?"

But, as always, there was no clear answer, merely an urgent insistence that she was supposed to do something, that the voices would never be quiet until she fulfilled some mission. What did it have to do with Helga Waltz? One of the voices had to belong to Dennise. She was sure of it. But which one? And what did she want? Like a fool she had ignored her apprehension and come to San Francisco. Now she either had to go through the slow and agonizing process of building new defenses, or . . . Or what? Or still the voices once and for all by finding their source. Actually, she had no choice. She had come too far to turn back.

After making a photocopy of the article, she began walking back to the hotel. She had no thought of taking a taxi or a cable car. She had to think and walking always helped her sort out her thoughts. Oh, God. Why had Dan Bradon betrayed her? She wanted desperately to ask him what she should do. The process of explaining to him what was happening inside her head would be a catharsis. Just feeling him there beside her, his shoulder brushing hers, their hands touching, would help her deal with the whispers that seared her mind like incessant flames.

She braced her shoulders and lifted her chin. The hell with Dan Bradon. She didn't need him. She would deal with this problem herself, just as she had dealt with problems all her life. The first thing to do was go to the site of the accident. If there were ghosts to be found, they would be there.

She cringed at the idea. There had been two terrible deaths. Any images she might find would explode with pain and horror. Should she subject herself to that?

But maybe there would be no images, no wrenching scenes. They never seemed to occur when she wanted them. It would probably be like that this time. Because she desperately wanted to know what had happened. She had to know or she really would go mad.

It was late afternoon when Sandi skirted a grove of pines and stopped her rental car beside the self-service pumps of a small gas station. According to her map, the station was located just west of a placed called Cahill Ridge on Route 92 that wound from San Francisco Bay over the mountains to Half Moon Bay. She had chosen the station because it looked as though it had been there for many years. Taking her credit card from her purse, she entered the station's tiny office. An elderly woman was sitting in a canvas director's chair behind a counter where she had a view of the pumps through a sparkling clean front window. The counter supported an old cash register and an assortment of candies, trinkets, maps, and a rack of dark glasses.

The woman looked up from a magazine in her lap, peering at Sandi through bifocals. "Self-service," she said. "Pay after you get your gas."

Sandi smiled at her. "Aren't you afraid I might fill up and just take off?"

"Better not." The woman's wolfish smile showed dentures. "I got your license number."

Sandi widened her smile. "And the sheriff is a friend of yours."

The woman's answering smile was as broad as Sandi's. "Son-in-law."

Sandi laughed softly. "Well, here's my credit card so you won't have to worry about me. You do take credit cards?"

The woman took the card without getting up. "Got to. Nobody's got cash any more, less'n it's pennies. Use 'em myself."

Sandi made a show of looking out the window at the forest of pine and spruce trees that crowded the station. Even inside the office the air was rich with the scent of pines. "You must love it up here. I'll bet you've been here a long time."

"Born here. Raised four kids."

Sandi took the photocopy of the newspaper article from her purse. "Would you by any chance remember this accident? It happened back in 1975"

The woman took the paper and peered at it through the bottom of her glasses. "Hit and run. Sure, I remember. Don't get many of them up here."

A surge of excitement tightened Sandi's chest. It was happening.

Until now the accident and her involvement had seemed like fiction, as though she was playing a part in a macabre story. But with the woman's words, the story became real. "Do you know where it happened?"

The woman made a vague motion toward the west. "About a mile down the road." She peered at Sandi, actually looking at her for the first time. "You know those people?"

"I want to find out what happened to the baby."

Hearing her own blurted words, Sandi caught her breath. Why had she said that? She wanted to find out about Dennise Winters. But the thought must have been incubating inside her head that Dennise Winters' baby might be the key. If she was still alive, and if Dennise really was her mother's sister, then she had a cousin she had never met. It gave Sandi a strange sensation to realize that some part of her could be out there in the world, unaware that she had living relatives.

"Yes," the woman said. "I heard that girl had a baby." She shook her head slowly. "Probably a drunk driver."

"Probably," Sandi said.

She went to the pump and filled the car's tank. After signing her credit slip for the purchase, she said as she turned toward the door. "About a mile, you said?"

"That's right. First canyon you come to. They put up a guardrail after it happened." She made a snorting noise. "Stupid. If they'd put it up before, those people'd still be alive."

As Sandi went out the door, the woman called, "If you're going down there, you better hurry. Fog's coming in."

"I will," Sandi answered. "Thanks."

What the woman had said about the guardrail occupied Sandi's mind as she drove west on the highway while keeping an eye on the car's odometer. If there had been a guard rail, if the people had not been killed, would her own life have been different? Probably not. Her mother had never mentioned Dennise. If she hadn't found the letter, she would never have known the woman existed.

By the time the odometer indicated she had traveled almost a mile, darkness was gathering and tendrils of fog, riding an on-shore breeze, were drifting up from the Pacific. Fortunately, there were few cars on the road so that Sandi was able to drive slowly without impeding traffic while looking for the canyon and guardrail.

There it was. The guardrail. She swung to the shoulder of the road and parked. She turned off the car's engine but remained in the car, staring into the fog-misted canyon. The canyon was more shallow than she had expected, dipping scarcely twenty feet below the level of the road. But it was choked with brush and several large pine trees. If a car was going very fast and hit one of the trees, the results could easily be fatal to its passengers.

It took all her resolve to climb out of the car and slowly walk toward the metal guardrail. Her legs were stiff, leaden, unwilling to move. Tension sent a dull pain along her spine. All her senses were locked on the canyon, shutting out all other sights and sound.

She stopped beside the low guardrail, staring down into the canyon, watching tendrils of fog swirl and twist through the shadows of the trees, expecting something horrible to flash into her head. In the gathering darkness, the silence was ominous, the trees looking like waiting gargoyles. Which one was the killer? What could it tell her?

She ripped her gaze away. She reached down and picked up a handful of gravel and squeezed hard so that the sharp edges of the rocks hurt her hands. Good. This was reality. She threw the gravel into the canyon and heard the rattle of rocks striking brush.

So. The canyon wasn't a doorway to hell. It was only a canyon.

She climbed over the guardrail and picked her way through the rocks and brush, watching for some indication of the accident. Cold fingers of fog crawled over her flesh so that she welcomed each painful scratch from the brush as her hold on reality.

Nothing. Not a sign of an accident. Was she in the right place?

She stumbled and caught her balance by putting her hand on the trunk of a large pine tree. Abruptly an explosion of brilliant red and white colors jarred her as though she had been struck in the head by a powerful blow.

She grunted with pain and jerked her hand back, falling to her knees. This was where Dennise had died in a brilliant explosion of pain. But buried in the pain was a horrible dread: her baby! What would happen to her baby!

She had to get away from here!

Half walking, half crawling Sandi clawed her way up the slope to the road. She dragged herself over the guardrail and braced unsteadily against a support post. Which way was her car? Gathering darkness and wisps of fog added to her confusion. That way. Back the way she had come.

Her halting steps sounded unnaturally harsh in the roadside gravel. There. The car, looking solid and real despite the metamorphic fog. She almost ran the rest of the way, stopping only when she could put her hands on solid metal. Her panting breath slowed as the coldness of the metal cleared her mind. She had found the scene of the accident and, except for the fact that Dennise Winters' last thought was concern for her baby, she had learned nothing new. Now she could put the accident behind her.

She opened the car door and when she saw her purse on the passenger's seat where she had left it, she shook her head in chagrin. What had she been thinking to leave the car unlocked and her purse in plain view? She must never again get so caught up in something that she forgot such basic rules of survival. She had even left the car keys in the ignition switch. Stupid.

She reached for the keys. Suddenly, a powerful arm reached from the back seat of the car and clamped around her neck. Her scream of shocked surprise ended abruptly as the arm tightened. In the car's rear view mirror she caught a glimpse of a man's face, young, coarse, a tangle of black hair, a stubble of black whiskers, staring, bulging eyes. The eyes of a maniac! She tried to wrench loose, bucking and heaving, clawing at the arm.

Oh God! He was too strong! She couldn't breath! He was going to kill her! And she could do nothing! As a pit of darkness swallowed her, the thought that echoed through her mind was fool! fool! fool!

CHAPTER 21

Throbbing pain. Pain in her throat. Pain pounding inside her head. Sandi's eyelids fluttered and faint light stabbed her eyes. Her chest heaved as air was forced in. Her mouth was open and her nose pinched shut. Lips were on hers. Someone was blowing air into her mouth. Lazily, as though in a dream, a thought penetrated the pounding in her head: C.P.R. Somebody was giving her C.P.R. Strange. She couldn't remember drowning.

Suddenly, memory rushed back.

The man! She had to get away!

She fought to sit up, pushing at the figure leaning over her. a mew of terror wrenching from her injured throat.

The hands shifted to grip her shoulders and a familiar voice said, "Easy, Sandi. Take it easy. You're okay. You're okay."

Bradon! Oh, God. It was Dan Bradon.

Strength went out of her and if it hadn't been for Bradon's hands on her shoulders, she would have collapsed. He sat down beside her and pulled her against his chest protectively. "It's all right." His voice was soothing, easing away the hurt and fear. "It's all right."

Bradon's chest felt so protective, his arms so strong and warm, that Sandi tried to keep her mind numb so she could make the pleasure last.

An image ruptured her pleasure. A man's face: young, course, a stubble of black beard. And eyes! Horrible, bulging eyes!

She stiffened and gasped, whispered, "Is he--is he gone?"

Bradon pulled her back against his chest. "He's gone. Don't worry. Just rest a minute."

Sandi started to relax and winced as pain cut her legs. She was sitting on the shoulder of the road in front of her car. Small pebbles and rocks gouged painfully into her buttocks and legs. The night had closed in, thickening the fog. How had she gotten here?

She pushed away from Bradon. "What is this?" Her voice was stronger now. "What are you doing here?"

Bradon rose to a kneeling position. He studied her face, his brows pulled into a worried frown. "I'm glad you're feeling better. You had me worried."

Sandi touched her throat. It felt bruised. It hurt to swallow. "He tried to kill me."

"I know. I got here just in time."

"It was stupid of me. I left my door unlocked."

"You had a lot more on your mind than locking your door."

Sandi glanced into the fog shrouded darkness in the direction of the canyon. "That's right. I was thinking about--" She stopped as she remembered why she was here.

"The accident." Bradon said. "It must have given you a hell of a shock."

Sandi leaned back on her braced arms, staring at him. "How did you know about it? What are you doing here anyway?"

Bradon got to his feet and held out his hands. "Let's go somewhere we can talk."

After he helped her to her feet, Bradon kept his grip on her hands until her legs felt as though they would bear her weight without collapsing. "We'd better take my car," Bradon said. "We can come back for yours when you feel stronger."

"The police," Sandi said. "We should report this to the police."

"Right. But first, a cup of coffee."

Hot coffee sounded good. She was tired, aching pain wracking her muscles. The thought of spending hours filling out reports, looking at mug shots was far from appealing. She had barely glimpsed the man's face in the mirror, and while she might recognize him if she ever saw him in person, she wasn't sure she could identify him from pictures.

"I guess I should report it," she said. "But . . . would it do any good?"

"I doubt it. He had a car. I heard it start after I ran him off. He's probably miles from here by now."

"Maybe later," she said. "I need to sit down for a while."

"There's a restaurant in Half Moon Bay. Have you had dinner?"

"No." She touched her throat. "I'm hungry. But I'm not sure I can swallow."

"Soup," Bradon said. "Chicken soup. It'll cure anything."

The Italian restaurant was small with the de rigueur red and white checkered table cloths. Bradon and Sandi were the only customers. With the sound of surf in the distance and a cold night fog held at bay by the front windows, the restaurant was warm and cozy. After Sandi had a glass of tart Valpolicella wine and a bowl of minestrone soup, her throat felt better and she ordered lasagna thinking it would be soft enough to swallow without hurting.

While waiting for their orders to arrive, Sandi sorted through a myriad of questions she had for Bradon. In the restroom she had managed to restore a small sense of order to her hair and to her makeup and clothing so that she felt ready to cope with anything he had to say. But despite her desire to appear unconcerned, the questions began to pour out in a rush, "What were you doing there? How did you find me? Were you following me? I told you I didn't want to see you anymore. So what are you doing here?"

Bradon help up both hands. "Whoa. Whoa. First, I wasn't following you. I never expected to see you--here."

"Then what were you doing?"

Bradon took a deep breath. "To tell the truth, I couldn't get you out of my mind."

"I'll bet. I'm probably in every page of your book."

"Not that way. I've, uh, I've decided not to write the book."

Sandi felt such an unexpected joy that she was sure it showed in her face. She ducked her head and took a sip of wine. With the book out of the way, his betrayal did not seem so horrible, so final. But perhaps he was lying. The only way to find out, however shattering it might be, was to ask. "Then why were you following me?"

"I wasn't. I've been going over government records--trying to find out what happened to Helga Waltz. I was investigating that accident."

Sandi almost dropped her wineglass. "Helga? What on earth did she have to do with the accident?"

Bradon gave her an odd look, a look of incredulity. "The woman who was killed in the accident, Dennise, was her daughter. You didn't know that?"

Sandi put down her glass. Her voice was a whisper. "Her daughter? Dennise Winters?"

"That's right."

"But her mother was Helen Winters."

"Helga von Luckenwalde changed her name back to her maiden name, Helga Waltz, after her husband was hanged at Nuremberg Prison. She was pregnant at the time. According to Army records, Helga came to the United States--to San Francisco. That's where she had their baby. Then she married a man named Joseph Winters. Oh yes, and she Americanized her name. Changed Helga to Helen."

Sandi closed her eyes. Helen Winters was Helga von Luckenwalde. Black spots swam in front of her closed eyelids and her body felt empty, lifeless.

Bradon thrust back his chair and came to put his hands on her shoulders. "Jesus. I thought you knew. I'm sorry." He reached for her wineglass. "Here. This'll help."

Sandi took a swallow of the wine and the pungent liquid brought feeling back to her body.

Bradon peered at her face. "That's better." He went back to his chair. "If you didn't know about Helen Winters, what were you doing there?"

"I found out . . ." Sandi took another sip of wine and started over. "My mother's maiden name was Winters. Gretchen Winters. That woman who was killed--Dennise Winters--was her sister."

Bradon made a low whistle. "Helen Winters--Helga Waltz--was your grandmother? My God. No wonder she was in your mind."

Sandi sucked in air, unable to talk. For once her mind was not churning with thoughts. It had gone blank, as though the night fog had taken over, obliterating every thought, every memory.

She felt burning hot, stifled. She pushed to her feet and went to stare out the front window. The fog swirling eerily beneath the streetlights was like her thoughts: nebulous, terrifying. She pressed her forehead against the cold glass. It was so confusing. Names revolved in her mind like pinwheels with no beginning and no end. Helga, Richard, Hermann, Dennise, Gretchen, Martin.

Bradon came to stand behind her. He put his arms around her waist, pulling her gently back against him. At first she stiffened, resisting his intrusion. She was not ready for new emotions, not now. She could scarcely cope with the thoughts that were already threatening to pull her apart. She could not face a whole new wave of emotions that Bradon's nearness could bring. And yet, his arms were pillars of strength that she desperately needed.

Gratefully, she leaned her head back against his shoulder, feeling his warm breath in her hair.

"Your mother's name is Gretchen?"

His words cut through the fog, and she began the painful task of sorting out the truth. "Yes."

Bradon continued, his voice low, speculative. "Helen Winters had two children. Gretchen and Dennise. Gretchen was the oldest. Hermann von Luckenwalde was her father. Otto Winters was Dennise's father. The girls were half sisters. Same mother, different fathers."

Sandi covered her face with her hands. "My mother had to know. Why didn't she tell me?"

"Maybe she was ashamed of what happened to her father. Helga was. That's why she changed her name, left Germany." He chuckled softly. "But she was smart enough to put the von Luckenwalde money in that Swiss bank first."

Sandi only half heard him. "Dennise's baby didn't die in the accident," she said. "I wonder what happened to her."

"Dennise? She never married. She didn't have any children."

Sandi stared at him. "Oh, you're wrong. Back there. At the accident. The last thing she thought of was her baby."

"The baby was . . ." Bradon paused. "You'd better brace yourself. The baby was Gretchen's. Her father was Gretchen's first husband, Richard Brooks."

Information was coming to fast for Sandi's confused mind to assimilate, and she turned to face Bradon. "The baby belonged to Dennise. It said so in the paper."

"The paper got it wrong."

"You said 'her'. A girl?"

"Yes. A girl." Bradon stared at her, a strange expression on his face. "The baby's name was Susanna."

Sandi shook her head, trying to make the truth go away. "Me?

Martin isn't my father?"

"Not if you're Susanna Brooks."

Sandi moved away from Bradon. Her legs were numb, the room rocking unsteadily. She had to think this through without the distraction of Bradon's arms around her. At the table she sat down and pressed the heels of her palms against her eyes. If her mother had been married before Martin--to Richard Brooks--if Martin was not her real father--why had they kept it a secret? She knew people sometimes kept family secrets from their children. Their reason was to spare the child from some ugly reality. In her case it was probably to protect her from the knowledge that her grandfather had been hanged as a war criminal.

But she would have wanted to know. No wonder they had been upset when she told them about Helga and that she was going to Germany to find her. The truth must have been a heavy burden for her mother through the years. But it was a burden she didn't have to carry. There was no reason for her to feel shame for anything that Hermann von Luckenwalde might have done. That had happened a world away, in another time.

Suddenly Sandi wanted to see her mother, to tell her that she loved her more than ever. "I wonder if I can get a flight out of San Francisco tonight?"

"Tonight?" Bradon sat down across from her. "I suppose you could. They have flights practically around the clock."

Sandi shook her head as she realized how impractical such a flight would be. "I've got to turn in my car and check out of my hotel. I'd better wait until tomorrow."

"I think that would be better. In fact, I'll drive you back to your hotel. You've got too much on your mind to be driving in this weather."

"What about my car?"

"We'll come back for it in the morning. You can drop it off at the airport. Where are you staying?"

Sandi smiled. "You might want to change your mind. In San Francisco. The Fairmont."

He made a face. "Ouch. I was hoping it was here in the Bay. Just kidding. I'm staying in the city myself."

During the long drive to her hotel, made even longer by the fog, she had plenty of time to ponder what she had learned. Her mother and father--correction, her mother and Martin--must have agonized over whether or not to keep the past from her. In the end, they had elected to protect her from the truth. All the time she had been in Germany, trying to find clues to her past, they must have prayed that her grandmother had covered her tracks well.

Now, she had a decision to make. When she arrived home, should she confront them with what she had learned? Or should she pretend that she had learned nothing and allow her life to settle into its previous rut?

She leaned her head back against the car's headrest and smiled to herself. Rut? A strange choice of words. But, of course, compared to the excitement of the past few weeks, her old life had been in something of a rut. After she was married to Jordan all that would change. It would be a totally new existence, with new friends, new responsibilities, and the excitement of making love with the man she loved.

She stared out the window at the fog and the darkness. The lights of passing cars swam out of the mist like specters and vanished back into the darkness. She knew she was avoiding thinking about going to bed with Jordan. Which was strange considering how many years she had fantasized about the glory of making love with the man she married, of feeling his lips on hers, of surrendering to his caresses and, at last, giving herself totally to him.

She turned her head to look at Bradon. He was hunched forward, staring intently through the windshield, concentrating on driving through the fog, oblivious to her steady gaze. He looked tired. His chiseled features seemed drawn. And there was a darkness under his eyes she had never seen before, as though he had not been sleeping well. She probably had the same drawn look herself. But her fatigue was caused by worry about her past. Then, too, thinking about her wedding had cost her a lot of sleep. Bradon's fatigue was probably caused by too many nights out with too many women.

Had he really abandoned his book? Sandi sat up straighter. If so, why? But if that was true, why was he here? Why was he trying to locate Helga Waltz? It made no more sense than anything else.

As though he sensed her thoughts, Bradon glanced at her. Embarrassed, she quickly looked away.

"What is it?" he said. "Something wrong?"

"No. I was just thinking--about Helga."

"Your grandmother. What about her?"

"You said you came here to find her. What did you find out?"

"Not much. Her last address was in San Francisco. But that was years ago. I assume she's dead."

"I suppose so. She'd be in her nineties by now."

His glance flicked toward her again. "Didn't your mother ever mention her?"

"No. Well, I mean, I knew I had grandparents. But I always thought they were dead."

"When you get home, why don't you ask her? If anyone would know what happened to Helga, she would."

Sandi was silent. She had not made a decision about what to tell her parents. Asking questions about her grandmother would bring everything into the open. She was not sure she wanted that. Sandi sighed. "What good would it do to open old wounds?

Bradon nodded. "If she is dead, maybe it would be better to let her go."

They had come to a particularly foggy area and Bradon again leaned over the steering wheel, concentrating on his driving. Sandi closed her eyes, allowing weariness to take over her body and her mind. She realized with faint surprise that the voices in her head were gone, probably stilled by truth. The only sound was the faint rumble of the car. Bradon reached down and turned on the radio and the sound of soft music replaced the rumble. Sitting next to Bradon, she felt warm and safe, able to let go of worry and fear. It was an intimate, sensual warmth, and she closed her eyes, letting the sense of pleasure take over.

The glare of lights awakened her. Bradon had pulled to a stop under the hotel's porte-cochére and the parking valet was opening her door. When she released her seat belt and climbed out of the car, her body felt stiff and sore. It was probably due to her climb down into the canyon. Then she remembered her violent struggle with the man in her car and she shivered.

Bradon was beside her, his arm around her waist, and again she experienced the odd sense of safety. He reached back in the car and picked up her purse and handed it to her. "I'm going to see you to your door."

Sandi nodded. She wanted to hold the warm fuzzy feeling as long as possible. She knew that as soon as Bradon left her all her troubled thoughts would come flooding back.

This time the ride in the outside elevator held no fear. It was as thought nothing bad could possibly happen as long as Bradon was close beside her.

When they reached her hotel room door, she was embarrassed to have to dig through her purse to find her plastic key. She half expected him to say goodbye and walk away, but he waited patiently, his eyes crinkling with amusement.

With a sigh of relief she located the square of plastic and reached to unlock the door. With a move that was so easy it seemed perfectly natural, he took the plastic card from her and unlocked the door. He pushed it open and held it for her to walk inside. He followed and closed the door, dropping the plastic key back in her purse.

She wanted to tell him to leave, that this was dangerous. But she was unable to voice the command. She felt drugged, her heart pounding, her thoughts spinning out of control. At the same time she was gripped by a languorous warmth that seemed to spread from her stomach until it suffused her entire body. Her lips were so dry she had to moisten them with her tongue and, as though it was a signal, Bradon cradled her face with his hands and gently kissed her.

When his lips touched hers, shock jolted along Sandi's spine, turning the heat to fire. A low moan of anguish escaped her. When Bradon released her face to put his arms around her, she could have turned her face away. But it was as though his lips had sized the fire within her and drew it to her mouth where he drank its leaping flames. Her entire being, was concentrated in the kiss. There was no hotel room, no night, no time. There was only Bradon's lips and the lean hardness of his body pressed against hers.

And yet, she wanted more.

Her hands went behind his head and she pulled his mouth against hers savagely.

His hands slid down her back, trailing fire, and she strained against him, wanting, somehow, to be part of him.

She protested with a moan when he broke the kiss. He picked her up, and she felt new sensations of pleasure when he cradled her against his chest and she locked her fingers behind his head.

He carried her into the bedroom and gently lowered her to the bed. Her fingers refused to release their grip and she pulled him down beside her, her mouth searching for his. His lips were soft, taking her lower lips in tender nips until she couldn't stand it a second longer and her tongue darted to meet his.

He rolled onto his back and pulled her atop him and his strong hands pushed at her shoulders. She whimpered in anguish when her lips were forced from his and she rose to her knees straddling his waist. Then his hands stripped away her jacket, his fingers fumbling at the buttons of her blouse. She rushed to help him, the sound of tearing cloth harsh in the quietness. With her blouse stripped away, cool air bathing her perspiring body, she leaned forward, offering her tender flesh to his lips.

She thrilled to his caress as his lips brushed her shoulders and plunged to the curve of her throat. His fingers stroked her back, and her body was wracked by shivers of delight. She arched her back as her bra fell away and his lips moved down the slope of her breasts.

She had to feel his chest against hers and she clawed at his shirt, pulling it away so that she could lean forward and brush her distended, sensitive nipples against the hair of his chest. He moaned and pulled her against him, crushing her breasts against his chest while his lips again sought hers, finding them in a frenzy of desire. His hands were stripping away the remainder of her clothing and she rolled aside to help him. Then his own clothing was gone and his hands and lips ripped moans of shivering pleasure from her. She was shuddering uncontrollably, unable to think, unable to reason, her mind and body surrendering to terrible desire.

She lay on her back, writhing in her search for even greater heights of sensual pain. He knelt between her thighs, staring down at her and she moaned, "Please, Dan. Please."

His voice choked in a raw cry of anguish and, abruptly, he was gone, exposing her sweating body to a shocking draft of cool air. She whimpered in disappointment, and her arms reached for him, finding emptiness. Her eyes snapped open. He was standing with his back to her, staring out the window at the fog-misted ocean of lights that ended at the dark waters of San Francisco Bay.

She went to him, drawn by an aura of pain. She put her arms around him, pressing against his back, wanting to soothe away his despair. "It's all right," she whispered. "It's all right."

"I'm sorry." His voice was so low and hoarse that she could scarcely hear him.

"It doesn't matter." His smooth skin was warm with a film of perspiration and she pressed her cheek against his back, trying to make him understand that it really did not matter. The emotions raging inside her had a much deeper basis than pure lust, however strong the burning desire might be.

She felt a sense of relief when, instead of hiding his shame with anger, he turned and put his arms around her. She expected him to tell her how much he loved her, but he surprised her by saying, "You were right about me. I have been using you."

A cold, hard pain stabbed her chest. "Using me? You mean, the book? I don't care about that."

"No, not the book. This is--something else--the reason this happened. I thought I had it under control, but--I guess I haven't."

"What? What is it?"

"One of my ghosts. Something that happened a long time ago."

"I can help you. Please let me help you."

He tilted her chin, and she parted her lips for his kiss of affirmation. Instead, he gently pressed his lips to her forehead. "You can't help me," he murmured. "I thought you could. But I've got to work this out for myself."

He moved away, leaving her standing, hurt and bewildered.

CHAPTER 22

Dan Bradon wanted to hate himself. There would be a certain purgative in taking full blame for the way his mind had destroyed his lust. But his intellect, his education, told him that the problem in his mind was beyond his control.

He snorted in disgust. Rationalizing. That's what he was doing. He should never have brought Sandi into his battle with guilt. It wasn't fair to her. Worse, it had backfired so badly that now she had lost all respect for him. He had damaged their relationship beyond repair.

The thought gave him a sharp stab of doubt; he desperately wanted their relationship to continue. If his only reason for wanting to be with Sandi was to use her, why should he have this terrible sense of loss? Was it possible that he was fooling himself, that he had not been using her at all, that the real reason he was so drawn to her was because he was in love?

If so, why hadn't he been able to make love to her?

"Damn, damn," he muttered. He was supposed to be a psychologist, someone who understood the workings of the mind. And here his own mind was so mixed up about the death of Kimberly Hill and his attraction for Sandi Boeckel that he couldn't sort fact from fantasy.

But his subconscious knew his real motives even if his conscious did not. It had to be that love had nothing to do with it. He was simply using her. And his body had rebelled. His subconscious had taken over, demanding that he walk away from her, that he allow her to get on with her life without him screwing it up to solve his own problems. For once, his intellect had to agree.

Now, in the bright light of day, driving back on the I-5 to Los Angeles, he was able to convince himself that he was glad it had turned out the way it had. Making love to Sandi would have been wonderful, but totally wrong. It would have added new dimensions to his guilt. It certainly would have been devastatingly traumatic for her when she learned the truth: that he was only using her body to see if his guilt was under control.

He pounded his fist on the steering wheel. Except that he did love her! Damn it! If he didn't, why would he feel such a depression of loss? It was as though something beautiful had been plucked from the dark and tangled field of his life leaving only weeds and scoria.

Maybe it wasn't too late to make amends. Would she listen if he tried to explain? How could he explain something that was not really clear even to him? Besides, it was now totally academic. After the way he had walked out, she would never speak to him again. And if she did, if he could find some way to explain, she would then know that he had selfishly tried to use her, and he really would lose her forever. So he was dead no matter what he did.

In her own bedroom, listlessly preparing for dinner, Sandi had never felt more depressed in her life. Her quest to find the answer to the voices in her head had ended in a dark and forbidding canyon. Then she had compounded her failure by allowing Dan Bradon to take advantage of her vulnerability, of her infatuation. The one bright spot was that she had been saved from making the terrible mistake of going all the way with him by his own psychological problems.

But she would have if he'd been capable. She had never experienced such arousal. She had been gripped by such intense desire that she would have done anything he wanted, given him all that she was capable of giving.

Could she give herself so completely to Jordan? And if she did, could his lips, his caresses lift her to such heights of desire that she could do anything, forget everything? Maybe she could. She had never really let herself go with Jordan. Or any other man, to tell the truth. Maybe it was not Dan Bradon at all. Maybe if she discarded all inhibitions, abandoned all adolescent notion that there could be no desire without love, she could reach the same heights of passion with any man.

Not her. She knew herself too well. She could never find such intense joy with someone she did not love. So, did that mean she loved Dan Bradon? Ridiculous. She had succumbed to an aberrant obsession. It would never happen again.

Marriage was the answer. Once she lost herself in Jordan's arms, once she had given herself to her husband in loving surrender, the passion would come. Then she would never think of any other man, including Dan Bradon.

When she went downstairs to dinner, she held the conviction with the intensity of a drowning person clutching a life preserver. Without it, she was not sure that she could confront the other doubts that were adding to her depression. She hated what she was going to do. Her mother and father would be upset and hurt by her confrontation. They had tried to protect her and she had gone behind their backs. Now she meant to open old wounds and she felt terrible.

Throughout dinner, she wrestled with ambivalent feelings. She might have dropped the entire matter if her father had not spoken with a heartiness that she knew was faked, "So. How was the trip to San Francisco?"

She considered simply smiling and saying that it was a lovely trip and that she had learned nothing. But that meant that for the remainder of her life she would always wonder.

"Eventful," she said. "It left me with a lot of questions."

Her mother pushed aside her dessert and picked up her glass of wine. The way she held it without drinking told Sandi that she was going to change the subject, "Have you talked to Jordan? We've got to get those invitations in the mail."

Sandi leaned toward her mother. "Why didn't you tell me your mother's real name was Helga Waltz?" She saw her mother's face sag as she turned to Martin. "Why didn't you tell me that you're not my real father?"

Martin rubbed a hand across his face. He glanced at Gretchen as though wondering whether he should admit the truth. Just as quickly he realized that he could no longer conceal the lie. There was no hint of guilt or remorse in his voice when he said, "Because it wasn't necessary."

"Necessity has nothing to do with it. Didn't you think I had the right to know?"

"What would be the point? We could not love you more--or give you more--if you had known. It would change nothing."

"I know that. It doesn't change anything now. I just want to know." She turned to her mother. Tears had gathered in her mother's eyes and it hurt Sandi to continue. She had to keep a quiver out of her voice as she asked, "Who was my father? What kind of blood do I have in me? What can I expect? I think I have the right to know at least that."

"I was young," Gretchen said. "I had just found out the truth about my father."

"You mean Hermann von Luckenwalde."

Gretchen nodded. "That's right. The Nazi traitor." Her nostrils pinched with distaste. "You can imagine, I was in shock. I married Richard to get away from home. I couldn't face my mother any more."

"Your mother, Helga?"

"Yes. I hated her for what she'd done."

"If she wanted to keep her past a secret, why did she tell you?"

"I came across her marriage license, when she married Otto Winters. I was born four months later."

"He still could have been your father."

Gretchen shook her head. "She had only been in this country three months. She had to have been carrying me when she arrived. I demanded to know my real father. She finally told me."

"He was hanged as a war criminal. Is that why you never told me?"

Gretchen nodded as she dabbed at her eyes with her napkin. "It could be worse." She pressed her napkin to her eyes with both hands.

"Worse? How on earth could it be worse?"

Gretchen could not answer. Her shoulders heaved with a suppressed sob. Martin said, "She means that Helga worked for that butcher Heinrich Himmler."

"I know about that," Sandi said. "She was a psychic. That's all she did. Hermann was the Nazi."

"Maybe not. She might have been Himmler's mistress."

Sandi's eyes widened in shock. She sat back in her chair, staring at her father. "Mistress? Are you sure?"

"It was only a rumor. But if it's true, maybe von Luckenwalde wasn't the father."

"Himmler?" Sandi turned huge eyes toward her mother. "Heinrich Himmler could be your father?"

"I'll never believe it," Gretchen said fiercely. "Never!"

"The point is," Martin went on, "we wanted to spare you even the rumor of something like that. So did Helga, your grandmother. That's why she changed her name and came to this country."

"But she didn't cut off her source of money," Sandi said slowly. "She kept control of her husband's Swiss account."

"Assuming it belonged to him. It might have been set up for her by Himmler."

Sandi put her hand to her mouth, trying to think clearly. She looked at her mother who was holding her soggy napkin to her eyes. "With Helga dead, you inherited the estate. That's been our source of money, hasn't it? Not the gallery. It never made that much money."

Martin stiffened. "The gallery has done very well."

"But if it was Himmler, that money belongs to the German people."

"Nonsense. There's no reason to reject the Luckenwalde estate because of some stupid rumor."

"We would have survived without it."

"I prefer to do more than survive. You've had a very good life because of that money."

A flash of anger brought heat to Sandi's face. "Not if I had known."

"Well, some day your mother and I will be gone. Then the estate will be yours. If would be interesting to see if you change your mind."

Sandi's gaze was level as she looked at him. "It doesn't matter whether it was Himmler's or von Luckenwalde's. We really have no right to that money. When the time comes, I intend to see that it goes to the people of Germany."

Martin smiled grimly. "I thought you might say something like that. You're too much of an idealist, my dear."

Sandi continued to stare at Martin for a moment. How different he seemed now that she knew he wasn't her true father. In the past, she would have cringed before his supercilious arrogance and said nothing. Now she realized why she had never felt that he loved her. She had no doubt that he had married her mother for her money. He had treated her civilly all those years. But never with love. She had simply come with the deal.

She turned to her mother and was more than a little surprised to discover that the fear she'd always had about her mother's disapproval had vanished. She was a fearsome idol with feet of clay. "Whatever happened to her?"

"To whom?" Her mother's voice was a sniff as though she sensed that something had been lost between Sandi and her.

"Helen. Helga. Your mother."

"That terrible accident. It took everything out of her."

"Then she's dead."

It was Martin who answered. "That's right. She passed away within a year. With Dennise dead, Gretchen was the only heir."

"And now I am.

Martin picked up his wineglass. "Not yet, my dear. Not yet."

Gretchen put down her napkin. She did not look at Sandi as she said. "I'm sorry that you had to find out like this. Maybe I should have told you, but I kept putting it off. Then you were grown and I . . . I was afraid."

"Afraid? Of what?"

"That you would hate me."

Sandi put her hand on her mother's shoulder. "I could never do that."

"I know. It's just that . . . well, you'll know when you're a mother."

"Speaking of that," Martin said. "It might be better if you didn't tell any of this to Jordan."

Sandi was silent for a moment. Jordan. She had forgotten about him. Would he still want to marry her if he knew that her mother might be the illegitimate daughter of Heinrich Himmler? He would if he really loved her. And he did love her. It was the one constant in this whole charade.

"He has a right to know," she said. "Besides, if he ever does find out that I knew and hadn't told him . . . well, I don't want to make that mistake."

Her chance to tell Jordan came the next night. He invited her to dinner, and to his delight, she suggested they have the dinner in his penthouse condominium. He had invited her to dine there several times, but she had always declined, knowing that it could put her in a position where it would be difficult to decline any amorous advances, although why she would want to do so she was never quite sure.

Now, sitting across from Jordan in his dining alcove, she wondered if she was making a mistake. Unvoiced in his invitation, but present nevertheless, was an expectation of sex. Well, why not? Their wedding day was rushing at them at express train speed, and having more or less offered herself by suggesting the tryst, there would be no reason why she should refuse to go to bed with him. Not that she wanted to refuse. Just the opposite, in fact. There was only one way she was going to extirpate the memory of Dan Bradon from her mind. That was by making love with the man she really loved and, of most importance, the man who loved her. Jordan would not be simply using her. He wanted her for his wife 'until death do us part.'

So why wasn't she feeling a mounting excitement as they neared the end of the dinner? The setting was perfect. Jordan had planned the evening with meticulous care. His sumptuous penthouse on Westwood's glamorous Wilshire Blvd. near UCLA, had cost more than a million dollars.

He had paid thousands more to an interior decorator to decorate and furnish it.

Sandi had only been in his condo once before and that had been with her parents. Then she had been struck by its sterile ambience. Predominantly of polished marble and stainless steel, it looked as though it was ready for a full layout in Architectural Digest. Daily maid service insured that everything was immaculate. Except that, hovering in the air like a miasma, was the faint odor of stale cigar smoke. For this momentous night, Jordan had employed an entire staff to make sure of absolute perfection. Soothing strains of a Mozart concerto wafted from strategically placed BOSE speakers. Beyond the pristine picture windows the lights of Los Angeles twinkling like a blanket of jewels.

The catered dinner had started with glasses of California Cote-Rotie and Buckwheat Crepes with Crabmeat Lobster Vinaigrette. It had progressed smoothly through a Mixed Green salad with Hazelnut Dressing and Grilled Lamb Chops done with thyme and rosemary. For desert Jordan had selected Creme Brule accompanied by a German Sauterne. Sandi knew that the wine was very expensive. Mentioning its price would have been gauche, but before the waiter poured, Jordan made sure she got a good look at the bottle's label.

Sandi eat sparingly. She didn't want to feel stuffed when she went to bed with Jordan. Besides, she really wasn't hungry. Were the strange qualms in her stomach caused by excitement--or dread?

Jordan watch her nibbling the Creme Brule with a smile. "You're very quiet tonight."

He had groomed himself for their rendezvous with the same care he had given in supervising the dinner. He was wearing a dark Armani suit with white stripes so narrow they were almost invisible. His snowy white shirt was complimentarily striped, white on white. His necktie was silk, midnight blue slashed with thin red stripes. His carefully groomed hair and clean shaven face looked as though he had spent at least an hour in a barbershop late in the afternoon. When she had arrived and he had kissed her cheek she noticed that he had switched his usual delicately scented after-shave lotion to something more masculine. She suspected it was something named Rogue or Commando. Beneath the Holmsund dining table his shoes undoubtedly shown like mirrors.

"I was thinking," she answered, "about all the things I've got to do before the wedding. I can't believe how fast time is flying."

"Not fast enough. I don't think December will ever get here."

"It will." She smiled, and said lightly, "Time enough to change your mind."

He slowly shook his head. "I'll never change my mind. I've waited a long time."

Sandi felt a wave of compassion. Jordan had waited a long time. He had always been loyal and loving. He would never betray her. "I know, my darling," she said. "But I'm glad we waited. It'll be that much more wonderful."

Jordan's gaze dropped to the cleavage of her blouse. Abruptly, he stood up. "Excuse me a moment."

He went into the kitchen and Sandi heard him tell the caterers to clean up as quickly as possible and leave; the maid would finish up in the morning.

He came back and held his hand out to her. "Let's go to the den. I have something to show you."

On the way to the den, he flicked switches on a wall control panel and when they entered the book-lined room, it was already romanticsized with soothing Beethoven sonatas. The sconced lights were turned low and, although the weather outside was warm, air conditioning allowed a fire in the fireplace to send forth dancing shadows and the aromatic smell of burning oak.

Jordan led Sandi to a huge couch upholstered in butter-soft black leather that faced the fireplace. She noticed that a low coffee table that should have been between the couch and the fireplace had been shifted to the side of the room and replaced by a thick, pure white, shag rug. Sandi almost smiled. Trust Jordan not to be so uncouth as to have a bear or tiger skin in front of the fireplace. This was where it was going to happen. In a way she was glad. She wanted to save making love in bed for their wedding night.

She sat on the couch and Jordan went to a small wet-bar and poured brandy into snifters. "I'm thinking about buying a house in Bel Air," he said. "We can live here for a few months while it's being remodeled."

Sandi's reaction was surprise. She realized that she had given little thought to where they would live after they were married. "Either one would be fine."

Jordan carried the snifters to the couch where he handed one to Sandi before he sat down beside her. "That's what I thought. Beverly Hills schools are within driving distance. At least three really good country clubs. And I could practically throw a rock to my office in Century City."

"Sounds perfect."

"It is. I've already got my real estate broker on the lookout. Which reminds me." He reached to set his brandy snifter on the coffee table, then realized he had moved it. He put the glass on the floor well away from his feet before he got up and walked to a large desk of dark oak near the door. He picked up a small jeweler's box from the inlaid top of the desk and brought it back to the couch.

Sitting on the couch, he opened the box. Inside were two wedding rings. The woman's had a large baguette-cut diamond surrounded by tiny rubies set in gold and platinum. The man's was plainer, with the single, equal-sized diamond in a setting of gold and platinum.

Jordan took out the woman's ring. "Try this on. We want to make sure it's the right size."

He didn't ask Sandi whether she liked the rings. She had not expected that he would. If he selected them, they had to be perfect. Actually, she would have preferred a smaller stone, less ostentatious.

He slipped the ring on her finger. "Hmmm. A little loose. A couple of millimeters, I'd say. I'll have Jacque make the correction."

Sandi took the ring off. "I was thinking--"

"Don't worry," he interrupted. "He'll have it finished in plenty of time." He held the ring so that the light of the fire made the diamond flame. "Beautiful, isn't it?"

Sandi decided not to make an issue of the ring. Jordan liked it so she could live with it. "Yes, it's lovely."

He put the ring back in the box and snapped it shut. When he got up to take it back to his desk, he said, "Finish your brandy."

Dutifully she swallowed the last of the brandy and he took the glass from her. He quickly drank the remainder from his glass, then took the glasses back to the bar where he rinsed and dried them. He took off his jacket and carefully draped it on the back of his leather desk chair before returning to the couch.

He sat down close to Sandi and put his arms around her. The thought that went through her mind was that this was it and she waited for her heart to begin pounding. But when Jordan kissed her she was chagrinned at how cool she remained. Even when his lips became more demanding, and he thrust his tongue into her mouth, she felt a strange detachment. It was as though she was standing off to the side watching critically.

The trouble, she decided, was that she was not letting herself go. She had to stop being subjective and become more active. Then it would happen. Then the excitement would carry her away just as it had with Bradon.

In an attempt to force the desired fire, she met Jordan's tongue with her own. He grunted with pleasure and his hand slid inside her blouse to cup her breast. He squeezed through her brassiere and mistook her gasp of pain for one of pleasure and squeezed harder.

She broke their kiss to say, "Wait." And she began to unbutton the blouse she had chosen to wear because it had buttons all the way down the front. Maybe he would be more tender if he could caress her bare flesh.

He smiled and leaned back against the far end of the couch. "Why don't you stand up?" he said. "I want to watch."

Sandi's fingers halted. He wanted her to strip for him. How could she become aroused without his help, without his touch?

Slowly she got to her feet. Maybe the act of stripping, of baring her body to his lustful eyes would induce the same passion she had felt with

Dan Bradon. Damn. Why had she ever allowed Bradon to kiss her? Was he to ruin her relationship with Jordan the way he had ruined everything else?

Impossible. She loved Jordan. They were going to be married and giving herself to him now was going to set everything right. Soon she would feel the heady exaltation that would make her forget everything, even Dan Bradon.

She slipped off her jacket and dropped it on a chair. Her fingers trembled so that she had difficulty unbuttoning her blouse. Were they trembling because of mounting excitement? If so, why wasn't her heart pounding and her flesh damp with perspiration?

She pulled off her blouse and carefully folded it before she placed it atop her jacket on the chair. Why had she done that? Why should she be concerned about wrinkles?

Oh Lord! This wasn't working! Instead of rising heat her body was cold. She felt every molecule of the conditioned air on her bare flesh.

While reaching behind her back to unfasten her bra, she caught a glimpse of Jordan's eyes. It might not be working for her but it was for him. His eyes were feverish, his face flushed. For Jordan. She could do it for Jordan. In a moment, her desire would surely rise to match his.

She took off her bra. Now! His eyes burned her bare flesh like hot coals. Now desire had to come. But the sensation that flooded her was not the heat of mounting desire, it was cold--the coldness of shame. She had never exposed herself this way to any man. Indeed, she had chosen a female physician because it was too embarrassing to expose herself even to a doctor.

Revulsion held her transfixed. She had to tell him. She could not do this. She had to make him realize that she needed time. She needed to feel his love, not his lust.

She stood frozen, uncertain about how to explain, resisting an impulse to cover her breasts with her hands. Abruptly, Jordan surged to his feet and yanked her into his arms. She did not resist when he lifted her and carried her to the couch. Thank God he had seen her embarrassment. He would now bring her to arousal with gentle caresses and lingering kisses.

He stood staring down at her as he stripped off his necktie and shirt. His chest was matted with dark hair, already glistening with sweat. She lay submissively as he bent over her, arching her back for his caresses, closing her eyes and parting her lips for his kisses.

The sound of him unzipping his pants made her ridged with shock. What was he doing? She wasn't ready! She grunted with pain when he threw himself on top of her.

His fingers clawed at her skirt, pulling it up with such force that she heard it rip. She was not wearing panty hose and he struggled to thrust his fingers beneath the waistband of her panties. His nails dug into the flesh of her stomach painfully and she gritted her teeth. She was acutely aware of hot breath on her bare skin, of sweat dripping on her breasts.

Oh, God! It was never going to work.

She would never feel the shattering ecstasy with Jordan she had with Bradon. Instead of being swept away in a rapture of joy there was only revulsion.

"No," she cried. "Jordan. Please, wait."

He paid no attention. His breath came in painful gasps as he struggled to tear her panties from her hips. She put her hands on his shoulders, attempting to thrust him away. It was like trying to stop a madman. When he was unable to force her panties down over her hips he ripped at them savagely, the elastic cutting into her flesh. Abruptly, her disgust gave way to an overwhelming flash of rage.

"No," she snarled, and pushed him so violently that he almost fell to the floor. With a desperate surge she sprang to her feet.

He stood up, his face flushed, his eyes bulging. He reached for her and she backed away. "No, Jordan," she gasped. "Wait. Please."

He stopped and stared at her, breathing hard. "What's the matter?" he said. "What the hell is this?"

"I, uh, I can't--I can't concentrate. There's something I've got to tell you."

"Tell me later." He took a step toward her, staring at her breasts so that she had to cover them with her hands.

"No. You've got to know. It might . . .it might change the way you feel about me."

His head came up and his eyes narrowed. "What?"

"Sit down," she said. He made no move to do so. Instead, he took a step toward her and she quickly said, "It's about my mother."

He stopped. "Your mother? What the hell are you talking about?"

She took the opportunity to take her blouse from the chair and shrug into it. "She's not who you think she is. Her father, my grandfather, was a Nazi, a war criminal. He was hanged in 1945."

The effect on Jordan was startling. It was as though he had been shot. His features went slack, his eyes widened, and he slumped to the couch. "What are you saying?"

"I just found out myself. That's why I went to San Francisco. Martin isn't my father. My real father was killed in an automobile accident. It was after the accident that they were married."

Jordan sat on the couch staring at her incredulously, his mouth half-open. Sandi buttoned the jacket, her fingers no longer trembled. For once she was in control. Her voice was strong as she continued, "My grandmother was married to a Nazi named Count Hermann von Luckenwalde. He was hanged as a war criminal. You can look it up in the history books. She left Germany right after the war. She was already pregnant with my mother."

As she slipped on her jacket, the stricken look in Jordan's face was so ghastly that a part of her hated herself for adding, "There was a rumor that she was the mistress of that butcher, Heinrich Himmler. It's possible that my mother is his illegitimate child. Maybe even of Hitler himself."

Jordan blinked at her as though she had struck him and he couldn't understand why. "Hitler?" he gasped. "Your mother?"

She sat down beside him and took hold of his slack hand. "But this won't make a difference, will it? That was a long time ago."

He stared at her, his eyes blank. She might have been a total stranger. "No, no," he muttered. "Of course not."

"Wonderful," she said. She got up and went to the door. "Call me in the morning." She opened the door and turned back. "Oh. You can keep my bra as a souvenir."

She was in her car and part way home before she began to cry.

CHAPTER 23

Sandi rather expected it when her private telephone rang as she was preparing for bed. It would be Jordan calling to apologize, to tell her that he was sorry for his brutish behavior. She was slow answering the phone's insistent ringing.

Should she forgive him? In all fairness, much of the blame for what had happened was hers. She had accepted his invitation knowing what he expected. It had simply not gone well. It would be different on their honeymoon.

Still, Jordan had given her the perfect excuse to call off the wedding. She wasn't sure she wanted to do that. What would be the point? There was no other man in her life she would even consider marrying. The best thing she could do was forget the past, let the wedding--let her life--proceed as planned. As for passion, that would come with time.

She picked up the telephone and said, "Hello, Jordan."

If he was surprised that she had anticipated his call, he gave no indication. "Darling," he said, using his deep and most sexy voice. "I want to apologize for my behavior tonight."

"It's all right, Jordan. Forget it."

"I'm not really like that. You know that. It's just that I'd waited so long."

"I know."

"And, uh, about the wedding--about us--tonight really made me begin thinking."

A faint temblor of shock tingled along her spine. When someone said they were 'thinking', it always preceded bad news. "What do you mean?"

There was a brief pause before Jordan said, "I, uh, I wonder if we're really right for each other."

To Sandi's amazement, a surge of joy shocked her. It was as though she had been relieved of a huge responsibility. Still, she didn't want to hurt Jordan's feelings so she said, "Do you want to postpone the wedding?"

"Postpone? Well, I wonder if that would be appropriate. Everyone would expect--"

He stopped and Sandi finished the thought for him, "They would expect that we were still engaged."

"Something like that."

Sandi had trouble catching her breath. Was she really comprehending what Jordan was saying? "You want to break our engagement?"

He mistook the faintness in her voice for despair, and he said, "I'm sorry. I'm really sorry. But I, uh, I think it's best."

Sandi's mind spun crazily with conflicting emotions. A part of her was incredibly happy that the wedding was off; another part of her was filled with dismay. Was she making a mistake to give up on Jordan? He was the perfect man for her. In time, they would get over the mistakes of last night. In time she could be for him all that he wanted her to be. Couldn't she?

Jordan's voice cut through, "It's not your fault. It all happened before you were ever born."

Sandi was not sure she had heard him correctly. "What? What happened?"

Jordan continued in a rush, "It's just that--well, you know how sensitive my work is. My clients are some of the oldest families in the country. Their patriotism is beyond question. Mine has got to be beyond question. And this situation with your grandfather. He, uh, he was a Nazi you said. Well, you can appreciate how they might--how they would react to that."

He paused, and Sandi murmured, "I can imagine."

"So, uh, perhaps it would be best if we just--well, if we just didn't see each other for a while."

"Can we stay friends?" Sandi put a bitter quality into her voice so that Jordan would not detect that she wanted to drop the phone and dance around the room.

"Of course," he said with a gratifying sound of guilt. "Although, I think it would be easier for both of us if we didn't see each other for a while. I--"

"Goodbye, Jordan," she said, and hung up the phone. It would not ring again, she was sure of that.

She stood for a moment not knowing whether she was going to laugh or cry. Jordan had behaved like a Neanderthal. He had practically raped her. She had been sure he would call to beg her forgiveness. True, he had apologized. But his primary purpose was to tell her that her family wasn't good enough for him. Well, thank God for that. To have found out he was such a snob after they were married would have been catastrophic. It went beyond his arrogance. It made her wonder again what sort of a father he would have made for their children. Would he be able to comfort a little boy or girl with a skinned knee? Would he spend a day at the zoo, or a museum or--God forbid--fishing? Would he be able to get down on the floor and participate in their games?

Probably not. It might chip a nail.

Strange how a failed sexual encounter could call into question so many aspects of character. There had also been a failed encounter with Bradon, but it had revealed a totally different person than had the encounter with Jordan. Bradon had shown a tenderness, a vulnerability that, she was sure, would always be foreign to Jordan's character. Bradon would never have forced himself on her. And he knew that her grandfather was a war criminal. "He's probably glad of it," she muttered. "Better for his stupid book."

Walking toward her bed she caught a glimpse of herself in her wall mirror. She stopped and examined her image. It seemed as though she was looking at a stranger. She had changed. Perhaps not so much on the outside, but there were major transformations on the inside. What had the situations with Jordan and with Bradon told her about herself? Only that she had her own problems.

Another thought intruded: suppose she had made love with Jordan and it had been wonderful? Would it have been because she was in love or simply because of lust? And if it was purely lust, what would happen to their marriage when savage passions died, as they surely would. Would there be a foundation of respect and affection deep enough and firm enough to sustain their marriage without the constant highs of unbridled passion? With Jordan, it did not seen likely.

She sighed. It was best that the relationship had failed. Now she would never have to go to bed with him; now she would never have to compare her love for Jordan with her love for Bradon.

The anomalous thought startled her. Love? For Bradon? How could she possibly be in love with him now after the way he had treated her? In his own way he had wanted to use her much as had Jordan.

Poor Bradon. Would he ever work out his emotional problems? Or would he need someone to help him? Another psychologist? More likely he needed the help of a woman who loved him enough to allow him to use her as a psychologic guinea pig.

But not her. Let him use some other sucker. He may have wormed his way into her heart, but she could control that. She was good at walling in ghosts. If her stupid id wanted to harbor him, let it. He was out of her real world forever.

She pressed her fingertips against the bridge of her nose. She was so tired. she climbed into bed and turned off the light expecting to fall asleep quickly. But her mind would not let go of its doubts and recriminations. They twisted through her mind like rampaging tornados, making her head feel as though it would burst.

What was her life to be like now? Would she ever marry? Had she made a mistake in not trying to change Jordan's mind? It was possible that she could have pretended love for a period of time--maybe even for years--but, in the end, her guilt for betraying herself would bring her down.

Until she met Bradon, she hadn't realized there were different kinds of love.

Her eyes snapped open. There it was again. Dan Bradon. Why couldn't she shut him out of her mind? Was he to be another one of those horrible ghosts that would not go away? There was already a pressure in her head that threatened to drive her crazy.

Maybe she could forestall the anticipated headache by taking a couple of aspirins.

She sat up in bed and glanced at the digital clock. Midnight. She'd thought it was much later.

She slumped back against her pillow. Oh God! It wasn't a headache; it was the whispering voices. They were back! Damn Bradon. He had made it possible for them to burst the walls of their captivity and now they were demanding to be heard. As usual, she had no idea what they wanted, why they were filling her mind with such darkness that she thought she would go mad. All she knew was that they wanted her to find the letter.

The letter? Was there something in the letter she had missed? Could it be connected to the voices she had suppressed most of her life?

She clutched at her head, more in consternation than pain. Where was the letter? Her mother or Martin must have found it and put it away so it wouldn't get lost. So, where would they put it? It was unlikely that they would put it back in the suitcase. More likely they would find a safer place, possibly with Martin's papers in his den.

Slipping a robe over her nightgown, Sandi went downstairs, moving quietly so that she would not disturb her parents. Strange, she thought, that she still thought of Martin as her father. And that was as it should be. He was the only father she had ever known, the one who had raised her, nurtured her, given her a home, an education, and had helped shaped whatever character she possessed. She would always think of him as her real father.

She closed the door to the den and turned on the lights. Where to begin looking? Even with the lights on the room seemed gloomy, possibly because of its somber furnishings. The carpet was a deep brown. There were heavy drapes over the windows. Dreary eighteenth century oil paintings decorated walnut paneled walls. The large desk and matching file cabinets were of oak so darkly stained they were almost black. Everything was, of course, scrupulously neat and tidy.

She moved behind the desk and switched on the desk lamp. She tried the top drawer. Locked. Odd. Why did Martin find it necessary to lock his desk in his own home? Habit, probably. The same habit that made him place every item on the desk in its precisely assigned spot. Even a letter to be mailed was stamped and propped in the exact center of a letter holder.

Her gaze was caught by something in the address on the letter and she picked it up. The Oberlon Sanitarium in Half Moon Bay, CA. Half Moon Bay? Near the site of the accident. Why on earth would her father be writing there?

The desk lamp was behind the letter and the back light clearly revealed that the paper inside the envelope was a check. She would have to talk to Martin about that. One should place a check inside a wrapping of paper to conceal it from potential thieves.

She reached to return the letter to the holder, then stopped. A check? To a sanitarium? Why? A charity? To her knowledge, her mother and father never contributed to charities. But what other reason could there be? One did not send checks to sanitariums to pay for office supplies.

It was the fact that the sanitarium was located at Half Moon Bay that was most disturbing. Could it have any connection with the nearby accident? Or with her mother's past?

The answer might be in Martin's checkbook. If she was not mistaken, his penchant for precision would force him to note the purpose for the check on the check stub.

Except that his checkbook was most likely in the locked desk drawer. She tried the side drawers. They were also locked. Locking the center drawer must also lock the other drawers. Where would he keep the key? In his pocket? No. It wouldn't be practical to carry it with him. Which meant it would be somewhere in the house, probably in this room.

She looked around the room for the most likely hiding place. It would not have surprised her to see a small box labeled "key". There was no small box, but there was a small empty vase on the top shelf of the bookcase nearest the door. It was an odd place for a vase. She took the vase from the shelf and upended it. A desk key dropped into her hand.

She shook her head with a smile. Poor Martin. A victim of his Teutonic genes that made him do the obvious.

She unlocked the desk and opened the center drawer. No checkbook. She opened the top right hand drawer. There it was: a large, three-check book with ring binders. She placed it on the desk and turned to the last check. The stub was notationed in Martin's small, precise handwriting. Oberlon Sanitarium. On the explanation line was written: 'For November'. The amount was $2,180.

She leafed back through the previous check stubs. For some reason her breathing had shortened to gasps and her fingers were distressingly clumsy. When she finished her search, she drew a deep, shuddering breath. Every month there had been a check for $2,180 made out to Oberlon. Martin had to be paying for someone to stay at the sanitarium.

It didn't make sense. Martin had stated many times that he had no brothers or sisters. And his parents were dead. The same was true for Gretchen. So who could be the beneficiary of the money?

The darkness in her head exploded into light! Helga Waltz! It had to be Helga! She was alive! Her grandmother was still alive!

Why hadn't she been told? Were there other secrets that her parents wanted to keep hidden?

Her hands trembled, clammy with perspiration; her eyes refused to focus so that it was difficult to return the checkbook to its place in the drawer. It took her several attempts to insert the key and relock the desk. Then, using Martin's desk pen and note pad, it was even more difficult for her clumsy fingers to copy the address of the sanitarium and replace the envelope in its precise place on the desk. She was so preoccupied with implications that she almost overturned the vase when she dropped the key inside.

Leaving the room she remembered to close the door carefully. If Martin wanted to keep his secret, she didn't want him to find out that she knew about it.

Back in her room she sank to the edge of her bed. What on earth should she do? Her mind reeled with confusion. Of one thing she was certain: She had to learn the truth. But should she simply telephone the sanitarium and asked if they had a patient named Helga Waltz? No. Not Waltz. The name would be Winters. Helen Winters. If they said yes, then what? It was, after all, a sanitarium. They would not allow her to talk to anyone unless she could prove she was a relative. She could not do that on the telephone.

And if her grandmother was alive, she wanted to see her. She had to see her.

She had to go there. Once she had her foot in the door, there was no way they were going to keep her out.

She stared at the address she had written. Her writing was such a tortured scrawl she could scarcely decipher it. Reading it, she was filled with such a sense of dread that she considered crumpling the paper and throwing it into the darkest corner. It was the familiar sense of doom she had experienced so often during the past few weeks. If only she could turn her back and walk away, return to her cloistered existence while she still had a choice. But she could not. Her only real escape was to confront this ghost from her past.

Damn Jordan. She needed his strength. She needed his support, his love. She needed him to tell her that she must go on no matter what the price. She needed him to tell her that she was not going crazy.

But Jordan could never have done any of that. She had always known that instinctively. That was why she had been so willing to accept the help of Dan Bradon. At least he understood her compulsion.

She cupped her face in the palms of her hands. Damn him too. Losing him hurt more than losing Jordan.

The realization deepened her pain. It also prompted another intrusive thought: she wanted Bradon to go with her. She needed him. Something in her nature made her desperately afraid to face the unknown alone. Did that make her a coward? Perhaps. But it was a part of her she could not change.

Should she, could she ask Bradon to go with her?

She sagged back on the bed. He would never agree, not after the way they had parted. Besides, she would have to abandon all sense of pride to ask him. So which was the most powerful, her cowardice or her pride?

She laughed grimly. That was a question easy to answer.

She found her address book in her purse and took out Bradon's card. Was it too late to call? Late or not, she had better do it before she changed her mind. She dialed his number, thinking as she did so that she was a total fool. He would probably make her grovel, then refuse anyway.

Well, she could grovel if that's what it took. If she had to give him permission to write his damn book she would.

He answered the phone with a simple, 'yes'. His voice sounded alert as though he had not been sleeping.

Sandi's throat was so constricted by doubt and apprehension that she could not force out a word. It was only the fear that he would hang up that brought forth a whispered, "Bradon."

There was a pause, and she half expected him to hang up. Instead, he said, "Sandi?"

She swallowed painfully and her voice sounded strange to her as she said, "I'm--I'm sorry to wake you up this late."

"I wasn't sleeping. I don't think I'll ever sleep again."

Was there humor in his voice? Her head lifted in wonder. If so, he couldn't be so terribly angry. Her voice was stronger when she said, "I found out something. About Helga."

This time she was sure that his voice was sharp with interest. "Oh? What?"

"I think she's alive."

There was an infinitesimal beat before he said, "You think?"

"I'm quite sure. Here. In California."

This time there was a pause. "Why are you telling me?"

"Because . . ."--her heart was pounding so hard she was sure he must hear it--"because I'm going to look for her. I want you to help me."

For a moment she thought that he had hung up the phone, and her heart seemed to pause in terrible suspension. It started beating again when he said softly, "I don't think that would be a good idea."

Sandi stifled a groan. She had to convince him. "Dan," she whispered. "I need you. I really need you."

There was another pause, shorter this time as though he had been waiting for her words. "Are you sure about this?"

"Yes. I've got to find out. I . . . I can't go on like this. It's all . . . my whole life is coming apart."

His pause was infinitesimal, but to Sandi it seemed like forever. Then his answer began her life anew. "Okay. When do you want to go?"

"Now." The word leaped out before Sandi could think, and it startled her as much as it did Bradon.

"Now? It's after midnight."

Her words tumbled out as though they had been waiting. "We've got to go. I'm afraid that something might happen to her."

"Okay, okay. Slow down."

Sandi took a deep breath and gripped the telephone hard as though she could make him feel the terrible urgency. "I'm sorry. It's just that I don't want to waste a minute."

"I understand. But I doubt if there are flights this late. Even if there are, there's nothing we can do until tomorrow."

The logic of his words filled Sandi with dismay. "I know," she murmured.

"You've waited this long, a few more hours won't make any difference."

He was right, of course. It would be foolish to go rushing off in the middle of the night. What would she tell her parents? By waiting until tomorrow she could concoct a plausible excuse. "Tomorrow, then," she said. "Can you make it tomorrow?"

"Yes. But it'll have to be late afternoon. I've got appointments most of the day."

So late? Could she possibly wait patiently an entire day without dying of suspense? How could she keep her mother and father from noticing? But she had little choice.

"All right," she said. "What time?"

"There are shuttles to San Francisco all day. I can make the five o'clock."

"Five?" She was breathless with disappointment. Then she realized he had not refused, and she clung to the joy. "All right. Five. I'll see you at the airport."

"Better be there by four. I hate running for planes."

She felt like singing as she answered, "Yes, yes. Four."

"All right. Terminal two."

"Terminal two. I'll be there." She would be there, waiting.

"Just one question."

She caught her breath, afraid that he had changed his mind. "Yes?"

"Why did you call me?"

"Why? I told you; I want to find out what happened to Helga."

"But why call me? You could have run this down yourself."

"Well, because . . ." He was right. If she had to, if Bradon had refused her, she would have gone to San Francisco on her own. "Because you were in on the beginning. I thought you would want to know how it ended."

Was disappointment in his voice when he said, "Oh. Okay. I'll see you tomorrow."

There was a click as he hung up, leaving Sandi holding the phone in surprise. Had he hoped for another reason? Had he hoped that she had called because she wanted to see him, whatever the reason? Was he right? Was she deluding herself? Was she using this trip as an excuse? Was her real reason for calling Bradon because she desperately wanted to be with him?

She dismissed the idea with a shake of her head. What nonsense. She had been over that ground a million times. It seemed that her every waking moment had been filled with conflicting thoughts about Bradon. And each time she had come to the same conclusion, his only interest in her had been to use her. The only thing that had changed now was that she would be using him.

CHAPTER 24

The plane had taken off and banked north across the placid waters of Santa Monica Bay and begun the long climb to cruising altitude before Dan Bradon settled back in his seat. He had to organize his thoughts.

Since Sandi's late night telephone call had sent his heart racing, his mind had bounced from thought to thought like a stone in a cement mixer. There was no way he could have refused to go with her. Every minute since they had parted had been agony. He had leaped at the chance like a starving man offered a steak. Admit it, he had told himself. You're in love with her. So how could the ghost of Kimberly Hill come between them?

But it had. After the way he had made a fool of himself in San Francisco, he had been sure he would never see her again. They had ended their relationship. If he was smart he would have let it stay that way. Just being close to her turned up the gas on flames that were already frying his brain.

So why had he agreed to come with her? An attempted catharsis? Or a death wish? The most stupid psychologist in the world would see in an instant that he needed Sandi much more than she could ever need him. What would the Dysfunctional Symptoms Manual say about this? Was there a category for simply being a fool? If there was, he could be an example.

The only way he had been able to keep any perspective at all was to remind himself over and over: Keep it professional. Don't let your emotions take over! If he could keep their relationship purely on a business level, he could handle the situation.

Even so, it was stupid of him to take the chance. Renewing their relationship could end up hurting both of them.

And yet, every resolution that he had pounded into his brain all day long had been driven from his mind the moment he'd seen Sandi waiting in the airport terminal. She looked so pale and wane that all his hard-won objectivity had drained out of him, leaving only a hunger to be near her. He wanted to take her in his arms and assure her that she would always be safe.

But it was the last thing she would want. It would ruin everything just as it had before.

His assessment was confirmed when she gave no sign of relenting from her air of cool detachment. The smile she gave him was apologetic but not forgiving. Obviously, she wanted to keep their relationship impersonal.

Good. That was what he wanted too. He would concentrate on the job they had to do. Be objective. That was the answer

Now, sitting beside her, smelling the clean spice of her perfume, feeling the gentle brush of her sleeve, watching her pale face, drawn with anxiety, he realized all his resolves meant nothing. He was hopelessly in love. Or, more correctly, in hopeless love. Because he had blown his chances. She could never return his love. Not now. Not ever.

Still, she was the one who had called him. That had to count for something.

With feigned indifference, he turned toward her. "Okay. "What's this all about?"

She sighed, looking small and fragile, her eyes luminous in the dim light. She twisted her hands together nervously and he had an insane desire to take her hands in his. He fought the impulse. She hated him. Worse. She probably pitied him.

"I--" Her voice broke. If she hadn't quickly started over, he was not sure he could have held his hands in check. "I was looking through some papers in my father's study. I found out that he's been sending regular checks to a sanitarium near Half Moon Bay."

Bradon clung to her words, but their meaning was blurred by the distraction of her husky voice, the scent of her body, the fear and pain in her eyes. He blinked and struggled to concentrate. "Half Moon Bay? Near the accident?"

She nodded. "It seemed strange. Why would he be doing such a thing?"

"A charitable donation?"

"Martin never gave anything to a charity in his life."

"Then it's obvious; he's supporting someone in the sanitarium."

"Yes. But who? As far as I know, we have no living relatives."

It took a moment for the impact of her words to sink in. When it did, his mind rushed to an incredulous conclusion. "You think it's Helga."

The way her hands moved to grip the armrests betrayed her anxiety--and her hope. "I don't know who else it could be."

"Helga? Alive? And in a sanitarium? That's hard to believe." Bradon ran his fingers through his hair. Her words had finally broken through, and he suppressed a mounting excitement. It wasn't just that Helga might be alive; of more importance, Sandi had come to him with the news. Did this mean that she had forgiven him his attempt to exploit her misery? More likely it meant that she desperately needed help, and he was the only one she could turn to without disclosing a nasty family secret.

"I know. It doesn't make sense."

"Well, don't get your hopes up. It's probably another wild goose chase."

"No," Sandi said. "I know it's her."

The conviction in her voice made him smile. "Oh? Woman's intuition?"

She shot him a quick look that told him that his question had no answer. "I just know."

A facetious reply died on his lips. She had been right too many times for him to dismiss her instincts out of hand.

"Okay." He glanced at his watch. "A quarter after five. Their visiting hours probably are only until eight. We should just make it."

"We'll make it," Sandi said. "We've got to."

It was going to be close. By the time they had rented a car at the San Francisco Airport and were driving over Cahill Ridge toward Half Moon Bay, it was already getting dark. Bradon drove with an unusual intensity. Generally, his driving was virtually automatic. Now he concentrated on the road so he could keep his mind off Sandi's disturbing nearness.

But maintaining an austere aloofness was a tremendous strain. However, it didn't seem to be a problem for Sandi. She sat quietly next to him, her slender fingers entwined in her lap. She stared determinedly straight ahead as though to lock out any stray emotions. Not even a glance in his direction.

To keep his mind from destructive fantasies, he turned to a subject he had been avoiding. On the pretext of adjusting the rear view mirror, he turned it so that he would see her face.

"So why are you doing this?"

In the mirror he saw her eyes flicker toward him. In their depths he saw calculation as though she was debating about how much to tell. And something else: fear. "To find my grandmother. I told you that."

"I'm not talking about just this. I mean why did you start this thing in the first place: going to Germany; coming up here."

"I wouldn't have if it wasn't for those regressions."

"People undergo regressions all the time. They don't start some kind of a quest." She was silent. He probed deeper. "Why did you take my class?"

"What does that have to do with it?"

"All right. Let's be empirical. You're working on a degree in art. You switch to psychology. Those are facts. What isn't known is why. Why the switch? Why psychology? Your background is art."

"Do you ask questions like this of all your students?"

"I'm asking you."

Again her eyes flicked toward him. She touched her lips with the tip of her tongue. Good. He was getting to her.

When she spoke her voice was faint. "I've become interested in psychology."

"Obviously. But why?"

Her voice was even fainter. "That's personal."

"Not anymore. It stopped being personal when you called me last night."

Her face had lost much of its color, and her fingers were clinched into a tight ball. But she refused to answer.

"I think you're worried about someone in your family, someone with psychological problems. But I don't think it's your mother or father. I think it's you. Is it because being psychic scares you?"

Her head shook almost imperceptibly. "I never knew I was psychic."

"Then it is you."

Her head jerked. She had been tricked and the color of anger came back into her face. But it quickly faded. "I didn't say that."

"You didn't have to."

She slumped down into the seat as though to escape. But he could not stop now no matter how much it hurt. "Let's look at the facts: you're out of college for two years. You have a good job. You don't need money. You have no connections with psychiatric institutions. Or psychologists, for that matter. Suddenly you're all gung ho for a degree in psychology. I'll bet your parents have some primitive notion about anybody who would see a psychiatrist. Ergo, you don't want them to know. You're going to cure yourself. But of what?"

In the mirror he saw her face close like a fist. She was not going to answer. Not now; probably not ever.

He shifted his approach with the smooth transition of a professional. He reached over and placed his hand over her clinched fists in a gesture of friendly concern. "I know you're concerned. But let me help you. Please. You don't have to face this alone."

He stopped talking and waited. It was imperative now that he remain silent, forcing her to respond. There was always the danger that she would retreat even farther. But he didn't see that in her. She was a fighter. She had proven that over and over.

After a moment of silence, he realized he was wrong; she was not going to answer. He wasn't wrong about her being a fighter. And it was that depth of courage, like an Aristotelian flaw, that keep her from answering now.

He also saw that her eyes were luminous with tears. He smiled to himself and took his hand from hers. Maybe she wasn't so tough after all. "We'll find the answers."

"I hope so. I really hope so."

So did Bradon, but not because the answers would be of any benefit to him. It was because he wanted to rid her of this fear he sensed. His foot pressed harder on the accelerator.

They had passed the old gas station at the intersection of Highway 92 and Skyline Drive and were approaching the canyon where the accident had happened so many years ago. Suddenly, Bradon noticed her shiver.

He looked at her sharply. "What is it?"

"Pull over," she whispered. "Now. Now!"

Instinctively he glanced over his shoulder to make sure the way was clear to pull off the highway, and his eyes opened in alarm. A huge pickup truck with dual rear wheels was bearing down on them. Desperately, he swung the steering wheel to pull out of the truck's path. Too late! Crash!

The truck's heavy bumper struck the left rear of the compact car sending it into a squealing, heart-stopping skid. Grimly, Bradon fought to keep from losing control.

But the big truck was close beside them, its engine roaring. From the corner of his eyes he saw its wheels begin to turn toward them. It was going to ram them, sending them crashing into the death canyon!

The brakes! Hard! Yank the wheel! Take a chance on rolling! The compact car skidded and struck the dirt shoulder of the highway, gouging clouds of dust, sending dirt and rocks flying. It careened up on two wheels and Bradon strained to keep it from going over. His abrupt move had surprised the other driver and the truck's tires screamed as its momentum carried it across the highway in front of the compact, missing it by inches. The truck hit the dirt shoulder, skidded wildly and slammed into the guardrail. There was an agonizing crunch of tearing metal and splintering posts and the truck catapulted into the air, spinning sideways until it smashed into the rocks and trees at the bottom of the canyon.

The compact fishtailed on the dirt shoulder of the road, leaving a trail of dust and the odor of burning brakes until Bradon brought it to a shuddered stop in a cloud of dust.

"Oh, my God," Sandi breathed. She released her death grip on the car's dash. "He tried to kill us."

"You got that right," Bradon gritted. He had no sense of fear. There was no room for fear in his burning anger. "Wait here."

He threw open the door and leaped out. He dashed back to the splintered and broken guardrail and looked into the canyon. The truck was on its side, some thirty feet down, its rolling plunge stopped by a stand of pines. Smoke poured from beneath the mangled engine hood. If the smoke was caused by power steering or brake fluid spilling on the hot exhaust there was probably no danger of fire. But it if was motor oil, it could burst into flame at any second. As if in response to Bradon's thought, the smoke diminished and flames appeared.

Bradon waited. The son-of-a-bitch would have to come out or be cooked. But the driver did not appear. And the flames were stronger, brighter.

Bradon muttered, "Damn," and began making his way down the slope, slipping and sliding on scree and grass made dry by the long summer. He was being stupid. The truck, tilted toward its right side, had to be leaking gasoline. It could blow any time! But he had to talk to that driver. Why had he tried to kill them?

By the time he reached the truck, flames and smoke were pouring from beneath the broken hood. The driver, blood streaking his face from a gash in his forehead, was struggling to unfasten his seat belt. But with the truck on its right side, gravity pinned his body over the release so he couldn't reach it. His eyes were wide with panic as he stared at flames that were only kept from him by the truck's intact windshield. When he saw Bradon, he screamed. "Get me outta here! Get me outta here!"

One glance told Bradon that neither of them could reach the belt's release, and he quickly dug his penknife from his pocket. He flipped open the knife's small, sharp blade and poised it over the taut strap. The man's eyes swiveled from the fire. "For God's sake. Hurry."

"One question first. Why did you try to kill us?"

The man licked his lips, his eyes wild. Heat was buckling the windshield and smoke curled from the plastic of the truck's dash. "It was an accident," he gritted. "An accident."

Bradon snapped the blade of the knife shut. "Okay," he said. "A fatal accident."

"No, no," the man screamed, his fingers clawing at the seat belt. "They paid me."

"Who? Who paid you?"

"I don't know. I swear, I don't know."

Bradon opened the knife's blade again and held it close to the strap. "I can wait longer than you can."

"Oh, God!" The man's face was red with heat and fear, his eyes bulging. "All right! All right!"

"Bradon! What are you doing?!" It was Sandi. She had plunged down the slope and was beside the truck, staring at Bradon in disbelief. "Cut it! Cut it!"

Bradon cut the strap. He couldn't carry through his bluff with Sandi so close. If the truck exploded it would take all of them with it.

With Bradon's help the driver pulled himself out of the window, his pants legs smoldering.

Bradon grabbed the man's arm. "Come on. That thing might blow."

The three of them were scrambling up the slope when two Highway Patrol Officers passed them carrying fire extinguishers. Reaching the highway, Bradon and Sandi half-lifted, half-dragged the driver over the broken guardrail, and he collapsed on the dirt shoulder of the road. In addition to the Highway Patrol car, two other cars had stopped, their drivers and passengers outside their cars staring at the burning truck. Two men came over to Bradon and Sandi and asked if they were okay. They replied that they were and the men went back to looking at the fire.

Sandi had been staring at the driver and she whispered to Bradon. "Dan. That's him. That's the same man who tried to kill me."

"Are you sure?"

"Yes. I know it is."

"All right." Bradon knelt beside the man who was sitting in the dirt, breathing hard, his head hanging, his face red and sweating. "Okay!" Bradon growled. "Who hired you?"

The man refused to look up. "Nobody," he muttered. "It was an accident."

"Come on, damnit! That isn't what you said!"

The man shook his head and clinched his jaws shut. Bradon stood up. "Damn."

"You think someone hired him? To kill me?" Sandi's voice was edged with shock.

"Don't you think so?"

"But why?"

The two Highway Patrol officers climbed back over the splintered guardrail. One of them said, "Who was driving the compact?"

"I was," Bradon said.

"All right. What went on here?"

"That son-of-a-bitch tried to kill us. I'll prefer charges."

"Tried to kill you?" The officer's voice was cold, impersonal.

The driver's defiance had returned and he snapped. "It was an accident."

One of the men from the other cars said, "He lying, officer. That man,"--he pointed to the driver--"tried to run them off the road."

The other officer had been looking at the skid marks on the highway. "That's what it looks like." He took handcuffs from his belt and went to the driver. "Put your hands behind you."

The only damage to the compact was a smashed left rear fender so after the Highway Patrol officers had completed their report Sandi and Bradon were able to drive away.

One of the first things Bradon did was readjust the rear view mirror. He had almost gotten them killed by using it to spy on Sandi instead of watching the road behind them. He wouldn't make that mistake again.

"You know," he said, "you saved our lives back there. If you hadn't told me to pull over," --he made a small shrug--"he would have had us."

"I don't understand," Sandi said. "He tried to kill us. What is going on?"

"Not us. You."

Sandi stiffened. "Me?"

"In your car. Remember? The same man."

"But why?"

Bradon rubbed a hand across his mouth. "Good question. Who knew you were coming here?"

"No one really. I didn't even tell my parents. They think I've carried on about this thing too much as it is."

"Well, somebody knew. Both times. Three really."

"Three?"

"In Switzerland. The man in the cable car."

She stared at him in disbelief. "But there's no reason anyone would want to kill me. No reason."

Bradon glanced at Sandi's pale face and tight lips and tried to think of something humorous that would dispel her tension. "You sure he's not an old boy friend? Maybe you broke his heart."

"Him?" The look she gave him was one of incredulity. "Are you crazy?" Then she realized his intent and smiled. "You are crazy." Her smile quickly faded, but some of the fear was gone from her voice as she said, "We'll never be able to prove he's the same man."

"Maybe not. But he won't be bothering you again. That we're sure of."

He didn't tell her that men like the truck driver, men who would kill for money, could be found easily. Whoever had hired the man could hire someone else. He would have to keep close watch over her. "It's too late to make the sanitarium now. We'll have to go in the morning."

Sandi nodded. In a way she was glad they would have to postpone the confrontation. Her mind was numb with shock. She felt like a fighter who had taken too many blows to the head. One more might put her over the edge. She needed time to think, time to pull her life together before she could chance another trauma.

"We shouldn't have any trouble finding a motel this time of the year," Bradon said. "We'll check in then find a restaurant."

The motel was California modern, with two floors of rooms opening off outside hallways. The water in a fenced swimming pool looked cold. When she and Bradon signed for separate but adjoining rooms, the elderly man behind the registration desk seemed vaguely surprised. He looked relieved when Sandi ask him directions to the sanitarium as though that explained why they wanted separate rooms.

"Too late," he said laconically. "They're closed."

"We know. We'll be going in the morning."

He told them to take State Highway 1 north toward Miramar about two miles. They would see a sign on their left directing them to the sanitarium.

Bradon had requested rooms on the quieter second floor and as Sandi unlocked her door, Bradon said, "I'll get your bag from the car."

"All right." The dullness in her voice distressed her but she could not seem to find the energy to give it life. "I'll leave the door unlocked."

"Okay. Be right back."

Inside her room, Sandi took her purse into the small bathroom intending to wash her face and redo her make up, but when she saw her face in the mirror, it was as though she was looking at the face of a stranger. Her eyes where sunken, tinged with red and shadowed by dark circles. Her cheeks looked drawn, their natural color replaced by a ghost-like pallor. Her lips were the color of raw liver. And her hair . . . A sob burst through her iron control, and before she could regain control she was crying. Her head drooping, she braced her hands on the edge of the cool porcelain sink as sobs racked her body and tears gushed from her eyes. She wanted to stop, to control her emotions. But it was as though all the shock and fear that had been bottled inside her for the past few weeks had burst the dam of her hard resolve and the flood could not be stopped.

She couldn't think. She could not reason. She could only cling to the washbasin and give herself to the purging tears.

She didn't know when Bradon came in and put his arms around her. She didn't remember turning blindly and burying her face against his chest. She was only aware of how good it felt to be held in his arms, to feel the wool of his sweater rough against her cheek, to smell the warm aroma of his body, and to have his cheek pressing her hair as he whispered, "All right, honey. It's all right."

She was dimly aware that he lifted her, cradling her against his chest, and she locked her arms around his neck, her tears staining his clothes. He bent to place her on the double bed and she clung to him desperately. "No," she gasped between sobs. "Don't let me go. Don't let me go."

She clung to him as, together, they lay on the bed. He brushed her wet cheeks with his lips as he whispered, "I promise. I'll never let you go. I love you too much. You don't know how much I love you."

His words warmed her like liquid gold and her shuddering sobs slowly died. Her lips came up, seeking and finding his and she tasted her own tears in his tender kiss. Then his fingertips were tenderly brushing the tears from her cheeks. His lips moved to the hollow of her throat and the sobs that had been wracking her body deepened into a new sound as a subtle sensation surged through her, driving the pain from her mind, taking control of her body. Her head lolled back exposing her throat, surrendering to his lips, surrendering to a mounting heat.

With a soft moan Bradon's lips moved to again capture hers, and his fingers curled in her hair, holding her in savage possession. Gently at first, his lips made love to hers, tasting their texture, savoring their softness. Gradually, their demand grew, pressing harder, aided by his seeking tongue. Her lips parted in answer, the tip of her tongue tentatively touching his as wary as a kitten responding to the touch of a stranger. But his tongue became urgent, demanding and she abandoned all fear, rushing to meet him, savoring a joy of giving.

His hands left her hair, but she did not pull away. She reveled in sweet surrender, giving him her mouth, her lips, her tongue.

His lips left hers and her moan of protest turned to a low gasp as his lips brushed her breasts, held captive by his hands. The stubble of whiskers on his cheek brushed roughly across her tender, distended nipples, and she quivered to new shocks of pleasure.

Her hands longed to touch his skin, and her fingers urged away his clothing until they had freedom to stoke the hard muscles of his back and thighs. And as she touched him, her brain responded with joyous wonder. How could she have denied herself the incredible pleasure of his body for so long? Her hands, her lips added to the joy by exploring the cords of his neck and the tender flesh of his sides and stomach.

He came up on his elbows and her arms circled his neck as she gave herself to the anticipation of ultimate joy.

Suddenly, he groaned and pulled away, collapsing on the bed, his forearms across his eyes. A moan of anguish was torn from her lips, and she reached for him, unable to comprehend what had happened.

"I'm sorry," he gasped. "I'm sorry; I'm sorry."

A chill swept her fevered skin. Her pounding heart missed a beat, seeming to stop. For a moment she was unable to move, trying to absorbed the unexpected shock. She swallowed painfully as strength returned to her body.

Bradon had turned away from her. He was lying on his back, his forearms covering his eyes, his body trembling. Instantly, her flood of disappointment vanished, replaced by a surge of tender compassion. She turned on her side and pressed against him. She slipped an arm beneath his head and pressed her lips to his cheek. "It's all right," she whispered. "Darling, it's all right."

She held him close while his trembling and his gasping breath slowly died. She stroked his cheek, astonished by the strength of her concern. The feeling was almost as powerful as had been the incredible power of her desire and she longed to hold him forever, to sooth away his torment and pain.

He pulled away, sitting up with his back against the headboard of the bed. "I'm sorry," he murmured. Then he laughed, his voice harsh and without humor. "A hell of a psychologist, I am. Can't even cure myself."

Sandi longed to put her arms around him again, to hold him close, to prove to him that it really didn't matter. But she knew he was not yet ready for her compassion so she, too, sat up, pulling the rumpled bed spread over her.

She sought desperately for something to say, som.. word that would take the place of a caress. "I doesn't matter," she said, knowing how hollow her words must sound even as she said them. "It doesn't matter."

To her surprise, Bradon muttered, "Damn her. Damn her to hell."

Sandi's hand went to her mouth in shock. "Her?" she breathed. "What are you saying?"

Bradon's head turned toward her and she could see the pain in his eyes. "I'm sorry," he said again. "It's my problem."

Her hand reached out to touch his arm. "No," she said, her voice strong with conviction. "Not any more. We belong to each other. I want to help."

"Help?" His gentle snort was rueful. "It's something I've got to work out for myself."

Sandi longed to question him. But she knew it would be a mistake. He was not in a mood to be pressured. "All right. But if you're in love with someone else, I think I have a right to know."

"Not love. My God, it's not love."

"Then what? Obsession? Infatuation?"

"Obsession. That's a good diagnosis."

"Maybe . . ." Sandi hesitated. How could she say this without making it sound stupid? "Maybe I can take her place. Whatever she does for you, I can do."

Bradon looked at her and the pain left his face. His eyes grew warm and he touched her cheek with his finger tips. "Oh, God," he whispered. "You don't know how much I love you."

"Then let me help. Please, darling, let me help."

He looked at her silently, and she was afraid, afraid that he would withdraw into a protective shell. Her fear intensified when he got up and went into the bathroom. He came back in a moment, knotting a bath towel around his waist.

"I was a lousy clinical psychologist," he said. "I was arrogant. Arrogant and lazy. When patients came in, I never really tried to understand them. I'd make a list of their symptoms and looked it up in the D.S.M. Then I'd give them the prescribed treatment. Everything by the book. I could have done it by mail." He smiled grimly. "I don't know how many people I helped, but I spent a lot of time at the beach."

Sandi remained silent, subdued by the anguish in his voice. He sounded so much different than the Dan Bradon she knew. Gone was the devilish grin; gone was the supreme self-control; gone was the subtle arrogance. He was a man in pain and she yearned to go to him, to hold him in her arms as she would an injured child.

But he had to work this out for himself, so she remained sitting up on the bed, willing him to continue, to break his debilitating barrier of silence.

"God!" he breathed. "I have no idea how many lives I ruined. I only know for sure about one."

Pain made Sandi close her eyes. "Her," she said. "It was her."

He nodded, and ran his fingers through his hair. "Yes. Her. Kimberly. Her name was Kimberly Hill. The first patient I ever allowed to get to me. And it killed her."

Sandi sucked in her breath. Her fingers clinched on the bedding as she struggled to remain silent. She had to give him time to control his emotions.

Bradon paced the small room, moving back and forth in front of the bed as though in a trance, his eyes filled with the pain of bitter memories. "She was depressed. Text book manic depressive. She fell in love with me. It happens. Patients often fall in love with their doctor. It doesn't mean anything. I knew that. It was psychosis driven. But, God help me, I gave in to it. She was so damned beautiful. I wanted her. I really wanted her. So I convinced myself I could help her by--by giving her what she wanted. God, what an ego. Instead of helping, she got worse. She'd come to me with these terrible depressions. And I'd apply my own little brand of macho therapy. One day after one of our little sessions, she went up to the roof of my building and jumped off."

He sank onto the room's only chair, his head in his hands and Sandi fled to him. Forgetting everything except his pain, she knelt beside him and put her arms around his waist, leaning her head against the cold flesh of his arm. "It wasn't your fault," she said. "She was unstable. She might have done it anyway."

"No!" His voice was so sharp it snapped her head back. "It was my fault. I took her because I could. I might just as well have put a gun to her head."

Sandi looked at him, her throat dry. "Were you-- were you in love with her?"

Bradon's raised his face from his hands. He laughed harshly. "No. I wished to God I had been. That would have been an excuse. But I used her. I used her. Like a God damned animal."

"Have you . . . " Sandi knew she was taking advantage of his susceptibility to pry into his mind, but she could not stop herself. "Have you tried--with other women?"

To her vast relief, he shook his head. "No." His eyes focused on Sandi's face as though he was suddenly aware that she was beside him. He touched her hair, his fingers gentle. "I never wanted to with anyone until I met you. And now,"--he took his hand away--"I've lost you too."

"No," she cried. "It isn't the same. I love you. I don't care if you never make love with me. All I want is to be with you. For always."

Bradon stoked her hair and his voice was warm and husky when he said, "Oh, Sandi. I really do love you." He put a hand under her chin and tilted her tear-streaked face. He touched her cheeks with his fingertips. "I don't want to lose you. I never want to lose you."

"You won't," she said. "You'll never lose me." She reached to pull his face down to hers, but he shook his head.

"No," he said. "I don't want to go through that again."

He stood up and went to sit on the edge of the bed, his shoulders slumped, one hand across his mouth, his eyes staring unseeingly. Sandi fought an impulse to go to him, to sit beside him with her arms around him. She sensed that at this moment he would resent her attempts at empathy. His mind had to be dark with guilt and self-pity. Right now he probably also hated himself for baring his soul to her; he might even resent her for being the cause of his confrontation with the truth. He was like an embarrassed child who would bristle at any attempt at comforting. It would be best to let him have his period of mourning.

She got up and went into the bathroom, closing the door behind her. She turned on the shower over the tub. When she moved under the stream, she scarcely felt the water. Her mind was filled with thoughts of Bradon. How could she help him? She felt helpless, shut out of his life at the very moment when he needed her the most. He was so lost in his misery that he did not realize he needed her. Her sense of urgency was so strong that she turned off the shower and only half dried herself before she wrapped a bath towel around herself and left the bathroom.

Bradon was sitting on the bed with his back against the headboard, the towel still around his waist, his hands locked behind his head. He looked so lean and powerful that Sandi caught her breath. It seemed impossible that anyone so strong and capable could possibly have doubts about themselves. She had to remind herself that the most powerful people often suffered from dreadful insecurity.

She wanted to hurl herself into his arms, to soothe his body and his mind with words, with her lips, with her hands. But he looked so tense, his eyes so fixed, that she knew it would be like touching stone. She paused awkwardly in the middle of the floor. Should she go to the other side of the bed? Or should she sit in the chair?

Bradon solved her dilemma by swinging his feet to the floor and standing up. "I'm just leaving," he said. "I wanted to tell you first that I'm sorry about--about all this."

He reached for his clothing, and Sandi quickly stepped in front of him. She put her hands on his shoulders, searching his face as she said the first words that came to her, "No. I don't want you to go. I won't let you go. Not now. Not like this."

His smile was crooked with bitter humor. "Why not? You know everything there is to know about me. All my little secrets."

"I'm not thinking about you. I'm thinking about myself."

He lifted an eyebrow as though he didn't believe her. "You? What on earth can I possibly do for you?"

"You can't see? You don't know how frightened I am?"

"You? You're the strongest person I know."

"I'm not. I'm not strong at all." Tears blurred her eyes and she wiped them away with her fingers, feeling like a fool for crying. "I'm scared all the time. I'm scared to death."

"Of what?"

"I'm afraid I'm going crazy."

He searched her face, puzzled by her unexpected answer. "Why do you say that?"

"It's . . ." She hesitated, fighting long-standing reticence. Her chin lifted and she took a deep breath. "It's the voices."

Bradon's eyebrows arched. "Voices?"

Sandi turned away. She was torn between the desire to tell him the truth and worry about the effect the truth would have. Suppose she was going crazy. Would she lose him forever?

She had to tell him. She could no longer fight the darkness alone. Maybe he would understand. He had told her his secret and she loved him more than ever. She had to take the chance. "Not actually voices," she said. "I just started to call them that when I was a child."

"So they've been with you a long time?"

"Almost as long as I can remember."

He sat down on the edge of the bed. When he spoke his voice had changed. It had lost its note of pain and doubt. Now it was warm and filled with concern. "Tell me about them. What are they like?"

She clinched her lower lip with her teeth. How could she describe the darkness so he would understand? She could not even articulate the feeling to herself "Like . . ." She paused, searching for words. "Like a darkness inside my head. More of a feeling than actual words."

"Like a sensation, a compulsion."

She turned her head to look at him, surprised that he understood. "That's right. More like a sensation."

"Can you single out any of these voices?"

"There is one that's stronger than the others."

"Can you tell what its message is?"

"No. It's never clear. Just--as you said--a compulsion."

"To do what?"

"That's the trouble. I don't know. But it seems as though I'm supposed to do something. They won't stop until I do." Her voice grew stronger, reflecting her frustration. "But how can I do anything if I don't know what it is?"

"Coming up here; did they tell you to do this?"

"I don't know. I don't think so. Nothing is clear. I just want to find out what happened to Helga."

"You don't connect them with your psychic visions?"

She paused before answering, thinking. She shook her head. "I'm not sure. That's why I went to Germany. But . . .I've had the voices as long as I can remember."

"So that's why you decided on psychology."

"Yes."

"You think if you find the answer to your regression you'll also end the voices. Is that right?"

"Oh, God. I hope so." She turned to face him and she could feel her lower lip tremble. "Dan, what's happening to me? I'm so scared."

In one quick stride he swept her into his arms. "Don't be," he said harshly. "I won't let anything happen to you."

She shivered, fighting the fear. "You're cold," he said. He picked her up and carried her to the bed. He pulled aside the covers and lowered her to the sheets. But when he attempted to release her, she locked her arms around his neck and shook her head.

"No," she said. "I need you."

For a moment she thought that he was going to pry her grip free. Then he saw the anguish in her face, and he moved in beside her, pulling the covers over them. He put his arms around her, saying, "This is really stupid, you know."

"I know," she whispered. "But I need you. I'm not afraid when you're here."

His answer was to tighten his arms around her. She lay quietly, snuggled with her head against his chest. She could hear his heart thudding and she put her palms on his chest so she could become one with the steady beat. She felt as though she could remain like this forever, locked in Bradon's warm embrace, his arms shielding her from the world.

And yet, she wanted more. She felt the heat from Bradon's body. She felt his soft breath caressing her hair. She remembered his pain when he had condemned himself for the death of his patient. And she was overwhelmed by such a feeling of love that she wanted to cry; she wanted him to know how very much she loved him.

She turned her face and pressed her lips to the hollow of his shoulder. She felt his body tense, but she did not stop. She moved her lips to the base of his throat, nuzzling beneath his chin with her cheek. Slowly she felt the tension drain from him. He stroked her hair and when her lips moved to brush his chin, he kissed her forehead.

He dug his fingers into her hair and began to turn her face to meet his lips. "No," she murmured, and he relaxed his grip in acquiescence. She moved down to nuzzle his neck and shoulders, trailing her lips across his skin as lightly as butterfly wings and she felt him shiver.

Without pausing in the caress of her lips, she pulled the towel free of her body and trailed the tips of her breasts across his stomach and she felt ripples of pleasure play across his lower stomach.

She released the knot securing his towel and pulled it aside. Gently, slowly, not touching him with her hands or her lips, she brushed her breasts across his lower stomach.

Tremors spread from his stomach to his thighs and he groaned. His hands clinched the sheets and his hips lifted. She moved her knees to straddle him and, meeting his seeking thrust, impaled herself. He gasped and shuddered and his hands came up to clutch her hips, pulling her down, making her totally his.

Only then did she lean forward, giving him her lips to use as he would, just as she gave him the rest of her body, just as she would for the remainder of her life.

CHAPTER 25

California's Highway 1 dips and curves along the shoreline where insistent waves of the Pacific Ocean play with the land. With a brilliant morning sun painting the water a deep blue and the land a verdant green, the view was spectacular. But not for Sandi. With every turn of the car's wheels her heart beat seemed to accelerate with anxiety.

Last night lying spent and warm in Bradon's arms, she had been certain that fear was gone from her life forever. But now, with each passing mile, pressure grew inside her mind. It was as though she was an antenna moving closer to a cluster of broadcasting stations. There were so many signals, and her mind was so cluttered with extraneous sounds, that she still could not make out the dominant voice. She fought against an impulse to put her hands over her ears knowing that it would not change the mounting dread. What terrible knowledge was waiting for her? Could there be a connection between the attempt on her life and her grandmother? Could there be a connection between the voices and her grandmother?

"Are you all right?"

Bradon's voice startled Sandi. He was staring at her, anxiety shadowing his face. She took a deep breath. "I think so."

He drove a moment more, unconvinced. Then he said, "How are you going to handle this?"

"What do you mean?"

"When we get to the sanitarium. Some of these places don't allow visitors."

"Oh. Well, I'm going to ask to see Mrs. Helen Winters."

"Instead of asking, you might have more luck if you tell them you want to see her."

"You mean, be assertive."

"That's right. Firm but friendly. Remember your psychology."

"Right. People tend to respond to authority."

"But not always. Be prepared for that too."

Rounding a bend, she saw a collection of low, Spanish-style buildings with red tile roofs that had to be the sanitarium. The buildings had been constructed around huge trees that looked like sycamore, oak and pine. Flower-bordered cement walks meandered beneath the towering green canopy. A short distance beyond the most distant buildings steep bluffs ended in a narrow, boulder-strewn beach. The bluffs muffled the constant sound of surf so that the effect was of pastoral tranquility, provided one could afford the very high price.

A head-high stucco wall surrounded the property. A discrete sign set low on a manicured lawn beside a gated entrance indicated it was the Sanitarium.

The gate was open allowing Bradon to drive in and park in a newly black-topped parking area. Winding cement paths flanked by flowers and ferns fanned out through the trees. Small plaques staked amid the flowers directed Sandi and Bradon along one of the paths to the sanitarium office. With every step Sandi was inundated by tides of dark voices followed by waves of light. It seemed as though one voice was calling to her, urging her forward while others warned her to go back. It took all her concentration not to stop and crouch with her arms wrapped around her head, shielding herself from words that struggled to rip her mind like claws.

At the headquarters' entrance spotless glass doors opened into a spacious lobby made warm and friendly by potted plants and colorfully upholstered chairs and couches. Mexican throw rugs decorated a floor made of large tiles. Sandi had never been to a sanitarium but this was certainly not what she had anticipated. This was more like a spa or an expensive Palm Springs hotel.

The illusion that it was a hotel disappeared when Sandi saw a middle-aged woman wearing a white nurse's uniform seated behind a registration counter and expertly typing on a computer's keyboard. She looked up at them with a smile. "May I help you?"

Remembering Bradon's advice to be assertive, Sandi stated, "I believe so. We're here to see Helen Winters."

Sandi held her breath, expecting the woman to say they had no such patient. Instead, the woman said, "Oh, Mrs. Winters. One moment, please." She turned to her computer and began typing. She studied the computer monitor. "Mrs. Winters is not specified for visitors."

"We're not visitors," Sandi said firmly. "I am her granddaughter. This is my consultant, Dr. Daniel Bradon. I'm sure you're familiar with his work in clinical psychology."

The woman blinked uncertainly giving Bradon time to extract a business card from his wallet. He handed the card to the woman. "You may call the State Board or the Association of Psychiatrists if you'd like to verify my credentials."

The woman held the card as though it was dangerous. "No, that won't be necessary. It's just that . . . it says she isn't to receive visitors."

"I told you," Sandi said, her voice edged with broken glass. "I'm not a visitor. My father is Martin Boeckel. You will find his name on all your checks."

Mention of the checks brought a worried look to the woman's face, and Sandi stabbed her with a sharp, "Up to now."

The woman quickly got to her feet. "One moment, please. I'll find someone to take you to her."

She went to a door labeled with the word DIRECTOR and knocked lightly before she went in, closing the door behind her. Sandi could hear the murmur of her voice as she spoke to someone.

She heard steps behind her and turned to see Bradon striding around the end of the counter. He went to the computer and peered at the monitor. "Room 36," he said. He had just rejoined Sandi when the door opened and a man came out followed by the receptionist. The man was slender with a full head of iron gray hair and thick, dark eyebrows. His sharply chiseled face was partially concealed by a closely cropped beard and mustache. He was shrugging into the jacket of a brown suit when he saw Sandi and Bradon and he smiled. His dark beard made his teeth look incredibly white.

He held out his hand to Sandi, "Hello. I'm Dr. Pavon. I understand you're Helen's granddaughter."

"That's right." Sandi took his hand, and he squeezed hard enough to make her wince.

Dr. Pavon released her hand and turned to Bradon. "And you're Daniel Bradon. I believe I've heard of you."

"That's gratifying," Bradon said as he shook Dr. Pavon's hand.

Sandi saw a look of distaste flit across Bradon's face when Dr. Pavon applied unreasonable pressure to his hand as though to prove that although he was an intellectual, he was far from being a wimp.

"I understand that you're Martin Boeckel's daughter," Dr. Pavon said to Sandi. "Would you be offended if I asked for some identification?"

"Not at all." Sandi took her wallet from her purse and opened it so that Dr. Pavon could study her driver's license.

He nodded with a broad smile as though she had relieved him of some troubling responsibility. "Thank you. This way, please." He walked with them across the lobby toward a rear glass door.

"Dr. Bradon," he said as they walked. "I can't help but be curious. What is your interest in Mrs. Winters?"

Bradon's reply was terse. "Psychometry."

Dr. Pavon's step faltered for an instant. "Oh," he said. "Interesting."

Outside Dr. Pavon was faced with a diplomatic conundrum. The cement walk was only wide enough for two and he had to decide whether to walk beside Sandi or beside Bradon with whom he obviously wanted to converse. He solved the puzzle by walking beside Sandi and turning his head to talk to Bradon. "Psychometry," he said. "I'm not terribly conversant with that regimen. My specialty is geriatric neurosis and psychoses."

Bradon rewarded him with a smile. "How apropos."

Dr. Pavon first looked puzzled. Then he glanced at their surroundings and laughed. "Right."

Sandi was having trouble following their conversation. The pressure in her head had intensified to a heavy throbbing. She wanted to scream, anything to make it stop. The only thing that made her continue to walk was a sensation that she would soon discover the reason behind the dreadful voices. But she had to do something to relieve the tension or she would not be able to continue. "How long has my grandmother been here?" she blurted.

"Several years. I've been here almost five years and she was here long before my time."

"Since 1975," Bradon said.

"Well, I don't have her record memorized, of course, but that does sound correct."

They approached a cluster of cottages situated near the bluff where the sound of the surf was louder, and Dr. Pavon turned off the main walk toward one of the cottages. Before he reached it, the door was opened by a portly black woman wearing a nurse's uniform. The receptionist must have called ahead and told the nurse she would be having visitors.

"Hello, Rose," Dr. Pavon said. "How is she?"

"Fine, Dr. She's on the patio."

She stepped back from the door and Dr. Pavon motioned Sandi and Bradon through. Sandi hesitated, putting her sweaty palm on the doorjamb to steady her trembling legs. Her heart was racing and her breath caught in her throat. Inside she would find all the answers--or none. She pushed away from the door and stepped into the room. She gasped as a wave of power tore into her brain. Bradon was instantly at her side, holding her arm.

"Are you all right?"

Sandi nodded, unable to speak. She had to harden her mind into a barrier before she could look around the room. It was a combination sitting room and bedroom made pleasant by sunlight slanting through several windows. The floor was of brick painted white, its center covered with a colorful Navaho rug. Several prints of flowers and floral arrangements decorated the pale pink walls. A daybed in one corner was neatly made and covered with a chenille spread of delicate pink that matched the color of the walls. A couch against one wall was upholstered in durable white Naugahyde. A small desk held several books and two small framed photographs. A TV set was suspended from the ceiling by a metal framework so that it could be viewed from the bed or the couch. Its remote control was on a nightstand next to the bed.

But Sandi scarcely saw the room. Her attention centered on an open sliding glass door that led to a roofed patio. Beyond the nearby bluffs the slate blue of the Pacific sparkled in the sunlight.

Seated in a wheelchair on the patio with her back to them, facing the sea, was a woman with gray hair worn in a thick braid. Her thin shoulders were covered by an afghan shawl.

Sandi began walking toward the open doorway, drawn by a terrifying urgency that spun through her throbbing brain. The woman in the wheelchair seemed to stiffen and her withered hands, moving with astonishing quickness, wheeled the chair so that she faced Sandi. Her pale blue eyes locked on Sandi's face with an intensity that was staggering, stopping Sandi in her tracks.

"Hello, my dear." The woman's voice was barely a whisper. "I've been waiting for you." Instantly, the darkness in Sandi's brain vanished, dispelled by a brilliant light of pure joy.

Sandi smiled. "Hello, Grandma. I'm here."

She went to her grandmother and knelt beside her and put her arms around her frail body. She kissed her on the cheek. "Oh, Grandma," she breathed. "I've been looking for you for so long."

"I know," Helga said. "I know."

Sandi leaned back to look into her grandmother's face. "You know?"

Helga nodded. From her lap she picked up a crocheted baby's bonnet. "This is yours. I've been trying to contact you for years and years."

Sandi's eyes closed and she tilted her head back, breathing deeply. Why hadn't she seen it before? Oh God. The wasted years. "The voices," she said. "They were all you."

Helga's puckered lips twisted into a smile. "Only one," she said. "There was always only one."

"Well, I'll be damned," Sandi heard someone say and she turned her head to see Dr. Pavon staring at them. "Are you telling me she was sending things into your head?"

"Yes. I've been hearing her voice since I was a child. But I didn't know what it was. It stopped just now, when I saw her."

"You see," Bradon said. "Psychometry."

Dr. Pavon rubbed his beard. "She always said she was calling someone. I thought it was a psychosis."

"He thought I was crazy," Helga snapped.

Sandi stood and took hold of her grandmother's hand. "Why didn't you write? Or telephone? You know my address."

Helga shook her head. "No, I don't. She never would tell me."

"Who? Who wouldn't tell you."

Helga raised a thin, trembling finger and pointed. "Her."

At first Sandi thought she was pointing at the nurse and she rose to confront her, an angry pulse pounding in her temples. Then she sucked in her breath. It was not the nurse. Helga was pointing beyond her to the cottage door where her mother and Martin Boeckel were standing!

Sandi stared at them, her mind dazed. "Mother. What are you doing here?"

"No!" Helga's voice was strong and clear as though she had dredged forth some long dormant source of energy. "She's not your mother."

Gretchen walked through the room toward the patio, her eyes narrow. "Mother," she said. "You hurt me when you talk like that." She looked at Sandi with a twisted smile. "She's been like this since Dennise was killed. We tried to keep it from you."

"Dennise wasn't killed," Helga snapped. "It was Gretchen."

"You see," Martin interjected. "She's not rational. Dr. Pavon, perhaps you can explain."

"Well," Dr. Pavon cleared his throat. "I thought she was hallucinating. But,"--he turned to Sandi--"you really do exist. Now I'm not so sure about the other."

"Other?" Bradon said.

"She's always claimed that it was her daughter Gretchen who was killed in the accident, not Dennise." He turned to Sandi's mother. "But you can see she has been--is--mistaken."

"She's not Gretchen," Helga insisted. "She's Dennise."

"Now, Mother." Gretchen took a step forward and Helga cringed.

"Don't let her touch me," she cried. "She'll kill me like she killed Gretchen."

Sandi dropped to her knees beside Helga and took one of her hands in both of hers. Helga's hands were hot, trembling. Sandi felt the wild beating of a pulse, and something more, something that seemed to emanate from the older woman's mind like a psychic force.

Sandi turned her head to look toward her mother, knowing that her face was drained of blood, wooden with doubt. "I don't understand," she said. "Is what she said true?"

"She believes it's true," Gretchen answered. "The accident effected her mind. That's why she's here." She looked hard at Dr. Pavon, her eyes hooded. "Isn't that right, Doctor?"

Dr. Pavon blinked before he nodded. "Her treatment should continue."

"Treatment!" Helga snapped. "They're trying to make me think I'm crazy."

Dr. Pavon's smile was professional. "That's not true, Mrs. Winters. You've been well-treated here."

Helga focused her eyes on Sandi's face so close to her own, and her voice was filled with despair as she whispered, "I tried to warn you. So many years."

"Warn me? About what?"

Helga's frail hand gripped Sandi's with surprising strength. "They want you to die."

Gretchen's laugh was a barb of derision. "Our own daughter? Why would we want that?"

"Because she's not your daughter," Helga said. Her voice was faint, without passion, as though her strength was draining.

"Ridiculous!" Martin growled. "She's not my blood. She knows that. But Gretchen is certainly her mother."

"Doctor," Gretchen said to Dr. Pavon. "This can't be good for her. We can discuss this somewhere else."

"Yes," Dr. Pavon echoed. "That would be best. We can use my office."

He started toward the door, followed by Gretchen and Martin. Helga was slumped in her wheelchair, her head down, as though she had given up. Sandi did not move. "I'm going to stay here for a while." .

"I don't think that would be wise," Dr. Pavon told her. "Rose can look after her."

Sandi shook her head. "I'm not going to leave her. Not now."

Dr. Pavon glanced toward Gretchen and Martin before he said, "I'm afraid I must insist."

Sandi's mouth tightened. "Insist all you want."

Blood rushed into Dr. Pavon's face and his hands clenched into fists. Before he could move, Bradon took a step toward him. "Before we go, Doctor, would you mind clearing up one point."

Dr. Pavon's glare swung toward Bradon. "And what is that?"

"You indicated that she's been hallucinating for several years. Is this hallucination always the same?"

Some of the fire went out of Dr. Pavon's eyes. "Generally. Yes."

"Let me guess what it is."

Dr. Pavon hesitated. Sandi could tell that his curiosity was piqued as he remembered Bradon's credentials. Then, too, Bradon's interruption had forestalled a messy confrontation. "I would be delighted to have your opinion."

Martin interjected. "Oh, no. You're not to be involved in this."

Bradon ignored him as he went to Helga and knelt beside Sandi. "Mrs. Winters, who inherits the von Luckenwalde fortune from you?"

Helga's head lifted. "Von Luckenwalde? Hermann?"

"Yes. Who inherits after you?"

"His daughter. Gretchen."

"There," Gretchen said. "I hope you're satisfied."

"And what about your other daughter, Dennise?" Bradon continued.

Helga slowly shook her head. "Bloodline. It has to go through the bloodline."

"So Dennise would get nothing."

"Bloodline." Helga's voice was a whisper, but it echoed through the room like a clarion. "It belongs to Gretchen's child."

Bradon got up and looked at Gretchen and Martin. "That would be Sandi. But she was just a baby. And with Helga in a sanitarium, non compos mentis, you took control of the estate."

Gretchen's eyes flicked toward Sandi. "You can't believe this."

Sandi stared at her mother, stunned. Her body felt leaden as she pushed to her feet. "You knew? All the time I was in Europe, looking for her, you knew?

"They knew," Bradon said. "They were terrified you would find out what had happened to Helga. That's why they tried to have you killed."

His words struck Sandi like bullets, tearing through her mind. "What?" she whispered. "What did you say?"

"That man on the cable car. The truck driver."

Sandi looked at Gretchen and Martin, seeing them through a haze of tears. "Is that true?"

As a child Sandi could remember the look on her mother's face when she was displeased with her. The same look was there now, hard, grim, without a trace of affection. Even her words had a familiar ring. "Stupid, stupid!" she snapped. "Why on earth would we do that?"

Bradon put his hand on Helga's shoulder. "She's been trying to tell us. You're not Gretchen. You're her other daughter, Dennise."

"That's not true." Gretchen's lips were drawn into a snarl. "I am Gretchen."

Bradon looked at Dr. Pavon. "Mrs. Winter's hallucination was that Dennise murdered Gretchen, then switched identities so she could get the von Luckenwalde money. Am I right?"

Dr. Pavon rubbed his hands together nervously, "Well, that's essentially true.

Bradon's eyes were chips of steel as he stared at Gretchen, "A DNA test would prove if you really are Sandi's mother. But I don't think that'll be necessary. When the police question that truck driver, I think he'll tell them who hired him."

Gretchen looked at Sandi, and Sandi watched her face change like an actress switching to a different role. She had seen her mother do this many times and she always wondered why she bothered. Her obsequiousness was appallingly apparent. "Sandi," she cooed. "You know that none of this is true. If we wanted you dead, we would have done it years ago."

"Oh, no," Bradon said. "The estate is in Helga's name but you have control. If anything happened to her the estate would probably end up in probate. They would find that Sandi is the next heir. And without Sandi, it could go to the German government. They knew at the bank in Switzerland." He turned to Sandi. "I'll bet they thought you'd been getting the money all along. It must have confused the hell out of them when you showed up and started asking questions."

"But they told her nothing," Martin said. "So why would we try to have her killed?"

"She was getting close to the truth. You had to take a chance that you could cover up her death just like you've covered up everything else." He smiled at Sandi. "If it hadn't been for your 'voices', no one would ever have found out."

Sandi's mind was reeling. Discovering that Martin was not her father had been a shock. But now, to find out that Gretchen was not her real mother, was staggering. It had to be wrong. Gretchen and Martin had never given her any affection, true. But she had always assumed that it was because they were not the affectionate type. Could the real reason be because they had simply been using her? Had they kept up an illusion all those years--because of money?

The truth was in their set expressions. And for the first time, Sandi realized why there had been so little joy in her life. She was not their child, only their insurance.

The realization brought tears to her eyes. So many wasted years. So much wasted love, love that she had tried to give them only to have it rejected.

Even now, her tears had no effect on the woman she had thought was her mother, who said, "Forget this nonsense. Come home with us. It will all be the same."

"I know," Sandi said. "And I deserve better than that."

Gretchen flinched. Then she snarled at Dr. Pavon. "We'll sue. We'll sue all of you."

Grabbing Martin's arm, she practically pulled him from the room. As she stormed away, Sandi heard her heels smacking the cement walk with a sound like gun shots.

Dr. Pavon, his face mottled with fear and distress, looked at Sandi. "This had better be correct," he said. "I don't want trouble."

"Don't worry," Bradon said. "If they make trouble, Sandi could take everything they have."

Dr. Pavon nodded toward Helga. "About Mrs. Winters. I'm sure you'll want her to remain here."

"No," Sandi said firmly. She put her arm protectively around Helga's shoulders. "We've had enough 'voices'. From now on she'll be living with us. Would you like that, Grandma?"

Helga reached up and caught hold of Sandi's hand. Her eyes were bright as she said, "I don't know. Who is 'us'?"

Bradon grinned at her. "She means me. From now on, we're all family."

Sandi reached for him with her other hand and Bradon took it in both of his, pulling her close, his lips seeking hers. When their lips touched, he felt a shock like a mild electric current and he pulled his head back in surprise. Sandi smiled at him with delight and glanced toward her grandmother. Then Bradon saw that she still clung to Helga's hand. Helga looked at him with twinkling eyes as though to tell him that he was now part of a shared secret.

"Bloodline," she whispered.

Printed in the United States
4821